FORK IN THE ROAD

Book 10 of
THE WARDEN

FELICIA JEDLICKA

For those who would like a second chance at a first impression.

FORK IN THE ROAD

FELICIA JEDLICKA

1

GYPSY WATCHED THE FUSION of the shimmering orb and blue lightning explode into blinding light. The pilot cussed and slammed into his rudder pedals, turning the helicopter away from the oncoming detonation. The blast wave hit, shattering the windshield. The pilot cursed again and frantically started compensating for their aircraft's sudden transformation into an open-top convertible.

"I need to land," he yelled through the headset.

Gypsy could barely hear him through the ringing in her ears. She pushed her fingers under the device to shake loose the irritating hum. "Keep going," she yelled before spitting a piece of glass shrapnel from her mouth. She could taste blood, but she couldn't tell what part of her mouth had been cut.

"What?" the pilot asked, baffled—or perhaps he hadn't heard her over his own earache.

"I need to get to the prison," she yelled, louder.

"Are you blind? That was an explosion! I can't land over there!"

"Then *you* can carry the comatose bitch six more miles to deliver her." She turned her head slowly to face him, eyeing his reaction carefully. He might have been afraid of her by pure reputation, but he was far more afraid of the woman she had brought on board. If she'd been smarter and joined the Air Force instead of the Marine Corps, she wouldn't need to put up with pilots that were so easily distressed. What was the military coming to if their men were startled by flying dragons and supernatural sonic blasts?

"I'll do a flyover, but if I can't find a place to land, we are leaving."

"Just land on the roof." She pointed out the building standing in the center of the walled-off installation.

"What the..." he mumbled and shifted the chopper back to its previous course. "How the hell is that still standing?"

The pilot circled once to survey the grounds. Gypsy could see three black hawks and at least six semi-trucks crowding into the open acreage surrounding the main prison building. The vehicles and outbuildings weren't in much better shape than their helicopter, with broken windows and mangled roofs. Only one outbuilding seemed to have been immune to the damage.

"Looks like I'm late to the party," Gypsy said, as she made a mental check of her ammunition. This volunteer mission was turning out to be far more effort than it was worth.

The pilot offered her a furtive glance and lowered them to the roof. Once they touched down, he adjusted his switches for shutdown. "Don't shut it down. You aren't staying."

"I can't go back with shattered windows," he objected.

"I don't think they have a helicopter repair shop. You need to go back immediately and report."

"What do I tell him?" he muttered.

"Nothing, just shake his hand. I'm delivering the girl to Danato. The others are coming in with the witch. By the looks of the parking lot downstairs, your project has arrived, along with some unwelcome guests."

"What do you mean, *my* project?" The pilot frowned at her as she reported to him as if he was an answering machine.

"Shut up and listen." Gypsy pulled out her handgun, and the man flinched. "There are three black hawks. I'm not familiar with the insignia. I'm assuming they are with the council." She checked her clip, doing a quick count on her bullets. "I'm also assuming that their presence has to do with that light show we just saw." She slammed the clip into place and shoved the gun back into her holster. "Regardless, this is probably a private party and I'm about to crash it. I doubt that I'm going to be welcomed with open arms, so if I don't make it out of here..." Gypsy shrugged. "It's been weird."

Gypsy grabbed her gear and hopped out of the chopper. "Oh." She turned back to the pilot. "And download this guy's flying lessons. I'm sick of dealing with panicky pilots."

The pilot's face scrunched with a new level of confusion. "Nutjob," he murmured as she moved to the back of the chopper. If she cared about the man's opinion in the least, she might have punched him for the remark, but it wasn't the first time her sanity had been put into question and it wouldn't be the last.

She yanked open the door to the helicopter's passenger section and was greeted with the oddest smell of floral dirt. She sighed as she looked over the tightly cocooned woman that lay comatose in the back. She would have preferred to have the woman travel with the others, but since Gypsy was the only one who could touch her, she had become the designated delivery girl.

She looped her duffel bag over her neck and maneuvered the petite woman from the back. She was light and Gypsy was strong, but she still wasn't looking forward to several flights of stairs with the witch and her heavy pack in tow. She could have lightened the load, but what would the warden say if she left a near-god-level sorceress just lying around? Someone was bound to trip over her.

Gypsy offered a lazy salute to the pilot and slipped into the stairwell. She had anticipated a group of guards to greet, detain, or otherwise annoy her, but there was no one around. She determined from the sound of the alarms that everyone was too busy to deal with her. Whatever the hell had just happened in the courtyard was taking precedence over her unauthorized visit.

2

THE FLUORESCENT LIGHTS HUMMED and flickered at half power in the main foyer. The bright white floor looked gray in the dim illumination. The ominous room looked like what Cori had expected to see the first time she'd walked through the prison doors. If a zombie came limping down the hallway from the docks, she probably wouldn't have flinched.

Everyone filtered in behind her. The invading military shuffled up the stairwell, overly concerned with prisoner containment. Her guards scattered to find and help their comrades. Renee, however, seemed more concerned with getting her cargo unloaded at the docks rather than prioritizing any human lives.

"Cori." Efrat pressed his hand on her back.

"Don't." She pulled away and started down the hall to Danato's office. She was angry with him—again. It seemed like she was always angry with him, but this time was different. They had made such strides toward civility the last two days. They had worked together, saving each other's lives and working toward saving their friends, but as usual, when it really counted, Efrat fell short of her expectations.

"We need to talk," Efrat said as he followed her down the hall.

"It's done, Efrat. I get it. You were following orders," she snarled, referring to his efforts to keep her from going back into the time bubble when it was threatening to destabilize. In the end, of course, he had saved her. His heroic subversion had turned her motivations from self-sacrifice to aggravated dissension. It was ultimately their combined power in a singular blasting bolt that had prevented the entity from completely retracting from this world. Together they had saved the prison, including everyone that was trapped inside.

"That's not what I mean," Efrat said.

"Never mind that it was the first order you've followed wholeheartedly since you've been recruited," she grumbled and gestured exaggeratedly as she walked. "Or maybe—"

His hand gripped her forearm, and he pulled her around to face him. She wanted to slap him with her other hand, but he pushed her shoulder back against the wall, limiting her movement. As irritated as she was by being manhandled, she could see a severity in his expression that gave her pause. The last two days had brought out a different side of Efrat. Without several dominating authority figures to buck and mock, he was forced to step up and play the part of sidekick, hero, and bodyguard.

It was a good look for him. Unfortunately, there was also another part that he wanted to play—a role that was already spoken for.

"Do you really think that was the only reason I did that?" He pressed her arm against the wall and pushed a little closer to her. "Did you think I was going to let you kill yourself?" His eyes glimmered with the sentiment he'd promised not to act on. She could feel herself trembling slightly in his grip. She wanted to believe that it was fear—remnants of long-ago abuses coming back to haunt her—but the truth was, she wasn't afraid of Efrat. She hadn't feared him in that way for a long time. The only thing she feared when she was around Efrat was herself.

"Or maybe you just didn't mind if the bubble swallowed them all up," she countered. "Maybe you're okay with a world without Ethan." She dropped the bombshell casually, but Efrat didn't take it that way. His face dimmed, and he brought his face that much closer.

"Stop it!" he hissed through gritted teeth. "What I mind is being in this ridiculous place without you." For a moment, they just stared at each other. His words should have been a prelude to a kiss, but Efrat kept his distance as he had promised. Despite her fondness for his lips, she kept her head pressed to the wall, refusing to tarnish her vows any more than she already had that day.

Efrat's face eventually dimmed as if he sensed the torment that he was causing them both. He stepped away from her, rubbing his face. "Let's just drop it." He clenched his jaw and walked on. "You can figure it out yourself," he mumbled as he distanced her.

She shook away her unwelcome hormones and followed Efrat into Danato's office. The small room was the same as always, but the drywall looked damaged and water spots littered the ceiling. She didn't think it could get more ugly, but apparently nearly starving the entity out of their dimension had warranted even further interior design retribution.

Belus was face down on the desk. She gasped and ran over to him. She checked for his pulse, but she could tell immediately that he was warm and still breathing. He was just asleep. She kneeled down and shook his shoulder gently so she didn't surprise him with her presence.

He coughed and sniffed before turning his sallow eyes to her. She smiled and caressed his cheek. "Morning, Yoda." He narrowed his eyes on her. She was about to defend the title as a term of respect, but his hands wrapped around her throat before she could get the words out.

She yelped and clawed at his fingers, but his small hands were like vices pre-designed for her neck. "Belus," she croaked at him, but his eyes were determined and glazed hypnotically on his task. Wherever he was, he wasn't in that room with her.

She tried to put him to sleep with the power of her rings, but it didn't affect him.

Efrat jumped in behind him and reached forward with electricity-streaked hands. She waved him off. As much as she preferred breathing, she didn't want to hurt Belus. He already looked sickly. There was no telling how much violence he could tolerate. Her choked "no" didn't sound like a word, but Efrat got the hint and growled.

Instead of electrocuting him, he came around behind her and helped pry at Belus's hands with her, so he didn't shock him. "Son of a bitch!" he griped, struggling with the man's dragon-infused strength. "Cori, I can't get him off. Just let me shock him!"

She was about to agree since she could already feel her deceptively dangerous water defense activating, but Duke walked in. "Cori, you're back!" His excitement quickly waned as he took in the scene. "Oh, damn! Hang on!" He jumped over to the water cooler and poured a paper cup of water.

"This isn't time for a drink, you damn hick!" Efrat yelled.

"It's all good, *spark plug*." Duke waved. "He's just sleepwalking... so to speak." Duke leaned across the desk with his full cup and splashed it into Belus's face. He immediately loosened his grip and Cori fell back against Efrat to catch her breath. "Belus!" Duke slammed his hand on the desk, drawing his attention back to reality. "She's not a dream. Cori's back. The bubble's gone." He gestured the description further and made a bubble-popping sound with his mouth.

Belus wiped the water from his face and looked at Cori. He still didn't seem to register the explanation. "It worked?" He stood, and she leaned back into Efrat a little more. His hands glowed with threat, but she pushed them aside.

Belus approached her carefully and touched her cheek, just as she had done to him moments before. Upon feeling that she was real, he smiled. "Hey, kid," he whispered.

She moved forward and gripped a hug around his mid-section. He didn't pull away. He just stroked her hair as she got her fill of the spectacle. She finally pulled away and pocketed any hurt feelings she might have about her mentor trying to kill her. She knew it probably wasn't her he had been trying to kill. The dream feeders had no doubt been torturing him about his past.

She stood up to report to him. "Duke's right. The bubble is gone. We used the taps to send for extra supplies, but, in addition, the board sent the flippin' auditor. She's got men running around the prison everywhere and she's bringing in enough cargo to renovate a stadium."

"She?" Belus's expression soured. "Renee?"

"Yes."

"Where is she now?" he asked.

"She was headed for the docks. What's this all about?"

"Unfortunately, I don't know, but I guarantee we aren't going to like it. Duke, where's Danato?"

"The infirmary," Duke answered.

"The infirmary?" Cori asked, wide-eyed.

"Blood draws," Duke assured her. "Good thing the dark side vamps stayed on the outside. Can't feed that many bloodsuckers."

Cori calmed at hearing that. She hadn't wanted to think about everything that Danato was going to have to do to keep his prisoners alive. Part of her knew that it would have been easier just to let them starve, but that wasn't any more right than letting his guards starve to death. After all, they were prisoners too, just with a different community service than the average convict.

"Come with me," Belus demanded and headed out the door.

Cori followed and stopped by Duke as he offered her leave to go first. "How are Ethan and the baby?"

He smiled, but there was sadness there, too. "Missing you something horrible." He glanced back at Efrat. Whatever exchange happened between them. His smile faded, and he rested his hand on her back to usher her through the door.

3

GYPSY CLIMBED DOWN THE stairwell as soldiers and guards filed past beside her. More than a few gave her questioning looks and even attempted to interrogate her about her presence, but the assaulting emotional vibe coming off her cargo kept them from troubling her too much. She wondered if she could bottle this particular magic and wear it around her neck. She rather liked the intimidation it offered.

She wasn't sure where to go, but luckily, the prison offered big sign designations for each floor. Naturally, it wasn't until she reached the second floor that there was a reasonable solution to her problem. She saw a sign that designated the level "Zoological" and "Infirmary."

The zoological subcategories offered more specific descriptions: Aviary, Aquarium, etc. However, she was more interested in the infirmary subdivisions, including Lab, Surgery, Radiology, and Transitory Holding Cells. She wasn't sure her sleeping beauty required a cell, but at any rate, this was probably the best place to find a bellhop for her baggage.

As she stepped out of the stairwell, she was nearly run down by a herd of passing goats. The bleating ensemble was tied together loosely with rope and led by an impatient guard. She wasn't sure where the goats were going, but she was pretty sure they weren't coming back from it.

A nearby elevator announced itself with a muted *ponk* and another guard exited the lift with a rolling cart. He struggled to pull the wheels over the slight rise in the floor transition, so she gave it an extra push with her free hand. The cart finally jarred loose and the stacked aquariums on board splashed water at her feet. She noted several thick eels barely being contained in the undersized tanks.

"Thanks," the guard said. He noted her baggage and pointed to the glass doors between the two main aisles. "Dead ones go to the infirmary." She nodded as he rolled his fish dinners away.

She strolled over to the infirmary and pushed through the heavy glass doors. Most of the exterior walls offered extensive windows, allowing her an open view of the area. The lighting here was better, indicating they had a separate generator. *Generators,* judging by the technology that she could see through the windows to her immediate right. More than a few people were in hospital beds, hooked up to IVs and heart monitors.

The nurse's station was empty, except for the gads of boxes piled on it. Several women were running around in the back halls yelling orders and trying to keep up with their patient duties. Gypsy thumbed open the loose cardboard flap on one of the boxes at the desk. Inside, she saw a stack of blood plasma packets surrounded by dry ice. Whatever had happened here, people were injured, and the staff was struggling to help them.

In a room labeled "Computer Lab," not too far down the hall to the right of the nurse's hub, she could see a man in a lab coat gesturing to his clipboard impatiently. She couldn't yet see who was on the receiving end of the ass-ripping.

A stocky nurse arrived at the counter, glistening with sweat from her effort to move fast. She grabbed one of the boxes, just as she saw Gypsy. She looked at the mummified body slumped over her shoulder. She frowned and put the box down again. "Oh, no, not another one." She sighed and moved to investigate the girl's identity.

"I wouldn't advise that," Gypsy suggested, but the woman was intent on seeing this potential victim.

The woman reached out before she could register the danger of her proximity. It only took one touch, and she recoiled from it. The traumatic emotional overload sent her backpedaling to the nearest wall. Tears streamed from her eyes and her body shook like a frightened child. Gypsy grimaced at the poor woman, unsure of how to apologize for her potent cargo.

"I'm not going to discuss this with you any further, Doctor," a rather burly looking man announced as he exited the computer lab. The man in the lab coat, apparently the doctor of this facility, persisted in following him with his ever-important clipboard in tow. "Your term is based on real time, not the den time."

"The timeline shouldn't matter, just the labor," the physician insisted with the arrogance Gypsy had come to expect from anyone who had achieved a doctorate. "I have been working non-stop for *three years*."

The larger unshaven man circled back to face him. "And I have been working non-stop for thirty-six years! Don't ever pretend that your burden is greater than mine. You will work your term in full, and you will feel fortunate to never remember it. Now get back to work before I requisition a term extension!"

Gypsy smiled as the squirrely doctor pinched his lips into an angry pout that didn't belong on anyone over the age of twelve. Much to her dismay, he walked away rather than stomping. That would have been the highlight of her day.

In place of that treat, however, the six-plus-foot man rounded the corner and spotted her standing at the front desk. She wasn't sure what had engaged his defenses first: the quivering nurse backing herself into a wall, the half-dead woman hanging over her shoulder, or the arsenal barely contained in her black duffle bag.

His eyes widened like a lion on the Serengeti prepared to pounce on his prey. If Gypsy had been a normal girl, or even a smart girl, she would have felt a wave of overpowering fear. However, all she felt was an adrenaline rush that primed her for two different paths, one of which was entirely inappropriate at the moment, but, nevertheless, she enjoyed the foreplay being offered.

"Who the hell are you?" the man bellowed with due contempt.

She couldn't keep the slow smile from spreading over her face. She already suspected that this was the warden, Danato Calibria, but the deep booming voice confirmed it. His eyes narrowed a little further, and he took a step forward, broadening his shoulders. "How did you get in here?"

Her instincts demanded that she reach for her gun, but she knew that *strong as an ox* was not an adequate description of the man's strength—perhaps *Babe the Blue Ox*. At any rate, she didn't wish to instigate a physical confrontation with the man, at least not under these circumstances.

His rough-cut look wasn't a deviation from the description she had been given, but he was a good deal trimmer than she had thought he would be. Much like the rest of the staff she had encountered, he seemed to be in a state of undernourishment.

His face was handsome, though slightly weathered by age and a little slack at the moment. His brownish hair was graying a little faster than it probably should have, but that was to be expected for a man in such a stressful position. He looked altogether unkempt: hair askew, wrinkled dress shirt, and untailored brown slacks. He looked more like he had purchased his wardrobe from Indiana Jones instead of Jones New York.

Despite all of that, however, he had a masculine appeal that Gypsy could get on board with, and should the opportunity arise, get into bed with.

"I seem to have arrived at a bad time," she admitted, glancing toward the filled beds in the other room.

"How the hell did you get into my prison?" Danato asked again.

"The roof." She pointed up.

Danato's eyes widened, and he grabbed for his radio and flicked it on. After fidgeting with the dial for a second, he seemed to find the main frequency that the guards were using.

"*What the hell is going on?*" a man barked over the radio. "*Why is there an elephant on four?*" he asked indignantly.

Danato frowned.

"There was an explosion of sorts," Gypsy reported what little she knew. He looked at her, waiting for more, but she didn't have much more to tell him. "More of a blast wave without the fire."

"*Who invited the stiff necks?*" a different man asked over the radio.

"Who are you?" Danato asked her. She could tell he was losing patience because his voice was getting quieter.

"I'm not with the *stiff necks*, if that's what you want to know. They were here already. I'm more of a subcontractor. Actually, I'm just an errand boy today." She nodded to the body slung over her shoulder. "Hope you don't mind that I let myself in. I had a lot to carry." Danato glanced at the body, but he didn't move to investigate. He probably would have thrown her in a cell or a headlock already if it weren't for the fact that she was a woman. His gallantry was slowing his reaction, or perhaps he was still evaluating her threat level before he pounced.

"Seriously! I am not cleaning this up. The flippin' thing just shit out a Buick!" the first guard continued to squawk over the radio.

"Ten-four, boys, we are just getting the report now," a man with a Texan accent jumped on the line. *"The bubble has popped, and we got some impromptu guests comin' in hot and heavy."*

Danato finally brought the radio to his lips. "Duke, who are they?"

"Cori says they're with the Board."

"Cori," Danato said to himself and took a ragged breath. He pressed the radio to his forehead. The relief on his face seemed to bring him close to tears.

"Boss, we got orders coming in from every yahoo with a gun and then some. Our boys don't know if we should be raising hell or putting out the welcome mat."

"All right, Duke, tell everyone to stand down and let them through. These are the good guys, at least for today. Send somebody down to the basement and get the power back to normal so we can have decent light. And I want a full report on the den stats as soon as possible."

"Will do, Warden."

Danato returned the radio to his side and looked back at the nurse cowering away from them. "Go on, Clare. I'll handle this." The woman was relieved to have permission to leave and ran down the hall. "What did you do to her?"

"Not me, the cargo." Gypsy tried to shrug, but the pressure from both sides made it near impossible. "She's pretty potent on closer inspection."

"Do I really have to ask you the same question three times?" Danato's eyes twitched.

Gypsy smirked and shook her head. "My name is Grace Gypsum. I'm a former U.S. Marine, honorably discharged—barely. I've been recruited by a private party to continue my services in the field of the supernatural."

"I know every one of my hunters, and you aren't one of them."

"I didn't say I was a hunter. The private party I work for is a budding organization. A sort of alternative business model."

Danato clenched his jaw and shook his head. "I would strongly advise you to find a new employer. My employers are a dedicated monopoly. I would hate for your budding organization to get acquired so early in its development."

Gypsy nodded. She liked this man. He knew how to flirt with her. Very few men knew how to do that. "I appreciate your candor, but we have no intention of being acquired by anyone. However, I think a merger might be of interest to us. Perhaps you and I could discuss our bottom lines."

Gypsy expected the man to meet her seductive gaze with leery interest, but his face fell and a weariness replaced his anger, extinguishing all hope that this flirtation was headed anywhere.

"Please tell me that you aren't with the Russians, because that didn't end well last time."

"No. I already told you, I'm here to give you this lump on my shoulder. I usually don't offer delivery services, but this was a special circumstance. Daniel McGrath sent me." His eyes finally glimmered with an inkling of understanding and he approached the body on her shoulder. She didn't bother warning him. She just held still so he could get as close as he dared.

To her surprise, he pushed through the teeth-clenching wave of passion to lift the veil on the woman's face. He pulled away as soon as he had witnessed what he wanted to. He looked angry, but that didn't stop the compulsory tears from dribbling down his cheeks. "That's Adrianna?" he asked her.

Gypsy nodded. "Your sorceress. She's in a coma, but alive."

Danato took several cleansing breaths, trying to get his emotions in check. "How are you able to carry her?"

"That would be the special circumstance that I was referring to. I seem to be the only one capable of touching her." She smiled, happy to see the befuddled interest on his face. "Seriously, though, I don't have superhuman strength. Can I dump her somewhere?"

He blinked and stammered, momentarily sheepish for his inhospitable behavior. "Follow me."

"Danato!" A woman's voice distracted him from his leading exit. His face brightened as he turned to see the origin of the glee.

Gypsy cursed her aching shoulder as a blond head bobbed past her and hugged Danato tightly.

"Cori, thank God you're okay." He lifted her from the floor in a long, tight embrace. He set her back down and released her.

"How are—?" Cori did a double take on Gypsy. "What the hell is *she* doing here?" Cori stared her down with the same mix of emotions she'd had when they'd last spoken. At least now Gypsy understood the woman's ambivalence, but the hatred that she exhibited still seemed excessive. After all, it's not like Gypsy had tried to kill her in *this* reality.

4

D ANATO COULD BARELY GET a handle on one situation before another arose. The food drops that arrived five months ago had kept everyone from making cannibalism a lifestyle choice, but that only solved the issue of nutrition. If he wasn't convincing hardened criminals to sacrifice their sustenance and blood for creatures they considered to be pets more than wards, he was arguing with the "voluntary" staff about their obligations to the prison.

Now he had the Board's hired thugs invading his prison to check up on him. He understood their concerns, but they could hardly control the entity better than him. Now the strange woman standing before him had brought a sorceress he was obligated to execute. Cori's reaction to her surprised him, but it wasn't nearly as alarming to him as the sinister smirk the woman cast back.

"Hello, Cori," the brunette said cheerfully.

"You know her?" Danato pulled Cori back protectively.

"This is Gypsy," Cori answered, sounding exhausted just to say the name.

"Gypsy?" Danato felt the weight of the day increase tenfold. He looked over the woman and she met his gaze with even interest. She was gauging him as much as he was her. He couldn't very well arrest her for a crime she committed in a skewed reality, nor could he make judgments about it. Still, from every description Cori had offered of the woman, she seemed insane. He may have to offer her civility, but he certainly didn't have to trust her.

"Danato," Belus called for his attention at the entrance to the infirmary. Efrat and Duke were at his side. "Cori says the auditor is here."

If Danato had been near a wall, he might have punched it. "You've got to be kidding."

Belus perked a brow. "*She* loves her bad timing."

"She?" Danato glanced at Cori and she nodded, probably not understanding the ultimate meaning behind his rising concern at the auditor's gender. "You're not kidding," he said to Belus. "This is Adrianna." Danato nodded to the body lying over Gypsy's shoulder. Belus barely reacted, but he knew the taciturn man had a thousand and one memories flooding his mind—as if the last eleven months hadn't brought enough of them to the surface already.

"*Danato!*" Ethan's voice finally came over the radio. Danato had presumed he was busy or had adjusted his frequency for a more private conversation with someone.

He ripped his radio off his hip. "Ethan, where are you?"

"Currently standing on the head of a very presumptuous, formerly armed man."

"They are with the Board, Ethan. Don't shoot anyone."

"I'd be happy to put down my weapon if they would do the same, but we seem to be at an impasse. And nobody is budging."

"What floor is he on?" Efrat asked.

"Where are you?" Danato asked.

Transmorphs. Section 5-A.

"Tell him I'm on my way." Efrat backed out of the infirmary doors before Danato could decide if that was a good idea or not.

"Tell him *we're* on our way," Duke added and jogged out the door after Efrat.

Danato dithered at Efrat and Duke's impromptu teamwork, but he presumed both men were above childish squabbles when real problems were afoot. Either that or they were both just up for a good fight.

"What are your orders, Danato?" Ethan asked impatiently.

"Hold your position. Efrat and Duke are on their way."

"Efrat?"

"That's right."

There was a slight pause on the line. *"Is she... okay?"*

Danato looked at Cori. Her eyes begged to take the radio out of his hand and speak to him, but she also seemed to understand that he was too busy for a reunion. "Yeah, she's fine." He paused and waited for the response. After a long pause, his voice cracked over.

"*Standing by.*"

Danato gave Cori a squeeze. He hoped she didn't take offense at his curt prescribed response.

"Danato, the girl," Belus interrupted again.

"Just give me a second to think," Danato snapped. He had too many people demanding his command.

"Do you want me to handle it?" Belus offered quietly. He stared down his adviser and friend. His offer was meant sincerely. And Danato was tempted to take him up on it, but he couldn't put any more blood on his hands, especially of young innocent women who had just made the mistake of trusting the wrong people with their safety.

"No, I'll take care of it." He broke away from Cori. "Wait here with Belus."

Cori backed away. "Danato, what's—?"

"Wait here," he said firmly.

"Yes, sir." She backed away, moving past Gypsy, who kept her in her peripheral view as she went by.

"Come with me," he commanded the militant woman.

5

GYPSY FOLLOWED DANATO DOWN the long infirmary hall, keeping a good distance between them. She could tell the girl's presence was already affecting his nerves, so she didn't want to make him more sensitive. Not to mention, she knew he didn't trust her. It wasn't necessary for him to, but it was going to make things very confrontational later.

They passed a line of exam rooms and at least three mammoth holding cells before he stopped in front of a steel door with a small eye-level window. He pulled a long key from his pocket and unlocked the deadbolt. He opened the door to the darkened room and offered her admittance. "Just lay her on the floor."

Gypsy peeked into the room, curious of its size, but she had no intention of entering a lockable room without assurance of her safety. She looked back at Danato and tipped her head to the door. "Gentlemen first."

He paused, staring at her a moment longer before shaking away whatever rebuttal was on his mind. He disappeared into the shadows of the room and she warily followed.

Inside, she could feel concrete under her feet. The acrid smell of bleach lingered in the air. "What is this room?" she asked.

"Just set the girl down and you can leave."

Gypsy checked his location in the darkened shadows and lowered the girl gently to the floor. Her veil slipped away from her face and she could hear Danato inhale sharply. She had probably been a beautiful young woman during her prime, but by now the magic that was slowly killing her had starved her body of all visible life. Her jutting cheekbones and sunken eyes were all the more pitiable because she was still breathing.

She moved the gauze back over her face to alleviate his discomfort. She stood and looked over the somber man hiding in the shadows. He was a strong man physically and his demeanor commanded respect, but his heart was possibly too big for the dirty job of an executioner.

"Are you sure you're prepared to do this?" she asked quietly, offering as much sympathy in her voice as she could. In a way, it was the only honest emotion she ever had. She truly did pity those that were burdened with intense emotions. It must make life so difficult. "You look a little green. When's the last time you had to pull a trigger?"

Danato shifted and moved back to the entrance. She might have been concerned, but he was careful to make his movements slow enough not to be a threat. He flipped on the light switch by the door and the gray concrete room was revealed.

"Holy hell," she whispered, looking at the wall behind him. Every manner of weapon from gun to blade hung from it. Unlike a personal collection that might hold polished, decorated weaponry, this wall held functional and often-cleaned hardware. She barely recognized most of the blades, but she assumed the array of varying sickles was particularly useful for larger prey.

The center of the room dipped down to a large drain, and a depository on the wall opposite the door provided immediate access to the incinerators. The wall behind her held varying chains, some high and large, others low and small. Vague blood stains flared from various areas on the wall where blood splatters had embedded too deeply in the concrete to simply wash away. This was a playground for psychopaths and serial killers. Real people didn't belong in here.

She turned back to Danato. He was no more proud of this room than a regular prison warden would be of their gas chamber. She recognized the determination on his face. He was willing to do what needed to be done, but it didn't mean he would enjoy it.

She moved to the door and slowly pulled the door shut, closing them into the small room. Danato narrowed his eyes, tracking the movement suspiciously. She took a step closer to him and he took the opportunity to look her over more carefully. He may not have trusted her, but he was not afraid of her. She enjoyed that.

She pulled the strap of her duffel bag over her head and dropped the heavy load onto the floor. It clunked, hinting at the number of metal components within.

She leaned down and pulled out one of the protruding objects from her pack. She moved slowly, and Danato's eyes remained on her the entire time.

She raised the sword and presented it to Danato before slowly sliding it from its sheath. The finely honed metal sang as it slowly slid from the scabbard. Even when the blade was fully exposed and reflecting the light in the room, Danato didn't attempt to intercept the weapon.

"I've heard the katana provides an almost painless death." Gypsy paused, waiting for him to give her permission to take the burden of murder from his hands.

He stared at her a moment longer, analyzing her like one of the many alien creatures in his facility. Without a word, he moved to the back wall and grabbed a handgun from the many varieties at his disposal. He popped the magazine out and checked it before slamming it back in place.

With no more than a few steps to reach the girl, Danato was over top of her firing three successive shots before Gypsy even had a chance to protect her ears from the echoing reports.

He looked back at her with a coldness that she only ever expected to see in a mirror. "Bullets work just fine," he said as he returned to the wall.

Gypsy looked over the body and observed the expulsion of blood filling the floor. The gauze bandages quickly saturated with blood.

Danato placed the firearm back on the wall and made a notation in a small book that hung from a chain on the same wall. She wondered if it was a log of the names that had been executed or if it was just an inventory of how many bullets he had used.

He turned to leave and paused a moment to look at the body. He looked ashamed of the achievement, but also relieved that he had ripped the Band-Aid off swiftly. If she hadn't been impressed by him earlier, she was definitely now.

He stopped in front of her and looked down at the samurai sword hanging at her side. "I don't think I'll need any more of your assistance. You are welcome to leave the way you came or I can set up a truck for you. Either way, I want you out of my prison." He pushed open the squawking metal door, but paused again to speak. "And to answer your earlier inquiry, there will be no discussion of mergers." Having given his final word on the subject, Danato disappeared back down the hall to get the chaos of the day under control.

Gypsy looked over the scene again, still in disbelief that Danato hadn't given the task more ceremony or contention. The blood was already flowing down the slope of the concrete, spilling into the drain. The bright red was always a surprise. It would eventually darken into the crimson that most people associated with carnage, but while it was fresh and warm, it was bright and... iridescent?

The shimmering sparkle in the blood was new to Gypsy. She squatted down and dipped her finger into the trickle, examining its consistency. The silver sheen in the blood was barely visible close up, but it looked like the woman had been injected with colloidal silver—or fairy dust; either was possible at this point.

The blood vanished from her fingers, seemingly absorbed by her skin. She checked the back of her hand to make sure it hadn't just dribbled away. It was an odd interaction, but it didn't worry her. She doubted the girl had any incurable diseases that she could contract.

Gypsy stood to leave, but a visceral wave knocked her back to the floor like a punch to the gut. A torrent of memories dripping with love, hate, joy, and fear slammed into her mind like a two-ton wrecking ball. Not a one was her own, but she felt them as if they were.

As the emotional overload faded, she rolled over and jumped up, searching for a physical attacker, but there was no one there. The confrontation had been internal.

Gypsy panted, now realizing that what she had just felt was what normal people felt—only perhaps times a thousand... or a million. It was definitely a fun rush, but the experience was unwelcome.

She cussed and shook off the sentiments like she would any physical assault. Despite the obvious danger of the blood, Gypsy kneeled down to inspect the red puddle again. She couldn't see the sparkling glow she had seen the first time. She reached down to touch it and noticed a slight glimmer in her hand. She drew it back, bending her fingers and stretching them. The glow appeared and disappeared in the creases of her hand, but then it was gone. Her skin was just skin, the blood on the floor was just blood, and her emotions were back to where they belonged—buried far too deep to survive.

She stood and grabbed her bag. Whatever had happened to her was either temporary, or more likely one of the many things that would ultimately bite her in the ass later. Regardless, there was nothing she could do about it now.

6

ORI HEARD THE MUFFLED shots and looked at Belus. He was watching her, waiting to see if her morality might explode under the pressure of reality. She wanted to. She wanted to be angry that her mentors could justify killing a young woman just because she'd dabbled too deep in the dark arts.

Instead, she reminded herself that Belus and Danato were good men. She ignored the seed of doubt, the part of her that wondered if their obligation to the prison was stronger than their love for her.

"You know it had to be done," Belus said quietly.

She nodded. "My first weeks here, Danato had to execute a mermaid to protect me."

"I remember."

"I never understood why he was so furious about it—" The door down the hall opened and Danato stomped back toward them. "—until now."

"Let's go, Cori!" Danato barked as he moved around the nurse's hub. It made her jump, even though she knew he wasn't directing his anger at her. "Let's go find out why my prison has gone from Fort Knox to

Disney-fucking-Land." He paused next to Belus and glanced back at the hallway. "Watch her. I don't trust her."

"I second that," Cori added, and Belus mock saluted her.

Cori followed Danato out of the infirmary and into the stairwell. She wasn't sure if it was his anger setting his pace or if his weight loss had just assisted his movement that much. Whatever the reason, she was barely keeping up with him. "Are you okay?"

"Not now, Cori," he threw back at her like she was nothing but a subordinate to him.

"Stop!" she yelled. She grabbed his shoulder and gave it a tug.

He turned back to face her. "What is it, Cori?"

Even two steps above him, she was barely taller than him. "Your eyes are bloodshot from fighting off the dream feeders. You've been offering up your blood to vampiric prisoners. You're at least thirty pounds lighter. And you just executed a woman."

"I don't have time for this! My prison—"

"You will *make* time for it!" Cori yelled at him. He raised his chin, ready to yell right back, but he didn't.

"I know you don't want to talk about it, and I know now is not the time if you were to, but... You need to tell me if you're okay. Or at least that everything will be okay." She bit her lip, waiting for his reaction.

His expression slowly softened, and a certain irritated smirk appeared. "Cori," he said softly. "The bubble is down; the sorceress threat has been dealt with; and you are alive and well." He wrapped his arms around her waist and pulled her in for another hug. He kissed her cheek and released her. "With the exception of my pain-in-the-ass job, I am actually okay."

"Good." She smiled with relief.

He started to turn away, but turned back. "What about you?" He looked her over. "How did things go with Efrat? Any... trouble?"

She opened her mouth to speak, but the only thing she could think about was the two stolen kisses with Efrat that had unfortunately been witnessed.

"Did he hurt you?" Danato's expression instantly turned dark.

"No!" Cori shook her head vehemently, but then she remembered Dirk, the man who had attacked her to win a bet that Efrat had stupidly made. Not that it would have taken a bet for the man to have an excuse to rape her.

"What is it?" Danato asked.

"There was an incident with one of the guards. Efrat and I handled it, but I'm not sure you'll be happy about how it was handled." Cori didn't want to get into the specifics of how she had frozen the man's member off in a fit of self-defense-inspired rage. "Now probably isn't the time for details."

He frowned. "I'm not going to like these details, am I?"

Cori shrugged. "You'll either be proud or perturbed, but I'm not sure which."

"All right, one problem at a time."

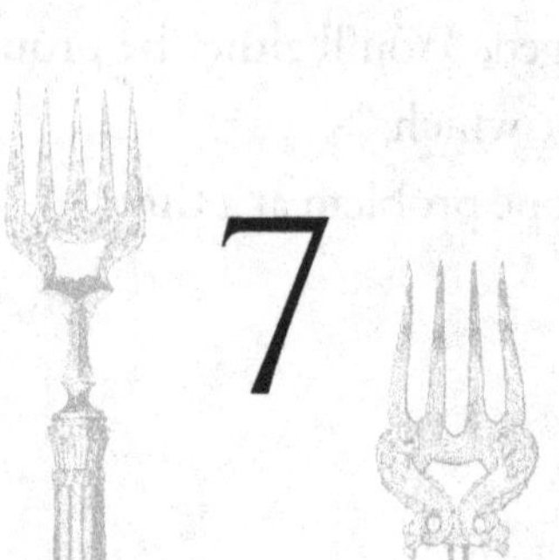

7

GYPSY STROLLED BACK DOWN the hall to the nurse's station. She glanced around, but didn't see the big man waiting for her. He must have been too busy to escort her to the exit. She headed toward the infirmary entrance and noticed a red-headed little man leaning comfortably against the wall by the door.

She paused to assess him. He wasn't as short as she had expected, but he would still have to stand on his tippy-toes to see down her shirt. He was surly looking, but his eyes sparkled with insight. He appraised her just as carefully, and when their eyes met she knew, he knew, he was looking into the eyes of his murderer.

At least from another reality.

She dropped her bag, and it hit the floor discourteously loud, but it didn't make the man jump. "I thought you'd be taller," she said, to test his temperament.

"I'm a dwarf. Everyone thought I'd be taller." She smirked at his humor. "I thought you would have purple hair."

She resisted reacting to his audacious show of his knowledge. "So I'm told."

"Really? And who would have told you that?"

Gypsy chuckled. He was smarter than she'd thought, too. "I'm not quite sure what to do now. I feel a little naked."

"Perhaps you could continue to disrobe." She perked a brow at his flirtation. "Metaphorically speaking, of course. Why don't you start with the elite group that you're part of and end with why you are so keen to get Leona in control of the Council of the Moon?"

"Ah, I hate to disappoint you, but I only follow orders."

"And who gives those orders?"

Gypsy bit her lip. "I can see why I had to kill you. You're too curious for your own good." He glanced down at the knife strapped to her thigh. "Don't worry, I'm not here to kill you." She picked up her bag and adjusted the weight onto her sore shoulder. "Those aren't my orders." She winked at him and pushed through the glass doors to leave the infirmary.

8

E THAN SHIFTED TO RELEASE the man under his foot. "Get up," he commanded.

"You have no idea who I am, boy," the one-handed man snarled and pushed off the floor.

Ethan adjusted his weapon to ease the threat against the six men surrounding him. He had yet to acknowledge any of them. All he was interested in was the man peeking into the cells of his transmorphs.

"It doesn't matter who you are. You just walked into *my* prison, so the only name that matters is mine."

"Which is?" He tugged his jacket down.

"Ethan Xavier Pierce."

"You're not the warden yet, boy."

"Call me boy one more time and you'll be eating through a tube for the rest of your life."

"Will I?" The man tipped his head to one side. "You've got six guns aimed at your head right now. What makes you think you can back up that threat?"

"Did somebody say backup?" Duke hollered as he entered the section with Efrat right behind. It was a strange combination, but Ethan wouldn't pass up the company. "Woo-wee! Looks like we're just in time for some fun."

Two men turned their guns from him to them.

"Maddox, I suggest you listen to me this time." Efrat stopped several yards away. "Stand down or fall down."

"And how exactly are two unarmed men going to intimidate me when a single man can't?"

"You're right, let's even those odds a bit." Efrat perked his brow and his hands lit with trickles of blue. He offered a slight pause for comprehension before he threw his hand out. The blast of energy cleaved the air above them, making everyone flinch, including Ethan.

He barely felt the tug on his gun before it was gone, right along with every other gun and knife within range of the magnetic field. Efrat ripped the ball of weaponry back and released them. They crashed into a pile behind him.

After a short pause, Maddox's men charged, primed for hand-to-hand combat. Ethan took out the first man with a single concussive punch. The next two, he eased back his strength, so he didn't inadvertently kill them. It made for a slower fight, but he didn't want Duke to miss the fun.

The Texan ran forward, but at the last second, crouched and slid past his first attacker. The second man in line was unprepared for the gut punch, let alone the head shot that quickly followed once he was balled up.

Maddox seemed content to go after Efrat. Ethan expected the elemental to take the man out with a single shock, but instead he fought him off slow. Give or take a few sparking punches, Efrat fought as normal and fair as he could.

When Ethan finished off his two attackers with a body-to-body slam, he grabbed hold of the last attacker, allowing Duke the privilege of socking him in the face. Ethan released the man to flop on the floor, now unable to see through his puffy eyes, let alone fight.

Rather than interrupt, Ethan and Duke watched Efrat and Maddox finish their fight. Despite Efrat having the upper hand most of the time, Maddox didn't appear to be affected by the encounter at all. No cuts and no bruises. Meanwhile, Efrat had a cut over his right brow and a red cheek. He seemed frustrated that his mortal defenses weren't producing the results he wanted. His hands ignited with bright blue energy threads and he grabbed Maddox's neck. He gave him one final hard punch to the jaw.

The combination of punch and bolt sent Maddox flying. When he hit the floor, he disappeared from sight. There one second, gone the next.

Efrat whipped around, searching for the man. "What just happened? Where did he go?" he asked.

Ethan shook his head. "He just disappeared."

"How did he do that?" Duke asked.

"I don't know. Maybe he can—" Ethan felt his scalp burn as a fist gripped his hair and yanked his head back. A blade pierced the skin at the base of his skull, but didn't go in.

"I told you, *boy*, you have no idea who I am!" Maddox rasped into his ear.

9

C ORI SHUFFLED BETWEEN RENEE'S men as they dragged random construction equipment off the dock from one of the semi-trailers. They didn't pay her any heed, but they offered deference to Danato when he passed. He was fuming, but he didn't stop any of the men to interrogate them. He seemed to know that there were bigger fish to fry. She also suspected he knew the exact fish he wanted to fry.

Cori noted the tools and blueprints in one freshly opened crate she passed. The heavy equipment was being loaded on the freight elevator, and the smaller items were being carried out by hand.

The dock manager was talking with Renee on the raised platform. He nodded, taking in every word she had to say with easy compliance. Cori was surprised he was being so accommodating towards her. He didn't even suck up to Danato and Belus.

When the woman caught sight of Danato, she ended the conversation and moved to the edge of the dock to meet him. The relief in her eyes disappeared and her arrogance smothered her scarce humanity. "Hello,

Danato," she said with a husky voice that wavered between sexy and masculine.

"Hello, Mother."

10

S INCE GYPSY WASN'T READY to leave yet, she thought she would take a tour of the facility. Since the next floor up was empty due to the lack of a full moon, it was on to the next. To her surprise, there was a storm brewing not far from the stairwell, literally and figuratively. By the time she arrived, the one-sided battle had shifted into a hostage negotiation.

"Pardon me, gentlemen," Gypsy interrupted the hostage situation playing out in front of her. Four heads whipped in her direction, and four brows buried into eight eyes. "I seem to have taken a wrong turn." She glanced down at the six men littering the floor with bleeding noses and swollen faces.

"Who the hell are you?" the man holding the hostage asked.

She chuckled. "You know, I've been getting that question a lot lately." She shifted her pack off her shoulder, letting it and its contents clunk against the floor. "Don't get me wrong, it's a practical question, but the problem is, if you don't recognize my face, how will my name illustrate my identity any better?"

The tall Farrah-Fawcett-haired man circled back, trying to get a better angle on her. He seemed to be checking her for weapons. Aside from the arsenal in her bag, the remaining few weapons were concealed under her clothing, but judging by where his eyes were lingering, he already knew that. She sensed he had some military training on his resume. For some, it was just an attitude, but for others, it was observation. If the military taught you anything, it was: *be suspicious as hell*.

"What you should really be asking me is: which side am I on?" she suggested, waving her finger back and forth.

"Which side are you on?" Farrah asked, biting on her verbal bait.

"So glad you asked." Gypsy leaned down and pulled her katana from her bag. "I was hoping to get a chance to use my sword today. My earlier opportunity ended..." She grimaced at the memory. "...prematurely." She unveiled the blade and swung it around to get a feel for it. "To answer your question, though, I'm not really sure whose side I'm supposed to be on here. I thought maybe I would just go with the majority and try to kill you." She pointed the tip of her sword at the man holding a hostage.

"My, my, you're even more arrogant than this limey prick. If *he* can't beat me"—the man nodded to Farrah—"what makes you think you can?"

"Because I train werewolves for a living. If I can handle them, I can handle you." The room stilled a moment as each man glanced at the next to see if this was even possible. "Now, if you wouldn't mind stepping away from the hostage so we can fight like civilized people."

The man ground his jaw and shoved his captive forward. He then turned to face her and disappeared... entirely.

Gypsy frowned. "That's new."

11

C ORI FELT HERSELF GASP, but fortunately, it wasn't audible. She hated being side-swiped by new information. It made her feel like an outsider. She was sick of being an interloper in her own home.

"What's this about?" Danato thundered. "Why are all those men roaming freely around my prison?"

"Is that all you have to say? Aren't you going to at least come give me a kiss?" Danato didn't move, but his lip twitched at her invitation. The woman seemed disappointed by this. "We are making some changes to your upper floor. These men are going to be my construction crew, and yes, they have my permission to roam anywhere they need to."

"I assume you have the paperwork to authorize that."

She crossed her arms. "Careful, Danato, I don't relish flaunting my authority over you in the presence of others, but I will if you press me. To answer your question, however, yes, I have the appropriate paperwork. The board has found a new renter and a lofty down payment has already been secured to start renovation of the level."

"Glad to hear it. I imagine that influx of money will put us safely back in the black."

"Very safely, but no, the audit has not been canceled," she said, glancing at Cori. "I will be going through your paperwork with a fine-toothed comb and interviewing your staff. The board believes that regardless of our financial situation, an investigation into the loyalty of your recruits is required."

Cori bit her cheek. She wanted to object to any doubt of her loyalty, but speaking at this point would only enhance that opinion. She needed to back up Danato, not undermine him.

"You will be conducting the investigation—yourself?" Danato queried.

"Yes. I'll also be overseeing the construction, so I will be here for a while. I've already had my bags delivered to your house. It'll be nice sleeping under the same roof again."

Danato's lip twitched again, but his voice remained civil. "Who is the renter?"

"I don't know. Some elitist snob who thinks himself an entrepreneur. Frankly, I stopped listening after the check was signed." She rolled her eyes at the memory of her encounter. "We can get started with the banalities of blueprints, staffing, and budget changes in your office. Your men should remain available to help your shipping staff. I have three more trucks coming, carrying equipment and supplies. I hope your elevators are in a happy mood."

"I don't have any control over that," Danato growled.

"Then I hope your men are in good shape, because six flights is not much fun when you are carrying drywall."

"They'll handle it," Danato seethed. "Now call off your dogs. The prison is secure. I don't need your help. My men know how to handle a crisis."

"Fine." Renee waved over one of her men and took the radio that was clipped to his belt. She wrapped her manicured nails over it and pressed the button to speak. "Maddox."

"Maddox?" Danato's head snapped up. "I told you I don't want *her* in my prison."

"Shush." She swatted away his objection. "Maddox, forget the check. Report back to the loading docks." She waited to hear for a response. "Odd." She shrugged. "He must be busy."

Danato reached for his radio, but seemed to think better of it and let his hand drop. He probably didn't want to give an impression of concern. If Maddox was the one stuck under Ethan's boot heel, he was probably taking care of the situation.

12

Ethan felt the man push him forward, but by the time he turned to defend himself, the man was gone again. "Watch yourself, he's invisible," he warned the brunette that had interrupted their battle.

"Great, just what we need," Efrat mumbled. His hands were armed with crackling blue. He circled around slowly, backing toward Duke and Ethan. They did the same, including the newcomer, until all four of them were back-to-back, watching the four corners of the room.

The woman kept her blade poised for attack, all the while listening intently to the movements around her. Ethan did the same, mirroring with his readied fists. He wasn't sure who this woman was, but so long as her sword wasn't pointed at him, he didn't have a problem with her.

"Maddox," a radio fractured the silence, but it wasn't his or Duke's.

The woman ducked and slashed her sword through the empty air in front of her.

"Maddox, forget the check. Report back to the loading docks."

She continued to pursue the noise of the radio and roundhouse kicked at thin air. Her foot got stuck midway through her kick and she nearly lost balance. Unfettered by the complication, she kicked with her free foot. Somehow she managed to barrel roll over her caught leg. Ethan heard a smack, as if her free foot had impacted something during the roll.

The woman's foot broke free of the grip on it and she landed in a squat. Wasting no time, she swung herself around and slashed her sword at waist level. Nothing appeared to hinder her graceful lethal movement, but as the blade completed its arc, he could see the tip was sweating blood.

Having once again correctly predicted the man's location, the woman jumped forward and slashed at him again. Ethan could almost imagine Maddox floundering backwards, narrowly missing a deadly evisceration with each swipe.

He heard a *thunk* as if something heavy had landed on the floor. The woman stopped and pressed her foot toward the ground in front of her. It hovered in place, stalled out by what was likely to be the invisible man's torso or groin.

She paused a moment, panting over her downed prey, no doubt proud of her accomplishment. Ethan was about to congratulate her when she raised her samurai blade high and brought it crashing down on Maddox, with no sign of stopping.

13

C ori wasn't surprised Renee hadn't invited her to the office party with Danato, but she was disappointed that he had sent her away to report to Belus. She didn't bother calling him on the radio, since he rarely kept it on. Instead, she just headed back up to the infirmary, hoping to intercept him. She also wanted to check on Gypsy.

When she found the waiting room empty, she turned around to leave again. A clipboard slapped against the counter of the nurse's station, drawing her attention back to the young doctor that was glaring at her. "You!" he seethed, jutting his finger at her.

He was in his thirties, slender with dark hair and high widow's peaks. Cori was certain that he had a name, but she had forgotten it. This man was just one of the many doctors who had served time in the infirmary over the years.

Cori wasn't sure if her dismissal of the medical staff started because she resented their short-term obligation or if she was trying to protect herself. At any given time, there were a half-dozen women on staff whom she could socialize with, but knowing that a deeper friendship would only result in a greater loss, there was no point getting too chummy with any of them.

"What about me?" she asked.

"What the hell did you do to that man?"

Cori frowned as she realized what might have perturbed the doctor. "I take it they brought Dirk in."

"Yes—most of him, anyway."

Cori bit her lip. "Yeah, we had an incident."

"Incident! You severed his genitals! He has third-degree burns from his belly button to his anus!" The doctor stalked toward her with every lecturing word. "Just because you have the power to hurt people doesn't mean you have the right to!"

Cori crossed her arms defiantly. She regretted what she had done to Dirk, but for this man to question her actions without even inquiring into her motives made her furious. "And what if someone hurts me first?" she asked coldly.

"Certainly, self-defense doesn't include removing a man's penis."

"That was the body part that was trying to hurt me," she said blithely.

The doctor paused a moment, as if putting the puzzle pieces together. Despite any sympathy he might have held for her as a potential rape victim, he was not content to lose his argument. "You need to get control of those things before you kill someone." He pointed at her rings.

"I *am* in control of them. That's why his dick is on the floor of the guard's quarters and not his head!"

"I'm going to report this to Danato." The doctor went so far as to waggle his head at her before he turned to scamper off and tattle.

"Report what?" Belus asked from the door of the infirmary.

14

"STOP!" ETHAN YELLED. THE harsh depth of his voice echoed around the hard walls. To his surprise, the deadly sword strike stopped millimeters from Maddox's head.

He had reappeared and was panting under the pressure of the woman's foot—which turned out to be pressing into his crotch. "Who the hell are you?" he yelled at her.

She balked in disgust and walked away. She picked up her sheath from the top of her bag and slipped the sword back into it. "Grace Gypsum," she answered unceremoniously.

"Gypsy?" Ethan questioned, all too familiar with Cori's recount of the strange woman who had helped her during the werewolf attack and sabotaged the prison during her wish reality.

Gypsy nodded. She offered him a little more inspection. "A nickname... from your wife?" She questioned the accuracy of the relationship. He nodded. "I liked it so much I thought I'd keep it. Seems like more people know be by that name, anyway."

"What are you doing here?" Ethan asked.

"When did your hand grow back?" Efrat asked Maddox, who was still lying on the floor among his rousing comrades.

Ethan looked at the man and saw that he was not only unbruised and uncut, but also no longer handicapped. "Transmorph," he whispered, frantically checking the cages nearby to see if the count was right. There were only two in this section, but they were both accounted for and happily impersonating the newcomer Gypsy. The woman looked over the mirror images of herself with momentary interest before turning her attention back to Maddox.

"I'm not a transmorph." He clutched his belly and pulled his hand away to show the blood. Ethan wasn't quite convinced since a transmorph could fake blood. "Transmorphs can't go invisible," he added.

"No, they can't," Ethan agreed. "So, what are you?"

"I'm here under the orders of the board members. Beyond that, I am none of your business." He grunted as he stood up.

"Is it deep?" Gypsy asked, eyeing his stomach as if their recent brawl was just a playground spat.

"Not deep enough," he muttered and started helping his men up.

Gypsy grabbed her bag and headed back to where she had come in.

"Where the hell are you going?" Ethan hollered after her.

"I've delivered my package already. No one is going to let me shed any blood. Not much, anyway." She glanced at Maddox. "I'm going to steal a truck and get the hell out of here while I still have the choice," Gypsy answered before continuing back the way she came in.

"What package?"

"The girl."

"Wait. Stop!" Ethan yelled after her, stopping her progress. She turned and tipped her head, waiting for him to ask the question that would inevitably follow such a succinct response. "Which girl?"

"The sorceress."

"Adrianna?" He moved toward her, ignoring the defensive shift in her stance. "She's here? Where?"

Gypsy glanced behind him and took a breath before she answered. "Listen, I don't know—"

"Where is she?" he asked resolutely.

"The infirmary."

Ethan pushed past the last of Maddox's recovering men and bypassed Gypsy to get to the stairwell.

"Hey, wait!" Gypsy called after him. "She's not exactly available for conversation."

He could hear her following behind him, but he ignored her. He needed to get to Addy before Danato. He needed to find some way to prove to him that she was good.

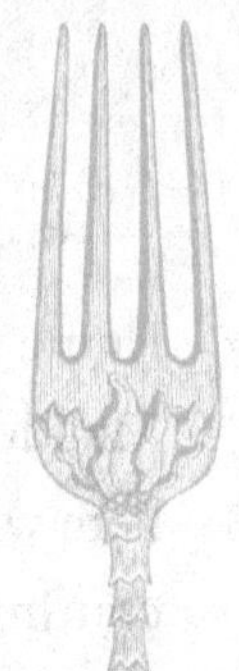

15

IT ANNOYED CORI THAT the doctor had effectively tattled on her. She'd had every intention of filling Danato and Belus in about the incident. She'd just figured she would wait until they were in better moods.

"Are you mad?" Cori asked, after she had finished reporting the bulk of the last two days to Belus. She had naturally left out the bet between Dirk and Efrat, and skimmed over the more intimate details of her interactions with Efrat. Belus wasn't interested in that soap opera.

Belus had listened to the story as he sat with her in the infirmary waiting area. He had yet to comment on any aspect of her account. Even her morbid admission about Dirk's dismemberment hadn't fazed him.

Belus sighed and glanced to the nurse's hub, where the doctor continued to eye them both indignantly while he finished his paperwork. "Will he live?" he called over to him.

"Yes, no thanks to her butchery," the doctor snarled.

Belus's face darkened, and he moved past her to approach the doctor. He didn't flinch at his arrival, but he stood a little straighter. "Heal him, wipe him, and send him back to a new prison with a reasonable medical explanation."

The doctor rolled his eyes and slammed his chart down. "She needs to be held accountable for her actions."

"Yes, she does, just as you need to."

"Me?" The doctor's chest puffed up.

"Yes, did you think harassing your superiors would be an excusable offense?"

"She isn't my superior!"

"She is your superior in every sense of the word. There are four people that command this prison, two of which are in the room with you right now. You will do as you are asked without question, and you will do it because it is the duty of your birthright."

The doctor opened his mouth to object, but he could see that the argument was not winnable. He shuffled his papers and walked away. Belus stomped back toward her. She smiled at his audacity, but he didn't share her amusement. He stopped before her and brandished a finger at her.

"The next time someone questions your authority or discounts your position in this prison, you will do whatever it takes to make sure it doesn't happen again. Do you understand?"

Cori nodded vacantly.

"There are only three people that are allowed to yell at you in this prison, and that mouthy bastard is not one of them."

"Yes, sir," she murmured. Belus walked out, and Cori followed him. "Is that it then?" she asked. She struggled to keep up with him at a casual pace, so she sped up.

"No." Belus turned back, and she nearly ran into him. "For the record, the next time someone attacks you, just kill them. Mutilation is far more paperwork than death."

"I can't tell if you're kidding or not," she stammered.

"Do I look like I'm in a jovial mood?"

"No, but I don't understand why you're so mad at me."

"I am mad because at some point you are going to have to make these men listen to you. Be it the Dirks that come through this prison, or those over-privileged assholes." He motioned to the infirmary.

Cori shrugged. "I know."

"I'm not always going to be there, Cori. Danato is not always going to be there." She nodded. She didn't want to think about a future without them, but life didn't offer exceptions to the grave. "You and Ethan will be the ones to take over this insane legacy. You have to be ready for opposition."

"Yes, sir."

"Don't *yes, sir* me, Cori. Tell me you hear me."

"I hear you," she insisted.

"There is no human resource office here to report harassment to. Danato's threats are meaningless if he isn't there to enforce them. These men have to know that you are not just eye candy. You need to be a leader so you aren't identified as prey. Do you understand?"

Cori felt the words like a slap in the face. He was almost blaming her for the attack. What was worse was that he was right. She was meant to be in a position of authority and she rarely, if ever, exerted any. She had had more control over the men in the last two days than in the last two years. How could she expect them to view her as anything more than a forbidden lay if she didn't give them anything more to think about?

Cori exhaled. "I understand."

Belus stared at her for a moment. His stern expression seemed to soften a bit. "Dirk didn't..." He stopped, unable to finish the sentence.

She shook her head. "No, he... I'm okay. Really."

A sort of relief poured over Belus that she hadn't expected. His tense shoulders relaxed and he let a breath out that he had been holding. As she'd suspected, his concern for her had fueled his bluster.

Cori heard the door to the stairwell open, and she looked back to see who had joined the level. She saw Ethan stride over to the infirmary. He looked determined to get there. She was about to holler at him when the infamous Gypsy Grace emerged and followed behind him. She immediately hated the woman all over again. There would never be a time that she tolerated that woman being near the people she loved.

"You don't want to see her, Ethan," she said as they disappeared out of view. Cori couldn't help wondering when they had gotten introduced.

"Cori, there's something we should talk about," Belus said.

She wanted to reunite with Ethan and go see their baby, but she already knew where he was headed. As selfish as it was, she didn't want his commiseration about Addy's death to sully her time with him. She decided it was best to avoid Ethan for a little while. Perhaps he could take his anger out on Gypsy and bring some pleasure to her day.

She turned back to Belus, prepared to discuss whatever topic he had in mind, but she realized she had a subject of her own to bring up. She tipped her head and narrowed her eyes. "Why didn't you tell me Danato had a mother?"

16

"E THAN, SHE'S NOT IN a holding cell," Gypsy said as he peeked in various windows. He looked back at her, and she raised her palms in surrender, but she wasn't offering him any peace. "Come on, you know why she was brought here."

Ethan stared back at the taciturn woman, shaking his head at her. "No, he couldn't have. Not yet."

Gypsy stepped closer to him. They met almost eye to eye, but she was a little taller. "Look, I don't know who she was to you, but if it makes you feel any better... it was a clean death."

He took in a deep breath, trying not to envision the pain that Levi would feel in knowing that his lover had survived the awesome power of the earth only to be killed by a lonesome human. "Why would that make me feel better?" he seethed in the woman's face.

"Because the girl was half dead—fuck, she was mostly dead. This was as much mercy as it was an offense."

"What do you know about it?"

"I know what Daniel and Heaton told me."

"Daniel and Heaton…" Ethan stepped back, feeling another pang of betrayal. "Why did they tell you about her?"

"They were assigned to retrieve her. They brought me and Callin along to help," she explained.

"Callin! What the hell, was *everyone* on board with this but me? Was there a meeting I wasn't invited to?"

"I'm not going to pretend that I know what you're feeling, cause I don't, but I will tell you this: that girl was dripping bad mojo like a waterfall. I don't know what she had inside her, but it wasn't good. No one could get near her without wanting to curl into a ball and cry. Ask your nurse; she practically started sucking her thumb after she touched her."

Ethan rubbed his face. He knew that the dark magic was still a part of her, but he didn't understand why the earth power hadn't balanced it out. "Where is she?"

"She's dead."

"Where *is* she?" he yelled. He could see that she didn't like the attitude he was giving her, but when push came to shove, he could still push harder.

Any sympathy she was offering him disappeared. She moved past him and led him to a metal door. Despite his tenure, he hadn't had the *privilege* of entering this room yet. He was aware of its existence and purpose, but there were a number of reasons why Danato didn't like going into it, the least of which was its lacking décor.

Gypsy opened the door, and he entered the concrete room. He had hoped to see a less dramatic scene inside, but that wasn't what the prison ever offered. The body of a formerly beautiful woman, wrapped in gauze, was lying on the floor with her brains strewn around her.

There was no way to make this seem right to him. He understood the duties of the warden. He had abided by Danato, even during Cori's incarceration, but for some reason, this was too much.

He knew in his heart that Addy had been a good soul. She didn't deserve to be lying dead on a cold, hard floor, bleeding out into a drain like a slaughtered animal.

Ethan kneeled down beside her. "I wouldn't if I were you," Gypsy suggested behind him, but she didn't attempt to stop him.

He lifted the blood-soaked veil from her face. He wasn't sure why he had done it. The only view it offered was of a destroyed face. He dropped the cloth and turned away to settle his stomach before he stood up.

When he turned around, Gypsy was watching him with some interest. She stopped him at the door and lifted his hand. His fingertips were covered in blood from the veil, but other than that, he didn't see what she found so intriguing. She glanced back at the body before moving to let him pass.

17

"I THOUGHT YOU SAID there were no more secrets, Belus," Cori scolded her mentor, who was thoroughly amused by her impromptu subject change.

With a soft snort, he walked past her and headed to the elevator, which appeared to be up and running again. "I was certain you were familiar with human reproduction by now, Cori. Of course, Danato has a mother. Shall I floor your comprehension by telling you he had a father as well?" Belus pushed the button for the lift and it opened promptly, as if it had been waiting just for them.

"You know what I mean," she said, following in behind him. She wasn't sure it was wise to be riding in it so soon after the bubble's shrinkage, but she assumed if the entity was satisfied enough to release the whole prison, it likely wouldn't retaliate with individual attacks. "So, tell me about Danato's mother," Cori whispered conspiratorially once the doors had closed.

Belus's mouth quirked at her enthusiasm for gossip. "She is his stepmother. She is a very wealthy woman who bought herself onto the board with her inheritances, and she is here to make our lives very difficult," Belus answered with a finality that she ignored.

He stepped off the elevator on the main floor, but she circled around to block him off before he could head to Danato's office. "So, if she's the stepmother, tell me about Danato's biological mother."

Belus crossed his arms. "She died when he was about fourteen. His father remarried when he was eighteen or so, but he passed away from a heart condition less than a decade after that."

"Why didn't you tell me any of this? I thought we were done with secrets."

"We *are* done with secrets; the rest is just stuff you don't know yet. I assumed Danato might have mentioned his family history, at least in part."

"Yeah, right. I just figured his entire past was a sore topic. Is that how he became warden? Because of her?"

Belus grimaced, either at the suggestion of her involvement or just his shock at her lack of knowledge. "Danato's father was warden before him. He was one in a very long line of men who were distantly related to our founder."

"Does that include you?"

"Yes."

"So, you and Danato are like... related." She smiled unapologetically.

"Distantly." He narrowed his eyes, but she was unfettered by his resistance to the humor and laughed whole-heartedly. "The torch was—are you listening?"

She softened her reaction to giggles. "Yes, sir." She kneeled down before him, crossing her arms so she could prop her hand in front of her still grinning mouth.

"The torch was passed down for many generations. Those families with the most enterprising lineages inherited the duty of financing the prison and protecting it from outside interests."

"The silver spoon generations," she joked.

"As privileged as they may be financially. There is far more treachery going on to protect this prison than there is running it. Don't underestimate what the board will do to keep this place safe *and secret*."

"What does that mean?" she asked, no longer amused.

Belus glanced over her shoulder. "I think it goes without saying," he said in a hushed voice, "but you must never tell anyone that your father is still alive." Cori's mouth suddenly went dry. "He is a loose end that some might feel the need to tie up. Do you understand?"

She nodded.

"As you already know, our medical staff rotates frequently." He went on, bypassing the veiled threat as if it were common water cooler dialogue. "The college-educated children of those upper-class citizens. They are essentially *paying their dues*."

"What about the not-so-wealthy families?"

"Danato and I are the last of them. Had Danato or I had siblings or produced heirs, the line would have gone on just the same, and our children would have taken over the prison, but as you well know, that didn't happen." Belus stared at her as if he was waiting for her to react to being the adopted infusion of a two-hundred-year-old bloodline.

"Why didn't *you* have kids?" she asked.

His brow furrowed, and he narrowed his eyes. "That's your question?" He moved past her.

"Okay, wait." She circled on her knee and he turned back, reversing their positions. "Why doesn't one of the rich brats just take over?"

"Shockingly, the board members are not willing to volunteer their grandchildren for such labor-intensive duty. Danato was advised to explore other avenues. As appalling as purchasing slaves was to both of us, the board found it far more appealing than indenturing their own kin."

"Why didn't either of you tell us this from the beginning?"

Belus shook his head. "Excuses, excuses, Cori. Danato and I weren't exactly going to be the good guys in your eyes at that point, no matter what."

"Maybe." She glanced down at the polished white floors, wondering if he was right. "But it does fill in a few blanks about your motivations." Cori jumped subjects when he started to look uncomfortable. "So, why isn't

Danato glad she's here? Shouldn't he be relieved that his stepmother is here and not some nameless bureaucrat?"

"No, because she's an insidious bitch," Belus griped.

"Well, hello to you too, Belus." Cori watched the aforementioned bitch step from the office hall and descend the steps into the foyer. She couldn't keep from gaping at the woman. She wasn't sure if it was the tone of her voice or just the look on Belus's face, but she half-expected her jaw to unhinge and eat his head.

"Hello, Renee." Belus turned and tipped his head, offering civility he might not have if he hadn't just stuck his foot in his mouth. Cori would no doubt have to take the blame for that later.

"Rutherford," Renee snarled, his rarely used first name with as much venom as she could muster while maintaining her phony smile. Cori suspected by the tense exchange between them that Renee already knew how much he hated the moniker.

"Wasn't expecting a visit from you," Belus said when his teeth successfully unclenched.

"Clearly." Renee looked Cori over. "I've gone over the basics of the new construction with Danato. I had some questions about Cori, but he said those would need to be directed at you." He raised his chin, acknowledging the truth of the statement. "He does like to pass off the dirty jobs to you, doesn't he?"

Cori could see Belus's jaw twist, struggling to swallow whatever defenses he had for Danato's behavior. If he had any. Renee no doubt knew his history, but more so, knew how taciturn he preferred to be about it. She was plucking his heartstrings with a razor blade, and she was enjoying it.

"Belus is my direct superior," Cori announced, taking a page from Belus's lecture to try to dilute the concentration of abhorrence between them. "However, I do take full responsibility for my actions. If you—"

Renee raised her hand, refusing further commentary as if she were being offered bad sushi. "Save your pandering. I just want to make sure my late husband's interests in this place are upheld. Either you are useful or you are expendable. No amount of shoe-licking will change that. Speaking of shoe-licking, what are you doing on the floor?" She looked over Cori's genuflected position before Belus.

"Nothing, I was just..." Cori stood, slightly embarrassed, though she wasn't sure why.

"Are you sure it's your late husband's *interests* you are trying to uphold, or his bank accounts?"

Renee's face darkened, but Cori could see her struggling to find an appropriate insult. "Careful, Belus. I'm more than happy to demonstrate the repercussions that come with those bank accounts." She glanced at Cori. "You aren't exactly without your weaknesses anymore, are you?" Her simper broadened as she turned back to Cori once more. "So glad you came to join us, darling."

Cori gulped at the not-so-obscure threat and watched the woman leave, returning to Danato's office. Belus headed after her.

"You're right, she's a bitch." She smiled at Belus when he glanced back, but he looked far more anxious than she was comfortable with. Apparently, no one was safe from this woman's claws. Not even Belus.

18

E THAN POUNDED DOWN THE stairwell to the main floor. He wasn't sure if Gypsy was following him, or if he even should have left her on her own, but now wasn't the time to worry about her. There were far bigger problems.

He made it across the foyer with a few strident steps and jumped the stairs. He was seeing red by the time he made it to Danato's office. Since he had long since forgotten his gun in the melee upstairs, he was free to barge into the office unencumbered.

Danato's face lit with concern as the door slammed against the wall. "Ethan, what's going on?"

The woman sitting in the chair across from him jumped at his sudden arrival. "Ah, the legendary—" she started to speak.

"Get out," he said definitively, without turning to look at her.

"How dare you!" she objected.

"Get out!" he said with more verve and volume.

Danato's ire for his rudeness quickly passed as his perception of the situation caught up to him. A moment of acknowledgment passed between the two men, and Danato rose slowly from his chair.

"Leave, Renee," he murmured.

"Danato," she once again tried to object, but the look he gave her stifled her words.

She stood, leaving her files on her chair. "Well, I can see you two... need to talk." Ethan didn't move as she maneuvered around him to get out. Once she was through the doorway, he banged the door shut behind her.

Danato's rage returned, and they both stood, mirroring the same disappointment back at each other. "You killed her," Ethan said, barely containing his own pained fury.

"I told you I would. I'm not going to have this same argument with you. You know what my job is."

"She was a good person."

"So was my wife, but I couldn't stay that execution either!" Danato bellowed. "Do you think I like the blood on my hands?"

"Doesn't look like you got any on *your* hands." Ethan raised his hands, baring the dried blood on his fingertips.

Danato's chest rose high, but the bluster that he had planned drained away along with his exhalation. "You're right, Ethan. I don't have any blood on my hands. You and Annette do."

Ethan pinched his lips, unprepared for this strategy of attack.

"You both knew that creating a sorceress was forbidden. Annette was the reason that rule was created. Her meddling in magic beyond her control helped create those damn wizards."

"It was the only thing that could save her."

"Save her from what? Death? There are worse things than death, Ethan. Like genocide at the hands of a being too powerful to destroy." Danato came around the desk. "I know she was your friend. I know that you wanted to protect her, but you had no right to go against prison rules to save her in the first place."

"You don't understand."

"Then help me understand. Help me understand why this was the one time you chose to neglect your position. Were you manipulated by magic?"

Ethan furrowed his brow and looked away. He wanted to tell him about the dragons. He wanted to explain the rationale behind his actions. If only he had told him earlier—hours, days, weeks. Perhaps then she would still be alive. What was the point now?

"She was... special."

"Most beautiful women are," Danato said softly.

Ethan huffed, trying to contain the anger, grief, and guilt. Danato rested his hand on his shoulder, and his eyes stung with hesitant tears. "I know that you need someone to blame right now." He squeezed his shoulder tight and Ethan wiped his eyes before they could belie his resentment. "But it's more important than ever that you remember your place in this prison."

"My place in this prison has been two steps behind you since the day I arrived." Ethan stared him down. "Yet, I have no say over anything that goes on here."

"I respect your opinion."

"Yes, but you don't trust it!" Ethan slapped Danato's hand from his shoulder.

"I only know what you told me, and it was not enough of a reason to risk keeping the girl alive."

"Just as you have always been open and honest about your motives?" Ethan narrowed his eyes. "I have trusted you blindly since the day I walked out of that village!" He pointed vaguely to the location. "Five years later and I ask you to return that trust, and you have nothing to offer me!" Danato's eyes wavered. "I saved her life, Danato. I had my reasons."

"What reasons? What aren't you telling me?"

Ethan opened his mouth to speak of the dragons, but that wasn't what came out. "And you killed her."

"Ethan? I need to know what is going on or—"

"Or what?" Ethan scowled. "People will die?"

Danato looked him over. He was debating how to handle this situation. This was not simply a matter of barking an order, nor was it something that he could just apologize for. They were at a crossroads. The next statement out of his mouth could make or break them.

"What's done is done. Report to your post," Danato murmured and returned to his chair.

Ethan stared at the wall, waiting for something more to be said. He wasn't sure what he expected Danato to say or do. He was right. He couldn't bring Adrianna back to life. All they could do was bury the memory and let it fester.

19

GYPSY LUGGED HER BAG back to the foyer of the infirmary. She was wondering if she shouldn't have asked the pilot to hang around. By the looks of the chaos in the prison, she wouldn't get a ride out anytime soon.

As she was leaving, the two guards who had assisted Ethan came in with Maddox—the man she very nearly skewered. She stood to one side as they entered. The taller of the two blond men entered through the proffered door, while the other dragged Maddox in by the arm.

"You two have no right to treat me like this," Maddox complained.

"What are you talking about? We're just getting you some much-needed hospitalization. Isn't that right, Efrat?"

"That's right, Duke." Efrat glanced back at him. "Unless you'd rather that I sear that cut shut right now?" He raised his hand, showing off a trickle of blue energy that sparked at the end of his fingertip.

"Oh, well, that's mighty generous of you," Duke said approvingly. "What do you say to that, Maddox? Save us some paperwork."

Maddox's face scrunched in disgust until he caught sight of her. They exchanged an evaluation that Duke and Efrat joined him in. After a moment, Duke cleared his throat. "Sure appreciate your help today, ma'am."

Gypsy turned her attention to the Texan and tipped her head as she looked him over. He could have been Efrat's younger brother, but his face was rounder and his muscles a little more pronounced. His hair was a good deal shorter, with a slight wave. "Not a problem." She allowed a small smile to warm her face.

Duke stared at her for a moment, only surreptitiously peeking at her body. He seemed to like what he saw. Or he just didn't get to see enough women to be picky. "Are you supposed to be here?" he asked carefully.

She looked around as if noticing the surroundings for the first time. "I keep getting left behind. I would have thought a woman walking around the prison with a mini arsenal on her shoulder would have demanded a little more attention, but everyone seems to be distracted."

"Yes, ma'am, we sure are. Been some activity going on. Everyone's a bit on edge."

"Mmm." She glanced at Maddox. "Can't imagine why."

"I am here to secure the prison," Maddox whined.

Gypsy glanced at Efrat and Duke. "I think they are securing it just fine." She adjusted her bag and headed to the door.

"Efrat, why don't you show the lady to the dock supervisor so he can help her with her departure," Duke said. Gypsy glanced back, catching the exchange between them. She wasn't sure what the extra implication was, but Duke didn't seem to think she should be on her own. At least someone at this prison had an interest in securing it.

"Yes, sir," Efrat said and followed her out.

20

CORI TRAILED BEHIND BELUS in the hallway. She didn't really want to see any more of Renee, but unless the audit miraculously got canceled, she wouldn't be able to avoid it. Ahead of them, Renee stopped outside the door to the office and backed away.

Ethan stepped out of the office. He didn't look happy—even less happy than the last time she had seen him. He barely looked up as he walked down the narrow hall. When he finally glanced up, he stopped in his tracks and met her gaze.

She stopped and smiled at him demurely over Belus's head. She had only been without him a couple of days. It was hardly a strain on her heartstrings, but she knew he had gone two months without her. She could see in his eyes that he had indeed missed her. It saddened her he had to do it, but she was pleased to see the longing in his face.

"Cori," he whispered and took in a deep breath.

Belus walked on, sidestepping his half of the stalemate. He disappeared into the office with Renee behind him. She offered them both a frowning glance before she disappeared.

"Hi," she said, taking a single step toward him. She wanted to embrace him, but he seemed overwhelmed. Much like the others, he looked overly tired, pale, and a little dehydrated.

His brow dipped and his eyes watered. He took two, maybe three leaping steps, and she was in the air. She could barely receive him with her arms pinned by his hug. He buried his face in her hair and set her down.

His hands moved to her face and neck. His kisses were urgent, fleeting, and repentant. She touched his hands, trying to keep up with the mounting affection he was offering. "Ethan," she mumbled between kisses.

He stopped and held her face. He looked at her as if he didn't believe what he was seeing. "I'm here, Ethan. I'm not going anywhere," she whispered.

His eyes flickered over hers, and he stepped away to inspect her more thoroughly. "Are you okay?"

"Yes, are you?"

He looked unsure of how to answer that. "Any trouble with Efrat?"

"Other than him trying to save my life, at your order, which almost cost all of you your lives?" She pursed her lips, thinking how angry she was and how close she'd come to losing all of them.

Ethan nodded absently, as if he didn't remember giving Efrat the order. "We should talk, Cori."

"I know; I want to talk to you too. I'm dying to see my baby boy, but this thing with the audit—"

"Audit?"

"They are starting the audit. That's why Renee is here."

"Now?"

"Yeah, great timing, and they are doing construction for a new renter on the top level. We should probably get in there so we don't get left out of the loop."

Ethan kissed her. "You go ahead. Danato and I need a little space."

"Why?" Ethan frowned at her and she realized why he looked so angry coming out of Danato's office. "Oh, that. Ethan—"

He kissed her again and pressed his forehead to hers. "I missed you so much, sweetness." She held his face, trying to return the love that he was exuding. "Go on in. I'll meet with you when you're done. Then we can have a proper reunion."

She smiled at his innuendo, but he didn't smile back. "Are you sure you're okay?"

"I will be. As soon as I have you next to me in bed tonight."

"I love you."

"I love you too." He brushed his finger along her cheek, then nodded to the office. "Go on, he's going to need some backup." He pulled away and walked down the hall. She wasn't sure how such a loving reception could seem so sad to her, but it was the only way to describe it.

She reminded herself that everyone had been under a lot of pressure, and some leniency for temperament was going to be necessary, but surely two months wasn't long enough to dismantle the morale of the entire prison.

21

"**S**O WHAT'S YOUR STORY?" Gypsy asked Efrat as they descended the stairwell together. Unconsciously or otherwise, they were matching each other's pace, step for step.

Efrat perked his brow. "Long story."

"Ahh." She grimaced. "I hate long stories. Why don't you give me the one-night-stand version?"

He glanced at her. She wasn't sure she detected annoyance, but she could already tell that Efrat was not the type of man that appreciated her personality type. In her experience, the men least attracted to her dominance were insecure with their own masculinity. However, in some rare cases, she simply fell through the cracks as a sexual prospect and landed squarely in the category of a nonsexual associate—otherwise known as: a friend.

"I'm a military lab rat gone wrong. I was being held here against my will until recently. Now I'm a recruit... I guess."

"Lab rat, huh? Is that what the scars are from?"

Efrat looked down at his forearms, where matching bracelets of puckered pink marred his skin. "Yeah."

"So, you can do what, exactly?" she asked as they arrived at the door to the main level.

"I wield electrical energy." He nodded to the door. "You mind?"

She looked over the door and then his hands. "What happens if you touch it?"

"Not much. Just a little zap, but it's usually unpleasant for everyone in close proximity."

Gypsy opened the door and offered him leave into the foyer before following behind him. "So it's activated by touch?" she asked, following him down the hall labeled "Shipping Docks."

"Yes, and no." He shrugged. "It's always active. I can't touch anything without electrocuting it, melting it, or burning it in some way."

"My God, how do you jerk off?" she blurted out.

Efrat stopped and looked back at her. She barely contained the smile, but only because she felt it was a legitimate question, deserving of an answer. "I don't." He narrowed his eyes, indicating that it was a sore subject that was best left alone. Of course, that wasn't the way Gypsy handled anything of a delicate nature.

"Well." She stepped to him and touched a finger to his chest. "You let me know if I can help you with that." She dragged her finger down his chest, past the waistline of his pants. He probably expected her to stop there, just to tease him, but she didn't.

When it was clear that he wasn't shy enough to pull away, and his indifference to her personality was no longer a turnoff, she cupped him full on. He took in a sharp breath, both in surprise and pleasure. He shook his head slightly, but she continued to rub him through his pants.

"You really shouldn't do that." He glanced around, no doubt embarrassed to be standing in the middle of a hallway getting an over-the-clothes handjob, but if he was even remotely honest about his handicap, it was probably the first contact he had had in a long time.

"Don't, please, I'm serious." He shook his head again as his breathing increased. "You're gonna get hurt." His hands sparkled with blue. He spread his arms out wide, trying to keep them as far away from her as possible, but as his length hardened in her hands, the output of electricity increased. The more she awakened his desires, the louder the snaps of static became. She looked cautiously at each of his hands, realizing that his celibacy was not because of his self-gratification handicap, but rather a lack of suicidal partners.

"You need to get away," Efrat groaned more than spoke. It was admirable that he was still trying to stop her despite being moments from completion.

Any normal woman would have stopped. Common sense was a tricky concept for Gypsy to grasp. What some called arrogance, she called fortitude. What some called dangerous, she called a challenge.

On one hand, the explosion exterior to Efrat's pants would likely stop her heart. But, on the other hand, she hated walking away from an unfinished project. As asinine as the goal was—to provide this poor, lame penis with a long-overdue ejaculation—it was still a goal she intended to achieve.

Unfortunately, the low growl that sounded in the corridor perpendicular to them was not a threat that she could ignore.

22

E THAN STOOD BEFORE THE dragon as she slept. He no longer feared the beast. He also no longer respected her. In the grand scheme of things, it was really her fault that Adrianna was dead.

Quick to blame, she responded to his thoughts as she stretched out in her pseudo-cave.

"Yes, I am, but there is blame enough for all of us." Ethan glanced at the door. He shouldn't have been speaking out loud, but he had too many thoughts to concentrate on just one. "She's dead because of what you made me do."

She's alive because of what we asked you to do.

"No, she's dead. Danato shot her."

Mortal death.

"Yes, and she is mortal."

The dragon twitched her tail. *Bury the girl.*

"We usually burn our dead."

Bury her. She is of the earth now. Return her to the mother goddess and she will know peace.

"Why did you do it? Why did you make us all go through this, just to have it end this way?"

There are many outcomes to one path. None are wrong, but most are not right. The conclusion is all that matters.

"That sounds like bullshit."

Bullshit is not audible.

"I mean, you are talking in circles again. You give me little bits of information and yet tell me absolutely nothing."

It is not my job to keep you apprised of our prophecies. Nothing I have told you is wrong; you have just interpreted it erroneously.

"What about my wife? You said she would betray me. She hasn't."

She will. Of that we can be certain, but you must feel the pain. You must endure the torment. For without pain, there is no growth. And without growth, there is no strength. And without strength, there is no protection.

"I don't know what that means."

Nor will you, until the time has come. You cannot make demands on the future when you are the instrument of its making.

"How am I an instrument of its making?"

You can only plan for the possible outcomes—of which there are many. You must accept that you are ignorant of our meaning, but endeavor to figure it out on your own, in time.

Ethan shook his head. He wasn't sure what the point of seeing the future was, if not to change it or influence it. The dragons were giving him so little to go on and yet they had demanded so much in return.

"I trusted you. I did this for you. I broke the laws of the prison. I betrayed Danato. And I lied to everyone about why. Give me one reason that I should still trust anything that you say."

Dragons rarely interfere with the dealings of man... unless it is for the protection of the Earth.

"The Earth? How does any of this have to do with the Earth?"

The dragon yawned, rolled her big head and lay it down on her paws. As soon as her eyes were shut, her nostrils started snorting rhythmically. Apparently, the Q&A was over, yet he was leaving with more questions than answers, as usual.

23

YPSY SHOVED EFRAT OUT of the way just as Callin leaped at him. Callin hit the wall, denting the drywall. Efrat hit the floor, baffled by her sudden change in mood and ignorant of the danger that he was in.

Gypsy pulled her sword, fully prepared to take on the brunt of Callin's aggression in Efrat's stead. Unfortunately, she didn't have time to grab her arm guards. That meant she was once again at the mercy of Callin's hair-thin temper. If she could get him calmed down, she might be able to walk away without any broken bones.

Gypsy didn't wait; she attacked him head-on before he could focus his retribution on Efrat. Which was for the best, since he was too thrown by the situation to defend himself. She slashed at Callin's neck with no intention of stopping. The samurai sword was the best choice when dealing with werewolves. It still didn't offer much more than a paper cut, but it did sting like a son of a bitch.

Callin punched her wrist before she could plant the blade in his neck. She yelped at the severe pain and dropped the sword. The finely sculpted blade clattered down the hall toward the main foyer. She backed herself into the side passage, closer to her bag.

Taking inventory of her wrist, she was a little more than disappointed to find it broken. She didn't have time for eight weeks of immobile healing.

She dove at her bag and ripped a gun out through the zipper opening just as she felt Callin's hands land on her. He picked her up by her neck and crotch. She fired three shots into his gut that made him roar in agony. He threw her down the hall, past the entrance to the docks.

She landed against the wall. She heard as much as felt the crack of bone. Slumping to the floor, the pressure increased, sending shooting pains through her leg and up her torso—to the point that she couldn't even tell what was injured.

She saw Callin stalking down the hall towards her—to finish her off. She searched for her gun, but it was well beyond her reach. Even with a dozen more small defensive weapons stashed on her person, there wasn't a single one that could fend off a werewolf, and Callin's pursuit of vengeance was not leaving room for negotiation.

She hadn't thought she would die this way. Death by handjob—or extension thereof. Then again, dying at the hands of a jealous boyfriend sounded right up her alley.

Callin stopped in mid-step, convulsing as sinuous streams of blue attacked his body. Gypsy had seen Cori's display of electricity, which had barely bothered

Frederique. However, this light show was enough to stop a normal man's heart.

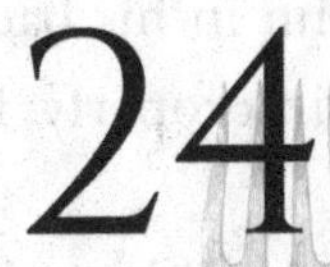

24

E THAN SAW THE SWORD skid into the foyer as he left
the gym. He knew exactly who it belonged to. He
didn't question the why; he just followed the sound of the
gunshots that soon followed. As he rounded the cafeteria
to the opposite corridor, he saw Efrat blasting electricity
down the branching hall to the docks.

He wasn't sure how Gypsy had incited his wrath,
but he ran down to see what was happening. As soon
as he rounded the corner, he saw Callin's familiar frame
shuddering under the barrage of lightning. Ethan didn't
bother asking Efrat for an explanation. He just punched
him in the jaw.

Efrat went down with one punch. His power regressed
to only a few lingering blue threads. He looked up at
Ethan, his face scrunched in confusion. "What the hell?"

"What the hell is right!"

"Look out!" Gypsy yelled from down the hall.

Ethan looked up and saw Callin barreling toward him
with deadly intent. "Bloody hell!"

Ethan bent down, taking the brunt of the impact with
his torso. His back hit the wall, and the drywall crunched.

Callin retreated momentarily, only to slam right back into him again.

Ethan elbowed him in his back, but he was in no position to fight Callin properly. He needed space and a safe word.

On his next retreat, Ethan threw a kick into his throat. Callin coughed, but was nowhere close to being incapacitated.

Callin grabbed Ethan's shoulders and threw him down the hall. He skidded across the smooth white hall until his momentum was halted by Gypsy's downed body. She winced as he hit her foot and bit back a potential scream of agony.

"What the hell is going on?" Ethan asked her.

"He's in a jealous rage. Just shoot him a few times. He should snap out of it."

"My gun is still upstairs."

Callin charged down the hall toward him. Ethan jumped up to intercept him, but Daniel stepped out from the docks just in time to meet him head-on. "What the feck is—?"

Daniel was cut off as Callin lifted him by the neck, well above his head. His lethal-eyed friend might have sent him through the wall for the assault, but unfortunately, the grip on his neck was preventing him from making the proper eye contact to aim his defense.

"Callin, stop!" Ethan leaped on his back, lassoing his throat in hopes of suffocating him into unconsciousness, but that was unlikely to happen.

"Grab my gun!" Gypsy yelled, no doubt irritated that her pain was preventing her from rejoining the fight.

"Move!" Efrat yelled as he stumbled down the hall to meet the ménage à trois. "I'll blast him again."

Ethan wasn't sure what was better, shooting one friend or electrocuting two friends, but he didn't have a chance to make the choice.

"Stop." The familiar voice was even and unperturbed. At first, the word didn't hold any impact. It was just four letters strung together to communicate a command. And yet silence seemed to surround the word, pushing through the noise of grunts and growls, until the only sounds were the heavy breaths of exertion.

Ethan felt the stillness overcome his desire to intervene, and he released Callin, sliding down his back before backing away.

He looked at Levi, meeting his somber gaze evenly before guilt forced his eyes downward. He hadn't anticipated seeing him. He hadn't imagined that he would have to tell the young man face to face that his girlfriend was dead.

Levi turned his attention to Callin, who was still holding Daniel by the throat. Levi raised his hand slowly and touched his arm. The werewolf turned a venomous stare at him and growled, but Levi didn't flinch.

"Let him go." Again, the words were nothing. They weren't a plea or even a demand. They were just a sequence of sounds placed in an order specific to a language that everyone in the room was familiar with.

Ethan had never fully understood what it was about Levi that had put him in such favor with Annette, but he was starting to now.

Callin's eyes glaze and though he maintained a steady quiet growl, he lowered Daniel to the ground and released him. Daniel sucked in some much-needed air and moved away from the werewolf. Ethan shifted his stance in case Callin only planned to change his attack to a new victim, but to his surprise and relief, the werewolf's rumble silenced and his tense shoulders dropped.

Gypsy's yelp shattered the room's silence. She attempted to shift or stand, but her injuries prevented it. She was significantly paler than she had been a moment earlier, and Ethan could see beads of sweat on her forehead.

Callin turned his full attention to Gypsy. His eyes widened, and he moved to her. He crouched down to inspect her, but Gypsy threw a scolding finger at him. "Touch me and I will rip your fucking eyes out!"

"You need a doctor," Callin insisted and made another attempt to get closer.

She pulled a knife from a holster on her thigh and brandished it in a downward stabbing angle. "Or do you prefer I neuter you?"

"Let me help you," Callin stated slowly, as if it were her ears that were damaged.

"I would rather die here than accept your help," Gypsy seethed.

"Put the knife away, Grace. I'll get you fixed up," Daniel croaked and pushed Callin out of his way. Callin looked at Daniel as if he might start another fight. Daniel caught the expression on his face and lifted his glasses to rest on the top of his head. "Don't get your knickers in a twist. I'm not the one who walloped her in the first place."

Callin's tension eased again, and he backed away to let Daniel do his work.

"What was all this about?" Ethan asked.

Callin turned his attention down the hall to Efrat. "Ask him."

"Don't look at me. She started it." Efrat pointed back at Gypsy.

"What did she start?" Ethan drawled.

Efrat's cheeks flushed, and he cleared his throat. "She was... being friendly."

"Overly friendly," Callin corrected and threw a glare at Gypsy over Daniel's shoulder. She returned the sentiment wholeheartedly with her own murderous look.

"And how does that concern you?" Ethan asked Callin.

"Because she belongs to me," Callin ground out.

"Since when?" Ethan looked at Gypsy, who rolled her eyes. "What about Leona?"

"Yeah, what about Leona?" Gypsy snapped, and Callin growled. Levi casually stepped into the path of his gaze before his anger could peak again.

"Leona is a controlling member of the Council of the Moon now. She is obligated to stay strong to protect her interests."

"She dumped him!" Gypsy cackled. Callin lunged at her. Levi did his best to press him back with the power of his mojo, but in the end, Ethan had to pull him back as well. Apparently, werewolves didn't respond well to diplomacy, even in a mystical form.

"Feck, woman! Shut up before you get us all killed!" Daniel barked at her.

"She did not dump me," Callin clarified. "We are committed to staying separated, so she doesn't get pregnant while she is still earning her position."

"Translation: she's fucking human men for a while," Gypsy mocked.

"I will not let you disrespect her!"

"Oh, no, of course not, *her* you put on a fucking pedestal. Meanwhile, *I* get a broken pelvis!"

Callin's anger faded, and he frowned at her. "Daniel?" he asked quietly.

"I don't think it's broken," he answered before the question was asked. "But her hip is definitely dislocated. It'll need a little torquing to get it back in place, but then I can try to heal the ligaments. We just need to get her to the infirmary."

Callin moved to transfer her, but Gypsy raised her knife again. "No! I've had enough of you for one day. *I decide when enough is enough.*"

"Always a sore loser," he drawled.

"Yes, a *very sore* loser."

"*Boss, I got the invisible man fixed up,*" Duke's voice came over the radio. Ethan looked down, surprised he still had it. Apparently, it was mostly plastic. "*What the hell do I do with him now?*"

Ethan yanked the radio off his belt to respond. "I'll be up in a minute, Duke." Ethan looked at Gypsy. "I'll take her." Ethan touched Callin's shoulder, but didn't push to intercept the woman until he gave him permission. Despite the obvious rejection on Gypsy's side, he still sympathized with the man's desire to care for his lover.

Callin nodded at him, and Ethan scooped up Gypsy. Her face pinched in pain, but to her credit, she didn't cry out, though he was certain she was close to passing out.

"Efrat—" Ethan's thought dropped out of existence as he passed by the entrance to the docks. Inside, avoiding the melee of drama, Annette stood between Heaton and Nevia. They were both holding the witch captive as they monitored the situation in the hall.

Ethan locked eyes with Annette, feeling yet another level of shame pass through his already aching heart. The stoic witch frowned at him and shifted her gaze to look past him into oblivion. The dismissal cut him deep, but he ignored it for the time being. There were more cuts to come.

He offered a nod to Heaton and Nevia that they returned. They seemed to sense that now was not the time for a cheerful hello; whether that time would present itself later was still to be determined.

"Efrat." Ethan forced himself back into work mode as he headed down the hall. "Report to Danato that Daniel's team has arrived and is waiting for him at the docks. Let him know that Daniel and I are assisting Gypsy in the infirmary. Also, if I catch you touching any more women that don't belong to you, it won't be your hands that will be on the chopping block."

Efrat scoffed and rolled his eyes.

"And Callin," Ethan added, turning slightly to look back at him, "if you attack one of my men again, warranted or not, you will be behind bars again. Understood?"

Callin nodded at him. "I will endeavor to keep my personal relationships... personal." He eyed Gypsy in his arms, and she eyed him back. He was surprised that even after a dislocated hip, there was still heat between them.

As Ethan turned back, he caught Efrat smirking—possibly pleased that he wasn't the only one to get scolded. "Well, get on with it," Ethan commanded.

"Yes, sir," Efrat said and jogged down the hall to do as he was bid. To Ethan's surprise, the phrase didn't sound nearly as sarcastic as it usually did.

25

"S o, it's going to be a lab?" Cori asked, turning the blueprints once more to read the tiny writing.

"Of sorts," Renee answered from the chair across from her. "It's designed to study the artifacts that are already in your possession, as well as develop potentially profitable pharmaceuticals and household products."

"You want to turn us back into a factory?" Belus asked from the file cabinet.

"I don't, but someone sees some potential in your little trinkets."

"Those trinkets are dangerous," Danato rumbled coolly.

"Yes, and right now, they are just sitting in a closet," she retorted with false merriment.

"She has a point," Cori said as she blinked away her cross-eyed vision. "They aren't very secure."

"They're secure when people leave them alone," Danato murmured and she bit back her opinion. She could see a slight amusement on his face, but that didn't mean he wasn't serious. It just meant the past was easier to laugh at when it was actually in the past.

"How long will the construction take?" Belus asked.

"A few weeks, maybe a month."

Danato exchanged a look with Belus and shifted in his chair. Neither of them was happy with that timeline.

"And who is the renter?" Belus asked.

"I don't remember his name."

"That's rather unlike you, Renee." Belus glanced at Cori, but she didn't know what she was supposed to glean from his hidden accusation.

"Yes, it is. Perhaps I was distracted by this endless list of misdemeanors, courtesy of your beloved understudy." Cori frowned at the blatant attack, but she fought the urge to defend herself—not that she had a defense. "A decade of paperwork tends to sap my attention span."

"Are you really going to bother with that?" Danato shuffled the endless documents that Renee had presented him with. "You have your renter. The money is covered."

"I told you; it's not about the money anymore."

"It's always about the money." He shoved the papers back at her.

"No, darling, it really isn't." She took them back and shoved them in her file folder.

"Cori hasn't even been here for ten years," Belus interjected.

"Yes, well..." Renee turned to look at Belus. "Will you get off that damned cabinet and join us? You're aggravating my vertigo." Belus debated his options momentarily, but he slid off the cabinet and stepped to the side of the desk. "Where was I?" Renee pinched her nose.

"A decade of reports," Danato said.

"Yes, it appears that there is some question about the quality of your leadership following your wife's death."

Cori could feel the room cool several degrees, coinciding with the menacing look that Danato was giving his stepmother. "My leadership?"

"Yes, Danato. Everyone in this prison is going to be under my scrutiny. This isn't about the money anymore. This is about what is best for the prison."

"Bullshit." He leaned back in his chair, making it squawk. "This is about six fresh new faces on the board of directors who don't want to risk their bank accounts and their freedom to keep caring for a prison that they neither understand nor give a damn about."

Renee shook her head and stood to look for something. "And why do you think I am here instead of one of those fresh faces? Your father wanted—"

"You never gave a damn about what my father wanted," Danato snapped.

Renee looked up from her search. She looked hurt by the comment, but the pain came and went. "Where the hell did I put my purse?" Danato pulled open his top left drawer and pulled out a bottle of pain pills, and set them within her reach. She took the bottle and removed three before replacing it on his desk. "Thank you."

"What exactly do they want, Renee?" Belus asked. "Surely they aren't stupid enough to think they can close us down."

Renee poured herself a cup of water and swallowed the pills. They appeared to offer her some relief just upon swallowing, but she pressed her hand to her head for a moment before answering. "The proposals on the table are exactly what I said. They are hoping to make the prison a lucrative business. Self-sustaining, as it were."

"We can't produce products here," Danato objected.

"Why not?" Renee shrugged. "You send out empty boxes all the time. Why not fill them with something? We can create a dummy corporation that repackages the product and ships it out through normal channels."

"It's too dangerous." Belus shook his head. "Someone will discover us."

Renee chortled wickedly. "Oh, you stupid twit. We are discovered every time a satellite rounds the Earth. We are discovered every time an accountant asks about unlabeled withdrawals. If either of you had any idea how much money and resources are put into protecting this place..."

"We've accepted this half of the burden, *Mother*. Forgive me if I don't sympathize with your side."

"You never did; why start now?" she sniped and sat back down. Cori got the impression there was more of a backstory to that little stab, but she wouldn't hold her breath for it.

There was a tap on the door, and everyone looked up. Efrat was on the other side. Cori moved to the door and opened it for him, so he didn't have to shock himself. He stepped inside and looked over the tense room.

"Sorry to interrupt. McGrath's team has arrived." Danato stood. "Ethan's gone up to the infirmary with Daniel to help Gypsy, so he told me to inform you."

"Help Gypsy? What happened to her?" Cori asked, more out of concern for Ethan than for her.

"There was a misunderstanding and Callin got a little defensive. She got hurt."

"A misunderstanding?" Cori furrowed her brow and Efrat glared at her.

"Should I have them wait for Ethan to return?" Efrat asked, and Danato shook his head.

"No, I should handle this myself," he said. "Renee, this may take a while. Feel free to rest up at the house. Belus, why don't you go check on the Gypsy situation. Cori, Efrat, you're with me."

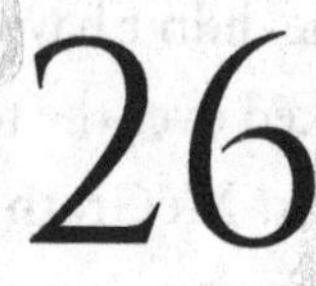

26

ETHAN PEEKED INTO THE exam room where Gypsy was biting into the pleather-covered exam table. The doctor shifted her leg around, searching for the correct angle to shift her joint back into place. He looked over at Daniel, who was patiently leaning on the opposite side of the open door. He looked preoccupied, to say the least.

"Hey, don't let him bother you. Callin is still an animal at the core."

"Hmm?" Daniel's brow lifted, and he shook his head. "No, I know, it's nothing."

"Something usually looks remarkably like that, too," Ethan said.

"Yeah," Daniel agreed. "What the hell happened here? Everyone looks half starved."

"The bubble grew. We've been in a while."

"Jaysus." Daniel turned to face him. "How the hell did you get out of that?"

"I have no idea. I haven't had a chance to talk to Cori about it. She and Efrat were stuck on the outside for a couple of days trying to reduce the power feed."

"How long on this side?"

Ethan frowned and looked around. "Just under a year." Daniel's eyes widened. "The bad part is Cori thinks it was only two months. I haven't broken it to her yet. Our son is over a year old now."

Daniel's mouth fell open, and he shook his head. "I haven't got any advice for that one."

"As if that isn't enough sorrow for one day, that guy downstairs, Levi, is about to find out that his girlfriend has been executed."

Daniel frowned and looked down. "I figured Danato wouldn't wait long. How are you doing?"

"I'm mad," Ethan admitted. "Madder than I've ever been." He looked away, trying to keep a grip on his emotions. "I want so much for this to all go away, but... I don't think it's going to."

"What do you mean?"

"I don't think I can do this anymore." Ethan shook his head. "Watch the people I love get hurt. It was easy when it was just my burden, but I have a son now. How can I train him to do the things that Danato is asking of me? How can I willingly put him in harm's way every day of his life and still claim to love him?"

Daniel licked his lips nervously. "You've got some pretty heavy questions there, pal. I'd love to tell you I have answers, but the truth is, I don't. All I know is that Danato probably asks himself those same questions every day about you and Cori."

Ethan looked at his friend. He was right, of course, but that still didn't disentangle his circling doubts.

"Get off me!" Gypsy yelled from the exam room. "It's in!"

"I'd better go finish up." Daniel chucked his shoulder. "Hang in there." He headed into the room. "Don't be a muzzy! It's your own damn fault for shagging a werewolf!"

Gypsy responded by spouting a special set of expletives, one that only the rarest of women used, before the door shut, cutting off the conversation.

"Woo-wee." Duke grimaced as he came down the hall. "That girl's got a mouth."

Ethan nodded. "Yeah, she's a handful. Where's Maddox?"

"Damn fool tried to disappear on me. I may have accidentally injected him with a strong sedative. I don't think he'll be going invisible now. He can barely walk."

"Good thinking."

"So, what in tarnation are we supposed to do with these guys? We can't house that many. Not to mention we still need a major influx of food, water, and, dare I say it, blood. I think they were only estimating for the original timeline."

Ethan rubbed his face. "Yeah, I know. Okay, we need to get the men together—and I still haven't spoken to Cori. I need to talk to her before she sees our son." Ethan glanced toward the nurse's station, where one nurse was making notations in her chart. "There's something else that needs to be taken care of first, though." He looked at the clock on the wall. "Gather the men, and our interlopers. We'll meet in the gym in forty to go over ground rules."

"Will do." Duke jogged back down to the room he had come from to collect his ward.

Ethan proceeded to the nurse's station to make preparations for Adrianna's burial before someone marked her down for cremation.

27

D ANATO STEPPED THROUGH THE door to the dock. He had met Annette there many times. Every time she had looked younger and more vibrant, but today she looked older and wearier. Her hair was flat and tawny. Her eyes were puffy and bloodshot. The most hateful look he had ever seen on a woman replaced her joyful smile—and he had seen many.

Heaton and Nevia were dutifully monitoring her, but he knew the only reason she was standing compliantly between them was because she had chosen to. She was a brilliant and powerful occultist and couldn't be forced to do anything she didn't want to. Of course, that was why she was standing before him. There was no leniency for the type of magic she had been experimenting with.

He stopped in front of her. Annette nearly stood eye to eye with him. Her glossy stare locked onto him and for a moment, he thought she might petition him for her release. Instead, she slapped him.

He didn't attempt to stop it, nor did he respond to it. He just let her anger deflect off his disappointment. She, like Ethan, was blaming him for the conclusion of this story, but who had written the first chapter? Who had broken the rules that he was obligated to enforce?

Who did they think they were?

Who did they think *he* was?

"Cori, take Annette to the seducers level," Danato announced. Cori stepped out of hiding and looked over the woman. When Annette didn't readily move to submit, she looked at him for further instruction. "Efrat, go with her."

Efrat stepped up on his other side. Annette took note of him. "You have an elemental working for you. My, how the tables have turned."

"I was just thinking the same thing," Danato agreed.

"I'm not going anywhere until I can see her," Annette insisted. Danato didn't speak, but Cori's sullen look hinted the horrific truth to Annette. "No," she rasped. "You heartless coward!"

"Coward?" Danato yelled back. "This happened because of *you*! I was just cleaning up your mess."

"I was trying to *help* her!"

"You were trying to help yourself! You were growing your powers, and she got caught in the crossfire! Just like Ogana."

"That was not my fault!"

"It's *never* your fault! Who shall I put in prison then, Annette? Shall I put Ethan in your cell, or your boy?" Danato gestured to her assistant, Levi, who was sitting on the edge of the dock, nearly catatonic from the inference about Adrianna.

"No," she said, determined. "No, I will go." She pinched back her anger and stepped toward Cori.

Baffled as to how to handle the woman, Cori just motioned Annette forward so she and Efrat could follow behind her.

"What about Levi?" Heaton asked when they were gone.

Danato looked over at the young man that he knew to be the girl's lover. Callin was standing behind him on the dock, guarding him or just staying out of the way. He assumed Callin had come along to help get them through Annette's defenses. Even with his assistance he was surprised the team had detained her. Once again, that had probably been her choice.

Danato approached the boy. He looked as young as Ethan had when he'd first arrived. He gulped as Danato towered over him. "I'm sorry things had to end this way."

His eyes fluttered over his and he shook his head. "Where is she?"

Danato closed his eyes and took a breath. "Don't do that to yourself." He opened his eyes. "It's over. Let her rest."

"I have to know for sure," he whispered.

Danato shook his head and turned away from him. "I don't have time for this. My prison is being overrun with drama," he announced to everyone before turning back to him. "If you want to torture yourself, then do it, but once you are satisfied with your grief, then you will return to China."

"I will stay."

"What?"

"I will stay by Annette's side."

"Annette is a prisoner now."

"Then so am I."

"I am not interested in imprisoning you for ignorance."

"Then I will serve my sentence in servitude."

Danato looked back at Nevia. "What is wrong with him?"

"Annette is all he has," she explained.

Danato huffed and paced the floor. "Listen up, everyone. My men need food, sleep, and more than a few need medical attention. I don't really care who is staying and who is going right now, so long as my prisoners stay locked up and my men get the care they need."

"Is that your way of asking us to stay and help?" Heaton asked.

"No, that's my way of asking you to stay the hell out of my way. The prison is being audited and I don't need any more insolent employees making me look bad." He looked back at Callin. "What's this about you getting out of hand?"

"It won't happen again," Callin insisted.

"Damn right it won't. There is a reason I only ever had one werewolf as a friend, and you are not him. Control your temper or you will be locked up."

"It won't happen again," Callin repeated. "You have my word," he added.

Danato let the issue rest. Callin wasn't nearly as composed as Vince was, but not many werewolves were. He could only assume that, like most werewolves, his word was not to be taken lightly.

"Heaton, you and Callin can take Levi to the infirmary to view the body." Danato sighed and looked back at the boy. He didn't like adding to the morbidity of the situation, but who was he to determine how he should handle his grief? "Jordan, if you would join me, please."

Nevia nodded and followed him out.

28

"WHAT DID YOU MEAN by a misunderstanding?" Cori persisted after Annette was safely deposited in a cell. She had missed meeting the witch the last time she was around, but she was almost glad about that now. As unhappy as she was that Adrianna had to die, seeing someone so personally affected by it made it that much worse. She wanted to apologize to the woman, but it wouldn't have made a difference. Annette wanted nothing to do with anyone in Danato's employ now.

"Nothing," Efrat mumbled.

"Why is Callin here, anyway? I hope Leona isn't here."

"Is that the fem-wolf that took over the Council of the Moon?" Efrat asked as they made their way back through the seducers level.

"Yeah, she and Callin have a thing."

"Well, apparently Callin and Gypsy have a thing now... or also?"

"You're kidding. When did that happen?"

"Cori, do I look like I keep up with gossip?"

"Oh, don't tell me that was the misunderstanding. Did you flirt with Gypsy?" Cori stopped before the section break to offer him a look of disgust.

He stopped and smiled. "Not exactly. Why? Does that make you jealous?"

Cori scrunched her face tight. "No!"

"Then why so interested?"

"Because she's nuts."

"Yeah, she'd have to be to make a pass at me."

"She kissed you? She doesn't even know you."

"She didn't kiss me."

"Then what did she...?" Cori shook her head.

"It was just a little hand action. I think she thought she was doing me a favor. A pity pump, if you will."

"Efrat," she scolded him. "I thought you couldn't do that. I mean, not that you can't, but... Is that why she's in the infirmary? Did you...?"

"No, no, it wasn't me. We got interrupted. For the best, I suppose. Although I don't imagine she's much better off. Callin is a pretty violent guy when he's angry."

"Yeah, I'm sure." Cori shook her head at Efrat again.

"Will you stop looking at me like I'm the jerk of the world?"

"I'm not."

"You are."

"I'm just trying to figure out what you were thinking, allowing her to do that to you."

"Um, I guess I was thinking how good it feels to be touched by a woman."

Cori crossed her arms. "But someone could get hurt."

"I know." Efrat glared at her. "I had a moment of weakness, Cori. After the last two days, can you blame me? Trust me, I am painfully aware of my sexual limitations. I am achingly aware of the Mount Everests all around me." He walked away, but Cori couldn't let it end that way.

"It's not impossible, you know."

"What's that?" He stopped and looked back at her.

"Mount Everest. I mean, with the proper precautions, people do climb it... successfully."

Efrat moved back to face her. "Are you saying what I think you're saying?" His eyes danced over hers.

"I'm not talking about me. I'm just saying that there might be some way for you to enjoy the companionship of a woman without potentially electrocuting her."

Efrat shook his head and shrugged. "Such as?"

"Can't you just tie your hands together, bondage style?"

"There would still be a lot of residual static. Enough to make things uncomfortable for both participants."

Cori swallowed hard and glanced around to see which of the prisoner seducers might be overhearing the conversation. It was embarrassing enough to give Efrat tips on electrified sex, let alone an audience. "I suppose the idea is to ground you during the act, so the majority of the electricity gets absorbed before it can hurt your partner."

Efrat nodded.

"Um, well then, if you had a tryst outside—"

"Tryst?" Efrat smirked at her unabashedly.

"Can you be a grownup for a second?"

"I'm not the one saying *tryst*."

"Okay, how about if you're gettin' some outside?"

Efrat chuckled and shook his head. "How about we split the difference and say making love?" He took a step closer to her, still wearing a devilish smirk. "So I'm outside, making love to... my female companion. Now what?"

Cori shifted and rolled her eyes. "You could bury your hands in the dirt. Let the Earth take the brunt of it. That might work."

"Assuming the ground isn't permafrost." Efrat seemed to consider this idea. "What do I do the other nine months of the year?"

"Another method would be to use a lightning rod. It would ground the charge and hopefully protect whoever you were with."

Efrat's smirk faded. "This isn't the first time you've thought about this, is it?" Cori shrugged. "You *have* thought about this. In your spare time, you've been imagining ways that I could have sex."

"Sure, just as I thought about glass utensils, adding a bidet toilet to the guards' quarters—"

"That was you?"

"Yes. I've also suggested anti-static clothing and blankets, a bedside generator, foot-handles on the section doors, and a ton of random ideas that might make your life slightly more pleasant in this place."

"You did that for me?"

"Yes."

"Why?"

"I'm just trying to help."

Efrat moved in a little closer. "That's very sweet of you. I was wondering who my ass had to thank for that toilet," Efrat teased.

"Well, you were burning through our toilet paper budget," Cori teased back.

Efrat laughed. The genuine smile on his face made him look young and human. It never lasted long, but she had been seeing it more lately. Unfortunately, there was a lot of pressure on her to keep those smiles coming. More than she would have liked.

"Can I ask you something?" Efrat said when his laughter had ebbed. "In these scenarios, where I'm leashed to a lightning rod, making love to a woman—for the first time in years..." Efrat tipped his head in exaggerated curiosity. "Who's on top? Me or you?"

Cori scoffed and tried to walk away, but Efrat jogged ahead of her and blocked her path. The lop-sided grin on his face was playful, but she knew this wasn't a game either of them should be playing.

"It's a legitimate question. I just wasn't sure how you were imagining my restraints. Is this full-on bondage or do I have a little wiggle room?"

"I don't know. I'm not *in* the scenario."

"Oh, come on, I can't just pick a random girl and hope for the best. You and I are going to have to do extensive research on positioning and rod strength."

"Why do you always have to put this back on me?"

"I never took it off you."

"Why can't you just appreciate the fact that I give a damn about your happiness?"

"I do appreciate—"

"Ever since I met you, I have wasted vital brain cells trying to think of ways to make your life more enjoyable. Why isn't that enough for you?"

Efrat chuckled and shook his head. "Just admit that you've thought about me—in that way."

"Why would that make any of this easier?"

"Because it would mean that I'm not completely alone in this odd-couple attraction."

Cori took in a breath, debating if this was one of those times where the truth was more dangerous than a lie. "I never said you were alone." Efrat's grin dimmed into an introspective smirk. "Can we not do this again, please? This day has already been too long. There is no need to repeat this argument." Cori continued walking.

"Oh, don't be so sour." Efrat walked beside her, easily keeping up with her quickening strides. "I know the answer is no. I know the answer will always be no, but my favorite pastime is still tormenting you. If you won't have sex with me, then you can at least offer me that." He ruffled her hair, and she slapped his hand away.

"Efrat," Ethan said as he entered the section just ahead of them.

Efrat raised his hands in surrender. "It was just her hair."

"We're having a meeting in the gym in thirty minutes. I need all my men there."

"Does that include me?" Cori asked.

"Yes, but I thought we might want to go see our son first." Ethan smiled as her face broke into an uncontrollable grin.

Cori rushed forward and hugged him tight. "Oh thank God, it's been killing me. Has he grown a lot?" She grimaced.

Ethan glanced at Efrat, losing some of his smile. "I can hardly say no. He's a healthy boy."

Cori looked at Efrat and saw the same concerned look he had before they left the bubble. "What is it? What are you two not saying?" Efrat stared at her a moment before turning his attention to Ethan. Apparently, he didn't want to give her the answer. "Is he okay?" she asked, bracing herself for the worst, even as her body began to tremble.

"He's fine, Cori," Ethan insisted. "Healthy and happy. We made sure he was well fed. It's just..." He stared at her, his eyes blooming with tears. "We were inside the bubble longer than a couple of months."

Cori shook her head, mentally calculating the hours versus the days. She had stuck to the timeline as planned. What had gone wrong?

"The bubble was bigger, so the differential changed. We've been inside for almost a year."

Cori stared back at Ethan, blank-faced, and blank-minded. She couldn't comprehend the months and weeks and days that everyone had endured when she had only been gone for a couple of days. She suddenly saw the weary, starved faces differently. Danato's once robust waistline, now trimmed, was a result of the food supply being cut off. Belus's sleep-starved mind had endured a year's worth of dream feeders, which further answered for his attack on her. Her friends and family hadn't just been rationing supplies and dieting; they had barely been surviving.

It took a moment for the word *year* to register in her mind. When it finally did, she realized what she had lost. Her baby boy had not seen his mother in a year. He was already past his first birthday. She had missed so much. So many pivotal moments.

"I'm sorry, Cori," Ethan whispered.

She nodded, trying to keep a grip on her emotions. She wanted to cry, but it was far from the worst news she could have heard regarding her child. There were too many dangers to count in the prison. Aging a year without incident was a blessing.

"I should leave you two alone," Efrat whispered and started backing away. Cori glanced at him and once again saw that same sympathy that he rarely offered her. His fleeting gaze returned, and she stared at him. All thoughts of tears vanished from her mind and the previous tremble in her body returned for a new reason. Efrat froze, seeing the shift in her demeanor.

"You..." Her eyes narrowed and shifted from one target to the next and back again. Ethan seemed to sense the change as well and shifted into his reserved soldier stance. "You knew about this before I left." Cori volleyed the accusation between them. "You had already predicted that the bubble's expansion would expand the time differential."

"Yes," Ethan answered in a mildly apologetic tone.

Cori scoffed, though it came out as more of a bark. "You ordered him to keep me out of the bubble, knowing this."

"It was too dangerous to navigate the exterior. There was no telling where you would have entered."

"Ethan told you about the time difference, didn't he?" Cori turned her accusation on Efrat. He stared back at her, refusing to answer. "You didn't tell me?"

"He ordered me not to," Efrat finally defended himself.

Cori laughed. She was still seconds from bawling or yelling, so the exhibition sounded more maniacal than sarcastic. "Once again, you astonish me with your impromptu loyalty. Congratulations, Ethan, you and Efrat have finally found common ground... against me."

"You know why he did it, kitten," Efrat said.

"Yes, I know why he did it. I just don't know why *you* did it."

"The same reason he did it, I imagine," Efrat grumbled, glaring at her. Cori could feel her hands icing over, but she was numb to the frostbite settling into her thighs.

"There's no reason to take this out on him," Ethan jumped in. "He had nothing to do with the decision."

Cori ripped her gaze from Efrat and stared at Ethan. "The decision?" Cori asked, mostly to herself. Ethan shifted uncomfortably. "Oh, of course. Of course." She shook her head. "Danato and Belus figured it out and discussed it with you." She smiled at this thought, despite the fact that it was bringing her to a new level of irritation.

"We didn't want you to have to make that decision."

"What decision?" Cori shrugged.

"Cori, if you knew the consequences, you never would have left."

Cori stared blankly at her husband. The laborious years of being her white knight were blinding him. All he could do was rescue her. She loved him for it, but Belus was right. She wasn't representing herself as anything other than the damsel in distress. Ethan might always be her hero, but that didn't mean she had to keep playing the victim.

Cori cleared her throat and stepped up to Ethan. He shifted his hands, not trusting her calm approach. He likely thought she intended to slap him. She probably should have, but that wouldn't help justify her condescension in this situation.

"I'm sorry that you think I wouldn't be willing to sacrifice a year with my son to save you. I would give my *life* to save each and every one of you. I almost did. *We* almost did." She glanced at Efrat, giving him some of the credit for their final efforts to keep the time bubble intact. "I'm sorry that you don't trust me with your life."

"That's not what this was about," Ethan objected.

"Yes, it was. It was about giving Efrat, a man that you are still struggling to trust, a better debriefing than your own wife."

"He made a choice, Cori," Efrat defended. Ethan glanced at him, probably surprised to have him on his side for a change. "He just saved you the guilt of having to make the decision yourself."

"Guilt?" She tested the word on her lips. "You think feeling deceived is better than feeling guilty? At least with guilt, I could still have some pride for my courage and sacrifice. Now all I feel is anger—and embarrassment for not making the connection myself." Cori tried to rub her face, but her icy palms kept her from shielding her misery.

Ethan moved forward, and she shook her head.

"No!" He didn't draw back, but the firmness in her words forced his hands back. Despite the emotions he emulated, he held her gaze, refusing to keel under her scrutiny. "I am your partner, Ethan—in everything. You should have told me. You should have trusted me."

"I'm sorry," he whispered, as his jaw clenched. "I was just trying to protect you."

Cori nodded, feeling the weight of that word like a lead vest. Protect. Coddle? Cloister? Restrict?

Imprison.

"And you." Cori moved to Efrat. "I still don't know what we are to each other. Two steps forward and one step back. Well, rest assured, we've taken several steps back today."

"What else is new?" Efrat grumbled.

"Save it. I'm going to go see my son. Why don't you give Ethan your report about the last couple of days?" Efrat's eyes momentarily widened, as if he anticipated his punishment for lying would be to confess his indiscretions against her. Her guilt for those stolen kisses gave her pause, but she didn't want to get into all that just yet. She was certain Ethan would find out about it since the incidents weren't without witnesses, but she was afraid an admission now would only serve to disrupt the one leg she had to stand on. "Don't forget to mention the incident with Dirk."

Efrat raised his chin as if catching onto her purpose. The corner of his mouth even tipped up a little as he remembered the playback. She wasn't sure how everyone else was going to take her impromptu penectomy, but at least Efrat was proud of her.

Cori bypassed Ethan's curious gaze and left Efrat to report to him.

"What about Dirk?" Ethan asked sternly, as she closed the door to the section.

29

"WOULD YOU LIKE SOME water?" Danato offered after Nevia had sat down in the chair in front of his desk.

"No, thank you," she said with a small smile.

He moved around the desk and sat down in his squeaky chair. When the smile hadn't faded, he furrowed his brow at her. "What is it?"

"Your leg is feeling better."

He smiled back at her. He kept forgetting the extent of her intuition. "Yes. Thanks to Daniel, I won't lose my leg. There is still some pain, but nothing like what it was."

"Daniel is a good man," she offered abruptly, as if he had insulted him.

"Yes, he is. I have no reason to argue otherwise. Not anymore."

Her small smile faded. "What do you need, Danato?"

He wanted to ask what had blanketed her mood, but he didn't want to get off topic. "I need to know what you think of Grace Gypsum."

Nevia leaned back in her chair. "I wish I could tell you."

"Why can't you?"

"I don't get a lot from her. She's human, female, heterosexual… mostly, and she has a strong affinity for danger. She demands a lot of herself, as well as the people around her. She has little tolerance for weakness or ignorance from men or women. She doesn't have the traditional emotional foundation like most people."

"What does that mean?"

"She is reactive to stimulus, but it's only her baser instincts. What little I read from her is directly related to aggression or… arousal."

"So Cori was right. She is a psychopath."

Nevia tipped her head thoughtfully at that description. "She doesn't seem to have the desire specifically to harm people, but she does like to put herself in situations that could cause herself or others harm. She's a thrill-seeker, be it sex or violence. She's a mixture of sociopathic symptoms."

"Is she dangerous?"

"In general."

"Meaning?"

"Fire is dangerous, but when properly managed, it can provide food, warmth, and even protection."

"I know how to handle fire, especially since I can just put it out, but how does one manage a sociopath?"

Nevia shrugged. "Traditionally, sociopaths rebel against authority. According to Cori, she used to be a nurse. Then she was in the military. Now she's working for a private employer. She's moving around, either to avoid attachments, or because her superiority complex keeps getting her fired."

"I'm not sure I can do non-authoritative." Danato sighed.

"No." Nevia crossed her hands gently on her lap. "I'm not sure you can." She paused to evaluate him. He wasn't sure if she was waiting for a reaction or just giving her critique the spotlight it was due. "I'm also not sure that she would respect you if you weren't imposing. I think you should treat her as you would any other member of your team." She shifted and cleared her throat. "And of course... just as with the fire, she *can* also be put out, if necessary." Danato leaned back and gave her a slight nod. He was pleased to know that at least someone else understood the measures that occasionally needed to be taken. He was just continually surprised by whom that someone was turning out to be.

30

Daniel stepped from the exam room with a hand under Gypsy's arm. She had insisted on walking on her own, but after the third wobble, he offered it anyway. "It still feels broken."

"You're just sore. I'm not much good with internal wounds yet."

"Well, aren't you just useless, then?" She feigned annoyance.

"Yup, pretty much just a waste of space."

She stopped and smiled. "I suppose I do owe you a thank you, though." Before he could stop her, she lassoed an arm around his neck and pulled his lips down to hers for a sensuous kiss that bordered on defilement.

He moved to push her away, just as he heard a familiar reprimand.

"Dude!"

Daniel raised his hands in surrender and backed away from the overeager woman. When he saw Callin next to his partner, he backpedaled and shook his head. "Easy man, she kissed me."

"It was a thank you," she said, unintimidated by the aggravated werewolf among the new arrivals.

Callin also looked indifferent to the display. "Yes, I can see that. Perhaps you could use your words next time instead of your lips."

"My lips are *my* business." She narrowed her eyes at him.

"So are mine," Daniel interrupted. "But I still got mouth-raped."

"Don't worry, I'm not contagious... anymore." Gypsy licked her lips and winked at him.

"What?"

"Daniel, let's just leave the honeymooners to sort out their shit," Heaton suggested. "We need to show Levi the body."

"The body?" Daniel frowned at the boy lagging behind Heaton. "Really, kid?" Levi nodded. He had the somber intensity of a broken man, but so far, it was only his heart that was damaged. "Feck, this job sucks sometimes." Daniel shuffled awkwardly between Gypsy and Callin, who were already radiating conflicting spectrums of passion at each other.

Heaton and Levi led the way down the far hallway, where a nurse intercepted them. "Can I help you?" she said, eyeing Heaton before settling a wide stare on Daniel. He offered her a smile and a wink, but it didn't help her composure.

"We're taking this young man to see the body," Heaton explained.

The nurse dragged her nervous gaze from Daniel and looked at Levi. She cleared her throat. "The execution was by gunfire," she whispered, as if saying it quieter might prevent the boy's heart from shattering further. When no one blinked at her detail, she looked around for someone to give a different order. "It's being prepared for burial right now, but I can show you the way."

"She," Levi corrected.

"What was that?"

"Her name is Adrianna. She was a human being not very long ago. The gender still applies."

"Oh," the nurse blanched. "*She* is right this way."

The nurse led them to a room that might have generously been called a morgue. It was, essentially, a mortuary laboratory used to dispose of bodily remains—human and inhuman alike. There were the usual metal cabinets lining the walls, designed to store human bodies when the need arose. It also had two oversized tables with deep rims to contain excess fluids as they were drained. The exception to the morgue appearance was the large crank lock door on the back wall. It was a crematorium for body disposal.

Daniel looked over the black bag on the table to his left. "Don't you usually cremate the bodies?"

The nurse bit her lip. "Yes, but Mr. Pierce has ordered us to bury this one. He was vehement."

Daniel glanced at Heaton. He returned the same look of concern. Danato wasn't likely to change his disposal routine, especially for a body. Even his own beloved wife had been turned to ashes rather than given an earthen grave.

Levi moved to the body bag and unzipped it enough to see Adrianna's face. Daniel caught a glimpse of the pale face with a permanent *bindi* and looked away. He wasn't a squeamish man by nature, but he had seen enough death to desire seeing less of it. Even in the most dire circumstances of self-defense, he hated the idea of taking a life. It was perhaps his only saving grace, but that was yet to be corroborated by the Big Man.

Heaton and Daniel stood back and waited for the lover's tearful non-reunion, but Levi didn't break down. He tentatively slipped his hand inside and pressed it against her face. He took in a sharp breath, as if unprepared for the feel of cold skin. He tipped his head down and murmured something resembling a prayer. When he was done, he zipped up the body bag and turned to face the men.

"Is that it?" Daniel asked, incredulous that the boy wasn't crying or wailing in emotional agony.

Heaton smacked his arm. "Do you need more time?" he asked sympathetically.

Levi shook his head. "No. I just needed to say goodbye."

Daniel could see the boy was in pain, but he had also shut down. He was numb to everything right now, but in a few hours or a few days, the reality would hit him. Then he would be destroyed: angry, inconsolable, and lonely as hell.

31

GYPSY SHOVED CALLIN INTO the wall and shut the door to the exam room behind her. She shoved her body against him and pressed her lips to his. She could hear him growl under his breath. He was still mad. This was one time when he probably legitimately wanted to talk to her, but she never had been a fan of honest communication.

She shoved her tongue forcefully between his lips, and his growl finally turned to a rough moan. He pulled her harder against him. He reached to lift her leg and spread her open around him, but her tender hip forced a cry of pain from her smothered mouth. He released her instantly and pushed her away from him.

"You are too sore for this."

"No, I'm not." She moved toward him again, but his hands gripping her arms were impassable. "Fine, never mind." She tried to pull away, but he wouldn't release her to leave, either. She glanced around the room for her weapons, but her bag had been abandoned downstairs. She had stupidly not re-holstered her knife before Ethan took her. She had a few more handy devices, but none that would work on a werewolf.

"Stop it." Callin pinned her with a disapproving stare. "Do you really think you need to defend yourself against me?"

"History tends to repeat itself," she retorted snidely.

He frowned and looked her over carefully. "And will you take no responsibility for breaking my heart?"

"Callin." She sighed, already exhausted by the conversation's direction. "I didn't know you had arrived."

"That's not what I mean, but I don't see how that is supposed to give me a more favorable opinion of what I walked in on. It also doesn't change the fact that I would have smelled him all over you when I did arrive. You can't hide your infidelity from me."

"Infi—fuck me! When did we become an old married couple?"

"I know what you are doing."

"You mean besides trying to get some strange?"

Callin's jaw clenched, and he took in a soothing breath. "You're pushing me away."

"Last I checked, *you* pushed *me* away." She glanced downward.

"Grace, don't play the fool with me. I deserve the truth." Callin released her and moved to lean against the door. He stared at her a moment before his face dimmed into pain. "I love you. Don't you have anything resembling that in your heart to offer me?"

Gypsy looked over his pained expression. Even in this hardened, animalistic man was the common thread of humanity. She didn't envy the turmoil that others faced in their day-to-day lives. She pitied them. She was free of the endless concerns and doubts that immobilized people in fear and made them powerless to love.

She let her mask fall away, and she showed him her unmitigated hollowness. "No," she answered with the same empty intent.

His gaze fell to the floor as he once again came to terms with the truth that she had never hidden from him. This was just the first time he truly believed it. He stood upright and turned away from her.

"You wanted the truth, Callin."

"Yes, I did," he said despondently into the door.

"Do you want the lie back?" She moved to him and stroked his tensed bicep. When he didn't shift, she pressed her face into his back and breathed in his scent before kissing the back of his neck.

He turned, and she gave him a sympathetic expression. He looked her over, still confused by her playacting. He said he wanted the truth, but the lie was so much more fun.

When he still wouldn't be baited by her allure, she stepped back and removed her shirt. In contrast to her militant style, her bra was bright red and satin. She slipped it off, but quickly turned around—only letting him have a glimpse of her breasts before she took them away.

She unbuckled her belt and slipped her heavy cargo pants down, leaving her matching red panties in place. She bent over the exam table, swaying her hips even though it hurt like hell to do so. She heard the door lock, and she waited for him to rip her panties off and slam into her from behind.

When his hand slid gently down her thigh, she almost jumped. He proceeded to carefully undo the endless straps on her boots and slip them off so her pants could be completely removed. "I didn't realize we had that much time," she said seductively.

He hushed her and slipped her underwear off as well. She braced herself for a familiar, satisfying invasion, but instead he scooped her onto the table. She chuckled as he slowly disrobed. "Seriously, Callin, they might actually need this room. It's pretty crazy right now."

He hushed her again and climbed onto the table with her. It wasn't unusual for them to be in a missionary position, but somehow, after his admission, she thought a less intimate position would be better.

"Callin," she started to object, and he pressed into her. She ignored her own thoughts and tugged him deeper. She wanted the pummeling of their usual encounters, but he went excruciatingly slow. "Callin," she persisted when it was clear that it would take days for either of them to be satisfied.

He hushed her a third time, and she felt dizzy from something other than euphoria. She shook it away, but that only made it worse. "Callin, stop."

"Am I hurting you?" he whispered into her neck.

"No," she said, trying to blink away her double vision. "Something's wrong. I don't feel right."

"Just let it happen, Grace," he said.

"Let what happen?" she asked, feeling intoxicated. "What the fuck is happening?" He kissed her, but she pulled away. "What are you doing?"

"Claiming you," he answered, but his words were a thousand miles away.

"Did you fucking drug me?" she slurred. She pressed on his chest, but unexpected waves of pleasure smothered her complaints and shattered her inhibitions. All she could do was lie back and be claimed.

32

C ORI DIDN'T THINK THAT her emotions could get any more raw until the elevator doors opened to reveal Belus standing inside. For a moment, she just stared at him, trying to balance the same anger and pain against her desire to command respect.

The command that Belus himself had just recently been lecturing her about.

Belus looked up and waited. When she didn't move, his brow dipped. "Going down?"

She clenched her jaw and stepped inside. Belus shifted back, allowing her to press the button for the infirmary floor. As the doors closed, she contemplated what to say to Belus. It was far more difficult to lecture the man that usually lectured her.

"I was just checking on the bubble," Belus informed her. "Looks like everything is in working order."

She kept her gaze straight, only glancing up to check the dial above the door. It wasn't taking as long as she expected it to.

"Looks like you and Efrat have appeased her for now. You did good." Belus glanced at her, no doubt anticipating her to be lapping up his kudos like mother's milk. On any other day, she would. "But we shouldn't get too comfortable. I think Efrat should steer clear of the bubble—at least for a while." Belus finally noticed her silence and leaned forward to get a better look at her face. "Cori? Any thoughts? Opinions? Objections?"

The doors mercifully opened, following the usual stunted *ponk*. She pressed her hand in the path of the door and faced Belus. "I'm not sure I'm capable of making any decisions that will affect this prison, sir. Maybe you, Ethan, and Danato should take a vote." Cori stomped out of the lift and headed toward the infirmary.

"Cori." Belus spoke her name without any demand, but she turned to look at him, anyway. He was baffled for a moment, but then his eyes revealed his illumination and guilt. "They told you about the timeline."

"Yes." Cori checked the imaginary watch on her wrist. "About a year too late, it seems."

"It wouldn't have made any difference when we told you. Knowing might have impacted your judgment. We didn't want you to risk trying to speed up the weaning."

Cori waved a finger at him. "You told me that I need to command more respect. How am I supposed to do that when the three of you are keeping me in the dark like an underling?"

"This was an abnormal circumstance. You are not the best at following orders." Cori opened her mouth to object. "I'm not saying that to piss you off. I'm just saying that your emotions play a greater role in your choices than logic—sometimes."

Cori groaned through clenched teeth. "How do you do this? I have every right to be mad at you, and you are still turning this around on me. I just found out I lost a year with my son! That should not have been kept from me."

"You're right," Belus stated, stalling her tirade. "That's why I voted to tell you."

"Then why *didn't* you tell me?"

"Because, unlike you, I follow orders, even when I don't agree with them."

Cori took in a breath, realizing that there was no room to argue with Belus on that point. "There should have never even been a vote. I should have been in on that conversation to begin with."

Belus nodded. "I agree on that point as well. Which only goes back to what I told you earlier. The staff aren't the only ones you need to start commanding respect from."

Cori nodded and turned to enter the infirmary. As her hand reached the cold metal handle of the door, she stopped and looked back at him. "Did you know there was a chance she would pull out? Did you know that there was a chance you would all die?"

Belus stared blankly at her for a moment. "Danato and I felt that the entity leaving was a certainty. You saving us... that was the chance."

"Then I guess you are all even stupider than I thought."

Belus's lip tipped up slightly. "And why is that?" he asked, playing into her bait.

"Because I do my best work during life-or-death scenarios." Cori marched into the infirmary, prepared to bathe her son in enough kisses to make up for the last year.

33

"Sooooooo." Daniel clapped his hands after they had determined that Callin and Gypsy were probably not going to catch up with them. "Now what?" He looked at Heaton and motioned to Levi with his eyes.

Heaton glanced down the halls of the infirmary, no doubt hoping to find someone to give them an order. "I don't know." He rubbed his face. "I just know that the longer we wait to talk to Danato, the worse this is going to get."

"Danato has bigger things to worry about than me," Daniel said.

"Which is why I don't think we should test his patience by keeping any secrets." Despite his declaration, Heaton didn't move. Instead, he twisted his jaw in contemplation—mulling over his only option as if there were a way around it.

Daniel knew Heaton was considering a cover-up. However, obliterating a human's arm was not something that was likely to be swept under the rug with ease. Eventually, word would get back to Danato.

Two years ago, Daniel would have done anything to stay out of prison, but now that he had earned an ounce of respect from the warden, he wanted to keep it. He was confident that Danato wouldn't put him in jail. Had he killed someone, yes, but Danato could at least understand defending the one you love with puerile revenge.

"What secrets?" Levi asked, innocently glancing between them.

Daniel had only begun to contemplate a response when the infirmary door slammed open. The glass in the door shattered as Ethan stomped into the area.

"Ethan, stop!" Efrat yelled as he crunched through the glass behind him.

Ethan stomped on, not giving a second look at the destruction behind him. Daniel and Heaton were instantly at attention, ready to back up their friend as needed.

"Daniel! Stop him!" Efrat yelled. His hands were glowing with a potential attack, but he was wisely keeping his power out of the intervention.

Daniel gauged the anger on Ethan's face and determined that whatever was going down was personal. Ethan's austere gaze didn't falter as he turned down the hall, heading toward the patient care section. Daniel shrugged apologetically at Efrat before marching side by side with Heaton after Ethan.

"He's going to kill him!" Efrat grumbled, staying hard on their heels. Daniel could feel the static charge raising his hair, but he ignored it, along with his warning. He wasn't sure what had incensed Ethan, but if he was mad enough to kill, then someone must have done something very bad. In which case, he and Heaton would be his backup with or without explanation or invitation.

Ethan surveyed the beds through the windows lining the hall until he found the one he wanted. He entered the section, managing not to break the glass door. He slowed his approach and stopped at the foot of one of the beds. The man sleeping in it was enormous, but that wouldn't protect him from getting his ass kicked by Ethan.

"You don't understand." Efrat pushed between them, but stopped just short of standing in Ethan's way. He kept his hands at ease, not allowing himself to become a threat. "Please listen to me. I know you're angry, but you don't have to do this."

"He tried to rape my wife!" Ethan seethed, and Daniel finally understood the anger in his eyes. Not only had this man taken liberties with his wife, but he'd dared to do it right under Ethan's nose. Who would be so stupid? Who would be that suicidal?

"Yes, *tried*," Efrat explained carefully. "But we stopped him—she stopped him."

"He'll never do it again," Ethan whispered sadistically, and approached Dirk. "Not to her or any other woman."

"He is not *capable* of doing it again." Efrat moved in a little closer to him, but still didn't attempt to grab him or subdue him. "He's been emasculated."

Ethan's head dipped, confusion reaching the level of complex math marring his features. He looked back at Efrat. "What do you mean?"

The trickle of blue on Efrat's hands ceased. "Ethan, she froze his freaking dick off."

Daniel snorted, unable to contain his amusement at the statement. However, the longer he let the idea absorb into his mind, the more treacherous it seemed.

When Ethan didn't react, Efrat mimed a vague interpretation for him. The visual of the snapping member seemed to wake Ethan up. His lip turned up slightly and there was pride in his eyes. "She..."

Just as Daniel's amusement died away, so did Ethan's pride. His eyes flickered over Efrat. "She can—she's capable of that much cold?"

Efrat nodded. "If she's pissed enough."

Ethan turned back to the unconscious man in the bed and leaned over him. He glanced down at the man's midsection. There was nothing visible under the blanket one way or the other, but Ethan seemed to be imagining his eunuch state. "You got what you deserved, you piece of trash," he growled quietly to the man. Satisfied with his insult, he rose and moved away.

Daniel barely registered the quick movement under the blanket before the man was up and extending his arm. He thrust a blade into Ethan's back. "So did she, you arrogant bast—" The man's final word was cut short as he disintegrated into a pile of dust along with the blankets covering him and half the bed.

34

34

D ANATO HEADED OUT OF his office behind Nevia without the first idea of where to begin undoing the mess his day had become. The last year had been hard enough, and he wasn't ready for guests, but perhaps he would do as Nevia suggested and just treat everyone as if they were his employees—regardless of who they were.

They stopped in the main foyer and waited for the elevator to arrive. He noticed Duke fidgeting in the hall leading to the gym. Danato caught his eye and nodded to him.

"Howdy, Warden." Duke moved to meet with him. "Got all the men together. Just waiting on Ethan to get here to give us some instructions."

"Maybe he got tied up. Did you try the radio?" Danato asked.

"Been trying for ten minutes. Wasn't sure how long I should keep these guys waiting. The tension's thicker than Mama's mashed potatoes in there."

Danato cleared his throat, so he didn't chuckle at Duke's metaphor. It was probably meant to be amusing, but he was not meant to be amused by Duke. "I'll try.

Maybe your radio is on the fritz." Danato pulled out his radio and turned it on. "Ethan, the men are waiting for you. You copy this?"

"*Danato.*" Belus's voice came over the radio.

"Belus? Where's Ethan?"

"*He's a little busy right now. You'll have to take over for him.*"

"Is everything okay?" Danato glanced at Nevia, who took a little more interest in the conversation.

"*I'll catch you up as soon as I can. I've got things under control for now.*"

"Okay." Danato clicked off and looked at Duke. "Well, looks like you're stuck with me." He looked at Nevia, who was waiting for orders. She probably wanted to get back to the others, but as long as he had her around, he might as well utilize her. "Why don't you join us, Jordan?"

Her brow perked slightly, but she nodded. He offered her a palm up to lead the way. At the last second, Duke's gentlemanly ways took over, and he ran ahead to open the gym door for her. She gave him a curt nod, which he returned before she turned into the doorway.

Danato paused as she stepped back suddenly, seemingly for no reason, and then proceeded again. He smiled, counting a couple of his steps before thrusting his hand out into midair. His fingers grabbed onto an invisible, bony neck. Without a moment's hesitation he slammed the transparent being into the wall. The drywall cracked under the force of the impact, but Danato didn't regret the strength he was exerting on this banished guest.

"Well, well, well." Danato spoke through gritted teeth. "Looks like you aren't invisible to bloodhounds."

"Damn it," Nevia whispered from the doorway of the gym.

"Show yourself or I swear I will crush your throat!"

The blurry image of a person appeared before him. After a moment, the mirage solidified into a woman. It wasn't the first time he had seen her, and it would doubtfully be the last. Her curvaceous hips and hefty endowments were his ideal image of a beautiful woman, and he had let his guard down more than once because of it.

"What's the matter, Danato?" She flipped her long salt-and-pepper hair over her shoulder before batting her icy gray eyes at him. "I thought you'd be happy to see me again."

"I told you to never come back to this prison, Maddox." He pressed on her throat to make his point, but she seemed to enjoy it, so he stopped.

"I don't work for you, Danato. You can't tell me what to do."

"As long as you are in this prison, I will tell you what to do, and you will do it!"

"Still mad, I see. You really should learn to let things go. Speaking of which, I really do need to breathe."

Danato released her, and she sagged against the wall, catching her breath. "Jordan," he barked.

"Yes, sir." Nevia approached them slowly.

"You see her, don't you?" Maddox looked at Nevia, trying to find the challenge in the petite woman. "You saw her when she came out of the gym, didn't you?"

"Her?"

Danato glanced at her. "He, she, it, whatever. Do you see…" He motioned to the woman before him. "…this person?"

"Yes, but I don't think that—"

"Good. I want you to stick around. This bitch is a spy and a thief, and I don't want her leaving my sight."

"A spy for whom?" Nevia asked.

"Yes, Danato, a spy for whom? What evil conspiracy theory do you have this week? Am I a double agent for the United States? Or is it Mother Russia that's trying to infiltrate? Perhaps it's your own people this time? Who, oh, who indeed pays me more this week than last?"

"I'm warning you, Maddox. You'd better be on the up and up this time, or I will lock you up."

"You know, that's the funny thing about stealing information. With a photographic memory, I don't ever have to get caught red-handed."

"I'm warning you—"

"No, I'm warning you!" Maddox stood up straight. "There are big changes coming. Changes you won't like. Changes that you are going to need me for."

"Don't pander to me." Danato scrunched his nose.

"And don't be a martyr to a system that is dying." Her face tipped to one side, and she looked sincere in her sympathy. "I asked for this assignment. I want to help you."

"Bullshit!"

"Shut up and listen to me for once in your life. There's a lot of talk right now, Danato. A lot. I don't know what the ultimate plan is, but money seems to be a lesser issue." She glanced to Nevia. "The issue is control."

"Control of the prison?"

"No." She took an exasperated breath. "Control of the entity."

"We have control of the entity." She perked a brow in disbelief. "This was a one-time incident. We just didn't understand how she would react to Efrat's electricity."

"Rationalize all you want, Danato, but you know damn well that the people on the board don't care about protecting people anymore. They especially don't care about protecting supernaturals."

"If they..." Danato frowned and looked for the lie on her face, but it wasn't there. "You and your men aren't here for an audit, are you?"

"No, the audit is an excuse to check you out, evaluate your weaknesses," she said somewhat sympathetically. "We're here to subdue you, in the event that you become uncooperative." Maddox frowned. "They're trying to shut you down, Danato."

35

"**F**ECK! WHY ISN'T HE waking up?" Daniel paced in front of his fallen friend while Belus took his vitals. "I healed him. He should be awake."

"Easy, man." Heaton patted him on the shoulder and tried to get him to sit down, but Daniel shrugged him off.

"He should be awake!"

"Yes." Belus eyed him from beneath his brow. "He should be, but clearly he is malnourished and weak, so we need to give him time."

"Maybe I should fetch a nurse," Heaton suggested.

"Fetch a nurse for what?" Gypsy asked as she arrived to the party. Callin trailed in behind her. He frowned when he noticed Ethan lying unconscious in one of the hospital beds.

"Where the hell were you two?" Daniel snapped, as if they were to blame for his friend being near death.

"What can I say? I love cock." Gypsy smirked.

Daniel couldn't stand her casual attitude at such a crucial time and didn't think twice before he shoved her across the room with his power. Callin growled and stalked toward him for another fight. Daniel ripped off his glasses and hunkered down for a linebacker tackle.

"Do it!" he shouted. "I double-DOG dare you!"

Callin hesitated, knowing the potential power that Daniel harnessed in his gaze. A quiet growl rumbled in his chest, but he rose from his attack position and moved to collect Gypsy from the floor.

"Daniel!" Belus scolded, but Daniel didn't look at him. He was too angry, and he didn't want to listen to his lucid mediating.

"Hurting others won't help Ethan." Levi murmured from the corner. Daniel kept forgetting he was even there, but his tiny voice burrowed into his mind. It made sense. He was only angry because he hadn't listened to Efrat and stopped Ethan in the first place. He was mad because he hadn't been a half-second faster. He was also angry because, despite his healing power, Ethan had still lost too much blood to simply jump back up.

"He needs a transfusion," Daniel announced, as if he had solved the world's problems with one sentence. To his disappointment, Belus had already been there and back already.

"We used all the blood stores, and he's type O," Belus informed him. "You two are both A negative. Cori is B positive." He motioned between him and Heaton.

"You know our blood types?" Heaton asked suspiciously. Belus acknowledged the question with a glance, but didn't confirm what he had already disclosed.

"I got some O," Gypsy contributed, twisting her shoulder around as she stepped in front of Daniel. "Of course, I'm not really sure I want to share it now." She twisted her jaw, proudly flaunting her position of importance to him.

He narrowed his eyes. "What do you want, Grace?"

She smiled and reached up to touch his exposed chest, but her hand stopped millimeters from its goal. Her eyes glazed in confusion and her smile faded. She shook away her stalled thoughts and dropped her hand. "Never mind." She looked at Ethan. "Let's just get this boy pumped up on some Grade A Certified Bitch Juice." She clicked her tongue and slapped her forearm before moving to his bedside.

36

CORI'S EYES WATERED AS her boy clutched to the nurse in the makeshift daycare in the infirmary. There was only one baby to care for, so the nurses spoiled him something terrible. After nearly a year, he now knew the nurses better than her. She didn't want to be mad at them for that, but she couldn't help it. She felt displaced.

"Now, now, girl, stop your crying," the robust nurse demanded sharply.

Her lack of sympathy for her situation surprised Cori.

"This young man doesn't want to be held by a sniffling woman. He wants to be bobbed up and down, and sweet-talked too." The woman pitched her voice high like a cartoon character. "Don't you, little one?" She smiled broadly, which made the little boy smile back.

Cori laughed, and he looked over at her. She could see what the nurse was saying. She wouldn't win back her son by moping over their lost time. She put on her mock surprise face before covering it with her hands. After a few peek-a-boos, he held a smile for her.

It was going to take a while, but a bond stronger than time linked her baby to her. One day soon, he would be reaching for her over anyone. She would just take a lesson from her husband and be patient.

A heavy pounding on the door disrupted the moment, making everyone jump. Efrat's voice beckoned her from outside. She rolled her eyes and moved to the door. She opened it and saw Efrat standing on the other side, looking uncomfortable.

"What?" She crossed her arms, staring at him with the venom she just couldn't let go of yet.

"You should come with me," he said somberly.

"Oh, really? And why is that?"

He frowned and looked back down the hall. "I reported to Ethan like you said, but he didn't take the news about Dirk very well."

"Oh, don't tell me he's mad about the castration."

"I never got that far. I mentioned the attempted rape and Ethan went into a rage."

Cori sighed, thinking that beating the man up now was just delayed overkill. "What did he do?"

"He found him in the infirmary. I finally managed to explain what you did, so he calmed down, but... Dirk got the drop on him." His eyes flickered over her perplexed face. "Dirk stabbed Ethan."

"Stabbed?" Cori stared at him. "How bad is it?"

"Daniel's healed him, but he's not waking up." Cori stepped into the hallway, shutting the door behind her. "Where is he?" Cori looked around as if she needed to collect her keys and wallet before she left.

"In the patient section." Efrat pressed gently on her back, helping her take the steps that some part of her was fighting against.

"Shit." She walked down the hall, but as her mind registered everything, her heart rate increased and so did her pace.

By the time she reached the patient ward, she was sprinting. She barreled into the room, greeted by several more sympathetic faces than she'd anticipated. She found Ethan propped up in a bed with Gypsy on one side and Belus on the other. Ethan was still unconscious. There was a long tube feeding blood from Gypsy's arm into Ethan's.

Despite the obvious benefit of the blood transfusion, Cori couldn't help being pissed off by the woman's infuriating, insouciant demeanor. Gypsy was nonchalantly passing the time by window shopping in a SkyMall magazine. Cori could almost picture her gnawing on a piece of gum, but so far, her vices seemed to be restricted to cigarettes and audacity.

"He's okay," Belus assured her, before she could choreograph her widow's immolation.

Heaton and Daniel were side by side, attentively waiting for Ethan's reawakening. Daniel caught her eye and nodded to the bed on the opposite wall. She glanced over at the dusty remains of what must have been Dirk on part of his hospital bed. She nodded to Daniel, giving him permission to ignore the guilt from that particular kill. However, judging by the muted ire still on his face, he didn't really need approval for this one.

Callin leaned against the wall by the door. He looked disinterested in the events, but she wasn't sure worry was something that all werewolves were capable of expressing.

Levi was in a chair on the other side. His mournful, comatose expression was familiar to Cori. She understood loss very well. She wasn't sure how he was keeping himself upright, let alone free from a deluge of tears.

Efrat entered the room a little late since he hadn't taken to running down the hall with her. "Any improvement?" he asked, looking over the scene of the blood donation.

"Hey there, sexy," Gypsy drawled when she noticed his entrance. "I was hoping I would see you again." She gave him a wink that seemed to elicit enervation from Efrat.

Given the description of their earlier encounter, Cori had expected Efrat to show more interest in the flirtation. Instead, he was hiding behind her, avoiding eye contact with the woman. It was then that Cori noticed Callin shooting a baleful look at the elemental and she realized Efrat wasn't hiding so much as keeping the werewolf in his line of sight. Callin didn't look pleased about the situation, but he remained composed. When her gaze lingered too long on the werewolf, Callin's eyes shifted, locking a predatory gaze on her. She looked away, returning her attention to more immediate dangers.

Cori watched Gypsy reveling, as she supplied her husband with blood. It was in no small way ironic. The last time she had seen Ethan in the same room as this woman, she had been spilling his blood. Regardless of how many times she reminded herself that this was a completely different reality, she couldn't keep herself from seeing Gypsy as a threat.

"Whose idea was this?" Cori asked, conferring some accusation of betrayal on Belus for letting Gypsy share blood with her husband.

"We need her blood," Belus said flatly, checking Ethan's pulse from his other side. "She's the only match that hasn't been drained to anemic levels already."

"Of course she's a match," Cori mumbled.

"Yeah, isn't that a kick in the crotch?" Gypsy teased and slapped her magazine down on Ethan's chest. "It's amazing how things change between realities, isn't it?"

Cori furrowed her brow. "What's that supposed to mean?" She knew exactly what it meant, but she wasn't aware that Gypsy would know.

"One minute I'm running amuck, the next I'm facilitating life. So unpredictable."

She could see Gypsy found great amusement in her suggested knowledge, so much so that it was causing Cori's defenses to rise.

The familiar static charge caught Belus's attention, and he moved to block her from approaching Gypsy. "Cori, don't. Not now."

"Easy, kitten," Efrat murmured under his breath and scooted closer to her back. "The puppy is already on high alert."

"This has nothing to do with him."

"If it concerns Grace, it concerns me," Callin called to her.

Cori looked at him, but he hadn't moved from the wall. She wasn't sure she could put up enough of a fight to beat a werewolf. Electricity and fire could certainly kill, but a broken neck was so much faster.

She didn't want to make an enemy out of Callin, but she also wouldn't allow Gypsy to repeat her rampage in the prison. She looked at Daniel and he gave her a nod. She was grateful that she had earned the man's friendship. He was the type of bodyguard that superseded any threat.

Cori took a step toward Gypsy, which caused Callin to stand up straight. Efrat grabbed her electrified hand, trying to draw her back. Meanwhile, Daniel took a leisurely step forward, putting himself at a better angle to look at Callin without obstructions. Gypsy volleyed her gaze around to all the men before landing back on Cori.

"I know who my money's on." Gypsy smirked and raised her eyebrows.

"The last time we spoke, you didn't seem to know anything about me," Cori said.

Gypsy's smile dissolved back down to her usual smugness. "Things change."

"What things?"

"I graduated from *need to know*, to *in the know*."

"And what do you know?" Cori asked.

Gypsy opened her mouth to speak, but Cori's favorite physician entered just then and interrupted the standoff.

"What the hell is going on in here?" The doctor looked over all of them standing around. "The nurse said someone was stabbed." He caught sight of Ethan and immediately jumped to his side. Belus shifted out of his way so he could check his heart and lungs with his stethoscope.

"How is he?" Cori asked.

The doctor turned to answer her and noticed the empty dust-filled bed on the other side of the room. His already small, slitted eyes narrowed even further. "What is that?" He pointed to the bed, causing everyone to turn their eyes to Daniel.

"Dirk is the one who stabbed Ethan," Belus explained.

"So you turned him to dust?" The doctor looked at Daniel.

"Aye," Daniel readily admitted. "That's what happens to someone thick enough to mess with my friends." Daniel confronted the man head-on, ready to listen to any argument he might have against his execution. Despite his effort to frighten him, the doctor was too high on his soapbox to recognize the impending threat of his gaze.

"I am sick of this anarchy!" The physician wheeled around to face Belus. "First, I have her severing a man's penis." The doctor threw his hand out at Cori, which made Gypsy snort. "Now I have him murdering a man right in my infirmary." Before Belus could respond to the man's rant, the doctor turned his attention back to Daniel. "You are a menace, Daniel McGrath!"

Heaton's fist came out of nowhere from behind Daniel and dropped the doctor with a single punch to the face. Everyone except Daniel seemed stunned by the abrupt violence from his partner. Heaton stepped out from behind Daniel and towered over the downed man. "And you're an asshole!"

"Heaton!" Belus attempted to scold him, but he was no doubt grateful for the gesture.

"You are too fucking cool, man." Gypsy chuckled appreciatively at Heaton's bravado.

"You broke my nose!" the physician squealed from the floor.

"Everyone needs to settle down." Belus looked over the whole room. "We have too many damn people here, and no one is abiding by anything resembling proper protocol. I understand that this is a chaotic situation, but that is no excuse for everyone to fly off the handle."

"If you want everyone to calm down, you should probably ditch that broad and be done with it," Gypsy suggested.

"What?" Cori was the only one to say it, but there seemed to be a general consensus of confusion around the room. Everyone turned questioningly to Gypsy.

"The witch bitch." Gypsy shrugged.

"She's not a bitch." Levi spoke softly from the corner.

Gypsy noted his turmoil, but didn't apologize for the verbal indiscretion. "That girl's got wicked mojo," Gypsy explained. "Nobody was able to touch her when we found her. She seemed to intensify everyone's emotions." Gypsy offered Callin a suggestive look.

"Yeah, but she's dead," Heaton said, sounding partly annoyed and partly sympathetic for Gypsy's obvious stupidity.

Gypsy shrugged, unaffected by his condescension. "I don't know. I got a pretty good zap off her even after she was knocking on the pearly gates."

"Zap?" Levi asked.

"A zap. A spark. I think whatever magic you idiots stuck inside of her is on a feedback loop. That's why everyone's so intense." Gypsy glanced at Callin again. Cori wondered what she was basing her accusation on. Aside from his reaction to her tryst, which was justified, Callin seemed to be rather calm.

"She may be right." Levi stood and moved to Gypsy. He sat down on the edge of Ethan's bed and looked her over. He swallowed and reached out his hand. "May I?"

"May you what?"

"I just need to touch you."

Gypsy narrowed her eyes. "How old are you?"

Levi shifted back and shrugged. "Um, nineteen. Why?"

"Just checking." She placed her hand in his and he looked it over carefully. "What are you looking for?"

Levi let go of her hand and stood up. "Just checking," he answered. It inspired a glare from Gypsy, but the boy didn't seem to be saying it sarcastically.

Levi looked over the circle of baffled faces. "As she said, Addy was resonating very strong emotions from her dark magic. Human magic. It can intensify all emotions, good and bad alike. I know you all felt that in the caves." He nodded to Heaton and Daniel before glancing back at Callin.

The werewolf's interest in the conversation seemed to wane, and he left the room. Cori looked at Gypsy to see if she was concerned about this, but she was more interested in what Levi was saying.

"Annette was mostly immune," Levi continued, "but even she was becoming more obsessive than usual."

"What about you?" Gypsy asked. "Wasn't she your girl? Shouldn't you be curled in a ball on the floor right now?"

Cori was disgusted with Gypsy's flippant question, but she was also curious why Levi was remaining calm in the face of such a crushing experience.

"I'm different. It doesn't mean I'm not feeling anything, though," Levi added, drawing another narrowed gaze from Gypsy.

"Addy's body isn't producing this magic. It's just a vessel to hold the power. She may not be alive anymore, but her body is still holding that power."

"Is she still dangerous?" Belus asked.

"Power could be drawn from her."

"How do we shut her off?" Cori asked.

"She's like a dying battery. Once the body... disintegrates, there is nothing left to hold the power."

"If that's true, we need to get her cremated as soon as possible." Belus looked at Cori. She nodded and moved toward the door to get that done.

"No," Ethan rasped as he revived to the party he had inadvertently started. "We have to bury her."

37

"E THAN!" CORI RUSHED TO his side, nearly toppling Belus as he maneuvered to get out from between their embrace. She touched his chest and face gingerly, as if unsure how much pressure she could exert. He was wiped out, but by no means in pain.

He pulled her into a one-armed hug and kissed her neck and cheek. "I'm okay, sweetness," he whispered in her ear.

"Why did you go after Dirk?" she asked, pulling back abruptly.

He moved his hand up to stroke her cheek. "You know why."

Her anger wilted. "I know you want to protect me, but..." Cori's eyes shifted to Gypsy, who was making no effort to hide that she was listening to the conversation.

"Don't mind me." Gypsy picked up her catalog again. "Ooh, video binoculars. I could save a bundle on porn."

Cori gave the strange woman a double take before continuing. "We don't have to get into this now, Ethan, but I wanted Efrat to tell you about Dirk, so you know that your constant protection is not necessary. You have to trust me. I can defend myself."

Gypsy snorted behind her magazine.

"Something to offer, Gypsy?" Cori asked, unable to hide her disdain for the woman. Ethan couldn't blame her for the grudge, but since Gypsy was currently saving his ass—again—he could hardly deny her some civility.

"Sorry." She popped her eyes over the rim of the catalog before dropping it into her lap. "That wasn't meant contentiously. I was just remembering the look on Frederique's face when you froze the shit out of her hand. Now *that* was a beautiful thing."

Cori looked as if she wanted to throw an insult at her, but she couldn't seem to find the gumption since the woman hadn't technically offended her.

"Cori, I'm always going to protect you..." Ethan swallowed hard, trying not to let any assumptions about his future influence his statement. "...no matter what. As far as trust goes? I *do* trust you to defend yourself. If I didn't, I would never let you leave my side. Please don't confuse my defense with disrespect. As far as I am concerned, you and I are a team."

"If we're a team, then we need to make decisions together."

"I know." Ethan nodded. "I shouldn't have let you go without explaining what was going on. I thought I was helping you, but I realize now that being surprised by bad news is far worse than being presented with it."

Cori nodded and touched his face. She was about to lean in for a kiss, but Belus touched her shoulder and she withdrew. "You can catch up on the rest later." Ethan glared at him for the interruption, but, as usual, it was a fruitless display. "What's this about burying the girl?"

"Adrianna," Levi corrected in barely a whisper.

"She can't be cremated. We have to bury her," Ethan elaborated.

"Why? What difference does it make?" Belus asked suspiciously.

"She deserves a proper burial."

"Proper is contingent on cultural influence and climate. The ground is rock solid right now. Burial is an unnecessary effort," Belus argued.

"We could use the lava man to dig the hole," Efrat suggested.

"Why would Rodan help us with that?"

"That's how we got into the basement," Efrat explained.

"You…" Belus's brow creased as he looked at Cori. She shrugged, as if he should be used to her tactics by now. "Never mind." He shook his head and turned his attention back to Ethan. "Even if we can do it, I doubt Danato will approve it, especially if her magic can still be sapped."

"The earth is a natural dampener of human magic," Levi said. "Burying her should sequester the remaining dark magic inside of her.

Ethan was impressed that he still had the state of mind to process anything resembling logical thoughts. He had to be dying inside. He hated himself for playing any part in his pain.

Belus eyed the boy, his lips twisted from the disgruntled internal argument. It was procedure to burn everything—corpses were no exception. In the end, Belus would let Danato make the final call, and he would choose to follow the rules. He wondered, if it had been Cori's friend that had died, if he would allow the leniency.

Ethan reached over and disconnected the tube leading to his arm. He sat up on the bed, pressing his hand into the wound as he surveyed the room. "Would everyone excuse us? Belus and I need to talk."

The room froze as if Ethan had just suggested guns at high noon with the man. Belus tipped his head slightly, no doubt surprised that Ethan would request a private conversation. Cori glanced between them, not sure what to do, but in the end, she dutifully led the evacuation.

Gypsy looked down at the other half of the IV in her arm and ripped it out, much as Ethan had. She pressed her hand over the puncture and looked at Ethan. He gave her a nod to thank her for the contribution, and she nodded back. "Who's got my juice and cookies?" she griped as she followed the line going out the door.

"What's up, kid?" Belus asked after the door had swung shut behind Gypsy.

"Do you remember the discussion about the radio?"

"Which one?" Belus asked.

"The one where I told you I wanted to use it to save Cori's life, and you wanted to protect everyone else's life."

"Oh, that one. As I recall, you won that argument."

"I don't think I've ever won an argument with you, Belus. I imagine I never will."

Belus scoffed and crossed his arms. "You're not usually one for flattery, especially toward me."

"It's not flattery. You're a stubborn ass and I hate that you're so damn clever. However, I need your help."

"My help? This must be serious."

"It is."

"Does that mean you're ready to tell me what's going on? Why is this suddenly so important to you?"

Ethan rubbed his face. As much as he wanted to admit the truth, he was still finding it impossible. There was still a part of him that was loyal to the dragons. He was certain that it would eventually wear off and he would come to his senses, but until then, he was stuck with an unwanted secret.

"Belus, you and I are cut from the same cloth. We follow the rules and only bend when the plan dictates it. I know this doesn't make any sense now, and trust me, it doesn't make that much more sense from this side of it, but I'm asking for a little latitude. I want you to back me up on this with Danato. Not because Adrianna deserves a proper burial or because I feel like I'm owed this for my years of devoted service, but because you know that if I'm not following Danato's orders, then I must be following someone's."

Belus's eyes widened slightly and Ethan held his steady gaze, demanding that he understand him without further inquiry. He took the hint and moved away. The small man paced the room slowly.

"Annette is a variable woman." Belus circumvented his question carefully. "I know she appears genuine in her concerns and devotions, but her ultimate motivations—"

"Annette has never superseded Danato in my eyes," Ethan interrupted.

Belus pondered again, letting his frustration show in his hesitant stride.

"I haven't asked you for much, Belus," Ethan added when it was clear he wasn't being sold on the *trust me* aspect of his request.

Belus paused and looked him over. "I can see that you're struggling with your obligations, Ethan." He took in a deep breath and looked over the glass-windowed room. His eye caught on something he spotted through the glass. "I'd be lying if I said that I hadn't doubted the morality of this place in my early days. Danato... I'm not sure his father ever left him room to question his duty. It was as much an honor as it was a burden for him." Belus glanced at him—he seemed to be expecting Ethan to roll his eyes over the *back in the day* story. When it was clear that Ethan was still rapt, he continued.

"For me, it was an unattainable position. I had a chip on my shoulder. I had something to prove." He chuckled. "I proved it, all right. I woke up one morning, and I realized that I had just fought to win a fight that I might not have wanted to win."

"You still feel that way?"

"To live the life you *want* to live is a luxury. To live the life you were *born* to live… is a privilege." Ethan waited for the speech about obligations to begin. "I will do this for you. Not because I agree with the concealment of your motivations or because I think I owe you anything, but because I know you wouldn't ask me for help unless you were truly desperate."

Belus let a small smile perk to his lips, and Ethan smirked at the juvenile amusement he got from his discomfort.

"You do realize that Danato doesn't always listen to me either?"

"No, but he does listen, and right now, that's more than he will do for me."

38

D ANATO PUSHED THROUGH THE broken glass door to the infirmary, examining it with some confusion. He assumed Ethan had caused it, but he could hardly reprimand him about the little demolition since he was not above the indiscretion himself. Whoever designed the prison had obviously done it prior to the discovery of dragon steroids.

"Yes, well, that wouldn't be a problem if you had stopped her in the first place," Cori scolded Efrat about something in a sidebar beside the nurse's hub. Callin was glaring at everyone, but most of his displeasure was focused on Efrat. Daniel and Heaton were having a private discussion on the other side of the station, out of earshot.

"Oh, cut me some slack, Cori," Efrat scolded her right back. "If I have to be lectured by you one more time today, I will gladly crawl into Callin's food bowl."

Gypsy clucked her tongue as she passed them. "You should have told me you were spoken for, Efrat. If I had known, I never would have stepped on Corinthia's toes," Gypsy apologized sarcastically from behind Efrat.

Cori's expression shifted from mild irritation to fury. She jumped forward, hands igniting with fireballs. Efrat barely caught her before she could fuse her super-heated hands to the woman's face. "How the hell do you know my full name?" Cori raged as she fought to get free of Efrat's railing arm.

Efrat rumbled and pushed her back harder, getting some distance between the women. "Must you piss off everyone around you?" he yelled at Gypsy.

Danato watched the scene play out, patiently observing Gypsy's performance. Her telltale smirk appeared as if she were proud of how easily she had flipped the switch on Cori's aggression.

"Someone has to put some personality into this place," Gypsy said playfully.

Efrat practically threw Cori across the room to free himself for his own confrontation with Gypsy. "You're not a personality. You're a plague."

"So that's a no on round two."

Efrat's fists balled up. Static energy poured off them, but he didn't raise his hands. Callin shifted in the background, barely restraining his own anger, but he also didn't attack. When it was clear, no one was going to attack, Gypsy chuckled and walked away. "I need a cigarette."

Gypsy approached the infirmary entrance, but Danato made no attempts to unblock her path. She stopped in front of him and held his gaze a moment. There was delight in her eyes, he thought. She liked this game, because she usually won. However, watchful eyes did not easily discomfit Danato.

Gypsy's gaze finally fell, and she looked him up and down, examining the impassable wall before her. Her eyes held on his biceps and her lips parted slightly. He may have shrunk down a few pants sizes while inside the bubble, but his strength had not been reduced. If anything, his leaner frame had defined the muscles that had always lurked beneath his extraneous weight.

It was obvious she was eager to pick fights, but the real question was whether she would risk bodily harm to do so.

Instead of trying to bypass him or even ask permission to leave, Gypsy just perked an eyebrow at him and pulled a pack of cigarettes from one of her many pockets. "Or I could just light up here." She pulled a cigarette out of the pack with puckered lips. Danato noted her coquettish gaze beneath her brow, as if he might find her vampish display alluring.

Amateur.

"Hey, Cori, you got a light?" She glanced back at her.

Danato's upper lip twitched at the woman's grating flippancy. It seemed to be never-ending. As if he didn't have enough to deal with, now he had to teach a militant teenager how to behave.

Before he could stop himself, he grabbed her shoulders and lifted her off the floor. Callin growled and moved to intercept him. Danato looked at him, and he slowed his approach. As per his promise, Callin bit back his anger and waited impatiently for Danato to make his point.

Gypsy glanced around from her newly acquired height and gave him an arrogant smirk. "What's up?"

He wasn't sure what his intention was other than brandishing his strength. He had never dealt with someone who couldn't be frightened. He wasn't sure that he knew how to be authoritative without inducing fear.

Before he could decide on the next step, he felt Nevia touch his back. She didn't say anything to undermine him, but the gentle touch reminded him of what they had spoken about.

He looked Gypsy over again, seeing her in a new light. The arrogance, the rude sarcasm, it was all just an excuse to create chaos. To incite the people around her. Like Nevia said, she liked danger. She also liked to play puppet with the emotions that she considered beneath her. She may not have successfully exploited his lust, but she had his temper firmly under her control.

Danato abruptly dropped her. She yelped and stumbled back, trying to regain her land legs. He hadn't thought the drop would harm her that badly, but he was in no mood to apologize for any pain he had caused her. "Everybody line up!"

Gypsy frowned at him, no doubt disappointed that she didn't have an opportunity to flaunt more of her dissident wit.

"We are not your employees, Danato," Callin pointed out as he wandered over to check on Gypsy.

"You are in my prison." Danato waved over Daniel and Heaton, who were too in depth in their conversation to break for his bellowing voice. He was curious about what took precedence over him, but he didn't have time for gossip. He needed to finish getting his prison in order. "Whether you are a guest, an interloper, or just a hitchhiker astray from the highway, as long as you are inside the walls of this prison, you will take your orders from me."

Danato stopped before Gypsy, who had ambled into line with Callin's help. He wanted to ask about her injuries even more now, but he didn't want to lose steam in his authoritative tirade. "Care to venture a guess why?" he asked, directing the question at her. Her brow tipped, double-dog daring him to say it. "I'm the warden," he whispered in her face.

"And if I have a problem with that?" she whispered right back.

"Then leave." He smirked.

"No problem, just get me a ride."

He put on his best fake pout. "The board has temporarily barred outgoing trucks while we are getting things back in order," he announced to the entire line. "Any exits within the next 48 hours will have to be on foot. So, there's the door if you don't like following orders." Danato motioned to what remained of the glass door. "It's only about 100 miles to the nearest active roadway. And I use the term *active* loosely."

Gypsy cursed under her breath.

Danato turned his gaze to Callin. "What about you? I have a cell upstairs if you think there will be any more issues."

Callin clenched his jaw. "Your house. Your rules. Besides, I wouldn't want anyone to get hurt trying to get me into that cell," he added, unable to resist the statement.

Danato threw back his head and chuckled sarcastically. After a moment, he threw his head forward again and stared at Callin. "Do you think you're the first werewolf to walk through my doors?" Callin narrowed his eyes, annoyed by the juvenile Q&A. "No, I'm actually asking you." Danato spoke slower. "Do you think you are the first werewolf to walk through my doors?"

The muscles in Callin's jaw and neck tensed. He was no doubt fighting every instinct in his body at this point. He wanted to attack, but he had made a promise. "No." The word came out as a rasp.

"Good, because we didn't install werewolf-proof cages and offer our services as babysitters without contingency plans." Danato took a step closer to Callin and put his face in his. Callin twisted his head, cracking his neck before tipping his head to look up at Danato. Down the line, Nevia let out a harrumph. But she wasn't warning him about anything he didn't already know. He could see the tremble in Callin's fists as he balled them up tight, turning the knuckles white.

"I can tell you're more man than beast. You are exerting excellent control." Danato spoke quieter, keeping as much of the conversation between them as he could. "As long as that remains true, you and I won't have a problem. But God forbid, if it doesn't… you will end up in a cell upstairs—and yes, before you can't resist your primal need to be the alpha male in this situation, I am fully capable of getting you in that cage." Callin's forehead glistened with the onset of sweat, but of course it wasn't from fear. "Are we perfectly clear?"

Callin took a long breath. "Yes." The word came out deep and throaty, like the wolf within was trying to crawl out of his mouth to get to Danato. "I am a man of my word."

"Good." Danato broke away from the confrontation before Callin's resolve broke.

"Anyone else object to following my orders for the next two days?" Danato looked over the remaining line—Heaton, Daniel, Nevia, Cori and Efrat—but none of them had any protests. He glanced at Gypsy just to make sure she was on board. She gave him a mocking salute with the cigarette in her hand that she had yet to find a light for.

"I've just spoken with the men downstairs. We've arranged to include Renee's men in the guard rotation so my men can get a break, which they are in great need of. The top floor is apparently being renovated for a new renter. I don't have much information on the tenant, just that he is going to be doing research on our magical artifacts and antiquities. That means we need to start organizing and cataloging the prop room. That's where you come in.

"As most of you already know, the prop room is full of some very interesting supernatural paraphernalia. Most of them are a nuisance, but many of them are extremely dangerous—especially in the wrong hands. You will not touch anything in that room without the express instruction from myself or Belus. Even we don't know what everything in that room does, so we will have to take it slow. Box by box and item by item. Most of it is before our time, so that means digging into the archives to find out where it came from and what it does. That means lots of lifting, lots of reading, and a fluffle of dust bunnies."

Danato glanced at the clock on the wall behind the nurse's hub. The day was getting away from him. He may have had a half dozen fresh faces to start the work, but neither he nor Belus was in good enough shape to supervise such a hazardous project.

"We will start first thing in the morning." Danato moved to leave, but Daniel raised his hand to get his attention.

"There's something we need to discuss," he said.

"What's that?" Danato asked.

"Sleeping arrangements." Heaton stepped forward, practically blocking Daniel. "We usually get an invitation, but..." Heaton glanced down the line. "We have a couple extra bodies."

"Damn it," Danato murmured under his breath when he remembered Renee had invited herself into his home. "Guest quarters will be maxed out with Maddox's men," he said, quickly calculating the number of new military faces and the number of available beds.

"There's an opening in the guard quarters," Efrat offered.

"Why is that?" Danato asked.

"Dirk is dead," Efrat answered.

"How did that happen?"

"I'd be happy to offer you a full report, but I can almost guarantee that you'll agree with the majority that it's an improvement," Efrat said gingerly.

Danato looked at Cori, and she nodded. "It's a long story," she said, either because it was indeed long or she just didn't want to discuss it in front of everyone.

"All right, I'll take your word for it now, but I will need a report at some point. Callin, would you mind sleeping in the guard quarters? I doubt you'll have any problems from the men."

"Guess that means I won't be sleeping," Efrat muttered to the ground. Danato ignored him. Whatever issue he had with Callin seemed to be of his own making, and regardless of blame, Efrat could take care of himself.

"If Jordan and Daniel share... Renee... that leaves one for Heaton." Danato twisted his mouth as he evaluated Gypsy.

She chuckled. "You've got plenty of empty cells. You won't even need a contingency plan for me."

"I'm not asking a guest to endure that," Danato said. He didn't really have an issue with putting her behind bars—in fact, he preferred it. However, without cause to lock the cell, it didn't do any good to contain her, and the last thing he needed was a volatile personality freely roaming around his prison for the night. He much preferred to have her in his sight. However, that left him searching for a bed, and he wasn't sure how Heaton would feel about sleeping on the couch.

"She can share with me," Heaton offered.

Gypsy smiled and leaned over to inspect him across Callin. She blew him a kiss, and he rolled his eyes back at her. Callin turned to scrutinize the tall black man who had designated himself Gypsy's bedfellow.

Rather than appease the man with promises of abstention, Heaton dragged his eyes up and down Callin's body. When Heaton's gaze returned to the werewolf's face, he tipped his brow suggestively. Callin's appraisal died along with the tension in his shoulders. A small smile perched on his lips before he turned away.

"Is that okay with you?" Danato asked Gypsy.

"Yeah, sure. I'm always up for a challenge," she said past the cigarette, which was once again hanging from her lip, waiting to be lit.

Danato sighed and looked at Cori. "Cori, I don't suppose you could get things going on the home front for our guests. Maybe some food. I'll catch up with you as soon as I can." Cori's lips were pinched tight, but she nodded. "Callin, I assume Ethan will be inviting you for dinner."

"Ah, Danato?" Heaton waved his hand. "We still need one more bed."

"Huh?"

Heaton pointed done the line and Danato wavered to see around Efrat where Levi was obscurely sulking.

"Oh, shit." He wasn't surprised he had forgotten about the boy, but he presented another problem. He was certain that he was not a danger to them, but his loyalty to Annette left room for him to be untrustworthy.

"He can stay with me," Belus announced as he entered the area.

Ethan followed in behind him. He looked pale and weak, but the expression on his face announced that he wasn't looking for any sympathy for what had happened to him. Danato nodded back at the broken door. "What happened here?"

"I can fill you in if you're done." Belus nodded to the lineup beside him. He could already sense the tone in his voice. Whatever Belus needed to discuss, he wouldn't like it.

Danato looked Ethan over. "Are you all right?" he asked. "You look faint," he added when he realized the question could apply to a good number of things.

"I'm fine. Daniel and Gypsy put me back together."

Danato glanced back at Gypsy, wondering how she had helped. Rather than flaunt her contribution or claim any debt of gratitude, she just nodded, confirming that the information was not false. He assumed Belus would get him up to date on those details as well. "Ethan, you and Cori can get everyone situated at the house while Belus and I finish up here."

"Yes, sir," Ethan said. It wasn't sarcastic or spiteful, but it still felt that way. "Cori, why don't you lead the way. I'll get the baby."

Ethan headed back into the far hall while everyone shuffled out behind Cori.

Danato turned back to Belus, but he shook his head as a nurse came into the station near him. "Let's go down to your office."

He *really* wasn't going to like this.

39

ORI WAS THANKFUL THE elevator didn't take as long as it usually did to arrive. Though everyone had simmered down since Danato's speech, there was still some tension in the group. She stepped inside the lift and held the door for everyone.

Heaton glanced over to Efrat, who was heading to the stairwell rather than getting in the elevator with everyone. "You guys go ahead, I'll catch up." Heaton jogged over to Efrat, signaling him to wait up.

Daniel popped his head out of the lift, slightly concerned. "What's up?"

"Nothing." Heaton lassoed his arm around Efrat's neck. The elemental nearly zapped him in defense, unused to the unfamiliar camaraderie. As it was, he gave Heaton a glare that he didn't notice. "I want to introduce Efrat to someone that might enjoy his electric personality," Heaton said with a sly grin and a wink.

Daniel paused, trying to figure out who he meant, but a smile emerged on his face. "Good luck, Efrat." He snickered and tucked himself into the lift with the others.

Efrat looked Heaton over a little fearfully. He glanced back at Cori, searching for an explanation for this sudden interest in matchmaking, but she didn't have one for him. Whether she should be demanding one was lost in the chaos of the day. So instead, she shifted back and let the doors close.

When the elevator arrived on the main floor, everyone spilled out and turned right. Except Gypsy, who turned left. Cori saw the deviation and followed her. "It's this way," she admonished.

"Yeah, I know, but my bag is this way."

"You don't need your weapons."

"Oh, but I do," Gypsy crooned and reached down for her samurai sword. Cori was surprised that she had left it haphazardly on the floor.

"I don't want you in my house with a bag full of weapons. Actually, I don't want you in my house, period."

"Then I will sleep outside," Gypsy grumbled.

"You can sleep in a—"

"Look!" Gypsy shouted and turned around. Despite the volume, she looked more exhausted than angry. She leaned on the hilt of her sword, rotating it once beneath her palm as she took a breath. "It's been a long fucking week, Cori. London to China, China to... fuck-knows-where. I have been beaten up by a dragon, two gigantic mongoloid gnomes, and a werewolf. I can't even tell you how much my ass hurts right now, but let me assure you, for once in my life, I don't want to fight.

"I know you don't trust me. It doesn't take nearly the broadcast you are giving for me to glean that. I also know that you have a good reason to distrust me, but these weapons have *saved* more lives than they've *taken*. They are coming with me wherever I go or I don't go. Now, is my invitation still good, or should I find a pile of hay in the stables?"

Cori narrowed her eyes at the woman. "How do you know about the alternate timeline?"

"No." Gypsy shook her head and waved a scolding finger at her. "You and I have a long way to go before we sit down and compare notes on that. This isn't about that. This is about where my bed is tonight and I'm in no mood to fight, so you make the decision and I will follow it."

Cori was taken aback by anything resembling a surrender by Gypsy. "How can I trust that you won't hurt anyone?"

"She isn't going to hurt anyone." Cori jumped at Callin's voice coming from behind her. She turned around and found that he had sneaked up behind her. His cold, hard stare was luckily aimed at Gypsy, or his proximity might have created an awkward situation. As it was, she was already gaping at the werewolf, bound somewhere between her natural attraction to strong men and her fear of them. She supposed that most women reacted that way to werewolves.

"Will you, Grace?" Callin asked, demanding confirmation of his edict.

Cori took a step back to remove herself from the path of dagger eyes and murderous intent. Gypsy cracked her neck, prolonging her answer as long as possible. "No, I'm not going to hurt anyone." She clenched her jaw, nearly choking on the next words. "Unless they fuck with me." She didn't bother waiting for Cori's approval before fetching the remainder of her gear from the hallway. She lugged her bag past them, giving them both resistant glares as she swung her sword with ambiguous threat.

"Don't mind her," Callin said as he started toward the exit.

"It's a little more complicated than that," Cori murmured behind him.

"Do tell," he said, glancing back at her.

"It's nothing."

"Ah." Callin chuckled and opened the exterior door for her. "That's my favorite female lie."

Cori paused at the door and smiled demurely at him. She wasn't sure how to take Callin. She hadn't really had a chance to interact with him since they'd both been incarcerated during his last trip to the prison. She owed him a debt for rescuing her, but that was practically meaningless now that nearly everyone she knew had saved her life at one point or another. It was as ubiquitous to her as someone passing the salt now.

The only impression Cori got from Callin was: money. She hadn't heard about any excesses of money in his bank accounts, but the werewolf carried himself with the elevation of class. His clothes were designer labels, and his hair always looked freshly trimmed. He even moved with a slow grace that on some men would have appeared feminine. However, on a man capable of amazing feats of strength, it was more like the grace of a hunting predator—slow, concentrated movements that at any moment could instantly become an attack.

"It's been a long time since I've socialized with a human woman," Callin said as they began walking back to the house. Cori looked after Gypsy, who was already over halfway there. "I mean one that isn't stone cold," he amended. "It's refreshing to be around an easy woman."

Cori's feet stalled, and she gaped at Callin. "I'm not *easy!*"

He shook his head and ushered her forward again. "Apparently, I am dreadfully out of practice. Perhaps I should stop trying to be suave."

"If that's your definition, then yes." She resisted the urge to shove his hand away. Until she had determined his tolerances, she needed to avoid physical confrontation.

Callin chuckled despite the slur. "I meant that your mood is easy to determine," he said, dropping his arm from her back. After a short pause he spoke again. "I wasn't lying earlier. Grace is a difficult woman, but I promise, she isn't a threat to you."

"I'm afraid I've seen her at her worst. Anyone capable of killing everyone they know out of preemptive revenge isn't someone I plan to trust anytime soon."

Callin's amusement in the conversation ended. "Grace mentioned that you had a history with her. One that didn't technically happen to her."

"It's a long story, but yes, it was my history, not hers. I know what you're going to say. If it didn't really happen, it doesn't count and I shouldn't hold it against her."

"Of course you should hold it against her."

Cori looked at Callin, surprised by his wavering loyalty. "But you just defended her."

Callin shook his head. "Grace is a wild animal. She makes werewolves look civilized. I don't mean that you should consider her a threat. I just mean that if you have indeed seen her at her worst, then it should be easier for you to determine what her triggers are."

"Triggers?"

"Yes, as I said, you have to think of her like an animal. You've seen her snap. Why did she snap? What threat did you pose to her? This knowledge is more powerful than any you'll gain from her in this reality."

"Because I can avoid pissing her off?"

"On the contrary, you can gain her trust and respect."

Cori frowned. "Why would I want to do that?"

Callin stopped and faced her. "Would you rather have a wild animal working with you, or against you?"

Cori stared at Callin's mesmerizing eyes. "If she's such a... difficult woman, then why are you with her?"

Callin smiled. "Because I can't possibly stay away from her. I've always been drawn to the difficult ones. I suppose it's really just my conquering instincts, but when I find a woman I can't readily master..." He paused, gazing at the house Gypsy had long since disappeared into. "Well, I'm sure you don't need me to explain attraction. We all have our propensities."

"I dated a werewolf before Ethan." Cori wasn't sure why she decided to drop that nugget of truth right then.

"Oh." Callin's brow perked, and his urbane demeanor returned. "And how did that work out?"

"He died," Cori said blandly.

"Oh," he responded, with far less charisma. "Well, that does tend to happen. I'm sorry."

"Thanks." They started walking again. "He didn't tell me that werewolves don't live much past thirty, so I was pretty distraught at having my happily ever after taken away early."

Callin nodded and glanced out at the grassy meadow. The sun was just setting, making even the drab courtyard of the prison look intentional instead of incidental. The black hawks and semi-trucks, however, sapped some of the beauty out of the scenery, as did the men clustering around them—guarding them, perhaps?

Cori shook her head at the audacity they had to come to the prison with guns drawn for a so-called rescue. It was laughable, of course, because the only people responsible for saving the prison were the ones who put it in danger to begin with.

"Maybe that's why I seek obstinate women," Callin murmured as he stared listlessly into the sunset. "I need to know that they will recover from my loss." They reached the house and stopped at the front door. He looked through it as if he were glaring at one of the residents on the other side of it. "Little did I know I would find a woman so wholly unaffected by my loss that she might not even notice when I'm gone."

"The attraction is wrong sometimes," Cori interrupted his angry contemplation.

"Pardon?" Callin shook his head as if he thought his ears were broken.

"The people we're attracted to. It doesn't always make sense. The threat of heartbreak or mortal danger should be enough to stop you from wanting someone, but it doesn't."

"No, it doesn't."

"Even so, we can't act on it."

"We can't?" Callin's head tipped to one side.

"No. Lust isn't love, and it certainly isn't compatibility. You don't just risk everything because something might feel good at the time."

Callin smirked at her. "Maybe it's a werewolf thing, but I would never deny myself sex simply because my partner's personality might not be compatible with mine. As much as I'm drawn to forceful women, I do still have a healthy appetite for the demure ones."

Callin caught her eye, and for a moment, they stared at each other. All at once, Cori realized Callin thought she had been referring to an attraction between them. Her mind blanked and her mouth draped open, searching for the words to rewind time. Simultaneously, the draw she had felt to his strength morphed into fear.

"Breathe, Cori," Callin whispered. She took in a deep inhalation, since she had indeed been holding her breath.

A small smile perked on Callin's lips. He took a small step away from her, no doubt smelling her fear. "I have to say, that is refreshing."

"What is?"

"You." He chuckled. "Come now, let's not have any more awkwardness. I'm getting hungry." He motioned her toward the entrance.

Cori was relieved that he was ready to go inside. As she reached for the doorknob, Callin growled at her back, sending a shiver up her spine. Before she could launch a fireball or conjure any lightning, Callin gripped her tightly and flung her away from the door.

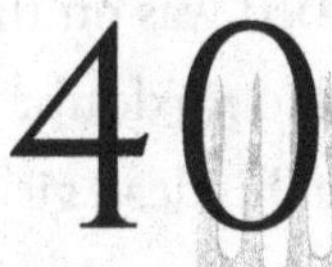

40

GYPSY ENTERED THE HOUSE, unencumbered by the trivial tradition of knocking. She instantly felt the warmth of the fire, which was a welcome change from the endless damp chill in the arctic air. Had she ever planned more than two steps in front of her, she might have brought along a proper coat. Then again, that would only encumber her movements.

She was momentarily stunned by the interior of the house. It was exactly as she had envisioned it, from the faux candle chandelier over the dining room table down to the knotty pine floors. Not that she minded the animal motif. It was honest and appropriate for the cold region.

It was easy to imagine Danato living in this home. The manly, rustic look was easy enough to match with him, but there was also a hidden luxury in the decor. The warden liked things simple and orderly in his home, something that he could never have inside the walls of his prison.

No wonder he hated her. Even if Cori hadn't tainted his opinion of her, Gypsy was certain the man would still have disliked her. She was not a simple woman. She was as disorderly as the prison he tried to maintain.

Gypsy noticed the young man, Levi, moving upstairs. He slipped into a bedroom on the second floor, despite the fact that his proffered bed was on the opposite side of the compound. The poor kid no doubt wanted a little privacy to bawl his eyes out over his dead girlfriend. No one would begrudge him that right, least of all her. It was true she could never truly empathize with the pain of others, but she could at least pity him.

"What do you mean, I can't cook?" Nevia complained to Daniel in the kitchen. They had apparently decided to pitch in and prepare dinner for the gaggle of people Danato was hosting for the evening. Possibly longer, if the board didn't get their heads out of their asses.

Daniel tugged a pot out of her hands. "I don't mean you can't, I mean you shouldn't," he insisted, raising the Dutch oven well over his head and out of her reach.

"You said you liked my cooking."

"Yes, but I do have some motivation to say that. Unless you're planning on offering your dinner guests a chance to squeeze between those beautiful thighs, I don't think they will agree."

Nevia's face froze in a horrified flush. Gypsy chose that moment to drop her bag. The loud *thunk* drew both their gazes. "Sounds like a tasty dessert to me," she said, giving the petite woman a wink. Nevia frowned and looked away bashfully, which made Gypsy smile. Women were almost as easy to fluster as men. At least that would offer some entertainment for the evening.

"Easy, lass, she's mine," Daniel said, dropping the pot back down for Nevia to take. "Then again, the three of us could come up with a temporary arrangement."

"Daniel!" Nevia snapped and kicked his leg.

"Ouch!" Daniel yelped. "No kicking with boots, woman. I already have a dent in my shin from flirting with that waitress in Dublin."

"Then quit suggesting threesomes," Nevia said with clenched teeth.

Gypsy moved around the island, closer to both of them. "Well, a threesome would certainly take the chill out of my bones. Are you sure you aren't just looking for another excuse to shove me against a wall?"

Daniel's eyes fluttered, as if he couldn't recollect what she was talking about. As the memory clicked, he lost all humor in his face. He glanced at Nevia as if she were the one that he needed to apologize to. "I have a temper."

Gypsy scoffed. "Join the club."

"I'm sorry."

Gypsy shrugged. "Don't be. I have the emotional memory of a goldfish." As much as she hated to be batted around like a cat toy, Gypsy knew better than to make Daniel her enemy. He was too valuable as a friend. "Now about this threesome..."

Gypsy looked over at Nevia, who was nearly panting, trying to maintain her composure about the topic. Perhaps having Daniel McGrath on a leash was proving more difficult than she'd expected.

Gypsy still didn't quite know where she stood with Nevia. She didn't consider the woman dangerous—sans gun. Even her intensified werewolf nose wasn't a threat to her compartmentalized mind. What did concern Gypsy, however, was the woman's more obscure werewolf quality. The trait that all werewolves, no matter how small, how old, or how smart, possessed: unrelenting determination despite the impossibility of success.

That was a dangerous trait to anyone who went up against a werewolf. And it was about time Gypsy found out what Nevia was really capable of when she was pushed.

"I guess we could just start things back up where we left off in the infirmary," Gypsy whispered seductively.

"What?" Daniel's face scrunched in confusion.

"Our kiss." She bit her lip as she watched Nevia turn from the stove to stare at her around Daniel's shoulder.

"That was not mutual." Daniel turned his head, saying it as much to his wife as Gypsy.

"Oh, I don't know about that. Maybe we should try again just to be sure. I mean, after all, Jordan will know if you're lying to yourself or not."

Nevia's eyes targeted her, but she didn't move to stop her. Gypsy smiled at the challenge the fem-wolf was unintentionally baiting her with. She latched her hand onto Daniel's neck and pulled his mouth to hers. She intended to leave her taste on Daniel's lips with a wet mingling of tongues. However, the moment her lips touched his, she felt a repellent surge that forced her to draw back.

Daniel backed away from her, keeping his hands up to block her should she attack again. "Knock it off, Grace! I'm not your fecking boy toy!"

"Your loss." Gypsy shook away the disembodied creepiness and queasiness that she had felt for the second time that day. She looked at Nevia, who was no longer glaring at her, but rather analyzing her.

She skipped the usual witty repartee and picked up her bag. "Which one is mine?" She nodded to the upstairs.

"The middle one," Daniel grumbled.

"I'll show you," Nevia offered, sounding sweet.

"Nevia." Daniel moved to touch her back. "She's just baiting you into a fight." He kissed her neck and whispered into her ear. "You know I was only joking."

"It's all right." Nevia turned and gave him a long, exaggerated kiss that barely surrendered his lower lip as they parted. "I can handle her."

Gypsy perked a brow at her confidence. "I think I've been hitting on the wrong half of this couple."

Nevia moved around the counter, leaving Daniel staring longingly after her. The petite woman stopped in front of her. "We need to talk," she said flatly before leading the way up the stairs.

Gypsy groaned and followed. She hated talking. There was always too damn much talking.

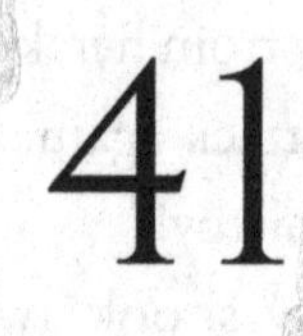

41

D ANATO LISTENED TO BELUS give a secondhand report for Cori and Efrat, leading up to the death of one of his employees. He didn't like that Daniel had outright killed Dirk, but only because that particular duty should have been reserved for him. He had been neglecting the less-than-subtle lessons that prevented his nearly all-male team from indulging in their baser instincts with the female staff. He would have to remind them of their priorities. However, the rumors of Dirk's castration would likely do the trick for a while.

Despite the complication of not having a body to return to the prison he had *borrowed* it from, Belus was right. No body was easier to explain than a man with a missing appendage, especially since Dirk would have had no memory of how he had lost it.

It wasn't until Belus reached the conclusion of his report that Danato discovered why he was being so sedate with his analysis of the day.

Danato leaned back in his chair and examined his friend from across the desk. They had been through a lot. The pain of the past had shortened Danato's fuse and ironically lengthened Belus's. They both did their best to give each other the space to deal with their grief in their own way. Belus was always careful not to incite his anger, but he also didn't leave any room for Danato to doubt his position in arguments. Belus was being no less cautious in this conversation, but there was something apologetic about his request.

"If what Levi said is true, then destroying the body is the safest option," Danato pointed out.

"Yes, that was my assessment as well."

"Then why is Ethan requesting that she be buried, and more importantly, why are you taking his side on it?"

Belus took a moment to contemplate his answer. "We're losing him, Danato," he said somberly.

"Who? Ethan?"

"Yes."

"He's just going through a rough patch. He just made a bad choice, and now he's bitter about the consequences of that choice. He'll get over it."

Belus cleared his throat. "I disagree." Danato perked a brow, silently asking for the remainder of his evaluation. "He's just spent the last year of his life away from his wife, watching his son nearly starve to death on the meager milk supplements we could offer him, and at the end of his hardship the man he respects the most in the world executed the woman he risked everything to save."

"I recall you ushering me to expedite that procedure."

Belus raised his chin indignantly. "And I would again. I'm not accusing you of doing anything wrong, Danato. I'm just trying to explain to you where Ethan's mindset is right now."

Danato smirked, trying to underplay the tension in his jaw. "I wasn't aware that you had that much insight into Ethan's behavior."

Belus shook his head and moved to the water cooler to pour a cup of water. "Don't make this a competition, Danato. Ethan is not Cori." He swallowed the cone of water in one shot. "He has always followed the rules. Why on this one occasion would his character change so suddenly?"

"I don't know, and he hasn't told me."

Belus turned back. "That's just it. When has he ever withheld information from you?"

Danato thought back to when Ethan admitted that he could hear the thoughts of the dragon. He could have kept it a secret until he knew for sure he wasn't just high as a kite, but he'd dropped the incident at Danato's door like it was part of his business as usual report.

"What are you suggesting, Belus?"

"He's hinted to me that he is following orders, just not ours."

"And whose authority surpasses ours?"

"That's the part he won't discuss."

"Is it Annette?"

"No, he denied that adamantly."

"Could she have put a spell on him? Tricked him somehow into doing her bidding and then deny it?" Danato leaned forward to fiddle with his pencil.

"You tell me. You know her better than me." Belus sat down again.

Danato's mind wandered to Annette's obvious flaws in judgment, but even if manipulation was her most reliable weapon, she had never outright used her magic to do it. "I don't think Annette would go that far. However, I also thought she would never get involved in making a sorcerer again."

Belus nodded in agreement. "That does seem to be an itch she can't help scratching. There is another possibility," he added. "Perhaps Adrianna was stronger than they realized and was manipulating them all."

"And now? Beyond the grave?" Danato raised his brow. "Why would he persist in hiding the truth from us? Her magic can't possibly hold that much power after her mind is gone."

"Levi described it as if it were a lingering radiation. He believed that the burial would prevent it from influencing us."

"So would cremation."

Belus nodded. "Are we certain this is the only secret Ethan is keeping from us?"

"What do you mean?"

"Ethan said that he was not able to communicate with the dragons? Perhaps that was inaccurate."

Danato frowned at this thought. "You think the dragons are convincing him to disobey us?"

Belus shrugged. "I don't think anything yet. I just know that we are running out of people to blame for Ethan's choices. So maybe it's not people."

Danato leaned back and considered that idea. The dragons were obviously intelligent creatures, but were they really capable of complex thought processes? Plots, schemes, and intrigues? "If the dragons were capable of communicating with Ethan; and if he felt obliged to obey them; what exactly would be their purpose?"

"The time bubble covered every part of this prison above ground level except the dragon's den. We assumed that their connection to the earth somehow made them immune. What if it's more than that? What if they aren't just catalysts for earth magic? What if they can also wield it?"

Danato frowned at this theory. He was always open to new ideas—the world of the supernatural demanded it—but frankly, the suggestion of dragons being capable of directing magical energy was as outrageous to him as cows being magical. There was just no evidence of sentience from them.

Danato rubbed his face. "I can speak to Annette now that she's here. Maybe she can once and for all shed some light on Ethan's lack of disclosure."

"Will she speak to you?"

Danato shrugged. "I don't know, but I have to try. As for the body—"

"No matter the reason behind Ethan's resistance..." Belus interrupted. "We need to do this for him."

Danato shook his head. "Why are you fighting me on this? Flouting protocol usually makes *you* the cranky one."

"Because I think it's the right choice, even if it is against procedure." Belus tapped the heel of his hand on the arm of the chair. "Look, Danato, if this was Cori, we wouldn't know what the issue was until shit hit the fan. That boy is *trying* to be honest with us, but for whatever reason, his obligation to another set of rules is preventing it. I think we need to give him the benefit of the doubt on this. And I also think you might win some points with Annette by doing this."

Danato didn't like the idea of appeasing Annette, but she was at least cooperating. He knew she had the power to break away from her captors. She could also just as easily walk out of the prison, unhindered by anything he would do to stop her. If she was willing to play by his rules, perhaps he could oblige her with this small concession.

Ethan, on the other hand, was a whole other issue. If Belus's evaluation of the situation was accurate, then Danato was in more trouble than he thought. Between the board trying to shut him down and his only successor becoming untrustworthy, he may not have many more opportunities to make the *right* choice.

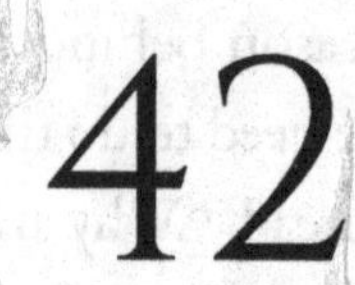

42

C ORI HAD NO TIME to react before she was repositioned behind Callin. He was growling at something or someone, but when she turned to help defend against the assailant, she saw nothing. She looked around for a hidden attack, but nothing presented itself. Callin was just staring at nothing next to the door.

"What is it?" she whispered, giving all her trust to the werewolf's instincts.

"There is someone watching us," he said, shifting to smell the air. "Show yourself!"

"Damn werewolves," a man said, and then Maddox materialized out of thin air next to the front door. His abrupt appearance made her gasp. Callin shifted, blocking Maddox from her path. She thought about mentioning that she wasn't afraid of the man, just the creepy unexpected entrance, but she doubted it would tone down his animal instincts.

"Who are you?" Callin grumbled, looking the man over. The black-on-black uniform was a little more sophisticated than the prison guard uniforms her men wore, but the real distinction in his look was the medals hanging on his left breast.

"This is Maddox," Cori introduced him blandly. "One of the Board's hired thugs, aka the uninvited guests. The invisible part is new, though."

Maddox nodded in agreement and smiled at her. "I didn't want to show all my cards up front."

"Why are you spying on us?" Callin asked, standing upright, though not really relaxing.

Maddox glanced back at Cori. "Just observing."

"Spying," Callin clarified again, letting a growl seep into his voice.

"Yes, well, I am a spy. A good one—usually," he complained and leaned against the house. As he did, his form changed into a Barbie doll blonde—though still wearing the same militant outfit. "Guess I'm losing my touch." The new rosy lips purred at Callin.

The werewolf shifted and glanced back at Cori. She didn't have an explanation for this any more than he did. "Are you a transmorph?" Callin asked.

"Do I smell like a transmorph?" Maddox's female form grinned.

Callin sniffed the air and narrowed his eyes in confusion. "You... smell... strange."

"Stranger than you could ever comprehend, my beasty." Barbie-Maddox puckered her lips into a kiss. "I would like to speak with Cori. Alone," he added in case that wasn't obvious.

Callin looked around, slightly confused, but determined that there was no danger. "Call if you need anything," he asserted firmly to Cori.

"Scout's honor," she said and raised her crossed fingers, which also happened to be ablaze with a tight licking flame.

He looked over her fingers with diminishing confusion, leaving only a solemn smirk of admiration. "I keep forgetting where I'm at." He perked his brow at her and chuckled at Maddox as he passed him to head into the house. "Good luck," he murmured to one of them as he shut the door behind him. "What do you want, Maddox?" Cori had missed his transformation back to his previous form. He was no doubt hoping to gain more clout with her as a man.

"I think we got off on the wrong foot, you and I."

"Which foot was that? The foot you used to invade my home, or the foot you stuck in your mouth after you ordered your men to shoot me? Which, by the way, I haven't mentioned to Danato out of respect for his already stressed year."

Maddox sighed and pulled out a cigar with his good hand. He halted his search for a lighter and looked at her. "You mind?" He raised the cigar in his fingers suggestively. She lit her fingers again, and he puffed the flame into his tip. He took several drags before looking out into the clearing where his men were perched on helicopters participating in similarly despicable habits, be it cigarettes, dip, or high-fructose corn syrup.

"I'll admit, you impressed me."

"That's not a compliment, you dick. That's just saying that I'm not nearly as useless as I first appear."

Maddox chuckled. "You're not going to make this easy for me, are you?"

"Why should I? If this is an apology, then start with *I'm sorry*. If this is something else, then just spit it out. I have a house full of people to feed, a year-long story to catch up on, and about a thousand reports to write."

Maddox nodded again. "All right, I won't flirt and flatter you then. I've come to tell you that I'm not your enemy."

"Could have fooled me. This audit doesn't sound like just an employee review. It sounds like a witch hunt."

"I have nothing to do with the audit. I'm just a hired gun."

"So you want me to trust a man whose loyalty is paid for?"

"Money can make a man do a lot of things: lie, steal, cheat. But there is no amount of money that can make a man betray his own heart."

Cori took in a breath and looked around. "Is that it? Is that your rationalization that I should trust you? Because your lying, cheating, stealing heart is ultimately good?"

"Well, when you put it like that..." Maddox took another puff off his cigar. "I don't expect you to trust that right now. That's not the point of this conversation. I wanted you to know that I trust you."

Cori could feel her tolerance for the man draining. "That's great, Maddox. I'm glad that one day is all it takes to win you over. I'm honored by your immediate, unprompted loyalty."

"Today isn't the only thing I'm basing my favor on. I've been following your work for years."

"Is that so?"

"Yes. You have a knack for getting into trouble, but you also have good instincts."

"I don't know. I'm still standing here."

Maddox smirked at her. "I know you'll protect this prison and your family no matter what the cost, and I respect that. That's a good skill set for you to possess in the near future."

Cori frowned at Maddox. "What the hell does that mean?"

"Loyalties can shift quickly in this type of business. Money and power are very potent influences." Maddox looked around the grounds. "This place relies on too many outside forces. There are some small steps being taken to change that, but I'm worried that the changes being implemented will come too late."

"What changes?"

"Never mind that. Just know that you and Ethan are not the only ones safeguarding the future of this prison."

"Are *you* helping to safeguard the prison?"

"I have always safeguarded this prison."

"And why should I believe you? I can't even trust your appearance."

He nodded again, finding some truth in that statement. "Very well," he whispered, and his form shifted from the militant man to a wispy non-corporeal... *blob?* Translucent yellow rivulets meandered from the core being before her, reaching twenty or thirty feet away in every direction.

Despite the obviously impalpable nature of the design, Cori reached out to touch a tentacle. Her hand moved through it, but the smoke curled around her fingers, warming them. The vision left as quickly as it had come, and she found her fingers wrapped in Maddox's human hand.

"You're beautiful," Cori said, unable to resist the compliment.

"Thank you." Maddox's gaze shifted shyly from hers.

"What *are* you?" Cori whispered, sensing that it was a secret only she could be privy to.

"I'm an angel," he whispered, pinning her with his sparkling eyes.

Her mouth gaped and her eyes widened. Her gaze naturally skirted his head and shoulders, looking for obscure wings or a halo that might match her definition of "angel." Her search ended abruptly when Maddox snorted and sputtered into an uproarious fit of laughter.

"You son of a bitch!" Cori ripped her hand from his.

"You should have seen your face!" he wailed, barely intelligible.

"I can't believe you! You..." Cori fumbled through her lacking vocabulary.

"Oh God, please stop! I'm going to wet myself if you make me laugh any harder."

"Is this your idea of a joke? I don't have time for this!"

"Oh, come on, Cori," Maddox pleaded between snickers. "You aren't the only one with skills."

"And this is your way of flaunting them. Ask me for my trust, then humiliate me with it." Cori moved to escape into the house.

"Okay, okay, wait." Maddox blocked her with his outstretched hand, but was careful not to touch her, which was wise. "You want the brutal truth? Here it is. I'm a spy. I've always been a spy. I will always be a spy, but..." His jovial outbreak simmered, and he looked around surreptitiously for unwelcome eyes and ears. "...I have always had the interests of this prison in mind."

"Once again, why would I believe that?"

"Because I'm showing you all my cards up front. Danato will warn you about me and he is right to do so. I'm not here to be your hero or your friend. I have my own agenda. I'm just here to make sure that you are the same Cori Reiger that I have been reading about in Danato's reports."

Cori took a step away from him. "Am I the Cori Reiger that bested a goblin, threw acid on a transmorph, and helped four elementals escape their unwarranted captivity? Yes, I am her. Will I defend the prison? Yes. Will I defend my family with my life? Yes. Are we done?" Cori moved to the door.

"I'm not worried about you defending your family. I'm worried about you making them weak."

"What?" She turned back to him.

"You are the weak link."

"Excuse me!" she squawked defensively.

"I don't mean *you* are weak." He motioned vaguely to her. "I mean that you are a vulnerability for more than one man at this prison."

Cori shrugged. "And what should I do about that?"

Maddox shrugged back at her. "I'm not suggesting that you do anything about it. I merely want to point out that the people that hire me are not always good at heart. They will use you against them if they have to."

"You mean Renee?" she asked quietly, thinking of how she'd flaunted Belus's partiality to her like a chink in his armor.

Maddox sighed and took a step forward. "Renee isn't the only board member I take orders from."

"And what are your orders?"

He shrugged. "That's confidential."

"What the hell? You'll warn about the potential for enemies, but not give me any information that might help me to stop them."

"You can't stop them." Maddox laughed. "I'm just telling you to be prepared for them. Don't let them use you as a weapon."

"How do I...!" Cori groaned. "Whatever." She shook her head and moved back to the house. "Let me know if you have more ambiguity and half-truths to share." She pushed through the front door, ready for the warm embrace of her cozy cottage home.

The sweetness of her arrival was quickly soured when she saw Gypsy raising her sword to chop off Callin's head.

43

"**S**HALL I DISROBE?" GYPSY teased, dragging her finger down her chest.

Nevia closed the bedroom door behind them and moved toward her. Gypsy tensed for an attack, but the petite woman stopped halfway. "Kiss me," she demanded.

Gypsy let her bag fall with the same unmelodious *clunk* that it usually did. "Wow, you are a bundle of surprises." She hissed through her front teeth. "I'll be honest with you. I wasn't really interested in the three-way without an interlude of cock. So, unless you're packing..." Gypsy tipped her head, searching Nevia for a stash of phallic surrogates.

"Doesn't seem like you're into that either right now." Nevia stepped closer. "Go on. Kiss me. Don't tell me you're shy?"

"I'm not shy." Gypsy crinkled her brow at the aberrant conclusion and approached her. "You sure you really want this? We're a little too old to call it experimentation."

"If you need me to punch you or something first, I can oblige."

"Funny." Gypsy stepped even closer, pushing her body against the woman's small frame. "I might strain my back bending over to reach your lips."

"Kiss me!" Nevia snarled.

Gypsy gave up on giving the woman an out and grabbed her face. She pushed her back harshly and smothered her lips with her own. She forced her tongue between them as further punishment for her impertinence.

The reaction was delayed, but it made up for it in severity. Before she could move her hand to grope or defile the woman in some way, she was on her knees, dry heaving and shaking away the worst heebie-jeebies in the history of bedtime monsters.

She saw Nevia's legs walk away, and she hoped she was leaving, but she heard the bed creak from the addition of her weight.

"Sorry about that," Gypsy said when the bulk of the sickness waned. She flopped onto her back and stared at the ceiling. "I must be getting sick."

"How much do you know about werewolves?"

Gypsy chuckled. "Oh, come on, do we really have to have the conversation about your invincibility versus my vulnerability? I'll stay away from Daniel, I promise. I was just messing around. Nobody has a sense of humor anymore."

"Werewolves have a matriarchal hierarchy."

"Oh, just shoot me."

"Unlike other mammal groups, our females are stronger than our males, so it isn't just a social structure, but an actual physical dominance that creates the pecking order. However, there are exceptions to our strength that help balance that inequality. For example, the female is at her strongest during her mating cycle and at her weakest during her pregnancy and before weaning."

"Yes, Dr. Spock, I understand all that." Gypsy leaned on her elbow. "I am kind of a werewolf expert. Can you get to the point?"It's during those times that the female needs the most protection," Nevia continued at an unfettered educational pace. "That's why a female must rely on males to protect her during this time. Protect her from other females who wish to control her pack, and other males who wish to shorten her weaning time." Nevia stood. "Outside of these times, however, a male has virtually no control of a fem-wolf. She is free to mate or not mate with whomever she wants."

"Sounds good to me," Gypsy drawled with an added yawn.

"The female has no contention unless a pack needs a new leader. If the female is disinterested in joining a pack voluntarily, the males will sometimes force the issue. They will coordinate and hunt the female until she is exhausted. This process could take hours or days. If she is strong and youthful, she could evade them long enough to get through her mating cycle without being impregnated. If she is not, she will be caught and the males will fight for the right of the first mating. The losers will follow subsequently as often as their virility allows."

"Aww, gang rape, how romantic. Why are you telling me this?" Gypsy narrowed her eyes. "Did Callin hurt someone?" She sat up and examined the woman. "Did he hurt you?"

Nevia's face muddled in confusion momentarily. "No, Grace. Callin is uncommonly gallant as werewolves go. My concern is that he may have hurt you, or at least overstepped his boundaries."

Gypsy smirked. "Um, no, trust me, there isn't a bruise on my body that I haven't begged him for. Well, the encounter at the docks wasn't exactly my idea, but he made his apologies." Gypsy rested back to the floor, remembering her recent encounter with Callin. It was by far the most explosive orgasm—orgasms—she had ever experienced with him. Just when she'd thought it couldn't get any better.

"Aside from a pack forcefully impregnating a matriarch, there is one other way for a male werewolf to compete with a female's strength." Nevia frowned at her. "Truthfully, I always thought it was a myth. Very few werewolves were reputed to have the ability."

"What ability?" Gypsy sat up, seeing the ending of the story coming to a fortuitous enlightenment.

"Some werewolves have the ability to mark their lovers."

"What does *mark* mean?" Gypsy glared at her, though it was meant for her lover.

"It's a hormone that the male can introduce into a female through intercourse. It essentially vaccinates her against any other pheromones, all but his own."

Gypsy stood up abruptly and stared at Nevia. The woman seemed apologetic, despite the fact that she had not wronged her... just her species. "So if I try to fuck anyone else, I will get physically ill?"

"Yes, and... you will be nearly uncontrollably drawn to him. He will have more leverage over you than ever before."

Gypsy pinched her lips, trying to take in that information. She had so few true joys in her life; sex and violence pretty much summed it up. Without the variety in one, she wasn't sure she could deny herself the variety in the other.

"Grace?" Nevia reached to touch her but stopped and pulled back.

"How long?" She paused, feeling her hands shake as she waited for the inevitable answer.

Nevia raised her hands again, trying to console her, but not willing to touch her. She could only imagine the sensory flood she was getting from her usually stale enigma.

"How long?"

Nevia took in several breaths and stepped away from her. "The hormone is designed to be broken down by hCG." She paused, but Gypsy let her say the words so there was no question what she really meant. "It won't dissipate unless you get pregnant."

Gypsy let out a guttural yowl before ripping her sword from its sheath and running out of the room to kill her lover.

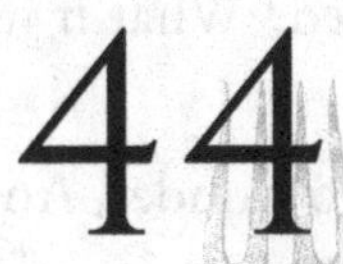

44

DANATO APPROACHED THE CELL on the seducers level slowly. He had never been afraid of his friend. Even with the power of the entire Earth bending to her will at any given moment, he had never been so unnerved by her as he was at that moment.

He stared down at the ragged blonde sitting on her cot. She stared right back at him through her painted bars. The stillness in her frame was more unsettling than her glassy-eyed gaze. Her beholden youth was slipping away, revealing the natural creases in her face and the silver in her hair. Her muscular tone, now slender and slack. Her bright eyes, though ablaze with anger, were tired. She was still beautiful, just marked by time.

"Hello, Annette." Danato greeted her coolly.

"Have you come to apologize for murdering my apprentice?" she snarled.

Danato clenched his jaw, refusing to react with anger. That was what she wanted. She wanted to mirror her ire onto him. Draw him into the misery with her. "Is that what you think I did?"

Annette finally looked away, putting all of her aversion into the dismissal. "I wonder what you would do if the situation were reversed? What if it was your dear sweet Cori?"

"You don't have to wonder, Annette. You've seen me bear the burden of killing the woman I love once. Twice would be the end of me." Danato approached the bars. "Is that what you want? My pain? Shall I invite the sorrow demons again? Maybe the weight will succeed in breaking my back this time."

"Don't mock my pain!" Annette yelled. Tears streamed down her cheeks.

"I am not mocking your pain, Annette! I am living it!" He slammed his fists into the bars, forcing her attention back to him with the anger he was unsuccessful in withholding. "I warned you that you would not be forgiven another indiscretion. You knew what my obligations were to this prison, and to the world! Do you think this is a hobby for me? Do you think I enjoyed destroying that girl?"

Annette pinched her eyes shut, and he leaned against the bars, hiding his own watery eyes. "Damn you, Annette," he murmured. "You play with magic, not even realizing that it's *fire*! This place is not here to punish you! It is here to protect the world from ignorance and *arrogance*!" Danato gripped the bars, nearly bending them before he contained his vehemence. "You are my friend," he said, pausing to give the statement justice. "No matter what foolish thing you do, you will always be my friend." He pinched his lips, controlling his thready voice. "But that doesn't mean that I won't hold you accountable for your stupidity." He waited for her to respond, but she offered him no response. "I need you to answer one question for me."

Annette laughed and wiped away her tears. "Interrogation time."

"It's not an interrogation, it's a question, and I want the truth." He gripped the bars again. "Did the dragons communicate with Ethan?"

Annette rolled her eyes. "Of course not. He was high as a kite on dragon's blood. He imagined it. Do you really think that beings as old and inscrutable as dragons would waste their time with your little runt? How dare you suggest such a thing? I've spent my life devoted to serving them. If anyone will hear the words of dragons, it will be me!" Annette smacked her chest, demanding it to be true. "ME!"

Danato nodded, accepting her fervor as honesty. He knew he should announce the burial to her, but Belus was mistaken that the token would mend their relationship. Nothing short of a dagger in his heart would please her at this point. Not that it felt any different to him to see her and Ethan blaming him for their misjudgment.

45

C ALLIN DIDN'T SEE THE attack until it was too late to react. The blade slashed through the air, ready to slice across his shoulders. Cori entered the house just then. She raised her hands to defend him with fire, but Daniel was certain the blade would reach Callin's neck long before the fire would hit Gypsy. He wasn't sure if Gypsy had the strength to make it through his abnormally thick muscle structure, but given the reputation and history of Japanese steel, he didn't want to risk it.

Before Daniel could knock her across the room, the katana ripped from her hands and embedded itself into one of the rafters above.

Callin belatedly flinched from the attack, while Gypsy checked her hands for some clue as to why her sword had disappeared. They both looked up at the sword in the rafter.

Daniel looked at Cori and she back at him. She looked at him, baffled, and he shook his head, taking no credit for the disarming. She shook her head as well, unable to account for the catapulting weapon.

The temporary ceasefire wore off and Gypsy slammed her fist into Callin's jaw. The werewolf grunted and backed away from her, annoyed but unharmed. "You son of a bitch!" She came after him again, but he pushed her away with ease.

"Gypsy, what the hell!" Cori yelled as she tried to get an angle to attack her.

"Let her be!" Nevia announced and intercepted Daniel as he came around the island to break up the fight.

Gypsy let out a virulent war cry and faked a punch to Callin's gut so she could get in a crotch shot. With no particular resilience in that muscle, he doubled over, allowing her another shot at the face.

"But, she—" Cori griped.

Callin grabbed Gypsy by the shoulders and threw her back. She skidded to a stop at the stairs. "Knock it off, Grace! You don't have your protective gear on!"

She charged again, but Callin batted away her attacks with lazy strength.

"What the hell happened up there?" Daniel snapped at Nevia. "Dear," he added when he saw her disapproval of his tone.

"Callin marked her." Nevia broadcast the statement to the room as if it might illuminate the reason for the battle taking place between the table and couch.

Though Daniel and Cori were only further perplexed, Callin froze. He gaped at Nevia while he held Gypsy's wrists in the grip of one hand. "How did you...?" Nevia crossed her arms and raised her chin, daring him to chastise her for revealing what she apparently considered indefensible.

Gypsy twisted and somehow managed to flip Callin over her back, which Daniel knew was not an easy weight to bear. Cori sidestepped the two wrestling on the floor to reach Nevia.

"What does that mean? Marked?" Cori asked.

Nevia shook her head. "It's a werewolf matter."

Daniel could see that Nevia was trying to be discreet, but he could also see that Cori was not happy about watching two people beat each other up in her living room without knowing the cause. "Nevia, my love muffin. Now is not the time to be cryptic. This isn't a tiff. She is actually trying to kill him."

"He's made it impossible for her to mate with anyone other than him," she answered.

Daniel couldn't help but smirk at his mind's interpretation. "My God, how horrible," he mocked. "Monogamy. How ever will she survive?"

"Seriously, *that's* what she's mad about?" Cori asked incredulously.

"Next thing you know, he'll be asking her to marry him," Daniel continued. "What an asshole?" Nevia turned a fearsome glare on him, but he refused to give up his amusement and she eventually caved and looked away to hide her smile. He leaned into her ear to whisper something inappropriate and ill-timed, but the sound of a nose cracking broke his focus.

"DAMN IT, GRACE!" Callin roared several decibels louder than most human voices were capable of.

Subsequently, he flung Gypsy off him, and she barely missed the stairs again. This time, she landed in the hall next to them. She stood up slower than before, no doubt feeling the effects of a dislocated hip being challenged so soon after its repair. She wiped blood from her mouth and glared back at Callin as his shoulders rose and fell, evidence of his own exhaustion.

"Shouldn't we stop this?" Cori asked, volleying her gaze between the parties in the standoff.

"Marking is viewed as deceitful among all werewolves," Nevia said.

"And that means we should let them beat the crap out of each other?" Cori asked.

"Marking a human is forbidden. It's a punishable offense since it's the equivalent of rape."

"I am not a rapist!" Callin's voice transformed into something barely human. He turned his anger on Nevia and made a move toward her. Daniel pulled her back behind him and squared his shoulders.

"Don't, man." Callin slowed and stared at him, wide-eyed and nearly feral. "I got no quarrel with you, but you lay one hand on her and you will be ash on the floor." Daniel could see his werewolf determination fighting against his common sense as he crept forward.

Cori's hands ignited with blue rivulets. She no doubt wanted to help subdue Callin, but when Callin's predatory gaze switched to her, Daniel pressed her hands down. She reluctantly complied and even stepped back with Nevia when he pressed her to. "You gotta back down, Callin," he said, drawing the werewolf's attention back to him. "I'm not an alpha male, I'm the Grim-fecking-Reaper, and I really don't want to prove that to you."

Callin shifted his gaze to the floor and eased himself back. Daniel was glad to see that he had more control of his temper than the average werewolf. Unfortunately, with everyone's focus on the impending attack, no one noticed that Gypsy had drawn her knife. Including Callin.

Gypsy directed the weapon through the slender valley between his collarbone and neck, where the overly fibrous muscles would not interfere. The six-inch blade sank deep into the vulnerable cleft. Callin's anger was instantly tamped down when the knife's hilt hit his clavicle with a sickening *smack*.

46

E THAN PULLED HIS BABY boy close as he followed the outline of Belus. The child was bundled up tight in one of Ethan's spare coats since he had long since outgrown his own infant-sized coat. He had also outgrown his little shoes. Aside from some socks that one of the nurses had made for him, the poor guy had been barefoot for months.

Ethan couldn't wait to get him home—his real home and not the stark interior of a prison cell. He wanted to feed him and bathe him and put him to bed, knowing that the long nights of nightmares were over. He knew Cori was unhappy about the time she had lost, but Ethan would never regret sparing her the indignity of blood draws and the torment of dream feeders.

Before he could take his son home, though, he needed to see Adrianna put to rest. It may have been at the dragon's request to put her in the ground, but he also wanted to do it for Levi. At least now he would have a place to mourn properly. It was better than nothing at all.

"What will happen to Levi?" Ethan asked. He saw Belus turn slightly, but instead of answering, he increased his pace. He apparently didn't want to get too deep into a conversation he didn't have the authority for.

"I don't know, kid," he eventually answered. "Friends are a luxury best kept at a distance to this place, as you well know."

Ethan considered that idea. He considered what his life would be like if he closed off his emotions like Belus, or wrapped himself in a cloak of anger like Danato. Neither sounded appealing to him.

"How did you do it?" Ethan stopped, unwilling to let the conversation be shortened by the pace or Belus's indifference. "I've always wanted to know. More so today than ever before."

Belus turned, shining the lantern on Ethan's face and illuminating his own in the process. "How did I do what?"

"How did you kill your best friend?"

Belus stared at him, offended or appalled. Ethan wasn't sure. "You're mistaken," he whispered, as if speaking louder might reveal the emotion in his words. His face, however, was stone cold with or without the intemperate climate. "Everyone keeps focusing on that moment, as if the bullet was what killed her. She was dead long before that. I was killing a vessel, Ethan. Nothing more." Belus continued to stare at him. "And as for my *best* friend, that title has always belonged to Danato. So perhaps the question you should be asking is: what would *you* do for your best friend?"

Ethan waited for him to walk on, but Belus's gaze remained pinned on him.

"Is that it?" he asked, revealing contempt in his tone. "No more questions to help justify your anger?"

"That's not what I was doing."

"Listen, kid." Belus stepped forward, shifting the lantern to his side. "I don't decide who lives and dies based on whether I like or dislike them. I balance the facts, measure the risks of containment, and the probability of escape. I don't go blazing into the infirmary when I find out they've hurt someone I love and dictate their fate with my fists."

"That's not the same!"

"It's exactly the same! If you are going to stand here and marshal your disgust against me for doing my job, then you and I are going to get one thing straight. You—"

"You can't tell me you have any sympathy for that asshole after what he did to Cori!"

"This isn't *about* Cori! This is about you! This is about the future warden of this prison. I just spent the last hour defending your actions to Danato and here you are, still casting judgment on both of us. If that's what I get for my efforts, then I have one thing to tell you. You are not the only one who passed that damn test!"

Ethan stared blankly at Belus, trying to understand his purpose. "What is this, a threat?"

"No, it's a reminder. You seem to be very comfortable with your position as of late. Comfortable enough that you are forgetting who the hell you are dealing with. You're a little late to be questioning your life choices now."

"Well, maybe I am just reviewing my options."

"And what options are those?"

"Maybe I don't belong here anymore."

"Your job isn't open to relocation, but it is open to a rehire."

"Won't do much good if Cori's gone, too."

"You like the idea of a complete memory wipe, do you? Or maybe you just want to skip all that and escape. I wonder who will get to you first, the hunters or the cleaners."

"What are you talking about?"

"Don't ask questions you don't want the answers to. And just for the record, Cori won't leave."

"Cori belongs with me."

"Then you'd better quit packing your bags, sport, because I promise you, she isn't meant for picket fences and poodles... never was." Belus started to move, but turned back. "And don't bring this topic up again. Danato isn't likely to take your threat of desertion as lightly as I did." His glare brightened and dimmed as he pulled his lantern around to light their way to the funeral.

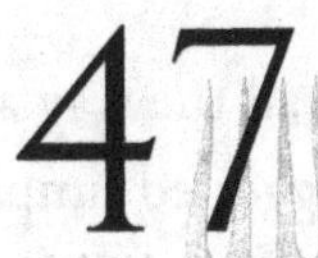

47

C ORI WATCHED CALLIN'S EYES glaze over, vacant of the anger they'd held only seconds before. The shock and disappointment of his lover's lethal aggression dominated his face. He fell to his knees, and she caught his torso in an attempt to keep him from hitting his head—as if that mattered at this point.

Daniel helped her ease his body back on the wood floors where his bright red blood was already pooling. "Oh, shit," she hissed and glanced at Daniel. "She got an artery."

The front door opened and Heaton walked in on the tail end of one drama and the beginning of the next. "What the hell?" He ran over, assessing the situation with the keen eye of someone who had experienced shit hitting the fan more than once. "What did you do?" His eyes landed on Gypsy, who was pacing, only dimly disturbed by the scene playing out before her.

"I'm so sorry, Callin," Nevia apologized, leaning over him as he coughed up blood. "I never thought she could…"

"Never mind that!" Daniel yelled. "Feck you people! How often do I have to tell you? Internal injuries are tricky!"

"So rip him open all the way and heal him from the inside out," Gypsy suggested simplistically.

"Shut up, you sadist bitch!" Cori yelled. She couldn't believe she had let a psychopath into her house. "Get out of my house!"

"She might be right," Daniel murmured.

"What?" Cori pressed her hands over Callin's wound, but most of the blood seemed to be bloating under his skin, and judging by his increased coughing, he was already drowning. She was familiar with that sensation. Far too familiar. "Let's just take him to the infirmary. He has a little time left."

"Surgical tools don't work well on werewolves," Nevia explained. "It will take them too long to cut him open."

"Then what, you rip him open and then put him back together?" Cori asked Daniel. "He'll lose more blood."

"I can do it fast."

"Werewolves don't generally pass out from shock," Nevia interjected again, though it didn't sound like she meant it as an objection, just general information. "He'll be awake for it. All of it."

"I can put him to sleep." Cori reached down, touching Callin's forehead, but the touch had no effect on him. "I don't understand. This always works."

"That big bad wolf's got enough adrenaline running through him right now to walk through a brick wall," Gypsy said with undue admiration. "He isn't going nighty-night for anyone."

Cori looked down at Callin's face. She expected him to be angry or frightened, but he seemed content. As if life had presented him with a noble death and he was accepting it with honor.

To hell with that.

"Do it anyway, Daniel. No one should die like this." Cori gave Gypsy a glower that made her turn away.

"He isn't just going to hold still," Heaton said. "Even with all of us holding him down, Daniel is just as likely to kill him if he moves at the wrong time."

"I can—" Daniel started.

"Don't say you can!" Heaton yelled at him. "You have limitations; you can't save everyone. Now everyone stop and think; how can we keep him still?"

Cori had long since stopped listening to the discussion. The frost forming under her hands gave her an idea. Her breath was coming out fogged, though the air warmed it away almost the instant she exhaled. She had never gone this far before. She wasn't sure it was wise—or healthy. Ice was easy enough for her to form, but it was the bulk amount that proved difficult. She had to not only create it, but maintain it.

"Jaysus, Cori! Watch the cool juice." Daniel jumped away, seeing the iceberg developing around the werewolf, limiting his movement and freezing him to the floor. "Well, aren't you just a snow princess? Do you make ice sculptures too?"

"Dude!" Heaton scolded him.

"Yeah, okay, I'm on it." Daniel paused and touched Callin's forehead. "I'm sorry, lad. I wish I could say this won't hurt, but from my experience, it's probably the most painful thing you'll ever endure in your life."

Cori could see Callin nod, giving him permission to proceed. Cori focused on the ice that had buried Callin and her arms right along with him. Her position was fixed and she couldn't plug her ears to block out Callin's roars of agony.

48

D ANATO WRAPPED HIS ARMS around Cori. Her catatonic state had frightened him far more than the blood on the floor or the pale-faced werewolf trapped under her mound of ice. She looked up at him, eyes red and cheeks clammy from tears.

"Cori?" Ethan kneeled beside her as well, kissing her cheek.

"Does someone want to tell us what the hell is going on?" Danato stood and left Ethan to attend to his wife. He glanced at the door and noticed Belus was still waiting for an invitation. He motioned him in along with a barely audible verbal invite.

Danato looked over the worried faces in the room. He had heard Callin's wails from across the compound. With the sorceress's body safely underground, they had rushed over to see what was going on. He was not happy to see Daniel slurping down water from the faucet like he had just walked through the Mohave Desert. He was even less happy to see signs of violence staining his hardwood floors.

"We had an incident." Nevia was the first to speak. "It was my fault," she admitted meekly.

Daniel popped up from the sink. "It was *not* your fecking fault! Gypsy stabbed him!" Daniel pointed at Gypsy who was casually lounging in Danato's chair, reading his newspaper.

"I shouldn't have meddled in their affairs," Nevia said sternly.

"Don't you dare take responsibility for this!" Daniel yelled at her. "You are not responsible for men who do stupid things for love!"

Silence ensued and Danato watched the couple stare each other down across the island. The stabbing had obviously sparked the prickling, but that didn't explain why there were tears welling in Daniel's eyes. He wasn't sure what had prompted the abrupt emotion shift, but he was certain he didn't want to get involved in it.

"Heaton." Danato looked at him for an explanation, but he was ensconced in his own thoughts next to the sink. "Heaton! Do you have anything lucid to report?"

Heaton snapped to attention. "When I walked in, Callin had Gypsy's knife in his collarbone. Cori used her ice to hold him down while Daniel did his thing. He had to go deep, so it hurt him more than normal, thus the yelling that I'm sure brought you here."

"Why in the hell did you stab him?" Danato turned his question to Gypsy.

"He marked me," she answered flatly.

Danato's anger diminished with her admission. "Oh, I see." He looked at Belus. He had put werewolves in prison for such an offense. Over the years, the incidents became less and less as the shame and stigma did their job to prevent the crime, but occasionally an oversexed werewolf would take delight in creating a human harem.

"That's it?" Cori stood, freshly freed of her icy confinement. "She stabs him and you say, *oh, I see*?"

"That is not it, Cori." Danato looked around. "I just need a moment to figure out an appropriate response to this situation."

"I need to see you in your office right now." Cori glanced at Belus and Ethan. "All three of you."

Danato watched Cori stomp off to his office and tried not to find amusement at the turn of the tables. He looked at Belus and raised his brow. "She's *your* successor."

"We'll see," he responded without the amusement Danato had intended to bring to the moment. He noticed Ethan didn't find much amusement in it, either.

He looked over the room and pointed to each one of the remaining five. "Where's Levi?"

"Napping," Daniel said. "I let him use our room. I didn't think you would mind."

"No." Danato couldn't begrudge anyone a nap right now. If he had his way, he would be in bed already, but by the looks of his closed door, Renee had probably set up shop in there for her own nap. "Do me a favor? Don't stab anyone else while I'm gone. I just can't impress upon you all enough how much I dislike overnight guests, so let's just not piss off the host, okay?"

"Yes, sir," Nevia and Heaton offered. Daniel gave him a sincere salute and Gypsy took a moment to look him over. Another evaluation or perhaps just checking him for weapons. She should have known by now that he didn't need any.

"Callin, are you going to live?" Danato asked as he passed by the supine werewolf.

"I think so, but I'd like to just hang out on the floor for a while to be sure," he answered hoarsely.

"Suit yourself."

Danato headed down the hall to his office. He half expected Cori to be sitting in his chair tenting her fingers, but she was leaning against the wall, mulling over God knows what. He shut the door and scooted past Belus and Ethan seated in front of the desk. He stopped next to Cori and rubbed her back. "Are you all right?"

"No, I'm not!" She twisted out of his grip and stared him down. For the life of him, he couldn't imagine what he had done to make her so angry.

"Cori, what is it?"

She motioned for him to take his chair, and he gave her a scolding look for the condescension. She graciously offered the chair again without the glare and he squeezed her arm before taking his place.

"Look, I get that my track history for good employee is a little marred. I also get that I am more prone to respond emotionally rather than logically." Cori glanced at Belus. "I also know that everyone in this room loves me and wants to protect me. Sometimes more than they want to actually listen to me." Cori looked at Ethan. "So, rather than letting my emotions get in the way, or acting impulsively, I'm going to consult with my superior, my mentor, and my partner about a problem that I feel needs an immediate solution."

"I think that sounds like a reasonable request," Danato interjected. "What is the problem?"

Cori looked them all over again. "I want that psychopathic bitch out of my house and away from this prison right now."

49

ORI LOOKED AROUND AT each and every despondent face. They weren't going to agree. Danato and Belus exchanged a glance, and she exhaled her frozen breath. This was why she didn't follow the rules—no one ever listened to her, and really, how often was she wrong... in the end?

"She just stabbed Callin," Cori whispered, containing her anger with the softness of her tone.

"I understand your perspective, sweetheart, but—"

"No!" Cori pinched her hands into fists and fought to keep her tone respectful. "You have no idea what it's like to be drowning in your own blood. Right now, the only person, other than me, who can understand that is Callin, because he was just experiencing it ten minutes ago."

"What happened out there was self-defense," Belus argued.

"How was that self-defense?"

"You of all people, should be sympathetic to a rape victim."

Cori froze, staring at Belus as she tried to formulate her objection to the word *rape*. She hadn't considered it to be a sexual assault since it wasn't the violent, forced encounter she had been subjected to prior to her arrival at the prison.

Then again, if Gypsy had no choice about her attraction to Callin, then it was forced. At the very least, Callin had denied Gypsy her freewill. Which may not be as traumatizing as a physical domination, but it was certainly just as violating.

However, even if Cori could find some empathy for the woman's situation, it didn't change the fact that Gypsy was a volatile and unpredictable woman. Someone she didn't want around her family.

"She is dangerous," Cori said.

"No more dangerous than Daniel or Ethan or you, for that matter." Belus nodded to her rings.

She was once again taken aback by Belus's sound logic. She hadn't expected him to agree with her emotionally fused request, but he was actually defending Gypsy. "The difference is I care about the people around me. Gypsy doesn't. She killed all of you, remember?"

"No. Because that didn't actually happen," Belus said.

"It did happen. I watched it happen. She may be in a different reality, but she is still the same personality. I know what she is capable of. Gypsy is a ticking time bomb and I don't want my child around her when she goes off." Cori narrowed her gaze on Belus and rolled her jaw, waiting for him to challenge her "mom card." He seemed to recognize that his logic would never win against an over-protective mother, and he relaxed back in his chair.

"What do you want us to do with her?" Danato asked. "You know the trucks aren't running."

"Why exactly aren't they running again?" Ethan asked.

Danato shook his head at Ethan. He either didn't want to answer or hated the answer he would have to give.

"Open the drawbridge and kick her out," Cori suggested.

"It's too cold. That would kill her," Belus said.

"I don't care." Cori raised her arms in defeat. "I know that's not my usual motto, but I am not letting that woman sleep under the same roof as my child. Either she goes or we do." She crossed her arms and looked over the now thoughtful faces. Danato tapped his pencil on the desk, inspecting her resolve. "I'm serious, Danato. Mother trumps warden."

"I know it does." He winked at her. "Obviously, she is unstable. However, I think, given Jordan's analysis of her, she is only as much of a threat as we make of her."

"You spoke to Jordan about Gypsy?" Cori questioned.

"Yes, sweetheart, we have already spoken at length about Gypsy and how best to handle her. Clearly, she is just as erratic as you have described from your wish reality, but kicking her out into an arctic tundra is not my idea of diplomacy."

"Since when do we need diplomacy with murderers?" she snapped.

"Since she saved your husband's life with a blood transfusion," Belus said. "And again, she hasn't technically killed anyone."

"That's what I am trying to prevent."

"Yes, but you already have expectations of a result based on evidence from a non-existent reality. You are letting your emotions dictate your response to her actions."

"Belus, I just lost a year of my son's life. Some invisible weirdo sex-change artist is giving me useless advice. I'm being audited by a plague of polyester—Danato's stepmother—whom I didn't even know existed."

"Your stepmother is here?" Ethan queried quietly to Danato.

"Yes," Cori continued, "and she has invited herself to stay at our house. On top of all that, my arch-nemesis numero tres is sitting in our living room. So, my apologies if I'm being emotional."

"If Levi's right about Addy, then we are all being a little emotional at the moment," Ethan said.

"That doesn't mean my concerns should be dismissed," Cori objected.

"That's not what I meant."

"Enough." Danato waved his hands, dismissing further discussion. "I will put Gypsy in the prison for tonight to keep her out of trouble. But Cori, you have to remember, she is not my employee, nor is she a supernatural being that I can dole out a prison sentence to. At best, I can kick her out, but that should be done by putting her on a truck. That way, we can actually get her away from us, instead of having her lurking outside the gate."

"I think our best strategy with Grace is to keep her on our good side. There's still a lot we don't know about her. Her sudden connection to this werewolf war seems a little suspect to me. I want to find out who she's working for. There is someone very knowledgeable funding this little coup and I want to know who it is. The last thing we need is someone trying to unite the werewolf community under a single political objective. Humans are bad enough."

"You want to casually interrogate her while she's here?" Cori asked.

"Exactly," Danato agreed. "I think we should take advantage of this situation to get a little insight if we can."

Cori couldn't disagree with that. Gypsy seemed to have some intimate knowledge of the prison. Things she shouldn't have known as a first-time visitor. "Fine. I'll play nice to keep her talkative, but if she so much as pricks the finger of someone else, I will slice her in two." Cori made a motion with her finger that made Danato's face muddle with concern. He either didn't realize she could do that—which she couldn't—or he was concerned that she actually would do it—which she would.

That realization even surprised Cori. She had always been an advocate of saving lives, but something about Gypsy made her abandon that morality. Then again, maybe it was just as Levi had said. Could the anger she was feeling be a result of overflowing magic? Or was everyone ignoring an obvious threat? Either way, she suspected Callin wouldn't be the only victim of Gypsy's hostility.

50

G YPSY WATCHED THE BAND of wardens and warden-wannabes enter the main room again. Cori went straight to the kitchen to help Daniel and Nevia with the meal. Ethan helped Heaton pull Callin off the floor, while Danato and mini-me arrived in front of her chair.

She glanced back at Callin when he let out a grunt of pain. She couldn't really say she felt bad about stabbing him. The truth was, she hadn't really given it much thought after it was done, but she was glad he wasn't dead. Maybe she didn't want to miss out on the sex. Or maybe she wasn't done beating the crap out of him. In the end, it was probably just the hormones he had inoculated her with, but she wouldn't worry about it no matter what the reason was.

"Callin, come over here." Danato beckoned, and he hobbled over. He stumbled once after the men had released him and Gypsy nearly jumped to his aid. Instinct, she thought, or hormones again. She wondered if his hormones would make her feel more. She supposed that was his plan. Force her to love him, even against her nature.

Did that make him an asshole, or just overly romantic?

"Grace—"

"Call me Gypsy, I like it."

"Gypsy, the offense of marking is very serious. Callin could be imprisoned for this crime." She smirked at Callin, who was still sulking from her attempted murder. What did he expect her to do, just lie down and play wife for him? "However, you must declare his guilt in the crime."

"How's that?" Gypsy's brow dipped in confusion.

"Some markings are consensual."

"Women actually *want* to be marked by werewolves?" she asked, trying to picture these pathetic servile women.

"Well…" Danato cleared his throat. "Given the side effects of the connection, some women participate voluntarily for recreational reasons."

Gypsy glanced at Callin, who now looked smug rather than angry. She raised a questioning eyebrow at him and he perked his suggestively back at her. The small flirtation was enough to spur her thoughts toward less homicidal activities. She took in a deep breath to calm her rising libido. "What are you going to do about my… reaction?" she asked, brushing her hand over her collarbone.

"We are going to place you in a cell tonight. Just in case your reaction isn't finished." Danato worded it just as carefully.

"I have to say, I'm a little disappointed, Warden." Gypsy stood abruptly, making all three men shift defensibly, which she loved. She stepped up to

Danato—ample breast to ample chest—and tipped her head back to look at him. He was less than a head above her, but it was enough that she felt overshadowed with or without his girth. "I was kind of looking forward to a little back and forth with you. A little push and shove, if you will."

Danato looked her over and took in a deep, chest-rising breath that pushed him further against her. "I think what you need is to get over yourself. That prison contains seductresses that are far more talented than you and I still haven't gotten trapped by their lure. If you want something from me, young lady, you are just going to have to pucker up your sweet cherry lips and say..." Danato puckered his lips for effect. "...please."

Gypsy heard Daniel snort in the background, followed quickly by Heaton's chuckle. She didn't like being played the fool, but she could see her usual routine was going to be lost on this man. Which was unfortunate for her, since she was really starting to like his blustery attitude.

"I'm not interested in pressing charges. He's gotten enough punishment from me." Gypsy looked over the still-bruised collar bone on Callin. "Am I being sent to bed without supper as well?" She rolled her eyes, knowing that he was now in control of her stomach content, as well as her sleeping quarters.

Danato glanced toward the kitchen, catching Cori's eye. She knew well that Cori was the one instigating this entire display, which made it so much worse. She honestly had no reason to hate Cori, but Cori had every reason to hate her. In fact, Gypsy's current annoyance with women aside, she rather liked Cori. She was ballsy. Kind of stupid, but definitely tenacious. It was fun to watch. Funner still to watch the men bend to appease her.

"The cafeteria is still open. I can send—"

"I can show her," Callin offered.

Danato frowned at the suggestion. "She just tried to kill you."

"Yeah, well, she's a bitch."

Gypsy chuckled at that. "That I am." She smiled at Callin. She was glad she hadn't killed his sense of humor either.

"I can show her the way and get one of the guards to lock her up afterward."

Danato glanced between them, trying to decide if this was wise. He shook his head, dismissing any concerns he might have had for their volatile relationship. "I assume I don't need to draw a picture of how unhappy I will be if this task is not completed to my approval." He stared Callin down.

"I give you my word, Danato. She will be contained in your prison for the night."

Danato sighed. "All right, but Gypsy, your weapons are officially off limits. I want you to empty the concealed ones before you go."

Gypsy bit her lips, reluctant to comply. She noticed Ethan shifting to intercept her possible escape attempt, even though she hadn't actually planned it yet. With three supernaturally strong men in her path, this was one battle even she couldn't win. "Fine."

She emptied her pockets and cleavage of several hidden blades and a very expensive garrote made of spider silk. When she hadn't received the shock and awe from her arsenal that she wanted, she pulled her blow pipe out of her side pocket and finished off her growing pile by removing the half dozen needle-thin darts she had pinned in her hair.

"Girl, you need a therapist," Heaton said, giving her the satisfaction that her display had been somewhat entertaining.

"Been there, done that," she responded before leading the way to the door. "Sweet dreams everybody."

51

Ethan caught Callin's arm before he could follow Gypsy out. He tried to exude his best silent reprimand for his stupidity, but Callin just squeezed his arm back and pulled away. Ethan had never understood his desire to fight for the love of temperamental women. His attraction to Leona, the mother of his child, could at least be passed off as parental instinct, but Gypsy? From what he had gleaned so far, the woman was cold as ice outside of the bedroom and too hot to hold inside of one. It certainly wasn't her maternal instincts that were drawing him in.

Heaton smirked and shook his head as he watched the werewolf leave. "That man has a death wish," Heaton said after the front door shut.

"That was beautiful, Danato," Daniel called over as he set the table for dinner. "I think you actually made her frown. I've never seen her without her simpering smugness."

"Well, I'm happy to have entertained you, but I'm not really sure that's a difficult achievement."

"Oh, damn!" Heaton chuckled.

"Ouch." Daniel feigned a knife to his heart.

Nevia stepped up behind Heaton, touching his back gently. When he caught on to her intention to speak secretly, he leaned his ear to her. "Who did you introduce Efrat to?" she whispered.

He chuckled, glancing at Danato and Belus. Deciding that it was unwise to continue the conversation in proximity to *grown-ups,* he drew her into a sideways hug and walked her back toward the island. Somewhere in the whispered details, Nevia started giggling nearly uncontrollably.

"Dinner's ready!" Cori announced, bringing what looked and smelled like spaghetti to the dining room table. "Let's get you half-starved men fed." Cori motioned for them to sit.

"I should grab Levi and get going," Belus announced and headed toward the stairs.

"Levi?" Danato asked, before clicking his tongue. "Damn it, that boy is forgettable."

"Belus, stay," Cori called over to him. "Daniel and Nevia made enough to feed an army."

"The cafeteria is stocked," Belus replied, immune to the social pressure of the request. Ethan could see his dismissal disappointed Cori, but she was in no mood to beg for his company.

"Oh, come now, Rutherford," Renee drawled as she slipped out of Danato's room looking refreshed—or at least her makeup had been refreshed. Belus froze on the stairs. "Stay for dinner." She leaned over the railing, catching him at eye level. "That's an order."

Ethan could sense the tension between them, but even more so, the levity in the room disappeared with her entrance. She passed by the Christmas tree, silently ba-hum-bugging some aspect of the spectacle. By the time she reached Danato, his lip was twitching.

"Hello, Mother. Did you rest well?" His voice rumbled in the lowest decibel he was capable of.

"Of course." She reached to his collar in a futile effort to flatten the never-been-ironed curling edges. "I've always slept well in your bed."

Danato's hand rose so fast Ethan instinctively tensed, ready to offer his protection. Who he intended to rescue was still up for debate. Danato gripped Renee's hand tightly and dragged it away from his neck. Ethan couldn't distinguish the conflicting expression on his face. Much like the rest of Danato's past, this woman brought out a fusion of emotions in him, none of them good.

"Let's eat!" Danato's voice boomed, and the room jumped into forced casualness.

Belus started up the stairs again.

"Belus," Ethan called after him, "I'll get him."

Belus offered him a knowing nod and headed toward the grub with the others.

Ethan climbed the stairs, listening to the bickering of his former partners.

"You'd best not be flirting with my wife, you poof," Daniel griped.

"And if I am?" Heaton retorted humorously. "What are you gonna do, tackle me and give my arse a good pounding?"

"Aye—*what?*—no! Ah, damn it, man, you can't make it gay! That's not fair!"

Ethan smiled as he tapped on the door to the guest room. He could barely hear Levi's admittance over Heaton and Nevia's laughter. He stepped into the bedroom and shut the door, leaving the cheerfulness outside.

52

GYPSY DIDN'T BOTHER WAITING for Callin. He was already steadily gaining on her. She wasn't one to be uncomfortable around anyone, but she didn't usually have to apologize for almost murdering anyone. Mostly because she never *almost* killed anyone she intended to. Her doggedness only allowed for *do* or *don't* in her duties.

She stopped to light up her cigarette, but the damnable breeze kept blowing the lighter out. She felt Callin slip up behind her and his large hands cupped around hers, freeing her to get a bright orange ember.

She sucked in a deep drag and let it out slowly. She was shaking from the cold even more with his proximal heat teasing her. "Are you mad?" she asked.

"I am," he said succinctly.

"How mad?" she asked, preparing for a fight.

He stepped incrementally closer to her. "If I wanted revenge, you would have been dead two seconds after you plunged that knife into my heart."

"It wasn't your heart," Gypsy corrected his exaggeration.

"IT WAS MY HEART!" he bellowed, forcing her to bend forward to protect her ears. Her instincts were on high alert, but she had no defense. Without her gear, she was useless against a werewolf—especially a pissed off one. Her only viable defense now would be to curl into a ball and pee on herself.

He grabbed her ponytail and yanked her head back, smelling her neck. His throat vibrated with a soft growl that bordered on a purr. "It's almost fear, isn't it? Accelerated heart rate and breathing, perspiration. It's almost an emotion, but not quite."

"Is that why you marked me? You were hoping that I might... *feel* something."

"No." He released her hair and walked around her. "I marked you because you're a fucking whore." He veered off the path and leaned against the concrete wall of the prison.

She didn't bother to feign offense from the insult. By common definitions, it wasn't inaccurate. She took another long drag of her cigarette to expedite her nicotine supplementation before her chattering teeth prevented it.

"I did sense anger on you when you attacked me." He spoke quietly, as if it were only an effort to break the silence and not a laden accusation.

"Anger is not beyond my grasp," she admitted. "It just takes specific... triggers."

"Being monogamous is your trigger?"

Gypsy took in the last of her cigarette and dropped her butt onto a snow pile nearby. "It's too cold for conversation."

"Yes, it is rather *cold* out here."

"Damn it, Callin. Don't make me the bitch in this scenario. When have I ever portrayed myself as anything but—" She motioned to herself. "—this. Stop trying to make me something I'm not."

"I don't want you to be different, Grace, but for God's sake, even dogs can elicit compassion for their owners. Doesn't it bother you at all that I almost died in there? Even if you don't give a damn that you stabbed me, can't you at least claim to be more enthused that I'm standing here instead of lying in a puddle of blood back there?"

Gypsy moved forward with the intention of walking away, but she couldn't do it. He wasn't asking about love or hate, simply her preference for his existence, and that was at least something she could offer him.

She clutched her arms around herself and turned back to him. "Yes, I am glad that you are not dead. I should not have stabbed you, but to be perfectly honest, I never in a million years thought that I would have gotten past you. Frankly, I'm a little disappointed in you, Callin."

He narrowed his eyes and stalked back to her. She was shaking so hard now, nothing short of an IV of hot chocolate would warm her. "My apologies. I won't let you almost kill me again."

"If your goal is revenge, the frostbite is already setting into my fingers."

"Mmm." He frowned and shook his head. "No, we can't have that. You have especially talented hands. Come now, my beautiful cutthroat. Let's get you warmed and fed. Then you can show me how sorry you are."

53

ETHAN SAT ON THE bed next to Levi. His eyes were red, but his tears were already dry. For a long moment, they sat in silence.

"I asked Danato to bury her, rather than burn her. The— She would have wanted that, I think. Back to the earth, I mean. Don't you think?"

Levi nodded.

"Tell me what I can do."

"Nothing." Levi's voice rasped as if his vocal chords were damaged from too much screaming. Perhaps he had been screaming. The house always sensed when to soundproof and when not. It was no doubt familiar with the agony of men by now.

Ethan cleared his throat, trying to surmount the rising emotions in him. "I see you sitting here paralyzed by grief and I find myself envious of you. I know this is all my fault and I have no right to feel anything beyond guilt... but I'm so angry, Levi. I'm being consumed by this, and I don't know what to do about it. I'm jeopardizing everything I've worked to achieve here."

Levi looked him over, and Ethan suddenly realized that he was pouring his problems into the lap of an already overwhelmed man. He wiped away a stray tear and stood up.

"I'm sorry, Levi. I didn't mean to pile my personal issues on you. I know your life is in complete upheaval. I just wanted you to understand that... I didn't want any of this. I thought I was helping her. I thought this was the right thing to do. I'm so sorry, Levi."

"We all decided this together," Levi whispered.

Ethan opened his mouth to explain that his decision had a backer. That this idea wasn't just something he had conjured from his own mind. However, as the words started to come, he realized it didn't matter whose idea it was. The dragons hadn't forced him to perform the ceremony. He'd chosen to do it.

Danato was right. He knew the rules. He may not have anticipated the consequences, but that didn't matter. His obedience has never been contingent on comprehension.

"I can show you where she is. When you're ready," Ethan offered.

"Thanks."

"We're having dinner. You don't have to come down, but I could bring you something."

"No, I'm not hungry."

Ethan nodded. "Okay." He moved to the door.

"Ethan," Levi said softly, and he turned back. "I never would have known that she loved me if you hadn't come. I know the whole *better to have loved and lost* line is cheesy, but I get it now. I mean... It would have hurt either way, but at least we had one night to show each other the truth. It would have sucked to have her die and never know that I loved her back."

Ethan nodded. Adrianna had been timid, but occasionally feisty, and Levi, though impatient at times, had a gentle determination that could calm her and draw her out. He would have very much enjoyed seeing their relationship blossom, but as with most things in his life, he didn't get a say in it.

54

GYPSY APPROACHED EFRAT AND Duke, who were seated at one of the long tables in the cafeteria. Duke was slouched against the wall before an empty tray and Efrat was happily gorging on a mammoth portion of mashed potatoes and gravy.

"I told you it was an accident," Efrat said over his mouthful.

"Accident, my tuchus. You nearly killed the breaker. We've got damn near eighty lights to replace up there. Do you know how much I hate working on a ladder?

"I said I'm sorry."

Gypsy sat down across from the men. Efrat looked up at her between mouthfuls and gave her a sour look. The expression deepened as Callin sat down next to her and handed her a bundle of silverware to go with her allocated supper servings. Gypsy smirked at the man's discomfort.

"Relax," Callin addressed him firmly. "If I was here to attack you, you would be dead already."

Efrat's eyes narrowed and his jaw tensed, no doubt offended by Callin's assumption of superiority. Most men had trouble adapting to the feeling of inadequacy.

Efrat's hands lit with thick blue rivulets that pulsed against his glass utensils. However, it was Duke who actually responded to Callin's threat.

"I don't imagine it would be wise for a werewolf to kill a man in a prison designed to imprison werewolves." A merriment filled Duke's voice that didn't match the challenge in his eyes. He hadn't moved from his relaxed position, but Gypsy could tell he was ready to jump from his seat at a moment's notice. "The way I hear it, you've already been told twice to keep your mitts off our men, so I would suggest not threatening one in a room full of"—Duke looked around—"eighteen of them."

Gypsy glanced around the room and noticed more than one man in black had put down their forks to listen in on the conversation. She looked back at Duke with new eyes. "My, my, aren't you a surprise, cowboy?"

Callin also noted the shift in the room and sighed. "Forgive me. I wasn't intending to threaten you, merely to acknowledge the facts."

"Ease up, Efrat." Duke pushed on Efrat's shoulder. "You're going to melt those damn things again."

Efrat threw down his glass flatware and leaned back in his chair. "For the record," he glanced at Duke as if he needed to permission to respond, "one bolt from me could fry this whole flippin' room." Efrat seethed. "It's because I'm *not* the biggest asshole in the world that I don't do that. This"—Efrat held up his lit hands—"is me controlling my damn self."

"He's right." Duke nodded. "He could kill us all, but he's a nice guy, so he doesn't."

Efrat gave Duke a dirty look. "Are you mocking me?"

Duke's mouth turned slightly, but he hid his amusement well. "I was actually agreeing with you. Truth is, I'd rather fight him than you any day." Duke nodded to Callin.

Callin dropped his fork. "Excuse me, did I hear that correctly? You'd rather fight a werewolf than an average-strength man?" he asked, notably insulted.

"No," Duke said. "I'd rather pull my gun and walk you to a cell, but if it was a choice to fight you or him, I'd have a better chance with you."

"Really?" Gypsy asked in disbelief.

"You can't be serious," Callin objected again. "A male werewolf is several times stronger than a man."

"Oh, I'm not denying all that," Duke said. "I just know that when push comes to shove, I can try to run from you. I can't run from his electricity. Spent more time fighting the elementals than we ever did werewolves. Pesky bugger this one was."

"So, you really were a prisoner here?" Gypsy tipped her head, examining Efrat. "And now you're a lackey. Kind of a sideways move, isn't it?"

"I beg your pardon, ma'am, but I think that statement is insulting to both of us, and I would appreciate if you didn't aggravate your hosts."

Gypsy bit her lip as she looked Duke over. "I would love to see you get mad."

"How can you be sure that you're not already looking at it?" Duke asked.

Gypsy laughed and shook her head. "You are just a pocket full of sunshine."

"It seems to me that we've all gotten off on the wrong foot," Callin said, putting his arm behind Gypsy to lean toward the conversation more. "I admit my part in that. I'm sure Gypsy can also confess to her own blame." Callin shook her chair when she didn't immediately take her gaze from Duke.

She sighed and leaned over her tray to speak with Efrat. "In regard to earlier, I'm sorry... that we got interrupted."

Callin growled at her and she felt his claustrophobic presence compelling her to obey.

"I'm not," Efrat spat back at her, making Callin lose his grip on her submission. He looked at Callin and shrugged. "Look, man, I'm not after your girl. She was pretty forward, and I was vulnerable to her attentions, but there wasn't exactly a discussion on boyfriends before she did it."

"I'm aware of Grace's lack of propriety. She's working on that."

Gypsy ignored the gaze she was getting from Callin and dug into her food. It was far from the worst food she had ever eaten, but she wasn't likely to go back for seconds.

"So, Duke," she said before she swallowed her mouth full of food. "You're in charge here, right?"

Duke didn't answer, but he nodded.

"Why don't you get me filled in on the latest gossip?"

"You aren't really on my list of superiors, ma'am."

"Not yet, anyway." She winked at him, making his eyes narrow. "That was quite a light show I saw when I arrived. You mind giving me the short version, just to catch me up?"

Duke looked at Efrat. He shrugged, not seeing a reason to keep the information a secret. They probably assumed she would be wiped before leaving, anyway. Fat lot of good that would do.

"This here prison isn't just for keeping things in. It's also for keeping things out," Duke began the "short" version.

55

DANATO SAT IN HIS usual spot at the head of the table, and Belus brazenly claimed the other end. It was a small defeat in terms of battle, but Belus was a tremendous fan of usurping Renee whenever the opportunity arose. He wasn't sure his irritation with her stemmed out of deference to him, or if the woman just pissed him off on a fundamental level. Either was just a likely, since Belus knew his background with her.

Danato had found a good deal of common intere with Renee during their early interactions. It was surprising, since she was closer in age to him than father. It wasn't until she'd seduced him on his birthday that he'd seen her true nature.

He had been drunk and naïve to the wiles of wo but he had been so ashamed of the affair that he'd told his father about it. However, Renee's insister repeat the encounter had finally revealed the truth.

His father had been far too entrenched in de Renee to place equal blame on her, and Dana been far too humiliated to take less than all of of punishment and a desire to secure his marr father had immersed him in training. Danato had never worked so hard in his life, but he'd taken on the endless burdens as his penance in a vain attempt to win his father's forgiveness.

It was in those miserable early days of his semi-voluntary employment that he'd met Belus, who had been training just as hard. He was a cocky upstart with something to prove. Though it had been clear that Belus would never be capable of the physical demands of the warden's job, he'd had no intention of completely missing out on his birthright.

Somewhere between healthy competition and camaraderie in desolation, they became easy friends. If it weren't for the bedlam of raw emotion following Olivia's death, it wouldn't have been such a rarity to see Belus at the other end of his table.

Cori had been trying, mostly in vain, to include him in more events. Danato wondered if his reluctance to be part of their lives was because he had not officially invited him back into his life.

"Cori." Danato caught Cori's waist as she leaned over to put more bread sticks into the basket on the table. She drew back, and he pulled her gently to him in a sideways hug. "Belus's glass is desperately close to being empty. Would you mind filling it for him?"

Cori glanced at Belus's one-third full wine glass and smirked at him. "Sure."

"Thank you, sweetheart." He released her to take the wine decanter over to fill Belus's glass. Belus seemed to understand the offering and nodded down to him.

"Thanks, kid," he said when Cori was finished pouring him a brimming glass.

"I wasn't aware that our budget allowed for such expensive wine," Renee interrupted the civil moment once Cori had seated herself to Danato's right. Ethan was on Danato's left, feeding himself as well as the baby. Renee had sat down next to him. Heaton and Daniel flanked Belus, leaving Nevia a spot in the middle of it all across from Renee.

"Has the audit started already?" He glowered at her.

"Actually," Ethan jumped in before Renee could respond, "this wine was made here, from grapes grown in the wizard's den. As you know, Cori's gardening project has saved the prison thousands of dollars."

Danato smiled at Ethan and perked a brow at Renee when she noticed his amusement.

"How delightful." Renee smiled at Cori. "Do you do anything besides pick vegetables all day?"

"Of course." Cori glanced around the table. "I do the rounds just as the guards do: meal delivery, prisoner recovery, logging, maintenance, and inventory. I've been helping to get Efrat's powers fine-tuned. There's paperwork, and—"

Danato placed his hand on Cori's, so she didn't persist to amuse Renee further. "Cori's workload is fully documented, Renee. You know as well as anyone that every day in this prison is different. When those *different* days arrive, that is when Cori's greatest assets are utilized."

"Yes, and who takes care of the baby while you're doing all of this?" Renee asked.

Danato could see Cori's hackles rise as she prepared to defend her motherhood as well. Danato squeezed her hand a little too tightly, and she relaxed back. "We all do," Danato answered for her. "We enlist the medical staff to babysit when we are all busy. So far, the nurses are enthused with the additional duty."

"I see." Renee paused to take a bite of her meal. "This is wonderful, Cori. Good cook, loving mother, a hard worker. You're the whole package. And your features are so *familiar*. You couldn't have been more perfect if Danato had purchased you out of a Stepford wife catalog."

Danato frowned and tended to his meal so he didn't say something he would regret. Cori, on the other hand, had no qualms about regretting her words.

"Well, there was a limited selection at the slave auction," she said cheerfully. "He just chose the only woman that actually defended herself. How many was it Danato? Three...?"

"Four," Danato said over a mouth full of food, even though he knew he shouldn't encourage her.

"Yes, four men I managed to subdue."

"Impressive." Renee smiled. "And what exactly are you trying to prove? That you're obstinate and violent?"

"That I'm not a Stepford wife," Cori snapped.

"Oh, darling, that wasn't meant to be an insult."

"Then apparently you have different standards than I do."

"Oh, I think that was clear the minute you sat down at this table in a t-shirt that says, 'Milk Factory.'"

Cori glanced down at the t-shirt she had slipped on prior to eating. Two milk cartons were strategically placed across her chest. Danato expected her to be wounded by the insult to her personal style, but she seemed lit by the challenge.

"Don't tell me the board is going to demand a better class of slave to be working in their facility, because I don't think we have a budget for overpriced polyester." Cori jutted her chin at the woman's expensive suit. "I think the expense of your hairspray alone would put us in the red, let alone that shit perfume you think smells elegant."

Daniel and Heaton snorted and ducked under their forked hands. Nevia, on the other hand, sat up straighter, already anticipating the reaction.

Renee's mouth twisted in disgust and she stood up. "You arrogant bitch!"

"Now, ladies…" Danato put down his napkin in preparation to break up the ensuing cat fight.

"Bitch?" Cori stood up as well. Danato could see the frost that had formed on her hands. He glanced at

Ethan and he nodded, scooting his chair back slightly and shifting the baby in case he needed to save Renee's life. "You walk into my house, sit at my table, and insult me, and then you dare to call *me* a bitch?" Renee opened her mouth to retort, but Cori didn't give her a chance.

"You may be a member of the Board, but understand this: when we are inside of that prison you can brandish and exert your authority all you want, but the minute you walk into my house you will treat me and mine with the respect that you would anyone offering you a bed to sleep in and food to eat. If you can't handle that, then I suggest you get your bags and get out!"

Cori whipped her finger toward the front door and it flew open, propelled by an unseen force. Everyone paused to look at the door, forcing the argument into immediate hibernation. Cori glanced at Danato, but she maintained her stern face so she could drive her point home.

Renee blanched at the open door, finding new credence in Cori's words. She took a moment to smooth down her outfit before sitting back down at the table. Cori moved to close the door, but Danato waved for her to sit. He grabbed the knob and gave it a tug, but it resisted his strength. He tried again, but he couldn't get it to move without damaging the door.

Renee cleared her throat and after a short pause, spoke. "You're right. I am a guest. My gratitude for that should be the only opinion I bring to your table. I'm sorry. My apologies to everyone. I didn't mean for my uncouth behavior to ruin this delicious meal."

The door finally released, and Danato closed it tightly. He locked it also, but he imagined that it wouldn't make a difference if the house was intent upon siding with Cori. When he returned to the table, he found everyone quietly nibbling on their food. Only the baby offered a consistent dialogue of squeals and blubbers brought on by the excitement of getting to share in a tangible spaghetti noodle experience.

He noticed Belus had a contented smile on his face, but when he caught Danato's eye, it vanished. He dipped his brow and nodded toward the door. Danato glanced at Cori and shrugged.

He wasn't sure if the house favoring Cori was a recent occurrence because of their interaction, or if it was just the inevitable result of occupying the home for so many years. After Olivia's death, Danato had been inexorably linked to the house, as well as his office and the elevators in the prison. The entity reacted to his emotions and even anticipated his needs on a daily basis.

Meanwhile, Belus had been permanently restricted. The home outright rejected his presence unless someone invited him in and the prison elevators were intolerably slow for him.

Danato had been concerned that Cori's interaction with the entity might have soured its opinion of her, but it was becoming increasingly obvious that her link was similar to his own. Perhaps stronger.

He just wasn't sure if that was a good or bad thing. The last thing Cori needed was another powerful being toying with her emotions and potentially manipulating her mental state.

"What is his name?" Renee asked civilly, offering a small smile to the baby, who had just discovered that spaghetti noodles were also enjoyable to the taste buds. He shrieked with joy, declaring the ingenious expansion of its worth a success.

Everyone chuckled. "What do you mean?" Danato asked.

Renee caught his eye and her annoyance seemed unfounded. "What do you call the child?" she clarified.

Danato smiled and shook his head, still baffled by the question. He looked at Cori for an answer, but she only rolled her eyes.

"Oh, don't tell me you haven't named him yet," Renee scolded. "He has to be over a year old by now. That can't be healthy."

Renee continued to stare him down, seeking the answer to her question, but all he could do was shrug and smile at the slobbering baby beside him. He supposed that there was a part of him that wondered why he didn't have an answer for her, but the more he tried to figure it out, the less important it seemed to be.

After all, there were far more important issues to ponder than...

56

"That doesn't exactly answer my question," Efrat grumbled to Duke. They had taken it upon themselves to lead Gypsy and Callin to her not-so-gilded cage for the night. Though the conversation was taking place in hushed tones, she assumed it wasn't so much a secret as just private.

"Like I said, she's a prisoner for a reason. Of course she's dangerous, but..." Duke waggled his head a little and Efrat eagerly waited for his response. "Ethan's trusted her with a thing or two in the past. Can't say as she's been much help to him, though. Cori hates her guts."

Efrat laughed. "Somehow I consider that a point in her favor."

Duke glanced over at him and shook his head. "She really gets under your skin that much?"

Efrat shrugged and looked away. "It's not her so much, just the situation. I can't get her out of my head sometimes."

"I can't say I blame you, but that's a dangerous fantasy."

"Tell me about it. I can't seem to find that balance of friendship, when all I really want to do is... touch her." Duke clucked his tongue. "No, it's not that. I mean—well—yes, obviously that, but... I think I just want human contact."

"Yeah, I think I used that line on a girl once."

Efrat paused and glanced back at Gypsy. She wasn't showing any particular interest in the locker room chatter, so he continued. "Speaking of that, though, how do *you* do it? I mean, hell, you've been here longer than me, haven't you?"

"You gotta remember, Sparky—"

Efrat groaned. "Don't call me Sparky."

"Fuse? Bolt? Charge?" Efrat shook his head. "It's gonna be something, Effie, so you might as well have a say in it. There is no way you can have a superpower without a superhero name."

Efrat smiled and shook his head. "Let me think about it a bit."

"You do that. In the meantime, you just remember that every guard in this place is a prisoner. We would all still be dealing with the burdens of confinement, whether we were here or not. And not everybody's in it for the long haul like me. However, to answer your question, I smile real nice at the nursing staff." Duke gave him a big broad smile that showed off his perfectly white teeth.

Efrat scoffed. "I bet that's all it takes, too."

"You'd be surprised how far a smile gets you in life." Duke stopped at the cell he had in mind for Gypsy and unlocked the door. "Anything's better than that curmudgeon look you got all the time."

"Curmudgeon?"

"Home sweet home, darlin'." Duke motioned to the cot within.

Gypsy stepped through the doorway, pausing slightly to look him over. She noted that he did not have a smile for her.

He closed the door, but Callin grabbed it before it could latch shut. "If you gentlemen don't mind, Grace and I have a little conversing to do before she turns in."

"Mind? I don't mind." Duke pursed his lips and looked at Efrat. "Do you mind, Efrat?"

"Nope, I don't mind," Efrat said on cue.

"You know who might mind, though? The warden."

"I've already given him my word that she will be locked up for the night." Callin paused and took a deep breath. "I really do appreciate your valor, boys, but I could just as easily take the key from you. I am trying to be civil."

Duke rubbed his chin. "Yeah, I suppose you are. Sorry about that. It's been a long damn year and frankly, there are too many outsiders telling us what to do." He exhaled, revealing some of the exhaustion his bout inside the bubble had brought.

"I have no wish to make an enemy out of either of you. My only interest here is with this troublemaker."

Callin jerked his head toward her and she smirked at the implication.

"Good luck with that." Duke grimaced and put out his hand to shake.

Callin shook his hand respectfully. "Thank you. I'll make sure she's contained before I leave."

Duke nodded and headed down the corridor. As he passed Efrat, the elemental didn't move to join him. Duke stopped and turned back to wait for him to give his farewell.

Efrat's usually embittered façade had turned mischievous. He stepped over to Callin and offered his hand to shake as well. "Bygones," he said, almost sneering.

Callin looked down at the proffered snake bite disguised as a peace offering. With as much ego being thrown around over the last hour, he could hardly refuse it. "Bygones," Callin said and took his hand.

After the initial curt shake, they held hands as tightly as their gazes. Callin's jaw tightened as he endured the electric shock. He squeezed tighter, making Efrat shift at the pain of his hand being caught in a vice.

Callin grunted as the electric blue became visible in their connection. Efrat, in turn, grimaced at the popping sound coming from his hand.

Duke chuckled and returned to the men. He put a hand on both of their shoulders. "Now, now, boys. We were doing so well. Let's not cause any broken bones or exploding organs."

"I can't really move anymore," Efrat admitted through clenched teeth.

"Stop shocking me and I'll release you," Callin said through similarly gritted teeth.

"He can't," Duke said. "Haven't you been paying attention? This is him *controlling his damn self*."

"And this is me not," Efrat said sinisterly. A spark erupted from their conjoined hands.

Callin yelled as he unwillingly recoiled from the energy Efrat released into him.

"Ah, hell," Duke mumbled and reached for his gun as he backed away.

Gypsy reached for her own, but realized that there was nothing to grab. She rolled her eyes at the stupidity of leaving the one person capable of controlling Callin unarmed. She slumped against the wall to watch the melee ensue. She didn't mind her cage so much anymore.

Callin's face seized in a familiar feral rage. He was trying to fight his baser instincts, but he wouldn't win. He rarely did when things got violent.

If Duke wasn't a very good shot, he was going to be cleaning his partner up off the floor.

To her surprise, however, Duke raised his gun and aimed it at Efrat. "You'd better get a grip on that anger, son." Once again, his words were aimed at the mere human.

"What do you mean, Duke?" Efrat taunted as he watched Callin. "I'm no match for a werewolf." He smirked at the certain death before him and dared to toss a glitter of miniature sparks at him.

Callin lost his battle with his ego and sprang forward. Efrat threw a bolt at him with an open palm that knocked him back again.

Callin recovered and tracked Efrat as he circled back to give them more space to fight. Curiosity flickered through his eyes and he charged again.

Efrat sent out another bolt, but this time, Callin dove and rolled under it. His shoulder impacted Efrat solidly, and the men went down. However, the short-lived advantage ended with Callin once again flying across the room, propelled by another jolt of electricity.

Gypsy pushed open her door and slipped out to stand beside Duke. He glanced at her disapprovingly, but didn't demand that she return to her confinement. "You still putting your money on Efrat?" she asked after Callin nicked Efrat's chin with his fist.

"He's not using his full strength," Duke said.

"Neither is Callin. If he was, Efrat's jaw would be on the floor."

Duke glanced at her. "With all due respect, miss, I've been working in this prison a lot of years. I know plenty about werewolves, but he isn't the scariest thing in here."

"And you give Efrat that honor?"

"No, ma'am." Duke's brow flinched, and she noted the condescension in his tone. He turned his attention back to the fight, which was turning bloody and slightly smoky. "Alston, finish this up. I still got paperwork to do," he hollered.

Efrat glanced at him and nodded. Despite being winded and bloodied, he was still smirking slightly.

Callin attacked during his distraction, but the room exploded in bright light and noise. Gypsy flinched at the light and plugged her ears while the rolling thunder continued to abrade her eardrums. Duke did the same.

When her eyes adjusted, she expected to see Callin lying on the floor passed out, but he was upright, quailing at the giant blue lightning storm swirling around him. He attempted to move out of the globe, but the potent shock it gave him was enough to still his movements.

Efrat, meanwhile, was no longer smiling. His eyes were dazed in concentration as he held the ball and poured a continuous stream of energy into it.

Gypsy couldn't keep from moving toward the ball. Duke put up a hand to block her, but she just pushed past it. She got close enough to draw Callin's attention. He still looked angry, but he seemed to understand that he was not equipped to fight this man. She knew he would be very bitter about it, especially since she had already bested him once that day.

She raised her brow, and he nodded, admitting his defeat to her. She looked at Duke and gave him a thumbs up. "He'll calm down now."

"You're good, Efrat," Duke hollered, but he also moved to grip his shoulder in case he was too entrenched in his revenge to hear him. "Ease up, partner," he yelled into his ear.

The energy reduced and dissipated. Efrat leaned over, breathing hard from the exertion. Callin approached him and he stood up straight again. The men looked one another over, but said nothing. A curt, barely noticeable nod was exchanged before they separated.

Efrat hobbled off with Duke, discussing the difference between *curmudgeon* and *pensive*. Callin returned to Gypsy and exhibited his leftover frustration for her. "Bad day, huh?" she asked.

"Bad couple of days." He exhaled and leaned his forehead against hers. "Come on." He took her hand and led her back to her captivity. "You can cheer me up." He kissed her hand. "Starting with a very ardent apology."

57

C ORI SMILED AT ETHAN from her outstretched position on the bed. He had just returned from putting their son to bed. Despite her eagerness to bond with him again, he still clung to his father something fierce. She tried not to let it bother her. Motherhood was, after all, an unbreakable connection, and soon enough, she would be his first choice again.

Ethan leaned against the parlor doors that separated their bedroom and living room. His eyes roved over her, plotting his attack strategy. She knew he would be eager to spend the night with her, so she'd put on her best lingerie. It wasn't much more than a pink nightie, but it did the trick. His eyes were hungry for more.

"Are you still mad at me?" he asked before he approached her.

She showed him her pinched fingers and scrunched up her nose. "Not enough to deny you the company of your wife. Especially since it has been so long."

"Yes, my goodness, however, did you survive without me for two days?" he teased.

She frowned and looked down at the bed. "I'm sorry you had to go through that."

"It's not your fault."

"Isn't it? My stupid rings fed the bubble."

"That's not your fault. I don't blame you for it. I know one year sounds horrible to your ears and seeing it on your son is painful, but in the grand scheme of things, all you missed was a bunch of men bickering about food, blood, and boredom. The hardest part was just wondering what you were going through out here."

Ethan moved to the bed and sat beside her. "You saved our lives," he said as he slid his fingers under her nightgown. "I knew you would."

"I had help."

Ethan nodded and looked down momentarily. "I know you did." His eyes flickered over her face. "Cori, if I left this place, would you come with me?"

Cori dipped her brow at the abrupt change of subject. "You mean get a different house?"

He pinched his lips. "I mean... the prison. If I decided to leave this life, would you come with me?"

"Ethan." Cori sat up against her pillow. "You know we can't leave. Even if we wanted to—"

"Just pretend that we didn't have to stay. If it was our choice. I'm asking you, who would you choose?"

"Who would I choose?" Cori squawked. "Are you actually asking me to choose between you and Danato?"

"No, I'm asking you to choose between the prison and your family."

Cori could see the gravity of emotion in his eyes. He wanted reassurance, but the question he was asking was an impossible one. How could she give up her entire life? How could she walk away now? After so many years?

"Why are you asking me this?"

"You really can't answer, can you?"

"Tell me why you're asking me this and I will answer you," she conditioned.

Ethan stood, breaking all contact with her. "I'm asking because I had to bury a friend today." He looked back at her. "I'm asking because I don't think I want to be a part of this anymore. I can't watch innocent people die."

"Ethan, she wasn't innocent." His eyes flared with anger, and she knew she was starting down a dangerous road. "Innocent is relative, I know, but she could have been stronger than a wizard."

"You're on Danato's side," he whispered the words like betrayal.

"Stop that. Stop tallying my words as votes. I love you, Ethan, but I never understood your connection to that girl. Frankly, it made me jealous as hell and at one point I even thought you might have had an affair with her."

"I would not do that," he rebutted quickly.

"I know that, but it doesn't mean I can't still worry about it. All I know is that you came back from China distant and moody. I thought..." Cori shrugged.

"I thought *you* didn't want to be part of this family anymore."

"No. No, that's not it at all."

"Then explain it to me. *All* of it. Why are you so angry? Why do I suddenly have to choose a different life just to be with you? Why is the death of a woman you knew for a few days more important to you than the happiness of a woman you've known for years?"

Ethan's face slowly melted in understanding. He looked down and shook his head. "You're right." He rubbed his face. "I'm sorry, sweetness. I didn't mean to make you feel less important. You and the baby are the most important people in my life. I guess I just wanted to know that you felt the same way."

Cori slipped off the bed and stood before him. "Of course I do. Ethan, the truth is, if you had a good reason to leave here, I would pack my bags and go, but I can't leave Danato just because you're angry. I've been mad in this place, and I've been sad in this place, but I've also been incredibly happy here. Most of that is because of you, but part of it is because of the life I have here."

Cori touched his face. "I do sympathize with you, Ethan; empathize even. Losing anyone you are close to is difficult, especially when you think you could have stopped it. However, I also sympathize with Danato. I know you want him to be the bad guy right now, but you know him as well as I do. He doesn't want to kill anyone.

He never did. All he wants to do is protect us and the world from the things that go bump in the night."

Cori kissed his lips, and he responded in kind.

"I think you need to get some sleep, Ethan. In your own bed, without the dream feeders."

He wrapped his arms around her and lifted her. He guided her legs to wrap around his waist. "I think I need something, but it's not sleep." He nuzzled kisses against her neck and she tilted her head to give him free access.

He dipped her down, and she felt the bed beneath her. She released her legs. The sudden tearing of her nightgown alarmed her, and she opened her eyes. Ethan paused in his movement and smiled at her. "You won't be needing this anytime soon."

He continued to rent the fabric, and he watched her for signs of objection. The gaping fabric soon enough revealed her breasts and panties. Rather than rip them off, he trailed his finger down from her bellybutton, stopping just where she wanted him to.

He leered at her playfully as he tickled his finger ever so gently over the fabric. "I missed this right here."

"Me too." She smiled, knowing that she couldn't compete with his need. She was impressed that he wasn't diving right onto her, but she got the feeling he was going to make the night last. As if he could make up for lost time.

58

"NO MORE!" GYPSY FELL on Callin's chest, nearly paralyzed from the waist down. The exquisite pleasure she normally got from her sex life with Callin was being put to shame with these new experiences. She was somehow outside of herself, intoxicated by his smell, his taste, his touch. As satisfied and exhausted as she was by the first three endless rounds, he had spurred her on to a fourth.

She felt him laugh more than heard it. "I didn't think I would ever hear that from your mouth." She could hear his heart racing, but his breathing was fairly steady since she had been the one put to work pleasing him. Not that she wasn't getting something out of it, but she was starting to see how marking could be considered a crime. It wasn't so much a mental control as a hormonal one.

"You shouldn't have marked me," she blurted out.

"You can say that even after I had to muffle your screams of ecstasy? You bit me, by the way."

She glanced up at him and he shifted his hand from behind his head to show her his boo-boo. "Sorry." She shrugged. "My ball gag was with my weapons."

He smiled and put his hand back. He stared up at the ceiling of the cell where who knows what fluids had stained the raw bricks. There were also more than a few claw marks on the painted cement surroundings. "Why did it bother you so much?" He paused, waiting for an answer, but she didn't speak. "I mean, other than the fact that you're a control freak."

"I function best under a very specific balance, Callin. Fighting and fucking are how I do that." She lifted her head and looked at him. "I can't have you interfering with that."

His gaze flickered over her. "Don't you think we work well together? You can fight me. You can fuck me. That's balance."

She sighed. "I almost killed you today, Callin. Does that answer your question?" He swallowed and leaned his head back again. She shifted off him to redress. "I think when you first met me, you decided that I was a woman you could conquer. Unfortunately, you only conquered yourself. When you realized you might not accomplish what you set out to do, you panicked, and you marked me." She paused, waiting for him to object to her summation, but he didn't. "So, what do you want, Callin?"

"What do *you* want?" he snarled.

"I want you to stop putting your heart in my hands. I'm going to break it. I don't mean to. I honestly don't, but that's kind of who I am. The only body parts you should ever trust me with are your cock and your back."

Callin sighed and stood up. "A heavy dose of hCG will stop the connection. I'm sure the medical staff can help you tomorrow." He somehow managed to get his pants up, shoes on, and shirt in hand before the end of his sentence. He slid open the barred door to leave.

"You didn't tell me what you want," she said, stalling his exit.

"Does it matter?"

"Yes. There are only two of us in this fucked up relationship and you do get a say in how it goes. Or *if* it goes."

"Is that what you want?"

"I asked you what *you* want. Just answer the question. Do you want a submissive little bitch?"

"No, I want you, Grace. I just need more than a punch in my face when I tell you I love you." She scoffed. "Goddamn it, I may be an idiot for falling in love with you, but it's a *compliment* to you, not an insult."

"It's an insult to yourself. You're a werewolf."

"Werewolves happen to love their partners very intensely. The fact that you cannot return that love is not an attribute of your strength; it is evidence of your weakness."

"*Love* makes you weak!"

"Love is what inspires strength!" He growled and sniffed the air. "There it is again. That anger. You do feel *something*. You may be emotionally stunted, but it's there, somewhere deep inside of you."

Gypsy smiled and nodded. "Yeah, maybe you're right. Keep diggin', doggy. Maybe you'll find some bones." Her smile dropped and she once again offered him the cold, vacuous truth. "Then you'll find out how deep that cold streak really goes."

Callin frowned at seeing that his desperation wouldn't gain any headway with her heart. "Good night, Grace." He stepped out and slid the door shut behind him.

59

"**YOU SHOULD BE SLEEPING** in," Cori scolded Danato as he made his way into the kitchen, fully dressed and ready for another day. The griddle she was manning hadn't even warmed up enough to signal breakfast, and the sky was barely pink outside.

Nevia neglected her first sip of coffee to offer him a nod as he passed by her.

"You've been dealing with dream feeders for nearly a year," she admonished him gently, in case it might be a tender topic.

Danato leaned in and kissed her cheek, giving her shoulder a slight squeeze as well. "I dealt with sorrow demons for years. The dream feeders can't compete with that. Besides, there are too many damn people here for me to sleep in." Danato frowned as he turned back to Nevia. "No offense, Jordan." She smiled knowingly. "Frankly, waking up to you two beautiful ladies is a blessing." Danato moved to the counter and poured himself a cup of the coffee that Nevia had brewed.

"Don't you mean three, Danato?" Renee's voice chimed from the stairs as she descended.

Cori could sense Danato's shift in spirits even before she glanced at Nevia.

"Hello, Mother." He spat out the word *mother* like it didn't belong in his mouth.

Renee stopped at the edge of the island close to where Nevia was sitting and overlooked the empty grill. "I was just about to start breakfast," Cori said, opting for civility rather than jumping right into a second helping of last night's cat fight. "Any requests?"

"No, I don't eat before ten, my stomach..." She trailed off. "Thank you, though." Cori could tell the woman didn't come by gratitude naturally. She wondered if it was her position, her money, or just too many years of people sucking up to her.

"Coffee?" Nevia raised her cup.

"No, caffeine sets off my migraines." She cleared her throat. "Danato, I am going to the upper level to check on the progress. Would you like to escort me?"

"You know the way," Danato grumbled. Renee's face slowly grew cold. "I'm enjoying my morning with my girls." Cori glanced at Nevia, offering her a slight smirk. She wasn't sure how the taciturn woman felt about being tucked under Danato's paternal wings, but she would soon find out that there was no arguing with the man's devotion. "Why don't you head up? You can report your findings when I get in."

"Danato." Renee spoke quietly, glancing at the two of them before speaking again. "This project requires your attention as well."

"Does it?" He sipped his coffee. The anger stemming from him surprised Cori. Danato was never a gracious host, but he was usually a little more genteel than this. "The board has been paid; the blueprints are drawn up; I didn't even get a notice before your militia showed up on my goddamn lawn."

Renee raised her hands and pursed her lips. "As I recall, the distress call was sent from here."

"For food, not soldiers." Cori couldn't help but contribute.

"Our plans for reconstruction overlapped. I do apologize for the uproar it caused yesterday. I assure you, after the bubble has been stable for another day, the soldiers will vacate."

"Do I have your word on that?" Danato asked, losing his sternness in lieu of subdued relief.

Renee nodded. "Yes, of course. You know the protocol.""Protocols change. *People* change," Danato said.

"Yes, Danato, people *do* change." Renee raised her brow, and he looked away. "Time changes the outside, and experiences change the inside. Except the heart... that stays the same."

"You have to have a heart to begin with, though." Renee's face fell, and she looked near tears. Danato nodded to the door. "Go on, Renee. You've got work to do." Her face hardened again, and she walked out the door with her coat in hand.

Cori exchanged a look with Nevia, then the floor, and then settled her questioning gaze on Danato. "So... you want to talk about it?"

"No!" he snapped before huffing out an exhale. "I'm sorry. It was a long time ago." He dipped his brow at her pained expression, which was no doubt because of his omission. "It's not a secret, Cori. I just don't want to talk about it. Okay?"

She nodded and looked at Nevia, who dipped her head into her coffee.

Danato chuckled. "She's my stepmother, Jordan, not my real mother."

"Oh." Nevia relaxed again. "That makes more sense now."

"You going to cook something on that, sweetheart, or just heat the kitchen?" Danato nodded to the empty griddle. Cori jumped back into chef mode and started on a batch of pancakes before Danato's stomach started to grumble.

60

"BUT WHAT THE HELL *is* he?" Cori asked, before she shoved a strip of bacon into her mouth.

Danato smirked at the balancing act Cori did in order to cut her pancakes while standing. The dining room table was completely empty despite the addition of two new hungry faces and only three stools at the end of the island. Since he was the first to be fed, he gave up his third helping to let Daniel and Heaton crowd around Nevia.

"I've never smelled anything like him before," Nevia said, giving him a look that was as near to horrified as he thought her subtle features were capable of.

He shrugged and pushed the button on the coffee machine to start another pot.

"Who are we talking about?" Daniel asked over a mouthful of pancake.

"Maddox, that military guy with a scar." Cori motioned to her own face.

Daniel licked his lips and looked at Heaton. Heaton shook his head, not recognizing the name or description. "Apparently we missed out on that introduction," Heaton said.

"I don't like him," Cori said.

"Neither do I," Danato agreed. "She's not to be trusted."

"She?" Daniel interjected, crinkling his brow in confusion.

"That's what he said you'd say," Cori said to Danato.

"Is this dude a dude or a dudette?" Heaton asked, shoving his plate away.

"Both and neither," Danato answered.

Nevia burped loudly, derailing the conversation. Danato tried to offer her a disapproving look for the loutish behavior, but he couldn't help but find amusement in the tiny woman burping like an ogre.

"Speaking of the crosswise genders." Heaton chuckled and patted her back.

"That's my girl." Daniel raised his fists in triumph.

"It's a compliment." Nevia shrugged and collected her plate and Heaton's to take to the sink.

Danato returned his attention to Cori. "What else did Maddox tell you?"

She put her plate down and faced him with crossed arms. "She... he implied that there was a problem with the board members. A money issue or power struggle. He said that the changes being implemented now are too late. What does that mean?"

Danato sipped his coffee before presenting the answer to the original question first. "The official name for Maddox's kind is *Phantosmia,* but the more common name is *"Blink,"* because they can change their appearance in the blink of an eye. Unlike a transmorph, though, he doesn't actually change. Maddox puts out pheromones that force the mind to rely on its olfactory sense to identify him instead of its visual sense. Even though your eyes see him as one thing, your mind translates it according to his scent. I can only imagine what he looks like to you, Jordan." Danato glanced at Nevia and once again she looked uncomfortable with her memory of him.

"How does he do it so fast?" Cori asked. "I wasn't even that close to him when he switched forms. How can airborne scent travel that quick?"

"Pheromones are a loose translation for his faculties. Proximity isn't a factor because he creates a connection with your scent receptors remotely, which means you could put him in an airtight room and you would still receive his visual misdirection. The link can last hours, but even after it's broken, his olfactory reach is well beyond human visual acuity. He could be a different face even before you could make out whether he was a person or not. In short, once he establishes a connection with you, all he has to do is think it and you will see it. He can make himself look like anyone he wants, just by adjusting his scent profile. He can even make himself appear invisible."

"Invisible?" Daniel glanced at Heaton. "I might have some uses for that skill."

"What's that, darling?" Nevia chimed from the sink.

"Nothing, dear." Daniel surrendered, but smiled at Heaton.

"You mean Maddox could be masquerading as one of us, just like a transmorph?" Cori glanced at the stairs as if she were already suspecting this.

"No." Danato shook his head. "He can't appear as one of us, because our minds are unconsciously hardwired to certain scents associated with the people we know. Closer contact would break the visual deception." Danato motioned to the short distance between them. "Also, he can't bypass the information coming from the visual cortex when the image is familiar. That's why none of us knows what Maddox really looks like. If we did, he would cease to have the power to trick our minds."

"How do you know he's not in here, though," Heaton asked, "just being invisible?"

Danato smiled slightly. "That would not be allowed. We may not sense his presence, but the house would, and she would not approve of him sneaking in here without my knowledge. Or Cori's, for that matter," he added, pinning Cori with a teasing scold. She shrugged slightly, not prepared to answer for her display the previous night.

"So, back to what Maddox told me," Cori evaded. "What does he mean about shifting loyalties? Why is he worried about the prison?"

"He means the people that are here to *protect* us might have another agenda."

"What sort of agenda?" Ethan asked as he hit the last step of the stairs.

61

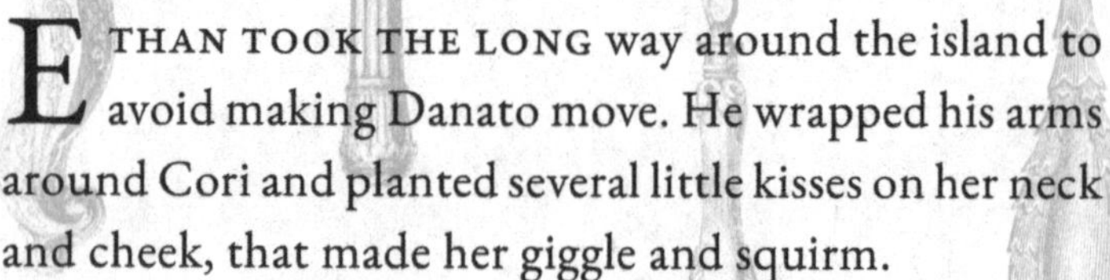

Ethan took the long way around the island to avoid making Danato move. He wrapped his arms around Cori and planted several little kisses on her neck and cheek, that made her giggle and squirm.

"Hey you two, get a room," Heaton teased.

"Let's not be too hasty," Daniel rationalized, which landed him a wet washcloth in the face from Nevia. He gave Nevia a wolfish grin and threw it back.

"We just so happen to have a room." Ethan scooped Cori up, making her laugh. "How long do we have?" He checked his watch.

"Stop, Ethan." Cori blushed.

"How long do you need?" Daniel asked, looking at his own imaginary watch.

"I'd have thought you would have taken care of all that last night," Heaton added.

"It's never enough, gentlemen." Ethan kissed her cheek again.

"Ethan, you're interrupting Danato," Cori whispered.

Ethan looked at Danato, but his face was not littered with disapproval for his garish behavior. He seemed pleased. "Not at all." Danato shook his head. "Ethan's missed you very much. I'm happy to see him in better spirits."

Ethan put Cori down and pulled her against him for a proper hug, all the while watching Danato. "Yeah, I think I just needed a night at home with my wife."

Danato nodded, acknowledging the small admission that wasn't quite impassioned enough to be an apology, but Ethan wasn't ready for that yet. He felt better, partly because of Cori, and partly because of a decent night of sleep, but he still felt betrayed. He still felt as if his years of service had meant nothing to Danato or Belus.

"I would happily give you the day off to tend to your lovely wife, but I'm not sure Belus will agree to offer her the same."

Cori snorted and pulled away to get another round of pancakes going. "Good luck with that. Although, he did try to strangle me yesterday; I could hold that over him."

"Strangle?" Ethan mirrored Danato's shocked response.

"Oh, never mind that. He thought he was dreaming. Duke splashed some water on him. It was all good."

"Remind me to thank Duke," Danato murmured.

"Efrat could have gotten him off, but I didn't want to fry him." Cori grimaced. "Again."

Daniel chuckled. "You lead a very eventful life, mama bear." Cori pointed her spatula at him, confirming that assessment.

"What's this about another agenda?" Ethan asked as he snagged Cori's plate to finish her leftover pancake. Although the space between Heaton and Daniel was free, he opted to stand on the opposite side so they didn't have to compete for shoulder room. He had gotten the gist of the conversation regarding the man with the disappearing act on the way down the stairs, but he was curious about the potential baggage that he had brought with him.

Danato glanced around at everyone. "This goes nowhere," he stipulated, and everyone nodded. "Not even Sophie," he added, looking at the men.

"Sophie's an underling." Daniel grimaced. "She couldn't possibly be part of anyone's agenda."

"Still," Danato reiterated. "Maddox is a spy and a very good one, as you might imagine. The board has used her more than once to peek in on me. In the early days, when my head was still easily turned, she got me into quite a bit of trouble. Fortunately for me, Belus's years of smoking caught up with him, and left his nasal receptors a little resistant to her tricks. The invisibility thing doesn't really work on him. He always senses her movement. After that, the board stopped using her."

"Why did they send him then?" Cori asked.

"This gender thing is really messing me up," Daniel griped.

"Maddox said she requested the assignment."

"And you believe him?" Ethan asked. Danato frowned at his distrust. "You just said that he's manipulated you in the past. Do you consider yourself objective enough to judge his motives as honorable or not?"

"Everything that comes from Maddox, be it her face or her words, should be taken with a grain of salt. The board knows better than to use her against me, so, yes, I do believe she chose this assignment."

"She did," Nevia whispered beside him. Danato looked at her, slightly wide-eyed.

"You could read her?" he asked. "Even with everything she was throwing out?"

"Not very well, but I don't believe anything she said was a lie. In fact, I get the impression that she is very dedicated to her current purpose. Dedicated enough to be trustworthy."

"What *is* Maddox's current purpose?" Ethan asked, trying to direct the conversation back to its initial target.

Danato looked him over. "Maddox came to warn me that the audit is just a ploy to evaluate the prison. The board is considering taking over the prison and shutting us down."

62

"**I** DON'T UNDERSTAND." CORI gave up on her griddle and faced Danato. "What would we do then? Where would we go?" Danato shifted under her gaze and averted his eyes. She looked at Ethan, but he seemed to have the same question.

"You gotta be fecking kidding me." Daniel stood from his stool and ran his fingers through his hair. Heaton, on the other hand, was stoic in his rage.

"I don't understand." Cori looked at Nevia, who was in mild shock. "What am I missing?"

"Sweetheart, this is a top-secret facility. They don't just send out pink slips. The only way to shut it down properly is to make the evidence disappear."

Cori touched her chest. "I'm *evidence*?"

"If the takeover was peaceful, you and Ethan could still be wiped. Some of the hunters could be wiped, depending on their cooperation." Danato glanced at Nevia.

"What about you and Belus?" Cori asked, already knowing the answer. He shook his head. "Say it."

"We are well past wiping. We would be killed, along with every prisoner housed here."

Cori's eyes watered. "If Ethan and I were wiped... Every memory we have of each other is here." Danato nodded. She looked at Ethan and found the same expression of mortified despair that she assumed she was wearing. She turned back to the griddle and scooped her overly brown pancakes onto a plate with more gusto than the task required.

"You said *if* the takeover was peaceful," Ethan murmured.

"The board knows I would never voluntarily sentence my wards to death. They would likely come in guns blazing and shoot every last one of us without negotiation."

Cori groaned and slammed her fists down, inadvertently sending her plate of pancakes flying. Ethan stroked her arm. She knew he was feeling the same torrent of emotions, but as per usual, she was the only one to actually let it show. "It's always something!" she yelled into the rafters. "I bring us back from the brink of utter destruction, and now it's on our doorstep again, only this time with an even more familiar face."

"Cori." Danato spoke softly. "None of this is certain. This is just a nasty rumor right now."

Cori turned back to face him. "That's not the point, Danato. The house, the bubble, now the Board. Not to mention my former assassin has stopped by for a visit. How am I supposed to raise a baby like this?"

"I will never let anything happen to you or Ethan or your baby," Danato insisted.

"How would you stop it?" she whined, not willing to be mollified by his reassuring words.

Danato closed the distance to her so fast that Ethan tensed beside her. "There's a short list of creatures in this world that I am afraid of, and humans are not on it." He brushed a tear from her cheek. "No one is taking over my prison." He glanced at Ethan. "*Our* prison."

"Damn right they aren't," Daniel added vehemently. "No fecking suit is going to ruin my life!"

"Easy, champ," Heaton mumbled.

"They have no right to do any of this!"

"Why would they do this?" Heaton asked, ignoring Daniel's now pacing rant.

Danato kissed Cori's forehead and moved around to put a hand on Daniel's shoulder. Despite Danato's calm façade, Daniel quickly found his seat again. After releasing his shoulder, he gave his back a pat and returned to leaning on the counter.

"This entire system is based on a discovery, a secret, and a noble purpose. The newest board members are young, privileged, and greedy as hell. There are too many years between my ancestors and these brats. They no longer care about their sworn duty of protecting the world. All they care about is dollar signs, and this place is one gigantic red number."

"This is about money?" Ethan scoffed.

Danato shrugged. "What in life isn't?"

"But Renee was talking about us becoming lucrative," Cori objected. "Isn't that what the top floor is about?"

"Yes, and I think if that works out, they might let this strategy drop. That's what we *all* have to remember. This conversation right now is about another *conversation*. No one has rolled any dice. No one has activated the plan."

"You have a fecking horde of black hawks sitting outside your front door." Daniel pointed toward the courtyard. "If that's not a threat, I don't know what is."

Danato laughed. "That is not a threat. That's a scouting party. If eighty Russians couldn't take this prison from me, forty Americans won't stand a chance." Daniel's brow perked at this new information. Cori knew the story well enough to recite it. It was like an old war story to Danato. She had always thought of it as just a tall tale, but now she realized Danato hadn't exaggerated any of it. He was more than prepared to fight for his prison, and consequently, his family. Maybe she didn't have as much to worry about as she thought.

63

"HUNGRY?" A VOICE ASKED.

Gypsy sat up on her torturous cot and stretched. She noticed the small man, Belus, at her door. He was eyeing her carefully, probably searching her for hidden weapons. Smart man. Too smart.

"Well, I was hoping for something a little bigger to slake my hunger, but I could give you a try."

"Sleep well?" he asked, hiding the amusement in his tone well.

She smirked and nodded. "Your dream feeders are a pretty pesky bunch, but... I'm immune to most things of that nature."

"Supernatural creatures or just emotions in general?"

"I suppose both." She stood and moved to the door. "I've never found the supernatural to be anything to get in a tizzy about, and attacking me with my own emotions is far less effective than a blade."

"Well, let's hope the ban is lifted before you have to spend another night in here." Belus unlocked the door and slid it open, allowing her to exit. "If you found them pesky last night, you will find them downright invasive on your second night."

"Is that so?" Gypsy rolled her neck around to get her cockeyed spine back into alignment. "I'm not sure anything could be worse than that mattress."

"The part-time human quarters are a little low rent, I admit." Belus led the way down the corridor. "They aren't exactly designed for long-term tenants, as you well know."

Gypsy found it difficult to keep stride with his short legs, but she eventually found a pace that kept her at his side.

"Speaking of things you know, who told you about our dream feeders?"

"Why do I get the impression you only ask questions that you already know the answer to?" Gypsy pushed open the section door, giving Belus permission to walk through. He paused at the gesture, once again checking her for weaponry before walking past her. She fell into line with him again, holding her hands behind her back. The intent was to put him at ease, but he seemed more unnerved, so she let them drop back to her sides. "Is that your cleverness? Disguising your intelligence with feigned ignorance?"

"My cleverness is knowing my enemy before they know me."

"And am I an enemy?" She kept her gaze forward, as he was doing. He was no doubt keeping her in his peripheral view, just as she was. It was a civil conversation, but not a trusting one.

"That remains to be seen." They reached the elevator and Belus pushed the down button.

"Don't you believe what Cori says about me?" Gypsy leaned against the wall for the indeterminate wait.

"I believe every word, but different paths in life can change people."

"Can people ever *really* change?"

"If the answer was no, then I would have arrived armed."

"Unless you knew there was a chance I could get the weapon from you. In which case you have come unarmed. Or..." Gypsy slid down the wall, bringing herself to his level. She reached out slowly for his pant leg. "...perhaps you just hid your weapon." She tugged up his pant leg and found the hilt of a dagger protruding from his sock. "Tsk, tsk, tsk, I guess you don't have as much faith in people as you claim, Ruthie."

Belus's calm façade melted with the abhorrent nickname. He reached down for the knife. Since she was already closer to it, she snatched it from his sock before he could grab it.

64

G YPSY SHOVED THE BLADE at his neck, just as Belus reached to still her hand. To her disappointment, the blade was as rubber as the bottom of her shoes. However, the blade poking her between her fifth and sixth rib was real enough.

She winced at the stinging penetration that was more than just a threat. She shifted slightly to bat him away, and he pressed harder, making her grunt. The grip he had on her forearm was strong enough to hold her. It also provided him with enough leverage to press his blade all the way in at the slightest hint of retaliation. Had she been standing, she might have still attempted to move, but as it was, he had played her like a damn fiddle.

"All I need is two inches and you bleed out," he informed her.

"Oh, sure, the one time size doesn't matter." She smiled and searched his eyes for something resembling weakness.

"You tell me, Gypsy. Can people change?" Belus stared her down, waiting for the answer.

She chuckled as best she could. "You would do it, wouldn't you?" She saw his eyes narrow slightly. "You would do whatever you had to, right?" He pressed the knife again, and she felt blood dribbled down the inside of her shirt. "Okay, okay, ease up. Fuck, I thought you would be the easy one," she seethed.

"Why did you think that? Who has been telling you about us?"

"Come on, Ruthie—" The blade twisted, pressing into her ribs. "—ahh-hhaa!" She grabbed his potentially lethal hand, but she couldn't push it back any more than she could disentangle her other hand. "Fucking dragons!" she slurred.

"My name is Belus, and if you think I won't kill you just for that nickname, you're wrong again!"

"Fine!" she yelled at him. "Damn it, Belus, I am not your enemy. I'm just doing my job."

"Who hired you?"

"I can't tell you his name." She saw his eyes flare with anger. "No, no, no!" She shifted her defensive hand to his forearm and squeezed it in hopes of mercy from his anatomical knowledge. "Seriously, I *literally* can't tell you his name."

Belus looked her over, figuring out if he should believe her. He suddenly ripped the knife from her chest and backed away. She groaned and covered the bleeding wound just to the left of her sternum.

"How does he know about the prison?"

"I can't tell you that either. Are you going to take me to the infirmary?"

"It's not as deep as it feels." Belus showed her his weapon, which was barely more than a pocket knife. He hadn't been lying that all he needed was two inches, but apparently two inches was all he had to give. "What can you tell me?"

She pulled up her shirt and examined the wound that was at best a scratch. The bulk of her pain had simply been from the pressure on her ribs. She hated being defeated, but what she hated more was being duped. "I can tell you that you're a son of a bitch," she said, pulling her shirt back down.

"I'm not sure you want to bring my mother into this, but if you insist, then I agree. When did you meet this man? In person?" Gypsy raised her hands in surrender. "What does he look like?"

"Okay, seriously, go back to killing me because your interrogation skills suck." Gypsy stood up rather than tempt him to take her up on the offer. "If I can't tell you his name, I certainly can't describe him." The elevator *ponked*, and the doors opened. "Just for the record, I still feel like you're asking these questions to verify a suspicion that you already have."

She stepped into the elevator and held the door until he joined her. He pressed the button for the main floor as the doors closed. He stayed by the control panel and she remained positioned on the other side. For a few seconds, they only glared at each other.

Finally, Gypsy gave in to the boredom of the tension. "I'm not here to harm anyone. It's only coincidence that our paths have crossed up to this point. A meeting was, of course, inevitable given our common interests in the paranormal, but I haven't sought you out. Daniel came knocking on my door about the girl. Granted, I owed him a favor, but it had nothing to do with you, and certainly nothing to do with Cori or this prison."

Belus said nothing.

"I'm not a good person," she continued. "I'll admit that. Truth is, I'm kind of a bitch most of the time, but it's not personal."

"You were able to touch that girl when no one else could. Why is that?"

"I told you, fighting me with emotions doesn't work. Call it whatever psychological crap you want. Bottom line is I don't function the same way everyone else does. The only thing I understand is rules and commands. And I don't take orders from just anyone."

"Cori thought she remembered you from a hospital in New York. Is that true?" Gypsy rolled her eyes. This man wouldn't be happy until he knew her as well as she knew him. "What made you leave that job?"

"Stupidity," she said. "I joined the military. Learned what I could, but it turns out following orders isn't enough for them. You have to be sane, too. After that, I found my current employment."

"Which thus far has been helping the werewolf coup?"

The elevator opened and Gypsy stepped out. "Yes."

"And what is the next phase of your agenda?"

"Agenda?" Gypsy headed into the cafeteria. Belus followed close behind. "What makes you think there is an agenda?"

"Forgive me if I doubt your altruistic intent. You said our paths were bound to cross. If the werewolf coup is over, aside from Daniel, what's the connection?"

Gypsy sighed as she reached the food line. She grabbed a tray and headed straight to the sausage and powdered eggs. "The truth is, I don't know what the endgame is. I don't really ask questions. Something I learned from my service."

"How did you meet Callin?"

"I was assigned to protect him." She glanced back just in time to catch his smirk. "Yeah, that was his reaction too. I did stop him from getting shot, though." Gypsy waved for another helping of eggs. "The bomb, however, was a surprise."

"A bomb?"

"Car bomb." Gypsy turned back and noticed that Belus wasn't eating. "Not hungry?"

"Just coffee."

She grabbed two cups and filled the first one to the brim. "Black?" she asked, handing it to him. He narrowed his eyes at her. "Just a guess. You didn't seem like a cream-and-sugar type."

He took the cup from her while she filled hers, leaving room for two sugars and a big splash of cream.

"You don't seem like the cream-and-sugar type either," Belus pointed out, and she smiled.

"No, I suppose not. My sweet tooth is probably the only thing sweet about me." Gypsy found a seat away from everyone and Belus sat down across from her.

"Was that the favor you owed Daniel?" he asked before taking a sip of his coffee.

Gypsy nodded as she swallowed her bite of eggs. "Callin was burned pretty bad. I had already gotten the rundown of Daniel's stats, so I knew he could fix him. I figured since I had helped him out of his werewolf debacle in Ireland, he might be inclined to help me with mine. The fact that he was honeymooning in Mexico was the only thing that made it remotely feasible."

"Daniel's healing ability is a rather recent change in his resume. I'm surprised that you knew about it already."

Gypsy chuckled to herself. "You aren't that bad at interrogation, after all." She leaned back and sipped on her overly sweet coffee. "What are you going to do with me after breakfast?" She perked a brow at him.

"You aren't a prisoner... yet," he amended. "However, we can't have you wandering the prison either."

"Oh, don't tell me I'm being recruited with the rest of them for the spring cleaning." Belus offered a not-so-apologetic shrug. "You could just lock me up. I wouldn't mind. Or are you hoping that I will inadvertently reveal my secrets through casual conversation?"

"Great minds think alike." He sipped his coffee.

"Yes. Yes, they do." She smirked and continued with her meal.

65

Gypsy accepted Belus's open door and stepped into the enormous room referred to as the "gym." Instead of being the location of a near-lethal grudge match with a dragon, it was currently being used as the location of an allergy-inducing rummage sale.

Gypsy snorted as she looked over the lines and lines of boxed junk that took up the initial spectator portion of the arena. In among the lines was the whole gang, sans Ethan. Even her two favorite blondes were taking stock of the uber important crap.

Her entrance, as unimpressive as it was without a heavy load of weaponry, drew the attention of the entire room. Especially Cori, who, despite basic self-control, was outright snarling at her.

"Should I bow or take my clothes off?" she asked her intrigued audience as she tugged at her shirt for pretense.

"Is that blood?" Nevia asked, drawing all eyes quickly to her and then back at Gypsy.

"What happened?" Danato's eyes moved to Belus as he passed her by.

"I cut myself shaving," she answered.

"Gypsy and I were just getting to know one another." Belus motioned for a sidebar with Danato, no doubt to divulge what he had learned so far.

She ignored the looks of derision she was now receiving from the whole prison clan. Apparently, almost killing her boyfriend had not improved their opinion of her.

As she waited for instructions, she looked over the inventory in the room. There was everything from jewelry, household utensils, and teddy bears, to furniture, ancient pottery, and bronzed or stone statues. One life-sized statue of a naked man caught her eye. She moved across the front of the gym to appraise the virility contained within a freshly opened upright box crate.

Just as she reached the strewn wood curls that were spilling out of the crate, Danato barked Duke's name. A half-second later, her favorite cowboy jumped to her side and placed an arm across her chest. She looked at the deputy guard who was giving her the same even gaze he had given her since she first arrived. He had no doubt heard about her debacle last night, but since she and Callin were already back on speaking terms, there wasn't much prejudice to be levied.

"I'm afraid that one's off limits. The no-touch zone starts with that monstrous piece of shit—pardon my French."

Gypsy dipped her brow and looked over the statue that more and more reminded her of Callin. "Monstrous?"

"That there is a living statue." Duke put down his arm and turned to look at the stone figure as well. "It shows you what you want to see. Draws you in."

Gypsy chuckled. "Why, so it can eat me?"

"No, ma'am, it turns you to stone if you touch it."

"Ahh, Medusa."

"Sort of." Duke frowned. "It's a tradeoff, though. Once you touch it, you become the statue, and you then must lure others to touch you so you can be free again. It's a hateful creation, and if it weren't unbreakable, I would have destroyed it years ago."

Gypsy looked at him to see if she was reading his tone correctly. "You know who's in there, don't you?"

Duke glanced at her, once again determining that honesty was still his path of choice. "Yes, ma'am, I do. I'm afraid I wasn't always as smart as I am now—if smart is even the word. At any rate, I was a piss poor excuse for a man and somebody had to pay for my mistakes. It took me a good number of close calls to finally hammer into my head that this shit—pardon me—that this stuff is dangerous." Duke glanced behind her. "I don't intend to let anyone else get hurt by this statue, or anything else in here. So, if you don't mind being bullied a bit, I'd like you to step a comfortable distance from this area."

Gypsy turned to face him directly. She took in a deep breath, revealing only the slightest of smiles when he raised his hand to his gun belt. "You know, Duke, I've never been one to take kindly to being bullied, but since you're the nicest damn bully I've ever met, I think I will do as you ask."

"I appreciate that, ma'am."

"You really do, don't you?" Gypsy chuckled at the anomaly before her. Since she had no desire to be turned into a living statue, she took her curiosities elsewhere. On the way back through the rummage sale tables, she caught Efrat's eye. Despite the fact that he averted his gaze right away, she stopped to chat him up. "That was quite a show last night."

He nodded. "Yeah, I got a little carried away."

"Don't worry. Callin has enough ego to recover. I seem to keep underestimating the people in this prison." Gypsy glanced at Belus, who was now having a heated conversation with Cori instead of Danato.

"Did you really try to kill Callin last night?"

Gypsy returned her attention to Efrat. "Yes."

"Why?"

"I could explain it, but it wouldn't make me sound any less insane to you. Speak of the devil." Gypsy watched Callin enter the gym with Ethan in his wake. They both noted her proximity to Efrat. A small smile crossed Ethan's face as he spoke to his friend. He patted Callin on the back before heading over to Danato.

Callin moved toward Gypsy. Efrat shifted back a little, unsure of the werewolf's mood. "Good morning, Efrat. Would you mind excusing us?" Efrat nodded and eagerly escaped the awkwardness in exchange for a conversation with Cori.

Gypsy took in a deep breath and prepared for the morning-after lecture that would inevitably result in another argument, sex, or business as usual. Unfortunately, they didn't have any business here and there wasn't enough privacy for the other two.

Callin took a long sip of his coffee before speaking. "I talked to the medical staff," he informed her. "They have a small supply of hCG in-house. Even a small shot should get you back to normal."

"Normal?" she asked.

"Yeah, as in free to be a whore. Or not, whatever." He averted his eyes as if he were disappointed that he hadn't delivered his news indifferently.

"Is that what you want?"

"You know what I want," he said, carefully containing his rage.

"All right, but when you look back on this moment, I want you to remember that it wasn't me that was being cold-hearted."

"This time."

Gypsy sighed and cracked her neck. She wanted to retort, but only because she liked getting the last word in. Thankfully, Danato's blustery voice stopped all conversation.

"All right everyone! Ethan, get off that!" Startled out of his contemplation, Ethan reluctantly moved away from the dining room table he had seated himself at. He joined the rest of the ranks to listen to Danato. "Belus and I will log the items and tell you how to box them. Everything that is known to be dangerous upon contact is behind the Medusa statue. That means *do not touch it*!" Danato looked over the room, checking for attentive ears. "No magic lamps, no rabbit's feet, no fertility statues—gentlemen, that means you especially!"

Heaton and Daniel snorted with contained laughter.

"Do you find painfully disproportioned penal expansions to be amusing, boys?"

Daniel turned red, trying to deny his amusement, while Heaton forcibly twisted his lips down and shook his head. "No, sir," Heaton said.

"Just to be sure, Duke and Efrat will be on guard to make sure no one forgets, and yes, they do have my permission to hurt you." As if sensing his cue, Efrat's fingers crackled with new energy. "Those items aside, everything in here has a purpose, and that purpose, be it useful or not, is in some way dangerous. That means don't break anything, don't open anything, and for the love of God, don't eat anything!"

"Eww," Nevia whispered from the other side of Heaton.

"Don't stare at your reflection too long in the mirrors. Don't write on anything, don't read anything, don't speak the names of your parents while in this room! You may encounter sprites, fairies, and/or nymphs as you are going through the boxes. They are naturally attracted to and, in some cases, bound to the items here. They may or may not run away. Don't try to make them, and don't try to communicate with them."

"Why?" Gypsy asked. Danato glared at her for interrupting his speech. She shrugged. "Just curious."

"The same reason we don't try to communicate with cows or fish."

"Not very perceptive, huh?"

"No, *we* are not." Danato leveled a judgmental stare at her before proceeding with his rant. "There are at least eight boxes of books in the mix here. Inevitably, a card or a page will fall out of one when you pick it up. I suggest that you place it right back in the book without reading it. And *especially* don't read anything out loud."

"Is he suggesting that fairies are smarter than us?" Gypsy whispered to Callin.

He glanced over at her. "Some believe the Fae have been around as long as dragons."

Gypsy looked back at the hangar door behind her. Somewhere within was a sleeping beast. "And how long is that?"

"It's highly debated, but some believe they are a sentient offshoot of dinosaurs, like man from apes. Others believe they are as old as the Earth."

"Are you two listening?" Danato barked, interrupting their conversation.

"I missed that last part where you said don't do... what was it?" Gypsy leaned in to hear his answer better.

Danato paused, evaluating her. "I said don't get cocky," he said far quieter than anything he had said so far. "Sort, clean, report, box, and distribute. Think you can handle that, Gypsy?"

"I think I can handle anything this place has to offer."

"Now that sounds like cockiness."

"No, sir, that's just confidence. Comes with the package." She motioned to herself. "If you don't like the package... well... Return to sender isn't an option yet, right?"

Danato paused, debating his next move or choice of words. "Everyone get to work!"

66

GYPSY STEPPED AWAY FROM her box and sneezed. Again.

"I'd like to believe that a talisman of hay fever is causing this, but I think your shit's just dirty," she complained to Ethan, who was on the opposite side of the table, some feet down from her. He glanced up, giving her a small sympathetic smile.

"Most of this stuff has been in there since they started the prison," he explained.

"And why exactly are we digging it out now?"

"I don't know. Some idiot thinks he can make money off of it."

Gypsy searched the room for something resembling a tissue. Her eye caught on a samurai sword with an ivory case. Even from this distance, she could tell it was an exquisite artistic achievement. She could only imagine what the sword itself could do.

"Yeah, I know the type. Capitalist with a penchant for world domination." She gave up on the tissue and did her best to wipe her nose without resorting to the seven-year-old sleeve option.

"It's a big mistake if you ask me," Ethan said.

"World domination?" she asked, poking through the wrist-deep dust bunny that was obstructing her view.

"No, using these items for financial gain."

"How could anyone make money off of crap?" She dumped out the box entirely and waved away the dust cloud that plumed from it. "I mean, you can't sell it. Too dangerous, right?"

"In the end, this stuff is just a specific spell trapped inside of an object. Releasing it is too dangerous; using it is too dangerous."

"So this particular endeavor is probably a crap shoot?" she asked, blowing away her dust bunny.

"Yeah, I guess," Ethan said, distracted in his thoughts.

Gypsy looked down at the remnants of her box. A broken stick, a dead, desiccated rat, and a stray fork from the cafeteria. She snorted at the collection of rubbish. "I don't suppose this is of any value to us." Gypsy picked up the rat by the tail and waggled it for Ethan to see.

He scrunched his nose in disgust. "I don't think so. You should probably check, though."

"What about the rest of this?" She motioned to the other two. "Oh, there's a dead spider in the bottom of the box, too. Do you want that?" Ethan's eyes landed on the objects and he stared hard at them. "Yay, nay?" she asked again. "Ethan." She snapped her fingers, and he regarded her with bewilderment. "Cafeteria fork and broken stick, anything worth hanging onto?"

He shook his head. "No."

"Okay," she said and tossed the stick back into the box.

"Here." Ethan moved down the table and took the box from her. "I'll take it to the incinerator. You can check on the rat."

"Thanks," she said, slightly suspicious of his generosity. He was no doubt trying to keep her in the gym. As if she could run amuck without her trusted entourage of weaponry.

She picked up the fork and stuck it in her back pocket for safekeeping until she had a chance to get it to the kitchen. She pinched the tail of the dead rodent and marched it over for inspection. Belus and Danato had set up card tables as makeshift desks for their inventory work. Since Cori was already logging her findings with Danato, she dangled her dead rat in Belus's face. "This anything?" she asked.

She fully expected him to narrow his eyes and scold her for the mockery. Instead, his eyes widened and his mouth gaped. He searched the stack of boxes behind him and pulled out a small black box that might have held a watch at one time.

With great care, he took the dried-up rodent carcass and placed it in the box. He closed it, taped it shut with orange tape, labeled it with a number that corresponded to a specific notation in his log. She noted that on the far end of the line, he placed a check mark under the category column "lethal." Despite the designation, Belus placed the small box in a pile with the rest of the sorted relics, giving it no further recognition.

She continued to stare at him, puzzled by his casual behavior. He looked up at her, as if her presence were a surprise. "Anything else?"

She dipped her brow. "There was a dead spider in the box. Do you want that too?" She motioned back to her table.

"Was it shiny, green, and encased in glass?"

"No, its legs were curled up like this." She clawed her fingers for effect. "And its face was like this." She tipped her head back and lolled her tongue from her mouth. When she looked back at him, he looked annoyed, but there was a sparkle of amusement in his eye.

"No, Gypsy. That was just a dead spider."

"And that was just a dead rat." She nodded to the box.

"Not quite. Back to work, kid."

Cori's gaze shot over to Belus, and then she turned it on her. Gypsy stood up straight and turned to face her. "Good morning, Cori," she said as cheerfully as she could, without sounding phony.

The woman stared at her blankly, before nodding civilly. "Good morning, Gypsy," she said, equally civil, and walked away.

"I don't suppose I should take that as an improvement in our relationship." She turned the question to Danato.

The big man's gaze followed Cori for a moment. "She believes you are dangerous to us and this prison."

"More dangerous than the military outside or the bubble inside?" Danato flinched slightly at the mention of the wizard's den, but ignored her bait. "Tell me something, Danato." She sat on the edge of his table. "Why is that fine samurai sword just sitting in this heap unused and unloved?"

"What samurai sword?" he asked.

"The one with the beautiful ivory case." She pointed her finger back to the general area of the exquisite instrument. Danato's eyes lit with understanding.

"It's not a katana, though I'm sure it's comparable. It's a bone blade. Two tusks of ivory from the same elephant. One was intricately carved into that beautiful case, the other was honed into a sword. With the help of a little magic, the bladesmith was able to make it as strong as steel and as sharp as a razor. Needless to say, it is not to be used."

"Sure, sure, I got the memo the first time, but what does it do?" Gypsy asked. "I mean, why is it here collecting dust instead of sitting behind glass in a museum?"

Danato paused, debating his answer. "The lore claims that any who wield it will fight with the strength and speed of two men."

"Nice." She smiled and glanced back at Belus. "And what does the rat do?" He looked at her and then at Danato. He shook his head slightly, indicating he didn't approve of her knowing the answer. "Oh, come on, boys. It's a dead rat. How dangerous could that little thing be?"

"Size is not always a good indicator of threat," Danato noted.

"As I'm quickly learning." She turned a wink on Belus that he didn't react to except to hold her gaze with equal audacity.

"The rat isn't a weapon," Danato clarified, "but it isn't something we prefer to play with. Let's just leave it at that."

"Fine with me. I'd better get back to work." She huffed. "So many more dust bunnies to cram up my nose." Gypsy headed back to her table, but a tremor beneath her feet made her stop.

"What was that?" she asked, though more than one mouth in the room uttered a similar question. Every face she searched had no explanation for the little aftershock, including the fearless leaders behind her.

"Did anyone touch anything?" Danato barked, and vacant stares answered.

Cori looked at Gypsy accusingly. She shrugged at her. "It's not me, Cori."

"Say again, partner, I didn't catch that!" Duke yelled over the commotion of interspersed questions and potential scenarios. Everyone turned to him. Danato brushed past her and froze as he saw Duke's face turn white. "Chuck. Chuck!"

"Duke, what is it?" Danato asked.

The Texan stared at Danato, tears brimming in his eyes. "I think Chuck is dead, sir."

"What? How?" Danato approached him, but Duke was too awestruck to answer. "Duke, how?"

Duke's face melted with the disgrace of the next word he uttered. "Ethan."

67

G YPSY WATCHED THE FACES before her transition from shock to confusion. Danato shook his head in disbelief. He pulled his radio from his belt and switched it on. "I need a report! Someone! Anyone!"

"What do you mean *Ethan*?" Cori asked. "It can't be." Her head shook with the same disbelief and she turned and ran from the room.

"Cori, wait!" Danato blustered uselessly at the closing door. "We don't even—damn it!"

"I'll go with her," Efrat offered and jogged after her.

"That isn't..." Danato growled, but didn't attempt to stop him. Not that Efrat seemed to be waiting for permission. "Someone report!" he barked into the radio again.

"They're out! They're out!"

Danato stared at the radio as a gargling noise filled the remainder of the transmission.

Gypsy looked around at the increasingly fearful faces around her. "Who is out?" she asked, trying to find the reason for such drama in an otherwise uninformed moment.

"The wizards have escaped!" another voice hissed over the line. *"Oh, shit guys! It's fucking Ogana!"*

Audible gasps filled the room, and Danato's face went pale.

"What level is he on?" Danato asked.

"Seducers!" a new voice answered back.

"He's going after Annette." Danato turned back to Duke. "What frequency is the military on?" Duke turned the knob on his radio and immediately picked up some banter about ordering new windows for the black hawks.

Gypsy noticed the door to the gym had opened once again. "The little guy's leaving. Is that gonna bother anyone?" She directed her thumb to the door behind her.

"Who?" Danato asked, locating Belus.

"Not me. Levi," Belus clarified.

"Oh, for the love of—someone needs to put a damn sign on that boy for me."

"He's probably going to try to help Annette," Belus suggested. "He's unarmed," he added.

"I'll go find him," Callin offered, but instead of charging out, he waited for permission.

"Fine, just... be careful. This isn't a fight you can win with persistence."

Callin nodded and rushed out the door to save the day on his end.

Meanwhile, Danato took Duke's radio with his own to broadcast on dual frequencies. "Attention everyone! The wizard's den has been compromised! I want every armed man up on the seducers level. Stay out of sight, but shoot when you can. They are still vulnerable to bullets." Danato stared at the faces around him, pausing on Belus.

"I'll head to the subbasement." The man said the words without ceremony, but they made Danato's head bow.

"Take a radio." Danato tossed Belus his and looked over the remaining faces again. "Daniel, Jordan, go with Belus."

Daniel glanced between the men. "But the wizards are upstairs. Don't you... I mean, Danato, I could—"

"I know, Daniel, and it may come to that, but you need to make sure Belus gets to his destination safely first. Do you understand?"

Daniel was about to object further, but Nevia placed her hand on his arm. "We understand." She nodded to Danato and followed Belus, who was already heading to the door with or without their protection.

"Watch your back," Daniel murmured to Heaton as he followed his wife out.

"The rest of you are with me. We'll head up and help the men hold off these nutjobs."

Gypsy turned to make her way to the elevator with the others, but Danato's hand latched onto her shoulder, forcing her to lag behind to the rear of the group.

"You know about wizards?" He spoke quietly as he pushed her forward.

"A little." She stepped over the junk at her feet as they went.

"So you know that they can control your body."

"Yeah," she answered succinctly, since that was really the only thing she knew about them.

"Then you know we are looking at a heavy body count."

"Yup." She would have guessed that by the panic in the disco, anyway. "I don't suppose I have time to go grab my weapons?"

He stepped from behind her, his jaw clenching tight. "We can pick one up on the way."

She climbed into the elevator with Danato, Duke, and Heaton and headed upstairs.

The air was thick with fear. Gypsy could tell by looking around at the men that this was an unprecedented occurrence for the prison. She imagined that Danato trained his men to be prepared for every scenario, but this was a scenario that couldn't be practiced or even described. Multiple dark-magic-laden wizards were tramping through the prison with nothing but human bodies standing in their way. Bodies that they could play with like puppets.

The ride was quicker than usual. The doors slid open without the usual ushering *ponk*. Danato paused in the doorway and turned back to them. He looked over each of their faces forlornly before speaking. "Whatever you do, stay out of sight. They may be dumb as rocks, but Ogana can influence them now that he has access to earth magic."

Danato turned to step out of the elevator, but Duke thrust his arm in his path. "Why don't you let me lead, sir—until you get a gun, I mean?" Danato nodded and let Duke take the lead. Heaton followed behind him, pulling a gun from the back of his waistband.

The vestibule of the first section looked fairly normal, except the broken glass door that led to the first section. Beyond that glass door, however, appeared to be the set of Dagobah. "It's raining," Gypsy observed through the misty veil before them.

"Annette must have sensed them coming," Danato said. "She'll use her earth power to defend herself."

Heaton and Duke led the way into the section and they followed. She noted a body lying just inside, presumably a cracked neck judging by the angle of his head. Danato kneeled over the man and snagged his radio and gun from his pinched fingers.

"Will Annette be able to fend them off?" she asked.

"The coven, yes, but not the leader. Ogana is different."

"Why is that?" Gypsy slicked back her bangs, that were directing a deluge into her mouth.

"The others are insane with dark magic fragments. Earth power always trumps dark magic, especially in that proportion. Ogana has very little dark magic left. He dispersed it to his coven members when he realized it was going to kill him. His magic still comes from the earth. It's not embedded, though. Not like they intended it to be. Since the bubble blocks out earth magic, it was the safest place to put him."

"Then how exactly did he get out?" She spoke quietly as they continued deeper into the mist. She could still see the two men ahead of her, but not as well as she preferred. The fog could protect them from the wizards, but it also hid the enemy. At this point, it would only be a matter of who had better eyes and a quicker trigger.

"I don't know. He doesn't have a source to draw from in there. Unless someone gave him his wand."

"Wand?"

"A stick he implanted with magical energy. He could have used it to break out."

Gypsy glanced at him, but didn't bother getting into the specifics of her broken stick. She wasn't about to make accusations against his successor before she had all the facts.

They came across another set of bodies. The heads had been ripped clean off. Gypsy looked down at the pool of blood they were walking through. She was used to looking at blood. It didn't bother her. Dead bodies didn't bother her either. The only thing that bothered her was the circumstances. This place should have looked like the aftermath of a war, but it didn't. It looked like a massacre.

"If Ogana and Annette go head-to-head, who will win?" she asked.

"She beat him once to get him into the time bubble, but only just. I'm not sure she will be up for this." Danato leaned down and did the vulgar duty of removing a gun from another corpse. He politely wiped the blood off the handle onto his pants before handing it to her. "It's not Annette I'm worried about, though. I'm worried about my men. Those wizard bastards may only have shards of dark magic, but it is as black as it comes and they will do whatever Ogana commands."

Gypsy checked the clip in the gun. Not many shots had been used up. Good for her, bad for the poor bastard it belonged to. "So, let me guess. Ogana wants revenge on you and Annette for locking him up."

"He wants revenge on me for locking him up. He wants revenge on Annette for betraying him."

68

ORI STOOD AT THE entrance to the room, looking over the body of a man she knew well enough to mourn for, and the man who supposedly killed him. Ethan's back was to her. He was facing the time bubble, frozen in place.

"Ethan," she whispered just as Efrat came in behind her.

"Cori what—oh, shit," he whispered at seeing poor Chuck on the floor, eyes glazed. There was no mistaking his lack of pulse. "Ethan, man, what did you do?"

Ethan slowly turned around and looked at them. His mesmerized eyes were cold and pitiless. Cori moved to intercept him, but Efrat held her shoulders.

"No, no, no," he whispered. "Let's just wait a second." He tugged her to the side and released her. "Hey, bud, you look a little... out of it." Efrat tiptoed verbally as Ethan followed his every movement. "Why are you here?"

Ethan paused to think about that. "I had to come," he answered distantly.

"Why?" Cori asked.

"Ogana needed the wand," he answered.

"The wand? Oh, God, Ethan, did you give it to him?" He nodded. "Are they really out?" He nodded again. Cori cringed, tears stinging her eyes.

"What? What's going on?" Efrat asked.

"He let the wizards out." The lights dimmed slightly from a distant power drain. "Ethan, did you kill Chuck?" Cori asked, despite the man's concave skull being her answer.

"He told me to kill anyone who tried to stop me."

Cori pinched away the tears in her eyes and stepped forward. Ethan reached for his gun but found it missing from his holster. "Ethan, what are you doing? Stop this."

"No one can survive," he said calmly, just before he lunged at her.

69

"**F**ECK!" DANIEL YELLED AS he hit his head into another pipe. "Yeah, let's send the tall guy down to the basement! Why are we here?"

"You are here to protect me," Belus answered as he unlocked a six-by-six cubical room randomly placed among the pipes and wiring.

"I get that, but why are we *here*?"

Nevia glanced back at him as Belus entered the room. "Contingency plan," she answered.

Belus glanced at her, either annoyed that she was answering for him, or just a general annoyance at her perception. "That is correct." He flipped a switch on the control panel in front of him and twenty more lights flickered on. A dull hum sounded as the device began to charge.

"What is this?" he asked, looking around the miniature control room. The walls were lined with tall metal containers. Their stickers were old and worn, but he could still read the flammable insignia. "What the hell are you doing, Belus?"

"The wizards can't escape."

Daniel shook his head. "I can kill every last one of them with one look."

"And now that I'm in place, you can. You'll have twenty-six minutes until the system is charged. If you save the day, then you can radio me to stop the explosion."

Daniel frowned at him. He didn't like time limits on heroism.

"Better hurry, Daniel." Belus nodded to the way they had come in.

Daniel growled and started running, dodging pipes, with Nevia hot on his trail.

70

G YPSY COULD HEAR THE crackling of lightning as they neared the action. The bellow of spells being cast from both Ogana and the witch Annette were shaking the floor and the walls. As they came to the next section break, the fog and rain were dispersed enough to see the fight.

Just inside, among the cells containing curious or frightened prisoners, was a scene from the old west, but instead of gunslingers, it was spellcasters. Annette would cast her blast wave of wind and ice shards, but Ogana would deflect with a shield of heat. When the elements no longer pleased them, they fought with pure magic: bolts and balls rippling with earthbound energy, each one more damaging than the last.

Seven stoic wizards stood guard around the battle, waving their hands to knock away the men that charged them with guns blazing. After several failed kamikaze attempts by various men, Gypsy turned to Danato.

"I don't understand. I thought you said the wizards could be shot. Those men just shot full rounds at them and nothing."

Danato looked at her. "I don't know." The worry etched on his face didn't immediately fade away. "Why aren't the bullets hitting them?" Danato asked into his radio.

"Because Ogana is protecting them." Maddox's voice sounded nearly directly behind them.

Gypsy whipped around, aiming her gun at the disappearing man. His image was not much different from before, just without the drama of a missing hand. He looked over her gun. "Easy, Black Widow," he snarled. "I'm on your side."

"What's happening, Maddox?" Danato pressed her gun down to her side.

"They've set up a protective ring. We can't get one damn shot into them. They just melt right at their feet."

"They can't do that." Danato shook his head. "They only have dark magic. That level of control—"

"I don't care what they couldn't do five minutes ago," Maddox snapped. "We got three pegged off and then, nothing. The damn things are stone statues now. We can't shoot them, we can't move them, and that battle isn't going to end in Annette's favor. She can't draw enough energy."

"What do we do?" Heaton asked when Danato hadn't spoken for some seconds.

"Ogana must be linking with the wizards, giving them his power to create a field around them. He doesn't want his revenge interrupted. We have to break the circle. Somehow."

"What breaks a magic circle?" Gypsy asked.

Danato grimaced. "There is… no, nothing that would work."

"What was that?" Gypsy perked her brow and shifted to face Danato. "You did think of something."

Danato glared at her.

"Whatever it is, Danato, we have to try it or we are all dead," Maddox insisted.

"Cori. Her rings. They might protect her from the power. She might be able to get through."

"What are we waiting for?" Gypsy prompted. "Let's call her up."

Danato ripped the radio from his belt. "Cori, come in." He waited for an answer. "Cori, come in now, we need your help right away."

"Cori can't come to the phone right now," an eerily vacant, but familiar voice came over the radio.

"Ethan? Is that you? Where's Cori?"

"Cori's—"

"Danato! The wizards are controlling him!" Efrat's voice filtered in from the background. *"Ahhhh!"*

"Oh, that's got to hurt." The radio clicked off.

"Ethan!" Danato yelled into it again. "Duke."

"I'm on it." Duke ran off.

"You've got to be kidding," Gypsy groused. "You are just feeding these men to him. We need a plan."

"I need Cori! Who else could possibly walk through a line of dark magic unscathed?"

71

CORI BARELY DODGED ETHAN'S diving attack. Efrat tried to push him back, but his strength wasn't of any consequence. "What the hell is wrong with you?" he screamed at him.

"I have my orders," Ethan answered callously.

"And I've got mine, sir." Efrat punched him in the face with a lightning punch. Though the hit didn't do much to him, the added electricity made up for it. "Cori, get out of here!"

"No." Cori backed away, trying to circle around to Ethan's back, but he turned to meet her gaze.

"Stick around; I'm not done with you."

"Ethan, don't do this. You can fight this," Cori pleaded.

"No, he can't." His voice changed slightly, adding more malice to his tone. "Because he's not running the show."

"Who are you?" Cori rasped.

"I am the sorcerer Ogana."

Cori shook her head. "No."

"Not in the flesh, but yes." Ethan waved his hand and Cori flew toward the lookout tower. Before she could stop it, everything went black.

72

DANIEL RACED UP THE east stairs at full speed. He could sense Nevia following behind, but he didn't care. He preferred to have her away from the battle, anyway. No one needed to see this.

"Daniel, wait!" she yelled from far behind him.

He reached the seducers level and burst through the doors in record time. He could smell blood and hear the explosions of a magical war, but nothing deterred him. He wasn't afraid of magic. His power never seemed to be hindered by it. He was something else entirely.

As he reached the section that contained all the action, he saw the battle raging in technicolor. There were only two true fighters, but that didn't reduce the firepower.

Daniel lit into one wizard after another. Plumes of dust were left in each man's place, a quick and easy death that extinguished their life and power with one angry glare.

Nothing could stand in his way. Not brick, not bone, not—

Before his destruction could span the entire group, one of the wizards raised his hand up high. With menace on his face, he clutched his fingers tight.

Daniel felt the pressure on his eyes and then his lids shut, blocking out his vision and trapping his only weapon behind a thin layer of skin.

Unable to reopen them, he struggled to lift his lids manually. He clawed at his eyes, all the while listening to the rolling laughter echoing around him.

"My, oh, my, what have we here? What a grand power you possess. Miserably ineffective without your sight, I'm afraid. Or is it? I wonder."

Daniel felt a tugging sensation deep within his head, like a migraine trying to take hold. Then the pain hit. He screamed as the searing agony and pressure increased. Blood dripped down his cheeks and into his mouth.

"No!" Nevia screamed beside him, shooting bullet after bullet at his attacker.

He heard the crack of bone and the gunfire stopped.

As his lids slipped away from his eyes, but before the optical nerve severed completely, he saw her body flop down beside him, eyes glossy and empty.

"Noooo!" he wailed, unable to cry anything but blood. He felt dust and ash rain down on him, but he was no longer in control of the devastation he created. His eyes, intact or not, were not the source of his power. They were only the filter.

Another shot rang out and darkness followed.

73

Danato watched as Daniel bravely charged the line. Within seconds, two of the wizards were gone, nothing more than dust being swept up by the tornadic winds of Annette's storm. The others were prepared, though. It only took one to close his eyes.

Danato waited for his head to twist in some awful direction or his back to bend unnaturally, but it didn't come. Daniel screamed, blood pouring from his eyes.

Nevia charged in at seeing her husband's torment and did what she did best. She fired bullet after bullet at Ogana's wizards. None of them landed. However, a simple finger snap caused her body to go limp and fall to the ground.

Daniel roared as his eyes became gaping holes in his head. The power that exploded from him killed one more wizard and destroyed the cells in his path—the prisoners they contained now mere casualties of the war. The ceiling disintegrated above him. Pipes burst, adding to the rain. The electrical wiring sparked. Men scattered, trying to get clear of his line of sight, but one man got caught up in his devastation.

Danato lifted his radio to his lips, uttering words he would never have anticipated. "Shoot Daniel McGrath."

There was only a slight pause before the shot rang out. Daniel flopped to the ground.

The faces around him looked at him in surprise, none so sternly aimed as Heaton's. Danato looked at him, but didn't beg for forgiveness. They would all join their comrade soon enough.

"Maddox, can you hide from them?" Danato asked the militant man behind him. It always bothered him seeing her as a man. He knew she was technically neither or both, but due to their more personal encounters in the past, he couldn't accept her as a man.

"Not as well as I would like," Maddox answered reluctantly.

"Everyone, listen up," Danato announced into his radio. "We go in together, guns blazing. There are only four left. Ogana has to be weaker. He can't stop all of us. On my count." He pulled the radio away from his lips. "You have to get to Ogana, Maddox. You're my only chance."

Maddox nodded. "I'll try, Danato." Her voice sounded more feminine, but nothing had changed in the male exterior.

Danato looked between everyone to make sure they were ready. He got the sense that everyone knew this was a death sentence, but somehow he'd always suspected the demise of his prison would come from the time bubble. It wasn't the exact threat he would have put money on, but the irony was more poetic than surprising.

"On my count. Three, two, one."

74

G YPSY CHARGED IN RIGHT along with everyone, shooting and racing toward the finish line—the finish line being the eye of the storm. In this case, however, the eye was more like a beehive.

She probably should have questioned the sacrificial orders. She should have held back and saved her own life. Unfortunately, the thrill of the attack was too deeply ingrained in her psyche. She just loved living on the edge. This time, however, she was pretty sure she was going to fall off.

She shot as she ran, as did the other men. A melee of black bodies flooded into the corridor from hiding spots inside the cells and just around the corners of the endcaps. More bullets than ever, but not a single one hit flesh.

The wizards flailed their hands, waving away the pursuing threats. Bones cracked, limbs came completely off. It was all that war was, but worse because the other side remained unharmed. She heard Heaton scream as he was hoisted high above the ground and slammed down. His body bounced unnaturally, offering no hope of survival.

Something about that bothered her. She liked him. Sex or not, he would have been a good ally. Gypsy focused her attack on that wizard, as men fell around her, snapping in half or twisting into knots.

The wizard she was targeting eyed her precise head shots that fell at his feet before reaching his skull. He reached out and gripped his fingers tight, as if strangling an imaginary neck. Her neck. She felt the force pressing on her throat. He twisted his hand, and her neck slanted slightly, giving her vertebrae a good cracking, but nothing more happened. Her spine was still intact, and she was still alive.

The wizard's face expressed the same curious shock she was feeling. He tried again, but this time she couldn't even feel the pressure of his magic.

Perhaps he just couldn't get a good grip. She slowed to a walk and dropped her empty gun. She was out of weapons, so she just waited for the wizard to finish the job. He concentrated on her and twisted his grip, but nothing happened.

Maddox appeared as he entered the circle. His blade came slashing down on Ogana's back. Gypsy smiled, happy that she would get to see the finale of this battle after all.

In a split second, Ogana was gone and replaced by one of the remaining wizards. Maddox slashed into the unsuspecting man, and he fell to the ground. Ogana appeared in the place of the man he had sacrificed, alive and unharmed. He made a sweeping motion across the room and everyone collapsed—everyone except the three remaining wizards, her, and Levi.

Gypsy did a double take on the boy, who was standing off to one side. She hadn't remembered seeing him prior to that, but apparently, he had come out of hiding.

Ogana also noticed him, but after a quick evaluation, his curious gaze returned to her. Levi took advantage of his disinterest and sneaked to Annette's side. The witch wasn't dead yet, but by the look on Levi's face, she didn't have long.

"What is this?" Ogana examined her.

Gypsy laughed. "This..." She grabbed a gun from a nearby downed man. It took her a half second to realize that it was Callin. She offered her lover another half second of remorse before pointing the gun at Ogana. "...is your death sentence."

As she pulled the trigger, a meaty fist slammed into her back, throwing off her aim. She tried to recover from the impact, but she could no longer move. She moaned under the intense, debilitating pain of her broken back.

She glanced back to see who had ramrodded her, and she found Ethan standing over her. His crooked smile was more than enough to convince her that he had switched sides.

He stalked around her and picked her up by the neck. She screamed as her rag doll legs tugged on her already strained muscles.

"Good job, Ethan," Ogana announced. "You are turning out to be quite the puppet."

Ethan barely acknowledged the accolade. He squeezed at her neck, cutting off her air. She knew she was dead, and frankly, without her legs, she *would* rather be dead, but that little part of her that liked the last laugh couldn't let it end quite so clean.

She dug into her pocket for the fork she intended to take to the cafeteria. She wanted her last memory to be of the four little tines stabbing out his eye. However, the moment she touched the utensil, it was all for naught.

75

GYPSY STOOD IN THE gym holding her coveted fork, minus one tine. The room bustled around her with small talk and rustling cardboard. The door to the gym was slowly closing, as a familiar head slipped through it. "Hey!" She pocketed the fork, grabbed the ivory tusk sword from its pile, and followed Ethan out the door.

"Gypsy, where are you going?" Danato called after her.

"Ethan!" Gypsy yelled after him as he entered the stairwell.

She ran after him, past the cardboard box he'd left at the door, and up the endless stairs. She knew he would be faster than her, but she was disappointed at how much faster. She heard her name being yelled and backup would be arriving to stop her, but she didn't have time to explain. Whatever this prophetic utensil in her pocket was about, it was at least giving her a second chance to right a wrong. And she wasn't in the mood to be killed today.

Gypsy burst through the double doors into the cavernous room that contained the time bubble. Even as she sought to protect the people downstairs, Ethan was already tossing the broken wand into the glowing dome. As it hit, the bubble shuddered, vibrating the entire prison with its displeasure at the added item.

"Ethan, what are you doing?" The guard on watch ran toward the bubble to grab out the item, but Ethan threw his fist at him. The man landed a short distance away. The side of his head looked dented, like a broken egg. The man reached for his radio and pressed it to his lips even as blood poured from his ears. He managed to speak the name of his killer before his eyes glazed over and his hand went limp, dropping the radio.

"Damn," Gypsy whispered. She wasn't happy with this outcome. She was tempted to reach for the fork again to see if it would allow her another do-over, but she decided to see how this would turn out. After all, all talent stems from practice.

Ogana's form emerged from the bubble, as did twelve gauzy-robed men to match him. The wizards looked her over curiously, but didn't attack. Ogana stopped before Ethan and touched his cheek. "Well done, my puppet. You..." His eyes flitted over his face. "Now, where did that come from? Well, it looks like you'll be part of my army for a little longer. How poetic."

"So, how's tricks, Ogana?" Gypsy asked before his private monologue could end in a clichéd maniacal laugh. Ogana's head tipped at her familiar address. "Oh, God, I know. I just hate it when your enemies know your name. It just throws the whole domination-over-the-inferior off."

"Enemy? Don't you mean prey?" Ogana raised his hand to squelch her existence, but as she suspected, the whole *master of the human body* thing didn't work on her. "Very interesting." He stepped forward, examining her. "You too." He raised his hand to touch her cheek, much like he had with Ethan. "My, it is my lucky d—" He ripped his hand away after only the barest of contact, as if he were in pain. He stared wide-eyed at her. "That is impossible. You should be insane by now."

Gypsy laughed. "Oh, Merlin, who says I'm not?"

"Who *are* you?"

"Grace Gypsum, but my enemies call me Gypsy."

"And *what* are you, Gypsy?"

Gypsy perked a brow at him. "I'm... a natural woman. What are you going for here?"

His brow dipped as he looked her over. He took a step back. "You're just a vessel, aren't you?"

"You're not really the best at witty smack talk, are you?"

"Fascinating. I might have some uses for you. I'll get back to you just as soon as I'm done with my errands. And if Ethan doesn't kill you first." Ogana brushed past her, ignoring her like a bothersome fly. As insulted as she was by the quick dismissal, the wizards followed right on behind him.

"Seriously, I'm here to kill you," she mumbled at the indifferent faces.

As the end of the line came around, she decided that she wouldn't let her skills go completely to waste. If self-defense wasn't on the table, she would have to play offense. She drew the tusk sword and stabbed it into one of the last wizards. Despite the bone being lightweight, the blade went in smooth.

The man barely yelped before he slid off her blade and to the ground. To her surprise, backup had arrived to kill the next man over. Gypsy stared at the woman standing opposite her, holding the very same blade, and the exact same face.

"Whoa," she and her mirrored self said together.

76

D ANATO BARKED ORDERS LEFT and right. He had already sent Daniel after Gypsy. He had barely stopped Cori from running out to go check on Ethan. He missed when Callin and Levi had slipped out, but he didn't have time to nitpick about following protocol when there was only one protocol for a wizard rebellion.

The debate had been long and arduous the first time around: Leave the wizards alive and kill Ogana. Kill all the wizards, including Ogana. Belus had suggested killing the wizards and leaving Ogana to serve his sentence. Annette had been too fearful of revenge to ask for anything but the heads of them all.

Danato had decided to let them live out their time in the bubble. He knew the passing time would kill them just as fast as they could, but that didn't happen. Time slowed for them, aging them no faster than he and Annette.

Now the worst had happened. They were out, and they wanted revenge. Belus was on his way to the only contingency plan available for this type of attack. Unfortunately, that left Danato very little time to stop what was happening.

"Cori, take Heaton and Jordan with you. Duke, Efrat, and I will head over to the east stairwell. Maybe if you two double dose these bastards with firepower, we can get a few clear shots without getting ourselves killed."

77

GYPSY DUCKED ETHAN'S ATTACK. Her other self was as much a helpful sidekick as a mirror image. She took a swipe at his head, only just missing it. She supposed it was going to be poetic justice that she had to kill the one person in the prison that didn't hate her very existence.

"I don't suppose there's a safe word for this," Gypsy's double said after she nearly missed getting her throat collapsed by Ethan's fist.

"I don't think he's a safe word kind of guy right now," she responded, unable to resist having a conversation with herself. She slashed at Ethan's ribs, finally nicking his flesh. "We might have better luck playing possum." Gypsy chastised herself when Ethan slipped in a hit to her chin. It was only a graze, but she had already experienced what a full strength hit from Ethan could do to her. She wasn't interested in a repeat of round one. Fortunately, her doppelgänger jumped right in to take the heat off her while she regained her balance. "I am really starting to like you, girl."

"Yeah," the doppelgänger agreed and put a deep slash into Ethan's arm. "We should see what else the two of us are good at later." She winked at Gypsy.

"Oh, I was sooo thinking that too."

"What the feck?" Daniel asked when he saw two Gypsys fighting Ethan. His ill-timed arrival momentarily distracted Gypsy. Ethan took advantage of the opening and grabbed her wrist. Daniel jumped in, lassoing Ethan's arm before he could land a potentially deadly hit.

Ethan released her and turned his fury on Daniel. He punched him in the face and Daniel fell back into Callin's arms just as he joined the party. "Dude!" Daniel touched the moisture on his lip to confirm that it was blood.

Ethan charged at him and Callin. Daniel wasn't about to take a second hit without retribution. He used his power to shove Ethan back into the time bubble. Gypsy and her double moved to the spot where Ethan's body was suspended in the enormous globe. When there was no sign of movement, they lowered their weapons.

"Huh," Gypsy said, "I guess that works."

"Not quite as much fun," her double observed.

"Yeah." Gypsy sheathed her sword, and her double vanished.

"I repeat!" Daniel righted himself and combed his fingers through his hair. "What the feck!"

"Ethan's been brainwashed by Ogana," Gypsy reported. "He threw a magic stick in and the wizards came out."

"The wizards are out?" Daniel's face went pale as he looked over the specific details of the two men lying before him. Then he noticed the third man—the one who had been killed by an impact to his head. His gaze moved to the bubble where Ethan was now in stasis.

"There's also—"

"We need to kill them all." Daniel's voice sounded cold and for the first time since they had met, Gypsy saw his pupils contract. It was there and gone, just a pulse.

"They're headed to the seducers level to kill Annette—"

Daniel pushed past Callin, and through the doors before Gypsy could finish.

"—but Daniel!" Gypsy shook her head and followed Callin out the door. Rather than waste time with another set of stairs, she tested the elevator. It arrived promptly, as if it had been waiting for her.

"What's wrong?" Callin asked as they situated themselves inside the elevator. "You're usually excited about this kind of stuff."

Gypsy shook her head. "I know, but this isn't going to end well."

"That's rather pessimistic for you," he said. "You're usually overly confident."

"Look, you're probably going to die, but just know I'll try to get it right the next time around."

"What are you talking about?" Callin asked.

Rather than answer, she exited in a dead sprint when the doors opened. She was ready for this fight and this time she at least knew what her weapons were.

78

DANATO DIRECTED HIS MEN to fire despite the lack of productivity in it. Cori's blazing blue was no match for Efrat's, but in the end, the wizards were engulfed in it. He could see Ogana struggling to maintain his battle with Annette while his servile sidekicks were in trouble.

Danato was happy beyond relief that Cori might once again save his prison. The oddity of it being with Efrat's help was not nearly as shocking to him the second time around, but it still had a strange ring to it.

Ogana faltered, and Annette saw her opening. She threw her magical attack. Danato rejoiced at the resulting hit until he realized Ogana had shifted his position with one of his underlings. Annette had killed one of the wizards instead.

Ogana's hands rolled, spinning a yarn of the electric blue before him. Danato watched him gather up the energy. "Everyone take cover!" he yelled into his radio. Danato expected an explosion from the growing mass in Ogana's arms, but he simply tossed the ball away.

The rills of electrical energy surrounding the wizards coalesced into straight streams. Despite their aim, Efrat and Cori's energy tangled in Ogana's ball. Efrat was on one side and Cori the other, each contributing a plentiful feed to the orb of coiled power between them.

At first, it was just energy meeting energy, but Cori's was only a copy of Efrat's. The source was far stronger. Cori's face muddled in confusion and concern as the growing ball of lightning came her way. The crackle of power was coming closer, spitting sparks in her face. She tried to step back, but her hands were stuck—glued to Efrat and the rising energy between them.

Danato shifted to do something. Anything to disconnect them. A sharp whistle brought his attention back to Ogana. He had a knife at Annette's throat. Danato opened his mouth to object or plead, but he was already cutting her. It was slow and Annette screamed, at first distinct, and then garbled.

79

GYPSY PASSED DANIEL ALONG the way and purposely tripped him. Several expletives reached her, but luckily, she disappeared into the fog before he could unleash his powers.

Every doorway was shattered, so a few well-timed jumps allowed her to keep her pace to the very end. She arrived on the scene to discover Cori and Efrat battling each other for the nickname *Shock Top*. Annette was screaming and struggling against Ogana's lacerating knife.

She unsheathed her sword, releasing her echo. Together, they ducked under the prevailing attack of lightning and slid between the circle of yahoos.

Unprepared for the barrage of gunfire, Gypsy felt a bullet nick her shoulder. It wasn't enough to stop her, though.

A new scream took the place of Annette's dying utterance. An explosion followed and Gypsy felt static energy raise every hair on her body. She didn't bother to look back. She had no time for details, just results.

Gypsy slid into place beneath Ogana. She thrust her bone blade upward, through his side, and up into his lung.

Another blade, from her twin, erupted from his chest, having gone straight through his back. Ogana looked thoroughly shocked at the view of his double evisceration. He stared down at his own dripping blood before his head lolled and the sparkle in his eyes faded into the afterlife.

Bullets fired all around them, and the remaining wizards—now unprotected—dropped to the ground.

Gypsy looked around at the dead men littering the corridor, some in black, and some in robes. The achievement was hard fought. Not entirely successful, but certainly less bloody than her first go around.

Annette's exsanguinated body slumped to the floor next to her, defying her previous observation of *less bloody*. Gypsy pulled her sword from Ogana and pushed him to the floor. Her mirror self stood and braced her foot on his back. With a little effort, she was able to extract her sword from his torso. Gypsy noticed the bleeding rent in her bicep, matching the one she had received from a stray bullet.

Her double clucked at the scene around them, no doubt coming to the same conclusion she had moments before. "Not quite right, is it?" She bit her lip.

"I agree." Gypsy stood and took another inventory of the chaos. "However, the bad guy is dead, and we have minimal casualties," she pointed out to herself. "Less, anyway."

"But look which one is in the casualty column." The doppelgänger pointed behind her.

Gypsy followed her gaze and found Danato cradling Cori in his arms. Efrat was kneeling nearby, head down and arms dropped to the floor. She couldn't see the expression on his face, but the abjection in his form told her it was his power that had killed her. It wouldn't matter to him that it was ultimately Ogana's fault. Nor would it matter to Danato.

Daniel and several others gathered around to witness firsthand what their hearts could not take on rumor alone. Cori's limp body was singed black; her hair was burned off. The only pink left on her body was what peeked out from her slightly gaping mouth.

"Shit," Gypsy grumbled.

"He's not going to like that," her mirror reminded her.

"I know, but can he really expect us to risk losing more people in exchange for her?"

"You!" Daniel spotted her and pointed an accusing finger at her. "I could have saved her!"

"You know he would," her twin answered, ignoring Daniel. "WWCD, girl," she teased as Daniel stalked toward them both with murderous intent.

"Well, if anything, it gets me out of this argument." Gypsy reached for her fork and the world was back to what it once was.

On the precipice of a disaster.

80

GYPSY THRUMMED THE TINES remaining on the fork before she put it in her pocket. Two more. The first time around, she'd followed orders and everyone had died.

That sounded about right.

The second time, she'd tried to stop Ethan before he could start the melee. That resulted in Cori and Annette and more than a few underlings dead. Even now, as the seconds counted down, she knew she couldn't reach Ethan before the wizards were released. She could risk the elevator, but only if it cooperated extremely well, and she had a feeling it wouldn't unless it knew that there was danger.

She had perhaps four minutes to choose a better path before someone chose it for her. Perhaps she could just announce it and everyone would follow her orders to the perfect result. Stranger things have happened.

"Attention everyone, in about three and a half minutes Ethan is going to chuck Ogana's wand into the time bubble, releasing the wizards."

Blank, suspicious faces looked over to her. Her audacious accusation had stoked amusement in more than a few of them.

"Ethan wouldn't do that," Cori said.

"He's under Ogana's control."

"How?" Danato asked, coming around from his table.

"Magic," she answered succinctly and continued before he formulated more questions. "They are going to trek up to the seducers level to kill Annette." Gypsy pointed her finger to Levi, who was already making a move for the door. "Don't move, kid!"

"How do you know this?" Danato asked, bringing his looming presence closer to her.

"No, time for that." Gypsy shook her finger at him. "I am immune to the wizards."

"How—?" Danato started again.

"No time!" Gypsy said again. "So is he." Gypsy pointed to Levi again. "Don't ask why! Ethan is on the opposite spectrum of this and has become complete brain candy to them, so avoid him at all costs." She glanced at Cori, since she was likely still thinking about rushing to save him. "Ogana is also controlling the wizards, so he can protect them while they proact them. It's a big revenge scheme on the witch, and we can stop it, but we have to intercept the wizards before they reach Annette. Once they get ponied up, we aren't getting through without serious bloodshed."

The room shuddered. Gypsy looked at Danato. He looked around, wide-eyed. If he didn't believe her before, he was starting to now.

"That's the wand going in," she said calmly. "They are stepping out in about thirty seconds. We need to go. You can call the cavalry on the way."

"What's that, Chuck?" Duke spoke into his radio.

"He's dead, Duke. Ethan killed him," Gypsy broke the news without ceremony. Duke's worry-etched face went blank, as if every ounce of optimism had drained out of him. "Danato." She touched his arm. "It's now or never. No time to deliberate."

He clenched his jaw as he stared at her. He didn't like the idea of trusting her, but she had been right so far. "Let's go! Everyone!"

Gypsy picked up the bone sword on the way out. Danato glanced at it, but said nothing. As they reached the elevators, Gypsy noted that Belus took the stairs going down, while the rest of them piled into the ready and waiting elevators.

81

"T HEY'RE OUT!" ANNETTE SAID fearfully as Danato reached her cell.

"Yes, and they are coming for you," he answered as he unlocked the door.

They had rushed to the east end of the building in hopes of beating the wizards, which they did, but with so few places to hide, they were sitting ducks to the wizards' power. He didn't understand why Gypsy was immune to it, or Levi, for that matter. To his knowledge, neither of them possessed any magic.

His mind was racing in the background, trying to figure out why Ethan had turned on them. He could only assume Ogana had gotten to him while he'd been in the time bubble, but what did that matter? It would take a great influx of power to manipulate his mind. Where would he have gotten it?

"How did this happen?" Annette asked, almost accusingly.

"Ethan," he answered somberly. "I don't suppose you know anything about that?" he asked, throwing the same indictment back at her.

"How dare you—?"

Before Annette's astonishment could be expressed, Gypsy pulled her out of her cell by her gray jumpsuit. She pushed her back against the bars. "Listen up, witch. No time. Ethan bad. Wizards coming. Lots of dead people. Me immune." Gypsy pointed to herself. "Him immune." She pointed to Levi. "You save day. What do we do?"

Annette stared at her. Her eyes dimmed as she reached for her, but her hand slid away. "I don't know how, but yes, you are immune. Which is impossible."

"Been there, had that conversation. I can stop this prick, but I can't stop him from killing every last person here before I do it. What can *you* do?"

Danato had so many questions, but he knew time was of the essence. Annette sensed it as well. She nodded and looked at Levi. "Levi." She reached out her hand to him and he moved to her. Danato let him through and Gypsy released her to do her thing.

Despite his announcement to stay clear of the level, he heard gunfire in the distant corridor. They were coming: a near sorcerer-level witch, and his entourage of vacant-minded minions that could kill all of them with the flick of a wrist. It didn't get much scarier than that. Even with Gypsy's foreshadowing, they weren't likely to survive.

"Everyone stay behind us," Annette announced as she gripped Levi's shoulders and faced him toward the oncoming battle. Her head tipped back and a slew of quiet words summoned the power of the earth to her.

The wind whipped around him as he ducked back behind the endcap of cells with Cori, Duke, and Efrat. He caught Gypsy's eye and motioned for her to join him. She glanced over the display, before backing herself toward him. He grabbed her arm and pulled her closer to his ear.

"How do you know about all this?"

"The fork," she answered. He loosened his grip on her arm. He already knew what she was talking about. The rumors of its use had tempted him more than once, but a do-over was never a guarantee of success.

"How many times?" he asked.

"Third time."

He nodded. "Any improvements?"

"I didn't die last time. I would call that an improvement."

"Who else?" Danato wasn't sure why he had asked. He didn't want to know how close they had come to being annihilated. Judging by Gypsy's rolling eyes, she had no intention of giving him a complete rundown on the body count.

"Don't worry, I'll get it right eventually. This version is going well so far," she said with forced enthusiasm.

"Just make sure you kill him."

Gypsy snorted. "Like you have to tell me twice." She drew her bone sword and her duplicate sword fighter appeared beside her. Danato looked between them and frowned. "This sword, by the way..." Gypsy smiled and walked away.

The duplicate took her place before him. "...awesome," she finished the sentiment before following her origin.

"What the hell was that?" Cori asked. "What is going on?"

"I don't really know, Cori, but we need to listen to Gypsy."

"What? Are you insane?" she objected.

"Enough!" Danato bellowed. Cori blanched at his forcefulness. "I know you don't trust her, but you do trust me, right?"

"Yes," she admitted guiltily.

"Then do as she says."

82

GYPSY AND HER DOUBLE looked over the line of wizards punctuated by the exceptionally tall Ogana. He looked more than pissed to see his surprise attack to be not so surprising.

The wind had not stopped, but the whistling sound it created had. Every movement it caused—the rustling of paper, the whipping of hair—had no sound either. As if the wind were not really wind. Or the sound not really sound.

Gypsy looked at the enthralled boy kneeling beneath Annette. His eyes were an unnatural white, fogged by whatever power the witch was running through him, but otherwise he was okay. Annette, on the other hand, looked to be in pain, as if the power she was harnessing took every ounce of her strength to hold on to. "Just stay behind us and you'll all be safe from the wizard's power." Annette spoke loud enough for everyone to hear.

Gypsy examined the barrier, searching for a specific line. She reached out to feel for it. As her finger reached the magic wall, she could feel a pressure on her finger, like water rippling around it in a fast-moving stream.

Slowly and carefully, Danato and his people created a line behind Annette. Newcomers dressed in black and heavily armed filtered in from the section behind them. All in all, nearly thirty men were ready for battle. An intimidating offense under normal circumstances, but Gypsy had already seen the quick work the wizards made of Danato's men during the first round.

"You're weak, Annette. That wall won't last more than minutes," Ogana said.

"That's all I need," Gypsy responded. She heard a curt throat clearing across from her. "Excuse me. That's all *we* need," she corrected, to include her other self in the smack talk.

"Are you sure about that?" Ogana asked.

Gypsy smiled and stepped forward, beyond the security of Annette's shielding. A torrent of wind whistled in her ear and whipped her bangs against her face. Her mirror was right beside her, duplicating her boldness. She stopped on the other side of the barrier and locked eyes with the head wizard. "Yeah, I'm pretty sure."

Ogana simpered and raised his hand to snap her neck. Much as in her first go around, there was a slight pressure, but then nothing. His smile faded, and he tipped his head to one side, examining her. His eyes widened. "No. This can't be." He looked at Annette, but the woman could hardly move, let alone converse with him.

"I must be pretty special to get two masters of witchcraft dumbfounded."

"You are an abomination!"

"Says the man trying to kill his wife," Danato said, not far from her. Gypsy glanced back at the big man, who was trespassing as close to the line of danger as possible.

"She stopped being my wife long ago," Ogana said.

"Was that right around the time that you stopped being human?" Danato asked.

A feral smile preceded Ogana's forward movement. Both Gypsy and her double flinched, raising their swords as he approached the line of scrimmage.

He barely acknowledged either of them as his newly formed boot loafers clacked on the white floor. The clothing transformation continued up his legs, changing his gauzy robe into black satin trousers and an untucked, collarless, white dress shirt. He twirled his wand—formerly identified as a broken stick—between his fingers. It transformed as well, growing into a gnarled but sturdy cane. As he came to a stop in front of Danato, he tapped it down hard against the floor. The echo of its landing sounded like a crack of thunder.

Ogana shifted his attention to Annette, who looked at him fearfully. "Bonjour, mon amour," he greeted her with veiled contempt. "Clever little trick you harvested, reinforcing the boy to ward off magic. My magic can't cross, and if I cross, I'll lose my grip on my coven. It's impressive, but a difficult spell to achieve. I mean, really, how hard is it to keep magic away... *with magic?*"

"Your magic may not be able to cross this line, but our bullets will pass over just fine. I'll give you one chance before this gets out of hand." Danato spoke quietly, intentionally reining in his anger.

Gypsy was impressed the man even had patience for diplomacy in the face of a threat this large. She would have preferred to just lop the jerk's head off, but for some reason, she felt like she needed to have a viable threat first. Apparently, being killed in the alternate timeline didn't count. If only Cori could get on board with that logic.

"Chance to what?" Ogana asked. "Go back to my prison? Live out my *endless* days in near solitude? Tell me, Danato, do you know how many years I've been in that prison? Have you ever calculated the number?"

"You—"

"TWO HUNDRED AND FORTY YEARS!" Ogana's face turned red as he spat the words out in an unnatural human volume. His voice echoed around the room, repeating the number until it was just a whisper.

Danato balked at the admission, as anyone would. Even Gypsy questioned the humaneness of a prison sentence that long. How had these men not died long ago?

"Now you tell me, would *you* go back to that willingly?"

Danato didn't answer. With the exception of his initial shock, he showed no sign of sympathy for the sorcerer.

Ogana took a deep breath before speaking again. "I'm not insane yet, though. I've kept my days and nights busy, thinking of ways to get free."

"How *did* you get free?" Danato asked.

Ogana's smugness returned, and he shifted to turn. Gypsy's counterpart tensed, ready to cut the man in two should it be needed. Instead of attacking, Ogana splayed his fingers and stretched out his arm, introducing Ethan, who was just now entering the section.

"Ethan!" Cori lurched forward, away from the established front line. Daniel tried to grab her, but he missed her arm. Callin took two bounding steps from his position and grabbed her before she could cross into unsafe territory. Cori fought the restraining arm across her shoulders, but only for a moment. "Ethan! What is wrong with you?"

Ethan marched past the line of wizards. His movements were mechanical. His face was stoic—sedate. He was on autopilot, except he wasn't the pilot.

"Ethan, snap out of it!" Danato demanded, but neither his wrath nor Cori's lamentations had any effect on him. His only interest was the sword Gypsy had aimed at his master's throat.

Ogana looked back at his toy and raised his hand to stall his movements for the time being. "Isn't he wonderful?"

"What did you do to him?" Danato's lip twitched as the rage within him started to bubble over. Gypsy wondered whose control would break first, Danato's or hers. However, Danato's questions were valid, and Ogana couldn't answer them if he was dead. And she still needed the lanky demon to make a move before she could kill him.

"It was a mistake, I think." Ogana turned to Annette. "A little leftover earth magic. Not much more than a piece of meat between his teeth, but enough. Enough to put a task in his head." He turned back to Danato. "I wanted the wand. He brought it to me. At any cost."

"How are you still controlling him?" Danato asked. "You can't impose this much control on him with earth magic."

"I didn't. He just slipped right under my thumb, along with these halfwits." Ogana motioned to his entourage.

"Dark magic," Annette whispered through her strenuous, magical efforts.

"Hmm." Ogana moved down the line to Annette. Gypsy's other half adjusted to compensate. "You sensed that as well? This one has it too." He looked at Gypsy, trying to decide what freak show she had just retired from. "Too much to fit under my thumb, I'm afraid. It's far too much for any human vessel to survive—I would have thought."

"What are you talking about?" Danato asked, glancing at Gypsy for the answer. She shrugged off his concerns. Whatever was going on inside of her couldn't be any worse than her controlling boyfriend's inoculation.

"Your little bodyguard here has gotten herself injected with dark magic." Ogana glared at her, as if she had somehow stolen it.

Danato looked at her, and she shrugged. She couldn't explain the situation, though she had an idea of when she might have gotten the injection.

"It's a wonder you're even standing, let alone sane."

"Who said I was sane?"

"It won't protect you, though."

"And why is that?"

"Because you are still vulnerable to human attacks." Ogana raised his hand and snapped his fingers. The sound brought Ethan to life, and he started forward again.

Gypsy smiled at the potentially lethal engagement coming toward her. "Oh, thank God!" she cried out, causing Ogana's brow to furrow.

Gypsy's mirror was just as pleased to be done with the bad guy banter and back to the battle. Before anyone could stymie her fun, she lowered her sword and stabbed Ogana right through the back. The sword emerged out of his side, ruining his white shirt. Gypsy was thrilled to get a second close-up view of Ogana's demise. Unfortunately, it wasn't enough to kill him.

A sweep of his hand followed Ogana's wail of pain. The movement fostered a blast of gale force wind that knocked her doppelgänger into one of the cells at her back.

Seeing her opening closing fast, Gypsy lunged at Ogana to impale him a second time, but Ethan reached her first. One punch to the chest and she was sent flying back across the magical barrier. The near heart-failing impact left her short of breath and pissed as hell.

Callin roared at the assault. He threw Cori to one side and leaped across the line to avenge her. Gypsy screamed at his stupidity, as did Danato, but he was only as smart as his instincts during a battle. She waited to hear the snap of his neck, but his body froze in near reach of Ethan's neck.

Ogana sauntered over to him, freshly healed and back in a pristine white top. Gypsy dragged herself from the floor to defend Callin, but Ogana's wand was up and tapping his shoulder before she could make it to the barrier.

A violent seizure racked Callin's body. Ethan grabbed him by the shoulders and threw him back over the line. Callin landed, spitting and frothing at the mouth.

Danato jumped through the line, tackling Ethan to the ground. "Fire!" he yelled back to his men.

"Danato!" Cori screamed, but the gunfire from the front line drowned it out.

Everyone took cover as the bloody duty was carried out, once and for all ridding them of the wizards and a wannabe sorcerer.

Gypsy stayed low, grateful that this round was going much better than the last two. She noticed her double waving at her from the barrier. She gave her a sour glare, then pointed at something behind her.

Gypsy looked back at Callin, who was still suffering from Ogana's attack. His muscles were spasming and bloating. She couldn't hear it over the gunfire, but she knew his joints were popping out of place in preparation for his transformation.

"Shit," she whispered to herself.

83

DANATO ROLLED OFF ETHAN and stared in awe at the results of the hailstorm. All the wizards stood at the ready, useless in their nearly automaton states, but unaffected by the bullets being shot at them. Ogana shook his head at his audience of enemies across the line.

"You really don't understand how powerful I am, do you?" He chuckled and dropped two handfuls of bullets on the floor beneath him. "My power comes from the earth. Metal comes from the earth. Therefore, I control metal!"

"What about bone, bitch?" Gypsy yelled as she ran back across the line. Her double joined her in the onrush and Ogana had two angry women to deal with.

Danato moved to get up, but a fist impacted his jaw, sending him right back down. Ethan came into view over him and grabbed his lapel, dragging him up for another punch.

After the third blow, Danato finally hit him back. He knew this wasn't Ethan, but he couldn't just let himself be pummeled.

The singular strike sent Ethan flying. He slid to a stop just short of Ogana's half-magical, half-physical battle with Gypsy... and Gypsy. He jumped up, snorting his anger, and strode back for more.

"Ethan!" Cori yelled from behind the line. He looked at her. She raised her hands with the usual threat of fire, ice, or electricity, but nothing came out. She looked down at her hands, baffled.

"They're magic. They won't work over there," Danato yelled at her as he got to his feet. Misinterpreting his statement as an instruction, Cori stepped over the line and raised her hands to attack. "Cori, no!" Danato bolted forward, but Ethan got to her first. He grabbed her wrists, disrupting her aim. Danato ducked the errant fireball.

Cori yelped as Ethan yanked her back against his chest. Danato moved to separate them. Ethan saw his movement and latched his hand around Cori's throat.

"Snap!" Ethan hissed.

Danato froze. There was no doubt of Ethan's strength. No doubt that he could snap her neck. The question was, would he?

Danato stared at his protégé, searching for some sign of humanity, but Ogana's control descended over him like a demon possession.

Danato held up his hands in surrender. "Ethan, fight this. You have to."

Cori freed a hand and reached up. She pressed her super-heated palm against his cheek, burning his skin with an audible sizzle. Ethan grimaced and wrangled her hand again. He pulled it up to his mouth and for a moment, Danato thought he was going to bite her finger off. By the looks of Cori's wide eyes, she thought the same. Instead, Ethan's devouring mouth slid right back off without so much as a nibble. Cori gasped and struggled even harder against his grip.

Ethan spat something at him. Danato looked down at the bobble that landed at his feet.

Cori's wedding ring.

The definitive ring in her defensive set.

Danato looked up at Cori's terrified face. She stared back at him, teary-eyed and shaking. He looked at Ethan and saw the snarl of delight on his face as his hands shifted into position.

"Ethan!" Danato leaped toward him and time seemed to slow down for him.

Ethan, however, was quick. He grabbed Cori by the chin. With one precise shoving twist, her head tipped to the side, inducing a loud crack that ought not be heard from the human body. Cori's eyes went dull and her body flopped to the ground in a heap at her husband's feet.

"No!" Danato threw his fist at Ethan, unable and unwilling to stop the rage. Before tears even had a chance to wet his cheeks, blood splattered on them. Ethan dropped to the floor and didn't move.

Danato looked down at the gory mess he had made of his apprentice's face. He was no longer recognizable.

He looked at Cori, lying there beside him, her vacant stare threatening to undo the last threads of his sanity. There was nothing to compete with this pain. Had the devil himself offered him exoneration, he would have signed his soul away in a second to save them both. Then again, maybe that was still an option.

Danato looked over at Gypsy, who was still battling Ogana. She noticed the bodies in front of him and mouthed a curse. She caught his eye and frowned.

"Fix this!" He yelled at her. "Whatever it takes! Save—"

84

D ANATO'S HEAD TWISTED ABNORMALLY, and his body slumped to the ground next to Cori and Ethan. Gypsy groaned in frustration. The heart and soul of the prison was lying on the floor in a triple heap. How had everything gone so right and yet ended up so wrong?

Ogana may not have had control of her body, but his earth magic did a fine job of defending against her attacks. Every thrust and jab was deflected by an unseen force. And since he wasn't technically fighting her, he wasn't wearing out nearly as fast as she was. With the odds already against her and a rising body count, there wasn't much more that could go wrong with this fork in the road.

A roar permeated the corridor, making Gypsy's eardrums vibrate. The sound made her stomach seize. For a moment, the battle paused, but she refused to turn around. She looked at Ogana, eyes narrowed with cumulative irritation. "You've got to be fucking kidding me!" she snarled.

"Moonlight, starlight, monsters will be out tonight," Ogana taunted her in a singsong voice. "You'd better go fetch your dog before he kills all your friends."

"Go!" her echo yelled at her. "I can handle him." Guile filled her face as she dove right back into the fight. The double even increased her speed to compensate for her withdrawal.

Gypsy slipped back over the line. As she passed by Annette, she could see the struggle on her face. She was no longer struggling to maintain the flow of magic. She was struggling to stay standing. At any moment, Gypsy was going to lose her shield, and the remainder of the prison would be done for. "Hang in there. This will be over soon enough," Gypsy encouraged her as she went by. "One way or another," she mumbled, too low for her to hear.

Gypsy stopped to stare at the feral, inhuman, and big-as-a-freaking-house version of Callin. He had risen from his painful transformation, angry and craving blood like cocaine. The men surrounding him fired bullet after bullet at him. Though he wasn't nearly as bulletproof in this form, they still couldn't penetrate deep enough to incapacitate him. As it stood now, the painful shrapnel was only pissing him off more.

The wolf swiped his hand over the line of men and knocked two or three of them aside while the others ran. His claws snagged on one of the men and he lifted him up off the floor. The close-up view of Callin's salivating jaws was enough to make the soldier scream in fear. The wolf pulled his lips back, growled, and buried his teeth into the man's neck.

"Callin! Stop!" she yelled, albeit with the knowledge of its futility. There really wasn't anything she could do to stop Callin while he was transformed. She barely kept him under control as a human.

To her surprise, the crunching of bones stopped. The wolf unlatched his teeth from the victim and turned his hooded eyes to her. The moment the wolf locked eyes with her, Gypsy felt a chill run down her spine. Something feral and dangerous and arousing stirred inside of her.

Gypsy looked at the blood dripping from his teeth. The razor blade claws and bone-snap strength in every appendage. He really was magnificent.

"Callin, come to me," she demanded.

She wasn't surprised the beast turned heel and walked toward her, but his lack of snarling, lunging, or bounding shocked her. He was simply moving in her direction. "Stop," she commanded, and the beast stopped.

Gypsy's mouth gaped, and she huffed out the excitement that only a rich girl getting a pony could emote. She assumed that this control was created because Callin had marked her, but she was shocked that the connection had transferred to the wolf. And more importantly, it was reversed. Callin may have been able to control her in his human form, but she could control him in his animal form.

This was too fucking awesome!

Gypsy laughed at the discovery, but even as her enthusiasm rose to jumping-up-and-down proportions, his body lurched and he howled. The massive animal before her turned to dust and dropped to the floor.

She stared across the powdery pile at Daniel. He was not happy to have done it, nor was she happy he had done it, but at least he'd done it to save the day.

"Get the feck out of my way," he ordered.

Gypsy may not have been smart enough to get out of a werewolf's way, but she was smart enough to stay out of Daniel's line of fire.

She shuffled to one side and watched the Irishman's face contort with pain that she could never and would never understand. He stepped forward to the battle raging across the midline, and with a sweep of his gaze, body and brick alike burst into drizzling dust.

Gypsy looked over at her duplicate, who continued to distract Ogana. At the last second, she sheathed her bone sword. She disappeared just before Daniel's obliterating power killed the remaining people in his path, including Ogana, Annette, and Levi. Daniel fell to his knees, overcome by the remorse of his actions, justified though they were.

Gypsy unsheathed her bone sword again. The mirror image appeared at her side, looking over the scattered ashes of microscopic death.

Gypsy turned to her and frowned. "We need to talk."

"Yes, we do," her duplicate agreed, and they moved to a more discreet area, away from the moaning of wounded men.

"Annette is the strongest weapon in our arsenal, but she can't fight Ogana if she is protecting everyone from the wizards."

Her double nodded. "And we can't get at the wizards unless Ogana is distracted or dead."

"It seems to me that the problem in this scenario isn't how to save these people. It's how to get them the hell out of our way."

"And how do you propose we do that?"

"Lock them in the gym," Gypsy proposed.

Her double smiled. "I think we both know there isn't a lock in the world that could stop them from getting out. Evacuation is laughable too. Danato won't back down from a fight."

"We only have one more chance to do this right. How do we stop everyone from leaving the gym and still get upstairs in time to free Annette?"

"You are forgetting one thing."

"What's that?" Gypsy asked.

Her double motioned to herself. "There are two of us now. We just need a distraction so one of us can grab the sword and slip out unnoticed. Then a little reboot with the sword sheath and voila, dynamic duo again."

"That's genius!"

"I know."

"But that brings us to another problem. How do we create a major distraction in under four minutes that doesn't draw attention to either of us?" Gypsy asked.

"I think I have an idea. It's a risk, but it might just work."

"You really think we can trust him?" Gypsy asked. "Or rather that he'll trust us?"

The double shrugged. "I suspect if you save his friend, you'll have his eternal devotion."

"Okay." Gypsy sheathed her sword, making her duplicate disappear. "Here goes nothing." She reached into her back pocket and grabbed the fork.

85

DESPITE THE ENDLESS COFFEE earlier that morning, Ethan dropped into the cafeteria for another when he noticed Callin in line for one.

"Good morning." Ethan grabbed a to-go cup and sidled up for a cup of the fresh brew.

Callin nodded to him as he filled his own paper cup. "Good morning. You look chipper. I take it being back in the real world agrees with you."

"You got the update on that?" Ethan asked, stepping up to the spigot.

"Yeah, Duke filled us in. How in the hell did you survive so long in here without supplies?"

"Well." Ethan grimaced as he added a splash of cream to his coffee. "I'll be honest with you, the toilet paper situation wasn't what I would recommend for civilized people."

"Oh." Callin frowned. "I'm afraid that's outside my scope of minimal hygiene."

Ethan chuckled. "No offense, man, but I get the feeling being without your cologne would be outside of your scope."

Callin's brow dipped at the slight insult, but it rose again with his smile. "I think you may be right. I suppose that makes me sound vain."

"No, you just know what your limitations are. And considering you're a werewolf, I guess that just humanizes you." Ethan motioned to the door. "Heading to the gym?"

"I suppose so. I doubt Danato will free me from my civic duty to his hospitality. Tell me, how did I go from being a diplomatic agent for the Council of the Moon to being Danato's errand boy?"

Ethan chuckled and headed out with Callin at his side. "He just wants to keep an eye on you. It's nothing personal, but I think he dislikes werewolves. Well, actually I think it's very personal. He had a very good friend once, but... well, you know how that goes." Ethan lost a little height in his smirk as he mentioned the unspoken inevitability of a werewolf's early death.

"Yes, I can see why he would be reluctant to want another werewolf friend." Callin glanced at him, but his expression was more bemusement than despair. "It takes a strong heart and a thick skin for a human to befriend a wolf."

"True," Ethan agreed. He wondered if one day he might also be reluctant to take on a werewolf friend. It's one thing to lose a friend abruptly. It's another thing to willingly get close to someone you know is going to die long before you. It's also another thing to do it more than once in your life. "I shudder to use any reference to dogs, but werewolves don't exactly fit into the nine lives category."

Callin surprisingly chuckled at the reference. "Oh, we do. We just use them up pretty fast. I'm sure my tagalong drama yesterday didn't help Danato's opinion of me, either."

Ethan stopped just outside of the door to the gym. "I gotta ask, what is it with the girl? I mean, I know that you are into strong women, but... she tried to kill you."

Callin sighed and shook his head. "I would love to tell you you're wrong, but for once in my life, I think I'm in over my head. I can't win her heart. Not ever. I never thought a woman, especially a *human* woman, could make me feel so inadequate."

"I'm sorry."

"Yesterday was my fault. The marking, I mean."

"What is that, anyway? I know I read something about it, but..."

Callin shook his head somberly. "Think of it as the human equivalent of getting a woman drunk to sleep with you. Only it's like keeping her permanently drunk."

"Oh." Ethan grimaced. He wanted to say something to support his friend, but it didn't sound like there was much room for justification.

"It was not my best moment. I don't condone her reaction, but perhaps you can at least understand it."

"Yeah, sure, I get it. Not so much the stabbing part, but maybe the punching and kicking."

"Anyway, it isn't the violence I have an issue with." Callin moved to the gym door. "It's the promiscuity. If I could just keep her away from other men, I could handle the rest." He stepped through and stopped midway in.

Ethan stopped behind him and looked to see who he was looking at. He saw Gypsy talking to Efrat in fairly close proximity. Apparently, potential electrocution wasn't a turnoff for her.

Ethan chuckled. "Good luck with that. I can't even get him away from Cori." He patted him on the back and veered off to speak with Danato. "Hey, I spoke with Annette."

"You did? Why?"

Ethan tipped his head. "Because she is my friend and because I wanted to tell her that we buried Addy."

"And was she happy about that?" Danato asked with a hint of resentment.

"No."

"I assumed as much. Annette is a very stubborn woman."

"Look, I know you're angry at her, but there's no reason to be a prig about it."

Danato's face blanked in shock. "Since when do you...?" He pinched back his response, glancing around the room. "I am not nearly as angry about this situation as hurt, but I can hardly compete with the pain of three people who are mourning over the loss of this woman. Since none of you will accept the sympathy of an assassin, all I have left for my defensive armor is righteous authority. Unfortunately, that doesn't work on Annette. We have been friends far longer than enemies. I think you're starting to grow out of it as well. Or maybe I am just a *prig*." Danato narrowed his eyes on Ethan, carefully containing his emotions, which again were not dominated by anger.

Ethan nodded. He understood the imposition he was putting Danato in by not explaining his motivations, but in the end, he was still disappointed that he didn't have enough authority to stop an innocent woman from being executed. "I suppose when this is all over, we should talk." Danato's face sobered. "About us. And the job I was hired to do. And when exactly I'm supposed to start doing it."

Danato frowned. "Yes, I supposed we are due for an evaluation."

"The reason I brought up Annette is because she has asked that we take on Levi."

"Levi needs to go back to his—"

"He has no one," Ethan answered.

Danato took in a deep breath. "I don't know, Ethan." He looked over at Levi. Grief aside, the boy looked lost and unsure of himself. "I don't want to subject another boy to this fate. It was hard enough the first time." Danato looked back at him, once again offering an apology for his sins of dedication.

Ethan had long since given up his resentment on that account, but he knew Danato never would. "I know, but like me, Levi has had a rough life. Annette saved him, and now she's here." Danato glared at him. "That's not a dig, Danato, just a fact. I don't know what your plans are for Annette, but we both know she's not as young as she looks. Without her, he had nothing anyway."

"All right, I'll take him on, but at guard level. I don't want him living with us. We have enough visitors in and out as it is. Let's not start passing out keys."

Ethan nodded, but he didn't agree. Levi was a friend, not a rented prisoner. He deserved more spacious accommodations, but he could argue for different accommodations when Danato's house was empty again.

He turned to see whether Cori was done speaking to Belus, and found her conversing with Efrat. He frowned at the sight of them gazing at each other. His mind rationalized that she had only been with him two days, but that was still too long for him to be alone with the only woman he could touch.

Ethan sat down in a nearby chair and rubbed away the troubles from his face. When he looked up again, he realized he was sitting at a dining room table. One of the many large furniture pieces that had been stuffed into their tiny prop room closet.

He looked over the length of the glossy red mahogany. Six chairs came with the set. He sat in one and a strangely familiar old man sat at the head, staring at him.

Ethan looked at him, baffled by his presence, but the old man stared squarely at him through accusing eyes. "Who are you? How did you get here?"

"Stop blaming her for your insecurities," the old man snapped.

"What? Cori?"

"She loves you, you damn idiot. If you want to keep her, then stop treating her like a ticking time bomb of adultery."

Ethan shook his head. "I—" A body slammed onto the table, out of nowhere. The choking, gasping upside-down face before Ethan was his own. A duplicate of himself was fighting a perpetrator that was invisible from the elbows up. Down from the elbows was a strong pair of hands that were strangling him. "What the hell?"

"Gun!" the upside-down Ethan rasped as he reached out for assistance. "Gun!" he rasped louder, expressing urgency with wide, bloodshot eyes.

"Well, you'd better give it to him," the old man scolded.

Ethan pulled his gun and handed it to his other self. His future self?

He disappeared off the table, and Ethan looked across the table at the old man. Was this his future self as well?

"Ethan, get off that!"

86

ORI COULDN'T HELP GLARING at Gypsy as she walked through the doors. The woman was starting to reveal her true colors. Last night was proof of who she was. The fact that they couldn't simply kick her out was more than an irritation. It was a mistake. Someone was going to get hurt because of this woman. She just knew it.

"Shall I take a bow or take my clothes off?" Gypsy asked, nearly beginning to disrobe. Cori shook her head at the audacious display.

"Is that blood?" Nevia asked, no doubt smelling it more than seeing it. Upon further inspection, Cori could see Gypsy's shirt was marred by a blob of darkness.

"What happened?" Danato asked Belus as he passed her by.

"I cut myself shaving," Gypsy's smart mouth continued.

"Gypsy and I were just getting to know one another," Belus said as he motioned for a sidebar with Danato.

Gypsy walked around, inspecting the prop room secrets. Cori joined the hubbub. As she approached, she caught the middle of Belus's discussion. "—then she turned the knife on me."

"What?" Cori whispered.

"It was just a ruse, Cori. She was testing me. And I was testing her."

"And what did you find out? That she might kill you, given the chance?" Cori seethed. "Duh!"

"Duke!" Danato hollered over at Duke.

Cori glanced back to see what trouble was starting. Gypsy was naturally getting near something she shouldn't. When she looked back, Belus was glaring at her.

"What did you find out, Belus?" Danato asked, releasing her from his shackled gaze.

"I found out that whoever she is working for has put a mental block on her. She can't reveal his identity, or even a description."

"That doesn't bode well." Danato pinched his lips. "Definitely a supernatural, then."

"Yes, and a rather informed one," Belus added.

"And we are adding to that information by revealing every secret we have." Cori motioned to the room.

"We will wipe her before she leaves," Danato pointed out, as if it shouldn't need to be.

"We should save ourselves the trouble and put her back in a cell," Cori grumbled.

"Cori," Danato scolded gently.

"May I speak to you a moment... privately?" Belus stared her down. She glanced at Danato as if he might protect her from the ass-ripping, but he only offered her a nod of release. Cori followed Belus to the least populated area and crossed her arms in preparatory defense. She might have normally bent to one knee for it, but she saw no need to be closer to eye level for this. "What is wrong with you?"

"How can you ask me that?" She nodded to Gypsy.

"Cori, this isn't about Grace Gypsum or Gypsy Grace. This is about you keeping your head on straight in the face of an enemy."

"I do have my head on straight. It's everyone else that is blind to the threat before them."

"Why are we blind? Because we aren't taking every opportunity to discredit her and dig up the past? The truth is, Gypsy is the least of our problems, and you know that. You need to get focused and get your emotions under control. And that is final," Belus warned with a raised brow before turning to leave.

"The hell it is," she murmured low enough for him to hear, but no one else.

He turned back a hard gaze that reminded her of the first time she had truly disappointed him. She had spent nearly a year regaining his trust and even longer his respect. She knew she was about to put herself right back to square one, but she couldn't let his command go uncontested. "What was that?" he asked, double-dog daring her to keep going.

"It's not final, because that was all bullshit."

His brow raised, and he stepped back to her. "What was bullshit?"

"You. Your bravado and reserved emotions. You want me to be like you, but the truth is, I already am. Just because you don't show your feelings doesn't mean that you don't have them. And it certainly doesn't mean that you're immune to them." She paused to let him counter, but he was waiting to hear the whole argument. "I saw the look on your face when you were strangling me."

He rolled his eyes. "I was half asleep."

"Doesn't much matter, does it? You took one look at me, saw Olivia's face, and attacked."

"That is different," he defended.

"No, it isn't. You had the duty of killing a monster and so did I, but my monster isn't in my dreams. She's on my goddamn doorstep!" Cori seethed low, so she didn't draw attention to the nature of their argument. "Now you tell me, Belus. Would you have control of your emotions if Olivia walked through that door?" Cori nodded to the door, where Callin and Ethan were just entering.

Belus looked her over, his own anger bubbling just under the surface. After a long moment, he spoke. "Yes," he said, deflecting her entire argument.

She pinched back her lip, trying not to let her chin shake as she regained control of her composure. "Then you must be horribly disappointed in me."

"Yes," he said again, putting another nail in the coffin of her dissension. The fact that he knew it made it that much harder to take. "Are we done here?" he asked, forcing her to avert her eyes, so she didn't cry.

"Yes." She smiled insincerely past watering eyes. "I think we are *done*."

Belus moved to his table and went about his duties without a hint of emotional discontent for their interaction. She, meanwhile, was ripped to shreds, barely containing her apparently overemotional reaction.

"Trouble in paradise." Efrat strolled over to her. She looked up at him with the intention of glaring, but she couldn't manage to hold it. He seemed to understand that she wasn't in the mood for his humor. "What's he on about now?"

"Nothing, I just made the mistake of picking a fight with a stone-cold man." Cori wiped her eyes discreetly.

Efrat hissed. "Ugh, many have tried and failed on that front. You can't really blame him, though. That guy's been fighting for respect his whole life."

"And where's *my* respect?"

Efrat shrugged. "He does respect you. You just can't see it because his reactions are more subtle."

"So he respects me, but he doesn't want me to know it. Good to know." She paused, waiting for Efrat to say something, but when the silence dragged on too long, she gave in. "Look, Efrat, about yesterday. I was out of line. I shouldn't have accused you of wanting Ethan dead."

Efrat nodded but didn't look at her. "I think I'm well past the point of being a good guy, Cori, but I'm not nearly the asshole you keep thinking I am." He looked at her, revealing the hurt her words caused.

"I know. I'm sorry. It's just... With everything you said before, I thought..."

"What? That I was willing to add murder on top of infidelity?"

Cori glanced to see if anyone was close enough to hear. "It was just a kiss, Efrat."

"*Two* kisses, and damn good ones," he murmured. "I take it from my still beating heart that you didn't mention it to Ethan."

Cori bit her lip. "No, I did that for you."

"Don't do me any favors. I can handle your husband."

"No..." Cori caught his gaze. "The kiss. That was for you."

"A sample of what I'm missing?" He narrowed his eyes at her.

"No, I just thought you could get it out of your system once and for all. I mean, you said it yourself; it's not really about me. It's about the rings." She lifted her hand.

"Yeah." His eyes danced over hers. "I think it was."

Before Cori could question his response, Danato started his "hands-off" speech.

87

GYPSY ARRIVED BACK WHERE she had started: fork in hand—only one tine left—and the door to the gym was swinging shut following Ethan's recent exit. Chaos would ensue in roughly four minutes. It was now or never.

She pocketed the fork and approached Duke. As she passed by Callin, she tapped her ear, signaling for him to listen in. He could probably hear just about everything in the small confines of the gym anyway, but just in case.

"I know you're trying to help, Cinder-fella, but you just keep burning boxes," Duke scolded Efrat, who was holding out his arms to be loaded up with cargo.

"Just put it in my arms."

"And who's going to..." Duke trailed off as Gypsy quite literally got in his face. Duke dropped his box to one side on the floor and grasped his gun. "Can I help you?"

"Yes, Duke, you are the only one who can help." Gypsy moved her hand slowly and grabbed the radio from his belt. His face was marred with confusion, but he didn't stop her. "I found out what the scariest thing in this prison is."

Gypsy put the radio to her lips. "Chuck?" Duke glanced at Efrat, but he was just as baffled by her behavior.

After a moment's pause, a questioning voice came over the line. *"Yeah."*

"Listen very carefully. In a few minutes, Ethan is going to walk through your doors and pitch Ogana's wand into the bubble." Duke's eyes widened fearfully. She lifted her finger up into his face to forestall his brewing questions. "If you want to live through this, don't try to stop him. When the wizards come out, stay clear of them too."

"Who is this?" Chuck asked.

Gypsy clicked off the radio and latched it onto her own belt. "Some shit is about to go down, but I can stop it. I can save everyone, but I only have one shot. I don't have time to explain. I need a distraction. A big one. Like last night." She glanced at Efrat, who was listening carefully. "Once Callin throws me clear, I want an all-out brawl."

"Why would he—?" Duke questioned her, but Gypsy smothered his query with a deep kiss. Given the serious and purposeful nature of the kiss, her gag reflex thankfully stayed in check. She was just beginning to rake her finger through his surprisingly soft hair when a deep growl sounded behind her.

Callin grabbed her shoulders and ripped her away from Duke. She vaulted through the air and landed just right. She came to a skidding stop right beside the bone sword.

At first, everyone's eyes were on her, trying to discern the reason for her abrupt but short flight. As instructed, Callin added to the display by throwing Duke across the gym into the arena zone. Danato rushed over, demanding Callin's obedience. Belus passed by her, giving her an exhaustive scowl. "Must you?" he asked.

She smiled and shrugged. As she rose from the floor, she dragged the bone sword right along with her, hiding it carefully behind her back as she shifted closer to the door. With all eyes on Efrat's electrical counter, no one noticed the appearance of a second Gypsy.

"Stay here," Gypsy whispered to her double. "Try to keep them all here."

She nodded, keeping the sword hidden, but in hand.

Gypsy was out the door. Only the squawk of the hinge would alert anyone, but how could they suspect anything when she was clearly still in the gym with the rest of them?

88

ORI GLANCED BACK JUST in time to see dark hair and a black uniform leaving the gym. Gypsy was standing very near the door, so it wasn't her. She was proudly observing the melee between the three men as Danato threatened them, in vain, to stop. All amusement left her face the instant she caught her watching her.

Cori moved over to her. "Who just left?"

She glanced at the door, then at the clock above it. "Ethan," she answered.

Cori looked around the room and noticed that Ethan was indeed gone. She assumed he had gone to retrieve more boxes from the prop room. As she shifted toward the door to check, Gypsy grabbed her arm.

Cori looked down at the pinching grip on her forearm, then up to Gypsy's stern gaze. "Don't leave this gym."

It took a moment for Cori to wade through the cuss words and retorts that lined up at the edge of her lips. "Let go of me or I will burn you to a crisp."

Gypsy's jaw tensed. Her eyes flickered over Cori's rings before she ripped her hand away.

Gypsy gave her a menacing look as she backed away toward the door. The more angry she looked, the more Cori knew she needed to find out what was going on outside of this gym.

Cori ran from the gym and peeked into the stairwell. She could hear someone stomping up the stairs well ahead of her. "Ethan?" she yelled up, but there was no response.

She took a chance and switched to the elevator. The doors opened, ready and waiting for her. She stepped inside and pushed the button for every floor. If her luck held out, she could get ahead of him and find out what was going on.

The doors closed and her ascent began. Between floors, the car shuddered, and the lights flickered. She feared the worst and braced herself for a sudden drop, but the elevator continued up. It skipped right past the first two floors and opened on the third.

89

G YPSY RAN NONSTOP UP the stairs and down the corridors toward the east stairwell. Annette's cell was still one more floor up and a few more sections back, but she was going to make it in plenty of time.

She hadn't really thought about how she would break her out, but she sensed that wouldn't be a problem for the witch. From what she understood, her incarceration was more about embarrassment than containment.

Gypsy felt a blast of heat at her back that knocked her to her knees. She grunted at her sudden joint-torturing stop. She wheeled around to see her attacker and saw Cori racing through the section after her. "Son of a bitch!" Gypsy yelled as she got up to face the woman. "I don't have time for this!"

Cori skidded to a stop in front of her. "Am I interrupting your plans?" she asked, her eyes bright with renewed vengeance.

"Yes, I have to go free, Annette."

"I can't let you do that." Cori shook her head. Two swirling fireballs blossomed in the palms of her hands, just waiting to be hurled.

Gypsy shifted, bringing her sword to the ready. "And I can't let you stop me," Gypsy said earnestly, hoping the woman could read the urgency on her face.

"Care to venture a guess who will win this fight?" Cori asked as she admired her literal fire power.

Gypsy sighed and clenched her jaw. She hated admitting defeat, but Cori was right. Just as Efrat could beat Callin, Cori could beat her.

That was assuming Gypsy fought fair.

"I have no wish to hurt you, Cori." Gypsy slid her bone sword back into her sheath. A misleading display of clemency. "But I will if I have to." She slid the sword right back out.

Cori turned her stance slightly, instinctively readying herself to parry even though she was armed with fire instead of a sword. As she shifted, Gypsy caught sight of her doppelgänger. The tall, sexy brute of a woman had rebooted and appeared right behind Cori.

The mirror smiled and raised her surgically sharp blade high in the air. She brought it crashing down on Cori. It slashed through the air with nary a pause, even when it hit Cori's left wrist.

Gypsy cringed at the hand that flopped to the floor between the two women. Cori looked back, first identifying the duplicate and then the bleeding stump at the end of her arm. She screamed, either in horror or agony. She dropped to the ground and grabbed her hand as if she might just put it back on. With the threat of fireballs no longer on the table, Gypsy and her duplicate ran on to finish saving the day.

"Damn!" Gypsy admonished her partner as they ran into the stairwell together. "I thought you were just going to put the blade to her while I got away."

"This works better." The double shrugged indifferently.

Gypsy frowned at herself. "Wow, I really am a bitch."

90

"THE WIZARDS ARE OUT!" Annette decreed when Gypsy got to her cell.

"Yeah, tell me something I didn't know an hour ago. Open this door." Gypsy flicked the lock. Annette barely closed her eyes, and it snapped open. "Can you handle Ogana?" she asked as she slid the door open the rest of the way.

"I don't—"

"Can you keep him off me long enough so I can kill the wizardettes?" Gypsy forcefully pulled her out of the cell.

"Yes, but the wizards will kill you."

"No, they won't."

"How will you...?" Annette noticed Gypsy's replica standing off to the side. With blood already staining her sword, she was looking a little more sadistic than necessary this early in the fight.

"Don't worry, she's with me."

"I can see that. How do—?"

"It's too late for questions, Annette! Get your Zen or center, whatever you need, cause we are going to war in a matter of seconds." Gypsy pointed to the general location of the soon-to-arrive rebels.

Annette paused as if she were trying to decide if Gypsy was trustworthy. "Whose blood is that?" she asked, nodding to the blood that was also spattered across Gypsy's face and neck.

Gypsy bit her lip, trying desperately not to smile at the serious query. "They'll live, but only if you and I work together. Right here, right now. *We* have to stop the wizards."

Annette seemed to accept that answer and readied herself by calling up a firestorm of wind. The tempest swirled above her—a mixture of wind, fire, and lightning. The woman's previously sorrowful appearance melted away as she took in the energy of her earth magic. When she was finished flexing her muscles, the power above her settled into a quiet threat, as if it were a loyal parrot perched on her shoulder.

Gypsy didn't know much about witchcraft, but if Annette was the exemplar of a *dabbler* in the occult, then she was pretty sure she understood why Danato had executed a potential sorceress. This was already a hell of a lot of power for someone claiming the title of human.

Annette turned to her and her duplicate, eyes glazed and slightly high from power. "He's coming," she said, her voice slightly deeper than it should have been.

"Don't worry about the wizards. Just keep King Cocky occupied." Gypsy moved into position ahead of Annette.

"And I thought *we* were scary," her double murmured to her before creating the other leg of their tripod.

"I don't like that you're funnier than me." Gypsy perked a brow.

"I don't like that you haven't complimented my ass yet."

Gypsy smirked and raised her sword. "All in good time, hot stuff." She faced the section door just as it exploded out at them. She shielded her face, but the glass hit an invisible barrier and dropped in a pebbled row near her feet.

She peeked up from her arm and examined the line of wizards backing Ogana like a badly dressed British lineup. The almost-sorcerer looked over her and her double with amusement before shifting his gaze to Annette.

"You're looking well, Mabel." Ogana's mouth twisted, chewing his words carefully before spitting them out. "Or is that just your veil?"

"You should have stayed in your cage, Ogana. Danato won't make the same mistake twice."

"Neither will I," Ogana snarled.

After a short pause for dramatic consensus, Gypsy interrupted. "I know you guys have a lot to catch up on, but I've heard this story once already, and frankly, I really need to kill these guys before anyone else shows up."

Ogana examined the strange challenge before him with annoyance.

"No, seriously. I just need someone to threaten me. It's apparently part of my quit-killing-innocent-people rehab program."

"If you are in such a hurry to get killed, then I can help you with that." Ogana raised his hand and snapped his fingers. Nothing happened, but her partner took the opportunity to have the spotlight and did her best interpretation of the Darth Vader choking scene. Ogana frowned at her theatrics. "What is this? How are you doing this?"

"Oh, did I forget to mention I'm hopped up on dark magic?" Gypsy said.

"That's not possible." Ogana's face squeezed inward in a mixture of anger and befuddlement. The combination made him look like a pissy three-year-old. "Stand aside, *vessel*, or I will destroy you!"

"Yes, that'll do. Game on!" Gypsy ran past Ogana to his front line of lackeys. The wizards were mostly entranced by their link to Ogana, but their hands rose defensively.

The first two kills were nearly simultaneous decapitations. Gypsy was once again surprised that the bone blade could cut as smoothly as her katana, but she supposed that was the benefit of magical honing.

"I love this sword!" her double remarked before burying it deep into the belly of another wizard. For a moment, Gypsy wondered how mad Danato would be that she was hacking up his prisoners. Then again, better them than his friends.

"You meddlesome bitch!" Ogana yelled at her, but an invisible force dragged his body across the white floor before he could attempt a physical confrontation with her.

Already behind on the count, Gypsy returned her attention to the wizards. The kills were easy; nothing like she preferred. The men weren't even fighting back. It seemed like a complete surprise to them when they started gargling their own blood, as if they were only just waking to reality at the moment of their death.

Gypsy checked in on her double and watched her kill the last man by slipping her blade through his chin and into his skull. She watched herself smile as she ripped her sword back out. The duplicate turned to her, eyes glimmering past the many layers of blood she had earned. Gypsy frowned at her. "I really am fucked up, aren't I?"

The double perked her brow. "Oh, yeah, you're bonkers."

Gypsy turned to see what she could do to help Annette. The witch and wizard were throwing magic at each other in the form of miniature hurricanes, hailstorms, fireballs, and pure energy. Despite the massive power being quite literally tossed around, Gypsy fought her way through the shrapnel-filled wind tunnel that had formed around the two of them.

"Just let them finish!" her twin scolded her for the stupidity.

A shard of glass ripped open her scalp. She yelped at the pain. She noticed her double cradling her own scalp outside of the storm.

As she neared the eye of the storm, she took inventory of her pain. She was bleeding badly, but nothing lethal yet. And she was still conscious. Good enough.

She raised her sword as she entered the private battlefield. Ogana saw her and turned a wide-eyed glare on her. "Impossible!" he roared. Before she could impale him, he shot a ball of pure energy at her.

She didn't remember her trip through the air, but she was certain the in-flight movie was just her life flashing before her eyes.

The landing, however, was extremely memorable.

Gypsy rolled to a skidding stop and hit the section wall. Her double crouched down beside her to inspect her. "I told you to wait."

"I almost had him," Gypsy rasped.

"Yeah, you did, but he called in reinforcements." Her doppelgänger jerked her head toward Ethan, who had just entered the section ready for a fight.

"Shit, I forgot about him."

Gypsy's mirror pulled her up, taking liberties with dusting her off. "You want me to take care of him? You can have another crack at Hurricane Ogana."

Gypsy looked over Ethan as he inspected the room with vacant eyes. Even in his relaxed position, his strength was well defined. He wasn't as strong as a werewolf, but the line was very thin. "No, I want this one. You give the whirlwind a shot."

"Oh, sure, take the hot one," she griped, but moved over to the other battle.

"You still got mad cow disease, Ethan?" Gypsy asked as she circled around to fight him.

He looked her over, his eye catching on the bone sword. He reached out his hand and the bars on a nearby cell started to vibrate, sending the unfortunate occupant ducking under her bed. One of the metal bars broke loose and propelled itself to Ethan's hand.

He caught it with ease, and Gypsy smiled at the accomplishment. "Ogana had better keep his power for Annette or he's going to get distracted."

The bar melted and morphed in his hand until it resembled a sword. Ethan smiled back at her. "I can take it from here."

Gypsy closed her eyes and sucked in a deep breath. She let out an ardent moan that was inappropriate for pre-battle circumstances and opened her sly eyes on Ethan. "I was so hoping to feel your long steel against my bone." She waved her sword at him.

"You'll definitely be feeling it when I'm done with you."

"Oh, stop the foreplay, I'm already wet," she insisted and set her stance.

Ethan leaped forward fearlessly. She deflected his first blow—that, as it turned out, was not his full strength. He intended to make this last. As excited as she was to test his endurance, she knew it was only a matter of time before someone arrived to break up the fight and she was pretty certain she would be on the breaking end of that.

91

DANATO ARRIVED BY CORI'S side just after Efrat. He feared the worst when he saw her pale face, but she was alive. She was barely conscious, bleeding excessively and in severe pain. "Daniel, get over here!" He hollered back as the others arrived in the section.

"Let me see." Efrat tugged the radio from her clutched hand and tried to unfurl her fetal position so he could see where the blood was coming from. She whimpered, cradling her wrist under her arm. "Come on kitten, what's... Oh, fuck! Daniel! Now!" Efrat gave him a worrisome look, but Danato still couldn't see what was causing his alarm.

"What is it?" Danato asked.

Efrat reached within the crook of Cori's body and pulled up a hand. A bloody severed hand. Danato's mind blanked, staring at the atrocity before him. It took him a moment to recognize the rings on the fingers and come to terms with what he was looking at.

"Daniel?" Danato looked over at the man, who was staring at the limp, pale appendage in Efrat's hand. "Yes or no?" Danato asked. "We need to know now."

"I... The bone..." Daniel gulped.

"I just need an answer, Daniel. We'll live with the result either way. Just tell me if we need a surgeon."

Daniel panted before pinching his face in determination. "I can do it."

"Daniel," Heaton said quietly behind him. "The surgeons can at least get it back on if it's too much."

Daniel glanced at him, but he shook his head. "Nah, I got it. Did Ethan do this?" he asked with a frown as he kneeled down beside her.

"What?" Cori yelped as Efrat shifted her hacked wrist from beneath her arm. "Why would *he* do this?"

"He—" Daniel started.

"Was this a wizard?" Danato asked before Daniel could explain what Chuck had reported to them. He didn't understand why Ethan had let the wizards out, nor did he understand why Gypsy had known he would. He especially didn't understand why his best guard would conspire to distract them with a ruse so she could get away from them.

"No, why are you asking me that?" She panted, trying to speak between grunts of pain. "Efrat, you're hurting me."

"It'll help, trust me," he whispered as tentacles of blue surrounded her bleeding forearm.

"Who, Cori?" Danato asked again.

She looked back at him in disbelief. "Gypsy!" she screeched. "The bitch I've been warning you about since she arrived! She's gone upstairs to free Annette."

Danato had already received reports that the wizards were on the seducers level. He had warned everyone to stay clear, but he had been too late for a few of the men. He suspected Ogana was headed straight for Annette. Apparently, Gypsy knew that too. How was a question for later.

"Get her put back together and down to the infirmary. Everyone else with me," Danato barked and led the way out of the section.

"Hold her still," Daniel instructed Efrat. "Keep your fingers back."

Danato missed the rest of the instructions Daniel offered as he crossed into the next section, but he heard Cori's screams well into the next.

92

As PROMISED, ETHAN'S PROWESS with a sword was not over-advertised. It only took Gypsy a minute or two to get a feel for his movements, then she was ducking and weaving his attacks. He was strong, but she was fast.

At first, she was worried that his steel would break her bone sword, but the elephant tusk held. She was even able to use the sheath as a shield.

She fell back as he battled her with increasing strength. She wanted to give him the appearance that he was winning.

As she angled back around, she could see her double fighting through the wind to get to Ogana. Despite her progress, she seemed to be caught in the gale. She wasn't sure if that was because Ogana had upped his game, or because as a double, she lacked the sheer will to surmount his offense.

At the far end of the section, Danato came tromping in with his army, such as it was. Without Daniel's eyes, Efrat's lightning, or Cori's rings of fire, it was just a bunch of guns and a werewolf. More of the men in black filtered in behind him, responding to the call to arms.

Ogana also noticed their arrival. His attacks increased in strength, forcing Annette to her knees. She was strong, but whatever flowed through this man's blood was stronger than the source she was drawing from. As soon as he killed her, the rest would die soon after. All the work she had put into this rescue mission was about to go down the drain.

Lucky for her, she had something pretty powerful running through her veins, too.

Gypsy ducked and rolled away from Ethan. Upon rising, she sheathed and unsheathed her sword. "Your turn!" she yelled at her body double as she magically arrived at her side.

Gypsy didn't bother to explain the change of direction, nor did her double question it, mostly because Ethan got the drop on her the moment she appeared.

Gypsy ran headlong at the tornado, no longer concerned for the shrapnel that had already permanently ruined her hair line. She no longer cared about pain or strategy, only winning. That was all she ever cared about. No matter the game. No matter the consequence. She had to win.

Gypsy cleared her mind of anger or expectations and focused on a singular goal. She pushed into the gale. The willful wind that had stymied her progress before now felt like a breeze to her. Even the shrapnel that she had previously flinched from was nothing but sand to her now.

She broke free on the other side and leaped toward her prey with vicious intent. Ogana's face turned, never more shocked than at this moment of his death. With a feral cry, she buried the blade deep in his chest, slashing through his heart and lungs. The winds surrounding them faded away, as did the magical gunslinging.

Ogana's staring eyes were vacant long before he hit the ground. Riding out his fall to the very end, Gypsy was left kneeling on his stomach, her hand still gripping the sword in his chest. She panted, relieved to finally have her victory.

"Ethan, look out!" Danato yelled from across the gym.

Gypsy's head snapped up. She didn't even have to look behind her to know what was happening. Her other self was taking advantage of Ethan's newly freed and dazed mind to get the drop on him. Never mind that he was no longer evil, or that the battle had just been won. She had her own game to win. And she intended to win it.

When she looked, she saw her double approaching Ethan from behind, unseen and shielded from the potential gunmen that were trying desperately to get a lock on her. Danato was running toward him, but he wouldn't make it in time. Her duplicate would hack off his head before anyone could get to her.

Gypsy looked around for the sheath, but it was pinned beneath her and Ogana's combined weight. She only had seconds before Ethan was headless. There wasn't enough time to free it and sheathe it.

"Son of a bitch!" she yelled and ripped the bone sword from Ogana's chest. Before she could remember which side her spleen was on, she rammed it deep into her gut.

She heard a scream, but it wasn't from her lips. She looked back to her other self, bent over on the white floor, turning it red. Ethan was already backpedaling away from her, giving them each a straight-line view of the other.

Gypsy wasn't sure she had ever felt fear—not the way others did—but as she stared into the eyes she only ever saw in the mirror, she felt an unfamiliar dread. The daggers in those eyes held not just a promise of vengeance, but of pain.

She mouthed an apology to herself—an apology that, for once in her life, she actually meant, but there was no absolution in the mouthed curse that her double offered back.

The bone sword ripped from her gut, causing a new level of pain that made her want to faint or vomit. The blood-stained ivory snapped back into its sheath above her. She turned her head to see what form her death had arrived in.

Danato.

She could live with that. Or rather, she could die with that.

She rolled over, flopping to the floor in surrender.

"Finish it," she whispered.

His angry eyes looked her over carefully. He looked at Ogana dead beside her and Annette passed out not far from them.

"How did you know?" he asked firmly, but she could tell her actions baffled him.

She reached into her pocket and pulled out the fork. As she brought it forward for him to see, the final tine disintegrated. The last of her do-overs were complete.

Danato kneeled down beside her and took the fork. Even as he examined the broken tines, they began to grow back. Resetting for a new player.

The remainder of the explanation no longer seemed necessary to him. His eyes searched the room. "Boys, we need an arm stretcher over here!"

A flock of men surrounded her and linked hands beneath her. She groaned as they lifted her up. At her new height she got a better view of Danato, who was looking her over curiously. "You just saved our lives, didn't you?" he asked.

She nodded.

"Why?"

"I had nothing better to do," she answered.

Danato frowned and ordered the men to get her to the infirmary. She didn't remember the rest of the trip.

93

Ethan sat in front of Danato's desk, staring at the pencil box. He had barely acclimated himself to Cori's potentially handicapping injury and his unintentional betrayal before Renee got her hooks into the drama and started yanking on fresh wounds. He glanced at Belus in the chair beside him. He didn't recognize the man's temperament. He seemed almost anxious, like he had bigger and better things to deal with than Renee's tantrum.

Didn't they all.

"You call this under control?" Renee paced along the far wall. "One minute the bubble is about to implode, the next your prisoners are escaping."

"Welcome to my world!" Danato vaunted with flailing arms.

"This is insane, Danato. Your first in command was even the one who let them out."

"Leave him out of this," Danato warned her.

"And I thought Cori was your Achilles heel?"

"Leave her out of this, too."

"Apparently she's just Belus's."

Belus glanced up at her. "Leave *me* out of this while you're at it."

"You need to get control, or I will."

"I *do* have control of the prison. This is what control looks like."

"I mean, control of your underlings."

"My *underlings* are doing just fine."

"Really? Because it looks like you've got one rebellious brat twisting you around her little finger, and one over-privileged fuck-up."

Ethan wasn't sure what his reaction would have been to the insult against him and Cori, but Danato's fist slammed into his desk before he could offer one. The metal top once again dented under the weight of his strength. The room cooled instantly, offering further proof of his intensity.

Danato stood up to face her. "I said you leave them out of this."

"I have the authority here, Danato." Renee wavered, gulping hard after her declaration.

"You have nothing here." Danato spoke quietly. His breath fogged with each word in the cold room. "*I* control this prison."

"I am on the Board." She tried to sound authoritative, but it came out more like a plea.

"There is no board here, Renee. It's just tiny little you, trying to stand up to a very big man with the backup of a very devoted entity."

"You wouldn't." Renee shivered.

"Try me, Renee."

Ethan was caught off guard by the threat in his voice. He wasn't bellowing at her like he usually did. There was real malice in his eyes. He truly hated this woman.

"Obviously, it's too soon for this conversation." She grabbed her purse from Danato's desk.

"Get the military off my courtyard," Danato demanded.

"When the time expires—" Renee yelped as he pulled her harshly back to him. Ethan flinched, once again prepared to defend the damsel, despite the fact that she was a bitch.

"Get... rid... of them... now." Danato managed to restrain his volume, but only at the expense of Renee's pinched arm. She squirmed under his grip until she finally whimpered in pain.

"Danato." Ethan finally stood, no longer able to resist defending her.

He glanced at him and released the woman. She glanced at Ethan, but since she didn't have a friend in him either, she didn't bother to thank him. Flushed and embarrassed, she moved to the door. "I will tell them to go, but that doesn't mean the audit is over. I will still be monitoring your—"

"Renee, you have got to learn when to shut up," Belus interjected, without looking back at her.

The woman looked at Danato and frowned before leaving. After she was gone, Danato released the tension in his puffed chest and leaned on his desk. "God help me, I will kill that woman someday."

"I'll be happy to bury her for you," Belus added.

"She's not wrong. I did fuck up." Ethan sat back down.

"From what we got out of Gypsy before surgery, you had no control of what you did," Danato said.

"I know, but..."

"There's no point casting blame at this point, kid," Belus said. "If anything, this incident will just bolster the need for our magical paraphernalia to be cataloged and secured. In the end, it doesn't matter. The wizards are dead. Ogana is dead." Belus shrugged. "It's a wash. All we need to worry about now is getting Cori's hand functioning again and maybe keeping Renee alive through this audit." Belus nodded to Danato, who was still bent over his desk, fuming.

Danato rolled his eyes and sat back in his chair. "The sooner she is gone, the better. I just can't stand that woman."

"Yeah, we got that impression," Belus said, still slightly amused.

Danato raised his hands over his damaged desk. "Damn it! I don't think I can fix this again."

"Danato," Ethan said.

"I know, I know, bigger picture. Where were we before Hurricane Renee got here?"

"I was about to apologize," Ethan said.

"Belus is right. The blame is irrelevant. We should have figured out a way to dispel the magic from that damn wand years ago."

"Not for that." Ethan paused, looking between them. "Adrianna."

Danato quieted, but he was already tensing for an argument.

"I was so focused on my own feelings that I didn't see what you were both trying to show me." Ethan glanced at Belus. "I don't remember everything I did while I was under Ogana's control, but I do remember enough to know that I wasn't me. It wasn't so much that I was a marionette, but like I was brainwashed. I was powerless against his influence, and I was following his orders.

"If he got out of here, hundreds—thousands—could have died before he was reined in. And he wasn't even a full sorcerer." Ethan looked expectantly at Danato, but he didn't speak. "I know in my heart that Addy was a good person, but who is to say that Ogana wasn't a good man at one point in his life? I see now the risk I was asking you to take by letting her live. I'm sorry that it took a near catastrophe to make me see it. And I'm sorry that I allowed it to come between us."

Danato swallowed and looked down at his desk, more than a little uncomfortable with the amount of emotion on his plate. "I appreciate that very much, Ethan. Your understanding means a great deal to me. I know I'm not always going to be the hero in your eyes, but it helps that I'm at least not the villain anymore." After a moment's pause, Danato cleared his throat and shifted back in his chair. "We'll need to get a round-the-clock rotation on Gypsy as soon as she is out of surgery. She may be our savior today, but she's still too erratic to trust. I know Callin is going to want to stay with her, but if we could politely ask him to get the hell out of my prison, that would be great."

Ethan smiled at Danato's devotion to his privacy. He wondered how he had ever come to terms with living with him and Cori. "What about Heaton and Jordan? They'll want to stay with Daniel."

Danato grumbled. "I'll see if Sophie has any easy hunts to keep them occupied while he heals. Hopefully, he'll be out of his coma in a few days."

"And Levi?" Ethan asked cautiously.

"Yeah, he can stay. I owe Annette at least that much for once again saving us from Ogana."

"I was hoping you would rethink putting him in the guard's quarters."

"Ethan—"

"Annette says he has some trust issues with men. I'm not sure what she meant, but I get the feeling that shoving him into a locker room style living arrangement with multiple men might be pushing his tolerances a bit."

Danato sighed. "I'll compromise with a dorm room in the volunteer building, but if not that, then you'll be making him a bed on the part-time level."

"The dorm is fine. I'm sure he won't mind."

"Of course he won't mind. He'll be surrounded by women running back and forth from their showers in nothing but towels," Belus muttered.

"Oh, don't tell me you're still mad that I built you a house. I put it as close to them as I could. Good God, man, pace yourself."

Belus chuckled and Ethan snorted at the ridiculous banter that had kept him entertained and sane for the better part of a year inside the bubble.

94

"HEY, NEED HELP?" ETHAN found Callin assisting Duke with the arduous task of moving their living statue. Getting the heavy sculpture on the dolly wasn't the hard part. The challenge was restricting contact to the statue's plinth. Touching the human portion meant a living death, and as Ethan understood it, gloves couldn't protect you from activating the curse.

"Nah, boss, we got it. Just stay back." Duke all but shooed him away. The Texan was never one to dismiss him so impolitely, but he was particularly protective of this artifact.

The item had been buried so deep in boxes that Ethan hadn't even known it was there until a few years ago. The story behind it was still pretty vague, but he had heard that the last man to touch the statue—the face currently looking down on him—was a friend of Duke's. The specifics of his transformation had yet to be revealed, and Ethan considered it a private matter, so he never asked.

"Shift it back a little more, Cal." Duke instructed as he pushed the dolly deeper beneath the base. "That's good."

"You want me to—?" Callin offered to move the dolly.

Before he could move around, Duke was shifting the heavy weight, nearly hitting his face against the knee of the sculpture. "I got it. Thanks."

Ethan jumped forward, nearly ready to knock his friend away from the dangerous situation he was putting himself into, but the dolly moved on with Duke right behind it, inches from life-altering contact. He offered a concerned and scolding look at him, but he resisted saying anything lest it disrupt his concentration.

"Hold that door," Ethan barked at one of his men leaving the gym. He glanced back and saw the burdensome load and eagerly held the door wide.

"He's a tough man to read," Callin commented.

"What, Duke?" Ethan looked back at Callin. "I always thought he was pretty straightforward."

Callin tapped his nose, indicating a different type of reading. "He's pretty mellow, but I think he's got some unresolved issues with the gentleman stuck in that stone."

Ethan nodded. "I'm starting to sense that myself. A conversation for another day. And speaking of awkward conversations, Danato is kicking you out as soon as the military gets out of here."

"Hmm, I'm not surprised. Have you heard anything more about Grace?"

"Not yet. She didn't hit anything vital, but there is a lot of damage, so we don't expect her out of surgery for several hours. Unfortunately, she'll have to heal the old-fashioned way, with Daniel out cold."

"He takes his healing very seriously."

Ethan shrugged. "I think he feels he owes it. Daniel is... a pretty dangerous man."

"Yes, I think there are quite a few dangerous men in this prison." Callin looked at him.

"Oh, no way, man." Ethan shook his head. "I have no energy for a fight today."

Callin laughed. "I wasn't flirting, Ethan. I was just going to point out that Efrat is probably among those dangerous men."

Ethan's brow dipped. "Yeah, I know what he can do," he said sourly. "He's more than willing to talk about it too."

Callin looked him over carefully. "I don't always partake in gossip, especially since I hear far more than people realize. Sometimes it's best to mind my own business, but in this particular case, I think I would be wise to advise you of a situation."

"What situation?"

"As I understand it, Efrat and Cori spent some time together outside of the bubble."

"Yes. Two days." Ethan frowned. "Why?"

"They were discussing a kiss that transpired between them."

Ethan took in a deep breath and gritted his teeth. "And?"

"I didn't get the impression that it went further than that, but I thought you should know."

Ethan nodded and swallowed hard. He was about to thank Callin for his honesty when Efrat walked in through the gym doors. He had gotten better at opening the doors with his forearms. There was barely a pause in his entrance anymore.

As he stepped inside and looked over the room, his eyes caught on Ethan. Whatever expression he saw on his face made his eyes narrow and his hands glow.

"I'll leave you two alone to... work things out." Callin sidestepped Ethan's tensed body and moved across the gym to Efrat, who was still not sure why he needed to defend himself, but was still ready to do so at a moment's notice.

When he reached Efrat, he paused as if he wanted to say something, but decided better of it. After the door clasped shut, Efrat moved forward slightly, not necessarily closer, but away from the remnant boxes still in need of transfer.

Ethan could see he was covered in Cori's blood. It should have eased his mind to know that he had helped save her, but it didn't. It was just one more time that he had been there for her instead of Ethan.

"What's up?" Efrat asked, annoyed.

"Tell me what happened with you and Cori outside of the bubble."

A small smirk played across his lips. "You want the dirty details?"

"Stop playing with me, Efrat. This isn't a game. This is my life!"

Efrat's smile faded, and he looked away. After a long moment, he spoke. "I made a pass at her."

"You kissed her?"

"Yeah, I kissed her."

Ethan refused to move or speak as he rationalized two sets of lips pressing together. It wasn't the same as hip to hip. It was just lips. "Why can't you just leave her alone?"

"Can you?"

"I love her." Ethan shook his head as Efrat looked away. "Don't. Don't pretend that what you feel for her is the same as me. You can't love her."

"Why? Because I am not capable of love? Because I'm the monster?"

"Because if you loved her... it would kill you to imagine her with another man!" Ethan moved forward, hands pinned to his sides, balled into fists but nonthreatening. "Is that what you feel right now, Efrat? Are you dying inside because you are afraid to lose her?"

Efrat looked at the intensity in his body, shaking and on the verge of tears. He took a deep breath and nodded his head. "I am terrified of losing her. She's all I have. She's the only normalcy in my life."

"Her *rings* are the only normalcy in your life!"

"Yes, that is the basis of our connection, but I'm sorry to inform you that I do care for your wife. More than I should. The fact that she is the only woman I can touch only makes me want her all the more."

"She doesn't belong with you."

"I know what you're saying, Ethan, and I don't want to do this. I don't want to be at odds with you, but you aren't just asking me not to sleep with your wife. You're asking me never to touch her again, and I can't do that. I can't continue to live my life without human contact. I can't... *live*... like this." Efrat displayed his hands, his face marred with the same emotion that Ethan's held. A pain that couldn't be satisfied with a single kiss or resolved with a fistfight.

"Cori said," Efrat continued, "that it was too much to ask, to break up her family just so I could have a reason to go on living. She's right, of course. But it's also too much to ask for me to stay in this facility and be a team player while I recluse myself from the only human interaction I am capable of."

Ethan stared at him, unable to pinpoint what he wanted to do about the broken man before him. He would never let him have Cori, but perhaps separating them was not the answer, either. He had made that mistake once already and his pride had almost cost him his marriage.

Efrat shook his head, giving up on the unwinnable argument. He lowered his hands, the blue long since faded away. "Let's get this over with. I don't even care about who can beat whom anymore. She chose you anyway. She'll always choose you. A black eye certainly isn't going to change anything."

Ethan relaxed and moved toward Efrat. To his credit, Efrat held his ground, willing and capable of accepting his punishment for the indiscretion. He even spread his arms to keep his power away, giving Ethan the perfect opening.

He threw his right arm around his neck and his other arm under his arm. Locking his hands behind his back, he pulled Efrat into a forced hug. He could hear Efrat start to speak and pause. "Uh... Ethan?" he finally managed to get out. "This is unusual."

"Yep." Ethan pulled back and clasped Efrat's face, making him even more uncomfortable. "I'm not going to beat the crap out of you, Efrat."

"I'm not sure I want to know what you *do* intend to do you me," Efrat said in earnest.

Ethan chuckled and slapped his cheeks, perhaps a little harder than necessary. He backed away. "I'm not going to deny that I want to smash your head into this floor, but I'm also not going to deny that you're just pathetic enough to feel sorry for." Efrat rolled his eyes. "However, a lost puppy you are not. You are a grown-ass man with mad skills, electrical or otherwise. You are going to do as Cori has been telling you for the last year and start cooperating... fully. You've made an excellent start already the past few days. I'm sure I haven't thanked you for that incident with Maddox, so thank you."

"Now," Ethan circled Efrat, "in regard to Cori." He placed his hands on Efrat's back and squeezed his shoulders. "I will not ask that you completely remove yourself from her life. I will, however, ask that your contact with her..." He pressed his thumbs deeper, causing Efrat's spine to crack. "...remain appropriate to friendship." Ethan released him and moved around to his front.

"I can't imagine your frustrations, Efrat, but it is unfair to ask Cori to satisfy *all* your needs for human contact. It's also unfair to ask me not to be jealous of the connection that has developed between you two. I think, in time, we'll find a balance. Or we'll kill each other. Either way, I think it's best that you and I just fake it until we get there." Ethan perked his brow, waiting for a response.

"I... ah... think that's fair. Thank you... sir."

"Do me a favor. Don't call me sir until you mean it."

"Okay."

Ethan started to walk away. "Oh," he turned back, "and check on Duke. Make sure he hasn't turned himself to stone."

"Will do."

95

ORI WOKE FOR THE third time, scratching viciously at her wrist. It was a painful burning tickle, and far from satisfying to scratch, but in the throes of a fitful nightmarish slumber, she couldn't tell herself not to do it.

"Don't, kitten." She felt Efrat's prickling touch pull her hand away. She opened her eyes and looked around the darkened infirmary. The nurse's station cast a dim light through to the patient section, but it wasn't much more than a nightlight.

She looked around at the other beds that were filled with victims of the breakout. She vaguely remembered the short report. Only a half dozen of Danato's men had been killed, which was impressive considering wizards didn't usually offer warning shots.

The specifics of Ethan's part in the escape were still being glazed over, but she clearly remembered Danato telling her that Gypsy had saved the prison. She didn't want to believe it, and in part, she still didn't, but only because she was lying in the infirmary with little to no feeling in her left hand.

"Where are my rings?" she asked, noticing that she was not being protected from Efrat's electricity.

"What do you mean?" he asked as he sat back down in the chair next to her bedside.

She looked down at her hands. They were still adorned with all ten rings. "Never mind." She examined the puffy red tissue that circled her wrist. The scar was the least of her worries. Her fingers were still numb and immobile. "Where's Daniel? We usually have a standing appointment for hospital bedside chatter."

"Third bed over." Efrat nodded down the line. "He's in a coma."

Cori leaned forward to see around her curtain. His face was turned so she couldn't see him, but she saw the familiar tinted glasses on his bedside table. "Oh, Daniel." She looked down at her rescued hand, no longer concerned that her fingers couldn't move. "Will he be okay?"

"His vitals are fine. I guess he's done this before. How's the hand?"

"Can we just skip the jokes about the irony of this situation?" She huffed and scooted deeper into her covers, shoving her limp hand out of sight. It wasn't until he didn't answer that she looked back at him. His jaw was tight, biting back whatever he initially wanted to say.

"There you go again. Assuming I'm..." He looked away. "I held you down while Daniel did a conscious bone graft on you. I listened to you scream and cry. In the end, my power couldn't do anything to numb your pain." She tried to speak, but he continued. "So, when I ask you how the hand is, it means I'm actually concerned about your wellbeing."

"Okay. I'm sorry."

"How is your hand?" he asked again vehemently.

"It's... numb, I guess. It hurts inside, at times."

"Any movement?" he asked more gently.

She tried to move her fingers again, but it was as if her hand was encased in cement. The signal was getting there, but it was too heavy to lift. "None." She grimaced. "What did they do with that bitch?"

"She's in the ICU right now."

"Maybe I should pay her a visit. Thank her personally for my handicap."

"You will do no such thing," Ethan announced, slipping in unnoticed as usual. He came in balancing two precariously full cups of coffee.

Efrat jumped up to alleviate him of one.

"Careful, it's hot," Ethan said as they transferred the cup. "Ouch," he seethed as a blue spark passed between them.

"Yeah, so am I."

"It's all good," Ethan said, drawing away after the transfer. "Is she behaving?" Ethan glanced at Cori, giving her a playful wink. She smirked at the impromptu flirtation.

"Of course not. She's still scratching the hell out of her wrist and plotting revenge. How's Gypsy, aka, the bitch?" He nodded toward Cori, to give her credit for the designation.

Ethan smirked. "Still asleep, but she's stabilized."

"And Duke?"

"Tired, but he says he can make it another hour or two." Ethan took a sip of his coffee.

"So, thirty minutes?"

"Yeah. Thanks for the break, man." Ethan touched his shoulder, not so much a pat as a squeeze."

"Who *are* you two?" Cori asked, trying to figure out when Ethan and Efrat had become so chummy.

Efrat nodded. "No problem. Goodnight, Cori."

"Goodnight, Efrat," she said, giving up on getting an answer.

"Now, where were we?" Ethan turned his scolding tone on her. He pulled the curtain around her bed, fully enclosing them. He set down his coffee and moved the chair right next to her bed. "Gypsy is off limits."

"Ethan—"

"No." He raised his finger instead of his voice, but the reprimand only served to annoy her. "That order comes in triplicate, sweetness," he said, softer. "Gypsy sacrificed herself to save me from... herself."

"That makes no sense."

"It will. I'll get you a more detailed report in the morning, but for now, you need to remember that Gypsy saved my life, and technically, although her methodology was extremely flawed, she saved your life as well."

Cori shook her head. "How did this even happen?"

"We are still investigating the specifics, but essentially, Ogana spelled me into bringing him the wand. Gypsy apparently found a magical fork that reset the timeline, and she used it to save us all. I guess the first few rounds must not have turned out so well. I think that's why she went to such great lengths to stop you from interfering. If it weren't for Gypsy, we would all be dead."

"I still don't trust her."

"That's fine." He nodded. "But you do need to stay away from her."

"And who's going to stop me?" she asked, slightly teasingly.

He smirked at her. "I think I might have a shot at it."

Cori glanced at her rings again. She tried to concentrate on making a flame, just for the sake of demonstrative humor, but nothing happened.

"Don't worry about your hand," Ethan said, misinterpreting the frown on her face. We'll figure it out. There is one other issue we need to discuss, though."

"What's that?"

"Efrat."

"What about Efrat?" she asked, already defensive.

"I know what happened between you two," he said sternly.

Cori shook her head, dismissing his unspoken allegation. "It's not what it seems like, Ethan."

"I know exactly what it's like. Efrat is struggling to maintain a grip on his humanity, and you are struggling to find a reason not to let him."

"I'm not struggling. He's just so damn... persistent. I just thought if he could understand that I don't feel that way—cause I don't."

Ethan chuckled at her befuddlement. "Listen, sweetness." He leaned forward, putting his elbows to his knees, and spoke even quieter. "I've been an idiot for the last, well, not counting *my* time, the last six months. I've been so afraid that you were going to cheat that I practically pushed you into it."

"Why did you think that to begin with?"

"It's complicated, but rest assured, I've made a lot of mistakes and I'm finally starting to see things more clearly."

"What are you seeing?"

"I'm seeing that I have a beautiful wife, whom I love very much. I'm seeing that I need to make sure you know how much I love you, lest someone else come along with a better offer." He winked at her and she was once again surprised by this playful mood during such a serious moment.

"Aren't you mad?"

"Of course," he answered honestly.

"But you aren't yelling at me, and Efrat's still breathing. You're kind of freaking me out, Ethan."

He smiled. "I'll deal with Efrat."

"And me?"

He took a breath and looked her over. "We almost lost everything, Cori. The wizards just hopped out of their cage and tried to wipe us out. Part of what I'm seeing so clearly is that Danato and Belus were right. There is no place in this world for anyone with that much power. I've been blindly seeking advice from... the wrong people. When it comes right down to it, this is my home, and my family. And nothing is going to change that. Not the death of a potential sorceress, and certainly not Efrat.

"You are mine, Cori. Not because I staked claim of you with a handful of rings, but because at one point, you actually gave yourself to me and I to you." He took her hand and kissed her wedding ring. "Is that still what you want?" he asked, almost hopeful.

"Of course. I never deserved you, Ethan, but if you still want me, then I'm yours."

His eyes sparkled as his mouth perked, pleased with her answer. He stood and crawled over her. He insinuated his body behind hers, pressing himself against her, and wrapping his arms under and around her.

"I would choose you every day and twice on Sundays," he whispered in her ear as he nuzzled against her neck.

"Me too." She smiled introspectively and snuggled in for her sleepover. She situated her hand to make sure she wasn't impinging the vulnerable appendage. She twisted one of her rings curiously, then pulled on it. The petite gold band slipped off her finger with ease.

96

"Leaving already?" Danato asked as he entered the loading docks.

Gypsy looked up at him, surprised that he was coming to bid her adieu. She had already collected her things and given her formal goodbyes to Ethan. She still half expected Cori to jump out from behind a crate box and exact her revenge, but so far, the woman was keeping her distance.

"You know, you can stay another week to heal," Danato said as he looked her over.

She knew she looked pale. She had lost a lot of blood. She was also in a good deal of pain, but nothing she couldn't handle.

"I think we both know you want me out of here as soon as possible."

His face dimmed. "Not at the expense of your life."

"Are you sure about that?" she asked. "I'm surprised you aren't more mad about Cori."

Danato moved to her side and leaned against the crate with her. "I probably would be, but you nearly sacrificed your life to save Ethan's, and that is worthy of a little wiggle room in my book."

"Is this your gentle teddy bear side? Because I think I like your grizzly bear side better."

"I'm trying to thank you, Grace."

Gypsy looked over at him and nodded. "Just doing my job."

"Your job?" he asked.

"I'm a heroine for hire." She heard the truck pull up outside the doors. "That's my ride." She turned back and grabbed her duffle off the crate. She winced at the weight as she slung it over her shoulder. She started to move away, but Danato held her shoulder. He pulled the strap from her shoulder, taking on the weight with ease.

"I'll walk you up." He nodded for her to head up the steps to the platform.

"This is new," Gypsy mumbled. Despite his gentlemanly behavior, she kept looking back to make sure he wouldn't stab her in the back on the way. She had enough puncture wounds to deal with.

"I must have told you about that bone sword you were using in one of your forks?" he asked as he followed her up.

"Yeah, I got the short version. One elephant, two tusks. I think fighting with the strength and speed of two men is a deceptive summary of its power, though."

"Yes, I suppose that was a little concise, but I'm sure I didn't want to intrigue you too much. I know how fond you are of weaponry."

Gypsy glanced back at him, catching him eyeing her overstuffed duffle. "What can I say? I have a soft spot for phallic objects." She turned and dragged her hand down his arm until she reached the handles he was gripping. "I think I can take it from here, big guy."

He stared at her, not moving to release the bag. "I didn't tell you why it's here, though."

"No, but I'm not really fond of backstories. I prefer to live in the here and now."

"The sword dates back to the 11th century." Gypsy sighed. "It first belonged to the Vikings. There is some debate about its origin, but I don't buy into god legends."

"Says the man with *something* trying to push through to his reality."

Danato raised his brow slightly at the remark, but continued. "The first owner of the sword was a great warrior, but he died a sudden and gruesome death in battle. The second owner was not a great warrior, just a fisherman. He kept the sword for many years, until one day, he too died a gruesome death."

"I'm sensing a theme," Gypsy offered in the hope that he wouldn't go through the sword's entire lineage.

"There's something intrinsically wrong about the relationship between the one that holds the sheath and the one that is controlled by it. The sword is here in my possession, because every owner of it has been killed by their double."

"Why would their double kill them, when they know it will kill them as well?"

Danato shrugged. "Call it a curse. Call it jealousy. Or perhaps our egos just can't stand to share. It doesn't matter. What does matter is that the bone sword is dangerous and eventually lethal to anyone that holds it." He raised the duffle bag for her to take.

She slipped into the shoulder strap and stared at him a moment longer before opening the bag. Buried among her braces, at an awkward angle, she found the bone sword and yanked it out. She sighed and shoved it towards him. "You could have just taken it."

"Yes, I could have," he confirmed as he took the weapon from her hand. "Have a safe trip, Grace." He nodded to the dock supervisor, who was impatiently standing by to usher her inside.

"Until we meet again." She offered her hand to shake, and he gave her hand a gentle squeeze before leaving.

She turned back to get on the truck. The dock supervisor was more than annoyed that her three steps to the door were slower than light speed. She stepped inside the truck and felt a slight thump on the back of her head. She turned around to give the man some kind of sarcastic response, but by the time she realized he was no longer there, she was already forgetting why she had turned around in the first place.

The truck interior she was being bounced around in was cold and dimly lit from the tiny holes in the siding. She couldn't quite remember where she was going, or where she had come from. It was so vague... A mission to deliver the girl, yes, but what happened after that?

"Fucking psychics," she groused even before she had the whole story. It was really no matter to her. She would get her memories of the last few days back soon enough. Including why she was in so much pain.

Gypsy sat down on the nearest sturdy box and let her bag drop. She pulled up her shirt, revealing a long gash. She had broken a stitch, and it was bleeding again. She tugged the useless stitch free with a hiss. She searched her bag for a bandage or clean cloth to dab the wound with.

As she leaned down, the filtered light glimmered against her blood-tinged fingers. She looked over the anomaly more carefully. Her blood, in fact, was the source of the silvery sheen. "Well, well, well, Gracie-girl, what have you gotten yourself into this time?"

97

D ANATO EXPECTED TO FINISH up his paperwork and head home for the day, but when he opened the door to his office, he found Daniel sitting in front of his desk. He looked back at him forlornly.

"Daniel, I didn't even know you were awake. How are you feeling?" Daniel didn't answer except to blink and swallow. "What's wrong?"

"We need to talk."

Danato frowned at the phrasing. As dooming as it was to hear from Belus, he liked it even less from Daniel McGrath's mouth. "Okay," he answered and shut the office door to give them privacy.

91 ½

CORI ARRIVED AT THE party screaming. The room of people turned and frowned at her seemingly unnecessary display. The memory of her pain quickly faded, and she realized she was unconscious, no doubt because of the pain that Daniel was causing to heal her. She looked down at her stump, hoping to find her hand once again intact, but instead of her hand she found a plastic mannequin hand poking from her sleeve.

"It's not real," she told herself, but of course it was all too real. Gypsy had cut off her hand. She was now twice the victim of the woman's blade and she was damned if she would allow it to happen a third time.

Cori looked around at the familiar surroundings and searched for Cleos. She barreled through the tipsy guests, disregarding the biting comments they made at her back. By the time she reached the fireplace, she was out of breath. She saw the back of Cleos's head, his long dark hair combed down as smooth as he could get it. Cori didn't bother excusing herself before pushing in front of the blond woman he was talking to.

"Cori?" Cleos's eyes widened, and he smiled. "Back again, I see. What sort of trouble are you in this time?"

"That bitch cut my hand off." Cori raised her plastic paw to show Cleos, but found instead a metal hook. She gasped, shocked by her sudden transformation to Captain Hook. "What the...?"

"Who cut off your hand?"

"Gypsy!"

"Oh." Cleos sucked air between his teeth and grimaced. "I take it you two still aren't getting along."

"As soon as I wake up, I'm gonna burn that woman to ash."

"Mmm." Cleos nodded absently.

"I'm serious."

"I don't doubt that you'll try. But if you want my advice, leave Grace alone. We have far more important plans for her."

"We?"

"You remember my latest acquisition?" Cleos motioned behind her.

Cori turned back to see which nameless guest was now being elevated to a name. She started to plaster a fake smile on her face until she saw the up-swept blond hair and glassy brown eyes. Her mouth dropped, and she took a step back, bumping into Cleos's chest.

"No. I told you to get rid of her."

"Why would I do that?" Cleos whispered into her ear.

"Because she is dangerous."

"So am I."

"This isn't a joke, Cleos!" Cori whipped around and slammed her fist on his chest. Astonishingly, her hook had been replaced by a rubber mallet that squeaked with every violent reproach. "You have to get rid of her before—"

"Hello, Cori," the woman said behind her. Much to her dismay, the dulcet tones sounded sweet, innocent, and motherly. She sounded like Olivia.

Cori froze, not wanting to look at her in case she might turn out to be Medusa in disguise. As it was, she was certain her voice was a siren's call, luring her subconscious through her connection with Cleos.

"I've missed you." The woman touched her shoulder and Cori batted her away. She raised her arm to poke a threatening finger at her. A long, sharp dagger replaced the rubber mallet. The woman stepped back, shrinking from the weapon.

"You stay away from me!"

"Relax, Cori, she's harmless in here."

"You still don't get it, do you?" Cori turned back to Cleos, shaking her head. "She's poking her head through a dimensional schism. Time and space bend around her. She creates matter out of nothing and her empathic abilities are the equivalent of demonic possessions. She will do *anything* to push through."

Cleos closed his eyes and took in a deep inhalation.

"And *you* still don't get it," another voice said from across the room. Cleos... the conscious one. He stalked across the room, parting the crowd until he reached her. He was in the same tuxedo, wearing the same hair, and yet he seemed clearer. Less like a dream. "I could swallow you whole in one bite. I could erase everything you are and replace it with anyone in this room if I wanted. It would be as if you never existed."

Cori's eyes wavered over his, wondering if he really could or really would do such a thing. He shifted and walked around her.

"Do you have any idea the amount of restraint it takes not to snap my fingers and make you what I want?" Cleos snapped his fingers in her ear. "I could have done it a thousand times!" he yelled at her.

"You're worried about her!" Cleos moved over to the woman and grabbed a fistful of her hair and yanked her forward for Cori to look at. She flinched, but didn't fight Cleos. "You're worried about the creature that I forcefully ripped from your mind." Cleos yanked his hand down and the woman disappeared from his grasp, leaving only a dress and blond wig. "She is nothing in here! She is an idea! An afterthought!" He dropped the clothes and ducked his head low to see Cori's drooping face. "But you... You're still connected. Laced into my mind by my own powers. The only danger to me in this room..." Cleos leaned in close and whispered, "...is you."

Cori had never considered the damage she had done to Cleos by linking into his subconscious. She had assumed her presence was as benign to him as it was to her, but how could it be? How could a union between two minds ever be without consequence?

"I'm sorry," Cori whispered. Cleos narrowed his eyes at her before walking away.

She was indeed sorry for the connection, and empathetic to his plight, but she was also angry that he was blaming her for it. There was no way she could have predicted the trouble her rings would cause, no way that she could stop herself from using them when she didn't understand them to begin with.

Cori rubbed her face briskly. She could feel herself slip away and was glad for it. The real world may not have had a better scenario for her, but at least Cleos would be out of her thoughts there.

She looked around the party, considering a civil goodbye to the unconscious Cleos, but she couldn't find him. She noticed the woman in the reflection of one of the mirrors. Cori turned to find her among the guests, but she wasn't there. She turned back to the mirror, but she was gone from the reflection as well.

Cori winked... Or rather, her reflection winked at her. Cori frowned, though the mirror did not show the expression.

Once again, Cori looked at her surroundings, trying to find the source of this mirage. When she looked back, her other self smiled mischievously at her. She raised a finger to her pursed lips and shushed her.

FELICIA JEDLICKA

DETAILS & DEADLINES

Book 11

THE WARDEN

Details & Deadlines

Sneak Peek

"**D**o you want the job or not?" Heaton asked again, quickly losing patience with his former partner.

Jack Macey looked up from his recent catch. At nearly forty-two, his scruffy beard, long brown hair, and thin slit eyes made him look at least sixty. His propensity for no sleeves left his muscular, artfully tattooed biceps exposed. Heaton was sure he had never seen the man clean, but that was at least a testament to his work ethic.

The ten-foot walrus slug lying behind him was not the type of creature Heaton's team usually hunted, but they were quite common in the swamps. Much like the variants of animals across the globe, each region also had its supernatural infestations to deal with.

Heaton would have chosen to hunt in the city over the swamps any day. Vampires may have been blood-sucking parasites, but at least they didn't stink like swamp creatures.

"Let me get this straight." Mace spit some of his tobacco juice just shy of Heaton's boot tip. Heaton glanced down at the intentional provocation but didn't react. Mace was always about a good show. There was no point in feeding into his need for validation. "You kick me off your team for being too unstable. Now Daniel—the kingpin of excessive force—gets thrown in the slammer again, and you want me back. Is that about right?"

Heaton paused, hoping he wouldn't have to repeat himself a third time. As much tolerance as he had for Daniel's potentially violent tantrums, he had none for Mace's. "Daniel's incarceration is only temporary. We just need a little extra muscle for our hunts."

Mace looked at Nevia on Heaton's left. "Little one not pulling her weight." He snorted and turned away from them both to drag his three-hundred-plus pound, fattened worm further onto dry land. The net encasing it wasn't actually trapping it, but since the creatures never scooted more than a few feet a minute, escape was hardly an issue.

Despite its weight, Mace moved it with ease. His 5-foot-7 stature had never impressed him or Daniel, but they had surmised he could bench press a baby elephant if his adrenaline was high enough. He had been a useful asset in the field. Unfortunately, he was too much of a loner to work well with a team.

Plus, he was an asshole.

"Mace, I'm sweating like I've run a marathon. I've donated enough blood to the mosquito population to warrant a transfusion. And your slug stinks to bloody hell. Do you want the job or not?"

Mace turned back and looked him over. "I want her to ask me." He nodded to Nevia. His raspy words sounded more like a challenge than a request.

"What difference does it make who asks you?" Heaton asked, no longer able to keep the irritation out of his tone.

Mace shrugged, not willing to offer any reason for the request.

Nevia stared Mace down with a venomous glare. Heaton wasn't sure she could smell him over the slug, but whatever she was sensing from him wasn't sitting well with her.

"Shall I say it slowly so you can understand the question better?" she asked him.

"Say it however ya want." Mace crossed his arms, refusing to budge until he got his way. Heaton suspected it was his way of establishing a hierarchy right out of the gates. The strange thing was it wasn't even about sexism for Mace. He just needed to know he was above someone—anyone. His attitude was the result of too many toilet swirlies and not enough friends growing up.

"We need—"

"Nah, just you," he corrected before she could finish. "You need me." He said with his usual deadpan expression that offered nothing of himself, least of all an inkling of his personality.

Nevia glanced at Heaton, but he didn't insist she continue. If she didn't feel like prostrating herself for the sake of convenience, he wasn't going to make her. As much as he hated Mace, he was his only living former partner. If they couldn't convince him to fill in, they would have to train someone new. It was a toss-up who would be more hazardous to them—his erratic ex-partner or a naive newbie.

Nevia stepped closer to Mace. He looked her up and down and snorted—obviously unimpressed by her brandished authority. Though her short stature and slender build made her seem diminutive next to everyone, it was her one-quarter werewolf heritage that gave her immunity against intimidation. Any woman who could stand tall in the face of Danato Calibria's wall-rattling lectures would be able to handle Mace's tantrums just fine.

"How about this," she proposed. "How about you ask to join us?"

Mace shook his head, still refusing without cause or justification. He was a spoiled brat with low self-esteem and a chip on his shoulder called high school. There was no reasoning with this man.

Mace lifted his upper lip, appearing at first to be snarling at Nevia. A fine stream of spit squirted from a gap in his front teeth. The spray landed on Nevia's white linen blouse. She looked down at the tobacco juice staining the cloth.

"God, that's disgusting, Mace!" Heaton griped.

Mace snickered at the shock on Nevia's face, taunting her with yet another level of derision.

Nevia didn't waste any more time with verbal banter and pulled her gun. Aiming her firearm at people was like second nature to her. Anytime she felt... well, any emotion on the bad end of the spectrum, she was liable to start shooting. Usually, Heaton enjoyed watching her wield her weapon, but Mace was not fond of guns. His former partner had never revealed to him or Daniel the cause of his repellent attitude. All Heaton knew was that Mace did not respond well to armed threats. Had Heaton been thinking ahead, he might have asked Nevia to leave her gun behind to prevent any incidents—such as the one unfolding.

Nevia barely got the gun out of its holster before Mace backhanded her and ripped the weapon from her hand. There was room to rationalize PTSD or depression as an excuse for the knee-jerk reaction, but Heaton wasn't going to defend any man stupid enough to hit a woman with femwolf blood running in her veins.

Nevia stumbled back, holding her face. She peeked at Mace from behind her hand—a wave of almost feral anger overtook her features. Heaton rarely saw the woman's emotion peak beyond haughty or pouty. Even her smiles were subdued. Seeing her raw fury now exposed was almost popcorn-worthy.

He wasn't sure what had pissed her off the most, the assault, the disarmament, or if it was still the defilement of her garment causing her to see red.

Nevia screamed and lunged at Mace. Heaton hadn't expected her to do much damage, and judging by his lack of defense, neither did Mace. However, she surprised them both.

Nevia hooked her arm around Mace's neck, drawing him down to her. She opened her mouth wide and sunk her teeth into his neck like a vampire.

Mace yelped and threw her off to one side. He cussed and groaned, grabbing at his bleeding neck. "Freaking bitch!"

Mace started to go after her, but Heaton intercepted him. "Fair is fair, Mace. You hit her; she bit you." Heaton frowned as Mace released his neck. Nevia had given him more than a love bite. There was a chunk of flesh missing from Mace's neck—and not a tiny piece.

"If you think I'm gonna help you now..." Mace's rant trailed off into silence as if he had lost focus on what he was saying.

"No, I don't think you are going to help us," Heaton said before he had to listen to more of the man's self-important rhetoric. "I think you are going to stay in this hellhole, dig up slugs for the rest of your miserable existence, and blame your problems on other people. That's what I think." Heaton ripped Nevia's gun out of his hand and turned to leave. "Come on, Jordan."

"Son of a bitch," Mace mumbled behind him.

Heaton looked back to see if Nevia had double-backed for a secondary attack, but she wasn't near Mace. She wasn't anywhere. He looked around the sloppy woods for her, but she was gone.

"Where is she?" Heaton yelled at Mace, but he just kept staring down at his most recent catch. Heaton looked at the walrus slug that was inch by inch trying to escape back to the swampy waters of the Mississippi. Either his eyes were playing tricks with him, or that damn thing was quite a bit fatter than when he had arrived.

Mace's face constricted in disgust even as his eyes remained glazed with shock. "Damn gluttonous thing. I've never seen it eat. I can't believe how fast she went in," he murmured.

Heaton looked between him and the overstuffed pile of pudge. "She…" He pointed at it in disbelief. "Is she in there?"

Mace lifted his gaze to Heaton. "She got too close to the mouth."

"Because you threw her over there! How do we get her out?"

"She went in like a wet fuckin' noodle," Mace said, in awe of the creature. "I didn't even know they could fit two people in there. I s'pose 'cause she's small."

Heaton grabbed him by the shoulders and shook him. "Just get her out of there!"

"I can't." He shrugged off his grip.

"What do you mean you can't?"

"I mean, there is no way, no how to get her out before..." The bastard seemed almost sympathetic now. "She's done for. That thing's like pure acid on the inside. It starts dissolving prey the instant it hits the stomach."

Heaton cursed and dug out his pocket knife. It wasn't long, but it was sharp. He leaped to the slug's side and started cutting at its belly—or at least the fattest part of its body. The blade caught on the initial layer of slimy tissue as if he were cutting tree bark instead of skin. He tried to stab the knife in, but it bounced off like he was trying to pop a balloon with his finger.

"You'll never make it through in time," Mace said. "I usually cut these things open with a chainsaw."

Heaton looked back at Mace. "I am not leaving her in there to die, you son of a bitch! Help me!"

"I don't know what to tell you, man. If she doesn't suffocate, the acid—"

"That is Daniel McGrath's wife!" Heaton rasped, pointing at the slug. "He will kill you for this!" He stared hard at Mace, demanding he understand what was at risk if he didn't help. However, even as he said the words, he realized it wasn't Mace who would suffer for this; it was him. Even if Daniel didn't kill him for failing to protect Nevia, it would destroy their friendship.

"I'm sorry." Mace shrugged. "That thing ain't letting anything out until it's a pile of bones and shit."

Heaton frowned and paced the water's edge. He considered shooting the animal, but that still didn't get Nevia out. The chainsaw would work, but Mace clearly hadn't brought it out with him.

He looked down at the slug, trying to fathom how to break the news to his best friend. How would he tell him the only woman he had ever opened his heart to was dead?

No.

He wasn't going to watch his friendship fester and die because of an ugly ass slug.

He tossed away his knife and Nevia's gun. He moved around to the rear of the slug—the end without teeth. He knelt and shifted the tail nub to expose the orifice.

"What are you doing?" Mace asked as if he had just walked in on Heaton doing something inappropriate.

Heaton clasped his hands in prayer and dove at the anus like a human speculum. Mace hollered out a protest as Heaton buried his arms elbow-deep into the creature's rear end.

Working as an underground bounty hunter, Heaton had experienced a good number of disgusting things. It was even gruesome at times, but nothing prepared him for entering the colon of a walrus slug. His final inhalation afforded him a bouquet of rotting flesh and feces. He controlled his gag reflex and pushed on into the darkness...

...down the rabbit hole...

...through the wormhole....

...into the slug's hole.

Thank you so much for reading. I hope you enjoyed the ride and if you aren't getting off here, I encourage you to sign up for my newsletter so I can return your generosity with new release updates and special offers.

Sign-Up

You can also find me on Facebook or visit my website. Keep reading!

Website

Facebook

AUTHOR

As a Nebraska native, and a small-town girl at that, I have very little to occupy my time beyond imagining a world outside of my own reality. By the grace of God and the seat of my pants, I have kept my waning attention span on the task of becoming an author.

So here I am, an indie author, peddling my words in cyberspace and enduring my comeuppances with an unwavering determination. I may not be a professional, and I certainly am not perfect, but if you've made it this far, you have to admit, this smartass yokel does spin quite a yarn.

From the self-inflicted sweatshop conditions of my unairconditioned childhood home, to the arthritis reaping positions of a sedentary lifestyle, I bring to you: my sarcasm, my oddity, and my heart. Take it with a grain of salt or a teaspoon of sugar, but take it for what it is: a story born of the mind, translated to paper, and gifted to you.

I thank you for your readership and even more for your support. Please recommend this book to your friends and family via any social media that you use. Word of mouth is still the best advertising and is greatly appreciated.

Most importantly, keep reading. I'll keep writing.